Dear Readers,

For me, part of the magic of the past lies in discovering the small, everyday details of living in another time. I believe that these details bring to life a world we can never visit except in our imaginations. However, because knowledge is passed on from one generation to the next, we have a legacy from those who lived long ago. Part of that legacy is food preparation, which has until recently been the special domain of women.

Cooking is an immediate and compelling example of our legacy from the past, one that holds a unique significance for women. As a special gift to my readers, I've included several recipes related to the story of *Lord of Enchantment*. This is my way of trying to bring to you some of the magic I felt upon writing the story of Pen and Morgan.

Please savor the enchantment with me.

Suzanne Robinson

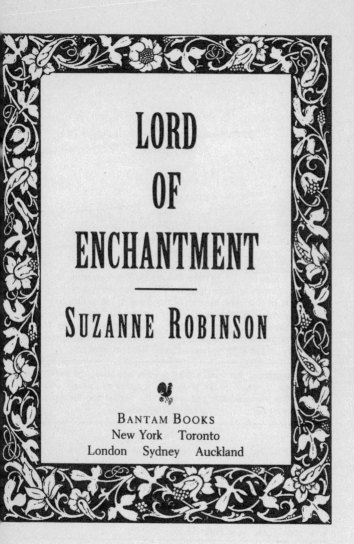

LORD

OF

ENCHANTMENT

SUZANNE ROBINSON

BANTAM BOOKS
New York   Toronto
London   Sydney   Auckland

LORD OF ENCHANTMENT
A Bantam Book / January 1995

ISBN 0-553-56344-0

Published simultaneously in the United States and Canada

Bantam Books are published by Bantam Books, a division of Bantam Doubleday Dell Publishing Group, Inc. Its trademark, con-
sisting of the words "Bantam Books" and the portrayal of a
rooster, is Registered in U.S. Patent and Trademark Office and
in other countries. Marca Registrada. Bantam Books, 1540 Broad-
way, New York, New York 10036.

PRINTED IN THE UNITED STATES OF AMERICA

RAD   0 9 8 7 6 5 4 3 2 1

This book is dedicated with love and admiration to a woman of great courage, style and wit, my aunt, Barbara Sodhi-Pieper.

ACKNOWLEDGMENTS

I would like to acknowledge my indebtedness to two works that have made writing *Lord of Enchantment* an experience in delightful discovery. The first is a book of advice and instruction called *The English Housewife* by Gervase Markham (1568?–1637) and edited by Michael R. Best. This wonderful book covers everything from the virtues of a good housewife to brewing ale. The second is a beautifully illustrated volume by Maggie Black, *The Medieval Cookbook,* which contains both original and modernized recipes as well as informative discussions of historical ingredients and practices. I highly recommend both to any reader interested in the history of cooking and housewifery.

So are you to my thoughts as food to life,
Or as sweet-season'd showers are to the ground;
And for the peace of you I hold such strife
As 'twixt a miser and his wealth is found;
Now proud as an enjoyer, and anon
Doubting the filching age will steal his treasure;
Now counting best to be with you alone,
Then better'd that the world may see my pleasure:
Sometime, all full with feasting on your sight,
And by and by clean starved for a look;
Possessing or pursuing no delight,
Save what is had or must from you be took.
   Thus do I pine and surfeit day by day,
   Or gluttoning on all, or all away.

                    —William Shakespeare

TANSY

An egg dish mid-way between an omelette and a pancake.

... for making the best tansy, you shall take a certain number of eggs, according to the bigness of your frying pan, and break them into a dish, abating ever the white of every third egg; then with a spoon you shall cleanse away the little white chicken knots which stick unto the yolks; then with a little cream beat them exceedingly together; then take of green wheat blades, violet leaves, strawberry leaves, spinach, and succory, of each a like quantity, and a few walnut tree buds; chop and beat all these very well, and then strain out the juice, and mixing it with a little more cream, put it to the eggs, and stir all well together; then put in a few crumbs of bread, fine grated bread, cinnamon, nutmeg and salt, then put some sweet butter into the frying pan, and so soon as it is dissolved or melted, put in the tansy, and fry it brown without burning, and with a dish turn it in the pan as occasion shall serve; then serve it up, having strewed good store of sugar upon it, for to put in sugar before will make it heavy. Some use to put of the herb tansy into it, but the walnut tree buds do give the better taste or relish; and therefore when you please for to use the one, do not use the other.

CHAPTER I

Isle of Penance, 1565

Pen Fairfax leaned out over the battlements of High-cliffe Castle and felt her skin prickle as if she wore a hair shirt next to her flesh. She had no cause to feel so skittish, and yet she'd left her tansy, bread, and ale to climb to the top of the Saint's Tower and scour the horizon.

Agitation tingled in her bones as she looked out at the sea. League after league of azure met her gaze, topped by a sky without clouds and riffled by a teasing breeze that burned her cheeks crimson. The glare of the sun, the sea's moisture, and the icy breeze combined to turn the air almost silver. Far below the steep cliffs upon which the tower sat, the surf foamed and crashed into the jagged black giant's teeth that were all the island could claim as a beach.

Again, the flesh on the backs of her arms prickled. Shading her eyes with one hand, Pen studied the sea. She didn't turn when Nany Boggs labored up the last stair and puffed her way across the tower roof carrying a cup of ale. Nany's generous chest heaved under the strain of hauling her bulk up the winding staircase. Teetering to a halt, she steadied her precious cargo and took a long sip. Then she wiped her face with her apron and tucked a strand of silver hair beneath her cap.

Before Nany could scold, Pen lifted a hand and pointed out to sea. "There's going to be a storm."

Nany Boggs looked up at the unblemished sky, at the calm sea, at Pen.

"Prithee, how do you know it?"

"We'll have to get the grain inside, and the hay, and the animals. No threshing this morn."

Pen avoided her old nurse's stare. She breathed in the fragrance of crisp sea air. The breeze caught a strand of her hair and played with it as she surveyed the blue plain of water that stretched from the island to the horizon. She shivered abruptly and rubbed her upper arms.

"Aha!"

Pen tossed her head and scowled at Nany, but the nurse only planted a fist on her hip and glared back at her.

"I knew it," Nany said. "I saw you go still in the hall and bolt like a frightened hedgehog. Left that tansy dish I made specially for you, you did. You're going all fantastical again, aren't you? Listening to spirits and fell creatures of magic."

Pen sighed. "Not spirits and creatures—"

"Hearken you to me, Penelope Grace Fairfax. If you rush about like a demented harpy, your secret will be out and we're all o'rthrown."

Pen took a deep breath of cold air, spread her arms wide, and lifted her face to the sun. "God's patience, Nany, I but warned of a storm."

"Under a cloudless sky, mistress."

"You're always complaining that I abandon sense too often by taking in unfortunates, yet when I give cautious warnings and thought to the protection of those under my care, you complain of that as well."

Never one to let logic impede her way, Nany drained

her cup and then shook a thick finger at Pen. "You're going all fantastical again."

Pen gave Nany pained smile and touched the end of her nurse's red nose with the tip of her finger. Nany swiped at her hand, but Pen danced away from her grasp. She left the embrasure, but paused to glance out at the tranquil water.

As she gazed at the sea, her uneasiness grew. Needles of apprehension pricked her palms. Suddenly she recognized the feeling. She'd had it before, upon the approach of danger—danger of a particular and most menacing sort. If she was right, she would need ward herself as never before. She would have to prepare herself for calamity.

Nany was still muttering. "Not a cloud."

Setting her jaw, Pen went to the old nurse and patted her shoulder as she headed for the stairs.

"There will be a storm," she said calmly, "a storm nonpareil, with waves as high as towers and sideways rain and sleet. A storm of trouble and wonder, Nany. A storm of trouble and wonder."

Out of sight of Penance Isle, a carrack chased a swift pinnace westward from the coast of England. On the prow of the carrack, Morgan St. John strained to keep sight of the pinnace while sailors shouted and scurried around him. He'd pursued the spy-priest Jean-Paul from England to Scotland and back again and wasn't about to give up because of a few clouds.

He glanced over his shoulder at the threatening clouds, then turned his gaze back to his quarry. As he stared at the retreating sails, he began to hear a faint hissing. He looked around, but no one was near him. He resumed his relentless vigil only to glance around again as he heard that same low, rhythmic whispering.

No, the sound seemed to come from somewhere ahead. But that was nonsensical, for there was nothing but sea ahead. Morgan gripped the gunwale and leaned out over the waves, straining as the whispers seemed to call to him. A tremor passed through his body even though he was wrapped in his warmest cloak—a tremor of expectation. What was this feeling of exhilaration? He hadn't caught the priest yet. He'd almost decided that the past few weeks' chase had played tricks on his hearing, when he felt the ship slow.

Whirling around, Morgan forgot the mysterious hissing as he raced across the deck toward the stern, his arm clamping his sword to his side. He veered around a coiled rope and swooped down upon the ship's master. Before he could speak, the master nodded to the boatswain, who began to shout.

"Stand by your lines!"

Morgan turned and gazed past the prow and the rapidly vanishing pinnace on the horizon. He rounded on the master. "You're not coming about."

Sunlight disappeared as he spoke, and the sea and wind picked up. The master pointed to the sky behind them.

"That be a black squall, my lord."

Morgan gazed up at a line of ebony clouds that seemed to fly across the sky, swallowing all light. The leading edge was as straight as a sword blade. Several men scurried past them and climbed up to loosen the topsails.

"You know nothing of the sea, my lord. A storm like that can slap my ship to the bottom of the sea. I know you want to catch that pinnace, but the squall will reach her before we can." When Morgan remained silent, the master pressed his lips together and continued. "After all, I got a wife to think of, and my men—"

"Mean you that you're turning this ship around because of a *woman?*" Morgan's eyes rounded and widened. "God's blood, man, that pinnace carries a French spy. If I don't catch the bastard, he's going to cause the death of more than just a few English sailors. A pestilence take you, man, that priest serves the Cardinal of Lorraine and the Queen of Scots, and you prate to me of a stupid woman? I'm trying to prevent a war!"

As Morgan finished, the wind hit them, and the boatswain began to yell again.

"Lower and reef the main course. Lower the mizzen course."

A driving rain mixed with sleet pelted them as the master's gaze darted from the topsails to the mizzen course and spritsail.

"Boatswain," the master yelled. "It's too late. Trim the spritsail."

A heavy swell pitched the ship, and Morgan gripped the gunwale. His feet began to slide out from under him, and he tasted rain and saltwater. Now the swells blocked out the sky. The ship ascended the next wave, and he caught a glimpse of the horizon before the deck rolled and pitched beneath him. Cursing, he got his feet back beneath him. Across the deck, sailors had uncoiled ropes and strung them down the length of the ship.

The master had worked his way amidship to join the boatswain. Morgan followed, but a great swell broke over the stern, dashing him to the deck. He landed facedown and felt his body begin to slide. He grabbed a cask as the ship pitched almost vertical to the sea floor.

When he'd gotten to his feet again, he gripped the gunwale and slowly maneuvered forward. He reached the master in time to hear him bellowing at a young sailor, little more than a boy, who was hugging the mast. The master pointed at the mainsail, which lay across the deck with its spars extending out past the gunwale.

"Get out there, you pissant cur!"

Morgan glanced at the men reefing in the sails. Wet sails were heavy and dragged, requiring great strength to haul. The master was still yelling. Morgan watched another swell nearly carry a man overboard, and made a decision.

Removing his sword and letting it fall to the deck, he lurched past the man reefing sail on the port side and climbed out on the spar. A swell rose up as he edged out over the sea. Morgan hugged the spar as an ocean of water broke over him. When it was gone, he straightened, spat water, and began to drag in sail.

To his right he heard someone yelling. It was the master, but he dared not take his gaze from the sail. A blast of horizontal sleet hit him in the face, and he gasped. The ship rolled, and the world turned sideways. Morgan clutched the spar again. He heard the master screaming at him. He couldn't see for the spray and the wind that blew his hair in his face.

Then he felt it—the crack and sudden drop of the end of the spar. Voices shouted at him, and he lunged in the direction of the gunwale. As he leapt, the spar broke. The sail tore as he grabbed for it. A gray wall of water loomed high above him, topping the mast. Morgan grabbed for the jagged end of the spar, and then plunged into the sea.

He hit the water like a pat of butter hitting a brick. The sea swallowed him. As he sank, he twisted his body and looked about, his lungs on fire. His clothing dragged at him as he fought his way to the surface. He popped, corklike, into the air and gulped in a deep breath. Another swell slapped him underwater once again.

This time it was all he could do to claw his way to the surface. A wave batted him again, and he went down into darkness once more. It was as if he were swimming in cold pitch. His muscles were stiff, and his chest burned.

Rapidly losing his senses, he broke to the surface. He tried to remain afloat, but his strength was fading. Another wall of gray rose in front of him, and he knew he couldn't survive it. The carrack had vanished.

In desperation, Morgan turned and tried to swim away from the giant swell. He threw out an arm, and it hit something hard—the end of the spar. Clutching the wood, he wrapped himself around it and braced himself as the swell hit. This time he went down, but the wood helped him pop back to the surface quickly.

How long he rode those swells, he couldn't judge, but his arms froze in their clutched position around the spar, and the rest of him went numb. Suddenly the blast of the wind dropped a bit, and the pelting rain let up. His vision blurred, and he could just make out great mountains of waves under a ragged black sky.

He fixed his whole attention on remaining afloat, and kept it there until he heard a sudden crash. Swinging his wobbling head around, he beheld sea foam and white tops. A wave rocked him. As he was carried on its crest, he saw the reason for the foam and the crash—rocks. Tall, jagged, and black, they littered the coast of an island.

Morgan tried to turn and swim away, but the swells were carrying him toward the rocks. He kicked uselessly, and a high swell picked him up as easily as the wind blows a feather. His body sailed high. Then he plummeted into the base of a pair of rocks that looked like giant's teeth.

His body slammed against pitted black stone. Air rushed out of his lungs. He lost his grip on the spar as he was sucked back out to sea by the return wave. Half conscious, he flailed his arms and legs only to be lifted once again and thrown. He saw black teeth and white foam, then cried out as his body was rammed between the two rocks. As he hit, his head smacked into stone. He felt the exploding pain just before blackness overwhelmed him.

The morning after the storm, Pen stood in the outer bailey listening to Dibbler and Sniggs. Her agitation had faded somewhat with the waning of the storm, and yet she still had vague expectations of calamity. Her gift seldom misled her, so she hadn't yet let down her guard.

Behind her she could hear the noise and catch the smells from the piggery, which backed against the south wall between two towers. Dibbler began shouting at Sniggs as the castle's herd of pigs trotted outside. Pen waved at the swineherd, a girl by the name of Wheedle, then winced as Dibbler cuffed Sniggs on his ear.

When the two were like this, she wished she'd heeded Nany's warnings about taking in homeless creatures. But there were so many who, like Sniggs, had been cast off their land by greedy noblemen, or, like Dibbler, possessed odd yet well-meaning natures that forced them into difficulties.

Dibbler and Sniggs were still scuffling.

"Stop it at once," Pen said.

Dibbler gave her a glance of pretended remorse and dug his toe into the mud. "Your pardon, mistress, but fell asleep at his post, did Sniggs. What if Sir Ponder had decided to attack last night?"

Sniggs reddened and burst into speech. "It were a fairy, mistress. A wee fairy with gold wings and silver hair cast fairy dust in me eyes and put me to sleep. I didn't even hear no thunderclaps nor nothing."

"Fairy dust," Pen said.

"Aye, mistress."

Pen's gaze traveled over Sniggs, from his grease-caked hair, patchwork jerkin and hose, to his worn and cracked boots. Sniggs rubbed his nose, which was pitted and shrouded in a network of tiny red veins. She caught a whiff of ale and cheesy breath, and stepped back.

Dibbler was making disgusted noises. Dibbler rivaled Sniggs in his tattered appearance. His doublet had once been of green and red velvet, but wear had made its nap all but vanish. The buttons that worked diligently to fasten the garment over Dibbler's paunch were tarnished. He had a ring of graying hair around his bald spot.

In order to keep his head warm, he wore a flat cap shaped like a kidney. Dibbler had an assortment of once-grand caps of which he was proud and which he guarded with his life against thievery. At the moment, he put one sausage-thick finger against his nose and addressed Pen.

"It weren't no fairy that put him to snoring," Dibbler said.

"No?" asked Pen, her already tried patience beginning to fail.

"Nah, mistress. Everyone knows that fairies don't come out in no storm. They hides under toadstools and leaves and such."

Sniggs sputtered. "Well, this one hid in my tower last night."

"It did not!"

Pen waved her hands and wavered between a sigh of exasperation and a smile. "Please, both of you. I like not this quarreling. No harm was done."

"But, mistress—"

"Dibbler, I thank you for your diligence, and now I must catch up with Wheedle. One of her sows took ill last night."

Pen left the two men to finish their quarrel without her and walked across the wet ground, avoiding puddles and lakes of mud. She passed the beehives and the dovecote, rounded the corner of the deserted woodshed, and entered the gatehouse. She passed beneath the rusting portcullis, through iron-studded double doors, and over the drawbridge. The moat was littered with dead leaves from the castle orchard and moss blown by the storm.

Free from the confines of Highcliffe, Pen emerged onto the stone outcrop upon which the castle had been built and hurried down the slanting path that led to the fields. To her right, nestling close to the castle, lay Highcliffe village.

Once again she fell to worrying about the future of her people. Regardless of her care, they remained vulnerable to disaster. This year's crops had fared well, but one late freeze, one plague, and they would all go hungry. Mayhap she should reconsider the marriage offer of her disagreeable neighbor, Sir Ponder Cutwell.

Pen gazed out at the countryside, torn between duty and her own inclinations. A patchwork of soggy mud stretched before her, and Pen thanked God once again that the harvest had been gathered and most of the grain threshed before the rain came. She was pleased, for her warning had come in time to shelter both animals and wheat. Highcliffe could ill afford their loss.

Nany Boggs wasn't pleased, though. Not since the recurrence of the gift. However, Nany would have to endure. Pen had arranged her life on Penance so that it was almost perfect, except for that annoyance, Ponder Cutwell. And if her gift warned her of a threat to that perfection, so be it. Of course, Nany resented their lack of servants, the shut-up and boarded towers, the plain food, the isolation of Penance Isle. Pen loved it for these very reasons. Here she was safe, safe from blood and terror and the contentious men who brought them.

Reaching the base of the Highcliffe Mount, Pen saw that Wheedle had already reached the edge of the forest that lay between Highcliffe and the realm of Sir Ponder Cutwell. She took in a deep breath of rain-washed air. She could ask about the sick pig when the girl returned.

In the glare of the newborn sun, yesterday's apprehension and prickling expectation faded even more, until they seemed but a whimsy. Her spirits lifted as she beheld the masses of gold and copper of the turning leaves of the forest. The sea breeze whipped at her cloak and skirts and danced in her hair. Another ordinary day in which she must needs see to the salting of meat, the making of preserves, the storing of grain and wood, all in preparation for winter. But first, a walk in the open air.

Pen skirted fields and gardens and took the path that bordered the cliffs. She would walk to the caves and back before resuming the day's chores. As she went, Pen glanced down at the surf breaking on the rocks.

Gulls and terns cawed and screeched as they sailed over the waves. She paused while three dolphins skimmed by, then took the path around a rock outcrop. As she walked she gathered stones. When she had a handful, she stopped and began tossing them over the cliff. She was determined to throw one out beyond the farthest rocks in the sea.

Three stones hit the fan of boulders that marked an old cliff slide. Pen grimaced and walked farther down the path, where the sea had carved more land from the island. She clamped a hand around a stone, drew back her arm, and it stayed there. Something white had flapped in the air. She narrowed her eyes against the sun's glare and peered down at two tall rocks that jutted out of the roiling surf like giants' teeth. It wasn't foam, this white. Was it a sail?

Pen turned abruptly and went back to the rock outcrop. Climbing it, she looked down on the jagged black obelisks swimming in surf. A shirt. And someone was in it. A torn shirt covered the torso of a man. Now she could see him. His body was wedged between the two rocks, lodged just above the water. His arm hung loosely, his fingers dangling in the waves at the base of the rock.

Pen glared at the figure trapped in the rocks. "I knew it. By God's perfection, I knew it."

She hesitated there on the outcrop. Every sense in her body screamed for her to turn her back and leave this castaway, leave him to chance and the elements. This, *this* was the peril of which she'd been forewarned. Hands clasped, fingers working, Pen scowled at the man caught in the rocks. She couldn't do it. By God's mercy, she couldn't leave a man to die—even if she knew he brought danger. There, she'd made the decision. And despite her misgivings, her conscience felt lighter.

Hopping down from the rock, Pen ran back toward Highcliffe Castle. She was breathless by the time she reached the drawbridge. She waited there to regain her breath, put two fingers in her mouth, and let out a piercing whistle. Dibbler's head appeared out of an arrow slit in the gatehouse.

Pen bent her head back and shouted. "I've found a man on the rocks below the south cliffs! Bring a litter."

Without waiting for an answer, Pen raced back to the cliffs. There was a terraced stair to the beach, but she had to scramble over rocks until she came to those upon which the man was cast. Leaping from boulder to boulder, she stood on a flat stone, bent her knees, and jumped onto the black rocks.

She lodged her feet in a crevice. With reluctance, she slowly reached out and touched his hand. It was cold, and at first she thought he was dead. Her gaze drifted to wet hair blacker than the rocks upon which he lay. She lifted his head, and he coughed.

"Saints!" Pen's hands slipped across his skin as the surf sprayed them. "Sir? Sir, can you hear me?"

He muttered something, but failed to wake. With his long legs and the bulk of his muscles, he would be far too heavy for her to lift. Pen glanced over her shoulder and saw Dibbler and the youth Erbut carrying a litter along the cliffside.

The surf had drenched her. She moved so that she could support the man's head in her arms and shelter against the rocks at the same time while she waited. Shivering, she felt the man lurch and flail his arms.

"No, keep still." Torn between the desire to flee and to give aid, she stroked his head and shoulders in an effort to calm him. "Don't move and hurt yourself further."

Of course he didn't hear her, but her caresses must have reached him somehow, for he stilled into her cradling arms. Pen shifted so that she supported his head against her breast. Glancing at the men carrying the litter, then looking back to her charge, she found herself staring.

She had never seen a man with perfect features. Mayhap not perfect, for the lips were those of an ascetic, a bit thin, and yet somehow in complete proportion to his nose and brow. A blue shadow beneath his skin told her his beard would be as black as his hair.

Why couldn't he have been an old man? Why couldn't he have been a leper? No, he had to be a young man. Young men were violent, they quarreled about trifles and then settled quarrels by drawing blood, by killing. Young men were unpredictable, rash, and they terrified her. And yet, this one . . .

Casting a covert glance at Dibbler and Erbut to assure herself that their attention was on the terraced stair, Pen returned to her perusal of the man. Caught between dread and fascination, Pen bit her lip and studied him. A little voice in her mind hissed to her, *Look, look now, while it's safe.* This might be her only opportunity to see a man's body. His shredded clothing left much of this one's exposed. Much of it was bruised and scraped.

Pen was touching the hill of flesh that formed the muscle of his upper arm and wondered at the silken feel of his skin when it bunched and turned hard. The arm came up, nearly striking her as he moaned. Her body lurched with the power of that movement, but Pen struggled until she captured his arm. Murmuring reassurance, she tried to hold his hand. It was too large, so she held his wrist instead.

His head had turned in his thrashing, and she noticed the purple tint of the flesh beneath his eyes. Without

warning, his eyelids lifted, and she beheld eyes as
startlingly black as his hair. His body writhed, and
she writhed with it. Her warm body slithered over his
cold one. His leg slipped between hers. Pen cried out
at the feel of muscle between her thighs and scrambled
away from the contact.

"Marry, I do believe the Lord has sent me a night-
black leopard in the guise of a man. Be still, sirrah."

Behind her, Dibbler and Erbut climbed over the
rocks with the litter between them. Whatever spell
his eyes had cast vanished with their arrival.

"Leave it there," she called to them. "Help me lift
him to it."

Their combined strength got the man off his rock
perch at last. Dibbler and Erbut lowered him onto
the litter, and Pen searched for broken bones before
covering him with a blanket. She waved at Sniggs and
his son, Turnip, who were hurrying down the terraced
stair to join them. At her feet, the man moaned and
thrashed about as Dibbler tied him to the litter. Erbut
was trying to lash his legs. He bent over the man's boot,
then straightened and held something up to Pen.

"Look at this, mistress. It were in his boot."

Lying in the youth's hand was a dagger. Not a yeo-
man's dagger, nor even that of a gentleman. This was
the weapon of a nobleman. A polished blade of steel
with an evil edge to it. A hilt wrapped with gold and
ruby enamel. A pommel inlaid with a faceted crys-
tal. On the crosspiece above the blade, writhing gold
snakes had been sculpted so that they curled in rich
malevolence, staring at her with ruby eyes.

Pen stared at the dagger, and as she stared, the snakes
began to twist and squirm. She stuffed her hands behind
her back as Erbut tried to hand the blade to her.

"No!"

Erbut jumped at her sharp cry.

"I mean, put it in your belt and we'll store it in the Saint's Tower after we've seen to this poor man."

Erbut gave her a confused look but did as he was told. Dibbler was stuffing the blanket tightly around the man's body.

"That be a lord's weapon, mistress."

"Oh?" Pen clasped her shaking hands together, hardly listening. She'd almost touched the dagger. Dear God, she'd been right about the storm, right about this man.

"I seen plenty of them kind of blades in London town when I were in service to that cloth merchant. That there is a fine blade. And this boy here, he's no sailor. Look at them hands. Palms got no calluses. Rough where he grips a sword. Got no sword, though." He produced a belt and pouch.

"Dibbler!" Pen said. "No filching and picking, remember."

"But we got to find out who he is."

Pen snatched the items from him and pointed at the stretcher. Sniggs and Turnip had arrived, and the four lifted the litter. Pen followed them as Dibbler resumed his treatise upon their castaway.

"He's a lord. Look at that shirt. Finest cambric, it is."

"And how would you know cambric from a camp stool?" Sniggs asked.

"Probably stole plenty of them, by our Lady," said Erbut.

Pen looked at the man on the litter. His head was turned to the side, exposing a gaunt jaw and a long, smooth neck. Somehow, regardless of her dread and apprehension, the sight of that exposed flesh turned her insides to custard. She studied the fan of black lashes against his cheeks, stumbled, and nearly fell. Catching her balance, she glared at the backs of her men, but none of them had seen her foolishness. And that's what it was, foolishness, near madness to allow the sight of a man's neck to nearly break hers.

Pen stopped for a moment and watched the litter and its burden. The storm had brought him to her. Erbut stumbled, causing the man to moan, and Pen set her will against the urge to rush to him. She clamped her teeth together as she watched his body writhe beneath the bonds that held him to the litter. Though he was covered with a blanket, she could follow the movements of his legs, torso, and arms.

Suddenly he arched his back, and his hips thrust upward, nearly sending Dibbler and Sniggs to their knees. That movement, its violence, its suggestion, attacked her senses. She felt as if the storm of last night had suddenly entered her body, and that he had put it there. As abruptly as he'd begun, the man lapsed into stillness.

Pen blinked, then shook her head. "Saints. God's patience. Holy Mother. . . ."

The storm had been a portent; she knew it. She knew it the way she knew so many things, things she usually didn't want to know. Only this time, these presentiments—they were different, more disturbing. Alarm mixed with desire; fear and wanting; the urge to flee and the craving to touch; all of these beset her at once. And they remained with her rather than fading like mist. They turned her world to gold, diamonds, and black fire.

She shook her head again, then lifted it to glare at the prone man. He couldn't do this to her. She wouldn't have her refuge and her peace destroyed by a man.

CHAPTER II

He woke to a haze of blue and to pain. Squeezing his eyes closed, he opened them again. The blue remained, as did the stabbing pain in his head and ribs. He tried to fix his gaze on one point above his head, and succeeded in making out a cherub. Confusion and the pounding ache in his head forced his eyes closed once more. He drifting into a realm where cherubs floated above his head.

The next time he woke, his vision had cleared, but the cherubs were still there. He lay on his back, head and shoulders supported by bolsters, and contemplated the sky above his head. This time he was able to recognize that the sky and cherubs were part of a fresco painted on the vaulted ceiling of a chamber. Angels and cherubs leaned over a circular balustrade with the sky above their heads, creating the illusion of a ceiling open to the heavens. Puffy clouds floated above the onlookers, while a peacock stared down at him in witless curiosity.

Suddenly, another face appeared above him, one surrounded by a mist of light brown hair streaked with gold. It had golden eyes to match, and an angular delicacy that drew his attention and kept it, in spite of his growing dizziness, and a pain in his head so severe as to make him fear puking. The arresting little

face frowned at him. He thought he perceived apprehension in those honey-colored eyes. Yet those eyes
held him anchored, supported him in the midst of a
sea of pain. He stared, but finally lost the battle with
pain and shut his eyes.

"How are you today?" asked the creature above him.
Such few words for so much ease to come from
them. No, it was the voice, chimelike, magically sooth-
ing. In but a moment his very being seemed to acquire
a craving for the sound of that voice—the voice that
banished the torment of his body. Its owner gifted him
again with its music.

"Have you forgotten me again? I thought so. Still,
you seem better, and should be after six days' rest. Can
you tell me your name this time?"

His eyes flew open again. His name. He searched
within himself, swallowing against nausea, and found
nothing. God's breath, he didn't know his name! He
searched again, and found a void, blank as foolscap,
washed clean. He licked his lips and tried to lift his
head. The jarring pain defeated him.

Hands pressed him deeper into the cushions. A damp
cloth passed over his brow.

"I feared it would be so, my lord."

Grimacing, he latched on to two words. "My lord?"

"Well, we think you're a lord. Dibbler says you're
one because of your clothing, and I agree. Even Sniggs
thinks it true, and Sniggs never agrees with Dibbler.
And then there is Twistle, she thinks it as well, and
Erbut and Wheedle."

His brain filled with nonsense names, which caused
his head to hurt all the more. "Please."

The pain receded a bit, and he risked looking at
his visitor again. This time he saw the same fragile
angularity of face and body, the same gold-tinged hair

and eyes, and a mouth blessed with a full lower lip. She was seated on the edge of a stool next to his bed, her perch precarious, as if she would take flight if he moved. Her body reminded him of some fragile water bird. There was about her a brittle slimness blessed with unexpected curves that drew even his suffering attention.

Gazing at the young woman who sat so near and yet seemed somehow unreachable almost made him forget that he didn't know who he was. Almost. The horror of blankness threatened to overwhelm him for a moment.

Again the angel-choir voice called him back from confusion. "Don't distress yourself, my lord. Twistle says you'll remember eventually. Marry, if Twistle says you will, it's a certainty. And we have a name for you anyway—Tristan."

He must have looked at her without comprehension, for she rushed on.

"After all, we must call you by some name, and I was reading, and—"

"I should be grateful you refrained from choosing Lancelot."

She didn't smile, nor did she answer. As they gazed at each other, he watched uneasiness flit across her face and vanish. Her gaze faltered.

"Know you if you're English?"

He tried to think, but ended up wincing.

"The reason I inquire is because I've tried speaking to you in French, and you respond in French. If I speak to you in Italian, you respond in Italian."

"But I think in English."

"*Bien,*" she said, "*parlez français.*"

"*Pour quoi?*" He stopped and stared at her as his thoughts began to flood at him in French. He pressed a palm to his forehead. "God's blood, don't do that!"

"You see," his visitor said in a tone that held suppressed agitation. "The same thing happens in Italian, which is why we think you're a nobleman, or a clerk. But then—" She paused to look at him and blush. "You don't have the shape of a clerk." Then she shifted topics again without warning, causing him more confusion. "But if you dislike the name Tristan, we can choose another."

He was beginning to know her, this young woman who was his only link with the world, and yet the more he discovered, the less he seemed to understand. For his hostess possessed a temperament more changeable than that of a monarch. She feared something, but tried to conceal her fear. And, ill as he was, he perceived that she found him as compelling as he did her. A complexity.

She distracted him from his appraisal of her by suddenly jumping up from her stool as if unable to remain near him longer.

"What about another English name?" she asked as she rubbed her palms against the plain wool of her skirts.

"Pardon?"

"There's Henry, Thomas, John, Richard, Edward, Christopher. Or mayhap you prefer Italian—Niccolò, Andrea, Leonardo, Claudio, Francesco."

"Please." He was drowning in names.

"And then there's French. Like you François, or Alphonse? Georges, Michel, Henri, Jacques, Louis, Guilliaume?"

"Tristan!" He winced and covered his eyes with his hands. A wave of pain made him bite his lower lip. "Please, I beg of you, no more names."

When he lowered his hands, she was still hovering at a distance, a wary gaze still fixed upon him.

"I understand," she said. Her fingers worked, twisted, tangled together. "I hate my own name too. I don't suppose you remember mine, though I've told it to you twice. I'm Penelope Fairfax. You may call me Pen, since I have been calling you Tristan."

By then he would have agreed to any name to forestall more rambling chatter. He clenched his teeth and tried to take her hand for a kiss of introduction. It was then that he noticed that his arm was bare. He glanced down at himself in disbelief to find his body clothed in a few bandages, cuts, scrapes, bruises, bedcovers, and nothing else.

Slowly he looked up at her. He'd expected to meet another look of agitation. To his surprise, he found her gaze on his body. It skimmed over his bare chest and down, down, down. He followed its course as it caressed his ribs, nestled on the flesh at his hip, and then softly drifted lower. During this examination, he remained still, caught in the unexpectedness of her interest. He found himself not wanting to breathe in case he startled her out of warming him with that captivated gaze. A wince of pain defeated him.

She started, retreated a step, and flushed. Then, as if to conceal her discomfort, she put on a smile that reminded him of moonbeams and revelry and adopted a tone of confident cheerfulness.

"I blame you not for misliking your name. I hate my other name. It's Grace. Such a rough-sounding word. Guh, guh, guh-race."

She wrinkled her nose, which made her resemble an irritated butterfly. His misery and sickness vanished for a precious moment. He chuckled, and this time didn't mind that he paid with a jab of pain.

"Grace," he said. "From the Latin *gratiana*, which means kindness or divine favor, which I'm beginning to think I have, else God wouldn't have given me into the care of so kind and lovely a lady."

All he got was a blank look. No smile, no blushing thanks. And yet he hadn't imagined that look of thirst she'd given him. He'd been right. She was a changeable mystery, one more palatable than his own dilemma, and certainly more enticing.

He didn't realize that they'd lapsed into another of those engulfing, timeless stares until the chamber door swung open and a serving woman entered the room. Jolted to his senses, he tore his gaze from Pen's. She blinked and did another of her retreating dances as if to escape his influence and ended up with her back against a wall opposite the bed. Jesu, he was the one with no memory and yet now she acted as if she'd given succor to a murderous dragon.

The serving woman carried a tray of food and cloths to the bed, set it down at the end, and scowled at him. Since she was small and round of body, with red hair, she managed to look like a disgruntled apple.

"Still alive? Too bad." She furrowed her brow at Pen. "Fie, mistress. You should have let me kill him."

He gaped at the woman and began to wonder if he'd landed in Bedlam and all the inhabitants were bedeviled.

"Hush you, Twistle." Pen shoved away from the wall. She walked stiffly over to stand a few feet from the bed, where she addressed him with that false cheerfulness. "Pay no heed to her."

"A little fairy cap or an infusion of lily of the valley, and he's off to the devil, where he belongs."

At this, Pen rushed at the woman and began shoving her out of the room. "Go away, Twistle. He's too weak to put up with your mad rantings."

When the door shut, he tried to sit up again, and

managed to prop himself up on his forearms. Pen picked up a bowl full of rich, dark green soup. Holding a spoon, she appeared to gird herself to approach, and came to him. Before he could stop her, she stuffed a spoonful of broth in his mouth and resumed her blithe chatter as if it were a shield against his presence.

"You mustn't attend to Twistle. Her father beat her and let her five brothers do the same. She lost a patch of hair on top of her head due to one of them. That's why she always wears a linen wimple. She's much better than she used to be. She does well with Erbut and Sniggs and Dibbler now."

He choked as he tried to swallow the broth and realized that Twistle had prepared it. He shove the spoon away and pointed at the bowl.

She jumped as his hand came near hers. "What?" When he made no attempt to touch her, Pen calmed. Then she looked at the broth. "Oh." She shook her head. "Fear not. Twistle wouldn't poison you. Not without my permission." She sipped from the spoon. "You see? No harm at all. It's only jowtes with almond milk."

He subsided against his cushions and turned his face from the proffered nourishment. His head reeled with the influx of unfamiliar perceptions. This woman confused him when he least could bear confusing. He gave up trying to make sense of her apprehension, of her unpredictable changes in temperament as weariness and discomfort gained hold of him. God, he didn't even know his own name. The more he tried to vanquish the mists of forgetfulness, the thicker they became. The magnitude of his own helplessness made him feel so exposed and vulnerable that he cringed.

"I've tired you."

That light, airy voice floated to him, wrapping him

in glittering coils and anchoring him to something tangible.

"Forgive me," Pen said. "I've gabbled on and on, when you're distressed."

He felt her hand draw up the covers to his shoulders and pat them. At least she didn't fear him when he was exhausted. Somehow the touch made the pain in his head and in his thoughts bearable.

"You mustn't worry," she continued. "Twistle says you'll remember who you are eventually. There is a supply boat due in a few weeks." She paused, then said as if to herself, "A long time, but it can't be helped.

"Meanwhile, there is a difficulty," she said. "I would send you to England, but I'm not sure you're English. If we're wrong, and you're French, well, it wouldn't do to take you where you might be arrested for a papist. But enough talk. I'll go and let you rest."

"No!"

He sat up suddenly and cursed at the wrenching in his head. She darted at him then, seeming to forget her own apprehension at the sight of his distress. Her hand went out and almost touched his shoulder, but stopped inches from his flesh.

Breathing heavily from the jolt in his head, he glanced at that hand, at the fingers tipped with pink nails. All at once he wanted that hand on his bare skin. He glanced up at her, not daring to move. She met his gaze, her lips slightly parted, eyes wide.

Still he waited, willing her to touch him. The hand moved closer. He could feel the heat of it. And then her fingers closed into a fist. She blinked at him as if waking from sleep. Her fist disappeared behind her back, and he almost uttered a curse. Her voice banished his frustration.

"Peace," she said.

He lay back. "Stay until I fall asleep. Your company banishes the—the emptiness of my memory."

She didn't answer at once, but just when he thought she would refuse and leave him, she resumed her perch on the stool beside him.

"Rest then. Trouble yourself no more. You'll be here but a short time. You'll regain your memory and quit this place. Yes, soon you'll be gone. Soon."

The words were said softly. They washed over him, and he paid little heed to their meaning, only taking comfort in the sound of her voice. It skimmed over him, featherlike, a sea breeze in summer, and he slept.

In the next few days he waited for his memory to return, but the only blessing for which he was able to thank God was his not forgetting Penelope Grace Fairfax again. No, he didn't forget her, but she vanished. In her place stood an old woman called Nany Boggs with a vermilion nose, who smelled of ale and possessed such bulk that she had a goose's waddle to her walk.

From Nany he learned that he'd washed up on this island and had been deposited in Mistress Fairfax's own chamber in the keep of Highcliffe Castle. Already he'd discovered that, except for Pen and Nany, Highcliffe was inhabited mostly by the slightly demented. There was that murderous cook, Mistress Twistle, and a pink lackwit of a youth named Erbut, and two who competed for the title of buffoon—Dibbler and Sniggs.

How one young woman could surround herself with so many crackbrains baffled Tristan. And if he'd possessed his memory, he might have been able to tolerate such a surfeit of lunacy about him. But his memory was gone. And his only anchor in a sea of emptiness was a creature of variable and mysterious moods who seemed bent on eschewing his company. At first he was too sick to resolve this difficulty. But the longer he had to wait, the more he craved sight of Mistress Fairfax.

Was it his custom to fall prey to such cravings so suddenly? He didn't know. All he knew was that he needed escape from the emptiness, the threat of a lost past, and he knew the path to escape. It lay in Penelope Fairfax, in her voice, in her fey moods, in her touch—and, mayhap, in her body.

On the fifth morning after Pen vanished, he woke feeling much stronger and the ache in his head much dulled. He stretched, feeling the brush of linens against his skin. He glanced up at the peacock. It leered back at him. He scowled at the plump, naked, and winged babes and felt the press of emptiness. Swearing, he thrust himself out of bed and dragged a sheet around his hips. The room's fire had been stoked so that he didn't suffer from the cold. Holding the sheet around him, he padded to the door and opened it.

He surveyed a bare landing and a length of winding tower stair lit by a sputtering torch mounted on a wall sconce. An icy draft whipped up the stairwell and burst upon him. He cursed again and called out.

"Mistress?"

The word echoed inside the tower only to be lost in silence. Where was she? Where was Nany? God's blood, his mind was blank enough without having to suffer from being abandoned and stuck in a black and deserted tower. He filled his lungs and bellowed.

"Penelope Grace Fairfaaaaaaax!" The name bounced off the walls of the stairwell. He threw back his head and filled his lungs again.

"No, don't!"

He looked down to find his hostess on the stairs below him, breathless and as skittish as ever. Her agitation grated on him. How dare she cause him to call out for her like a frightened child.

"Where have you been?" he snapped. "Jesu, woman, my stomach is shriveled with hunger."

At last he'd reached her. Her hesitant demeanor vanished in a flare of answering temper. She marched up the steps and stood in front of him, arms folded across her chest.

"If you're strong enough to bellow like an ox in rut, sirrah, you're strong enough to descend to the hall and eat with the rest of us."

Tristan narrowed his eyes and took in the rise and fall of her breasts. He hadn't felt so stirred in—he had no idea in how long. Letting his sheet fall a little lower on his hips, he stepped close to her, so close he could feel her heat, and said on a growl, "By the cross, lady, if you'll have me in this sheet, I'll oblige you."

Pen's gaze flew from his eyes to his chest, and then down to the warm, smooth skin of his hip. She made a little sound, then stumbled backward, her color rising. Her step took her to the brink of the stairs, where she tottered and cried out. Her fragile features contorted with terror. Tristan swore and grabbed for her with both hands. The sheet fell as he grasped her by the arms and swept her against a wall and pressed against her as if to prevent her from plummeting down the black steepness with the force of his weight.

They remained pressed against each other, him panting with relief, her shivering with leftover fear. Then she gave a squawk and shoved at his chest.

"Don't touch me!"

She writhed against him, and he felt himself stir.

Heedless of the blows with which she was now buffeting him, he set his jaw and tried not to succumb to this sudden arousal. He heard her curse him. Her body twisted. Her hip ground into his unruly part, causing it to leap and buck. He gasped. If he didn't stop her, he would lose all chivalry and lift her skirts right there on the landing. He felt himself twitch again. Catching hold of her upper arms, he lifted her abruptly and gave her a gentle shake that bumped her head against the wall.

"Be still, damn you."

She gaped at him, quivering. Slowly he lowered her to her feet. Their bodies slid over each other, and he gritted his teeth as the slight curve of her breasts caressed his bare shoulder and chest. Her legs slithered down his own, and his rigid sex danced into her skirt, seeking her warmth. Wordlessly she continued to stare at him in consternation.

He couldn't help it. As she settled on her feet, he pressed against her and lowered his head and whispered hoarsely to her.

"You should take better care, Gratiana." He moved his hips against her and elicited a quick indrawing of breath from her. "Look you what happens when you neglect me."

She squirmed and turned her head aside, but he found her mouth anyway. She tried to keep her mouth closed. He smiled against her lips and snaked his hand up to cup her breast. When her mouth opened for a gasp, his tongue invaded. She stiffened, then caught her breath as he began to suck on her.

Tristan felt her body soften, felt her lips open to him. He was brushing his hips back and forth against her when she tore her lips from his.

"No, please."

He heard fear. The music of her voice was drowned by it. Whatever he might be, he was certain he wasn't a man of rapine and forced submission.

"Aye, Gratiana. A moment."

Tristan turned his face away, setting his hot cheek on hers, and gulped in deep breaths. Then he lifted his head to look into her alarmed eyes and gave her a pained smile.

"If you wish to avoid such encounters, I advise you to find me clothing, Mistress Fairfax."

"Oh."

"Aye, chuck. Now, if you will close your eyes, I'll return to my chamber. But if I'm not clothed and fed in the space of an hour, I'll come looking for you as I am, with no sheet."

"No!"

Her outrage made him chuckle. He stepped away from her. Pen's glance darted down, as he'd known it would. She turned the color of a rose, gave a small whimper, and squeezed her eyes shut. Taking pity on her, he turned, picked up his sheet, and vanished into his chamber. She must have opened her eyes quickly, for she banged the door shut after him.

He heard the tap of her slippers on the stone stairs as she fled. Glancing down at himself, Tristan sighed. He went to a washbowl resting on a sideboard and splashed icy water on his face and chest. He spent the next few minutes calming his rampant urges. By the time Mistress Fairfax knocked on his door, he was resting in bed again with the covers drawn up to his chest.

"Enter, Gratiana, if you dare."

CHAPTER III

After her encounter with Tristan in the stairwell, Pen
fled as if hell's fires licked at her heels. Avoiding the
bustle of the hall, she took refuge in the solar, where
she'd been preparing clothing for her unwanted guest.
She dismissed Nany Boggs and shut herself inside.
Shaking, she tried to warm herself in the sun's rays
that beamed through one of the open windows.

She had feared this young man, but for the wrong
reasons. How could she have known? In her experience, young men strutted about with their manhood's
pride on display. They took offense at the cheeping
of sparrows and provoked quarrels that lead to duels,
blood, and death.

How long ago had she learned this lesson? At least
seven years, for she'd been but fourteen. She, in her
impulsive innocence, had followed a pretty young cox-
comb named Will into the streets of the market town
near her parents' manor. It had been a madness, the
madness of a foolish maid's captivation with an older
youth.

She'd gone but a few yards, when her quarry met
a group of young men. Swaggers led to jeers, which
turned to buffets. A glove sailed through the air to land
in the dirt at their feet. Pen shrank into a doorway as
the singing of metal heralded a duel. The jeers rose

to shouts. She was jostled and crammed against the threshold, her face rammed into the back of someone's leather jerkin.

Then she was free, in time to see Will backing toward her. His opponent rained sword blows at him. Will parried, then dodged, but he wasn't quick enough.

The tip of a sword slashed in front of Pen's eyes. It jabbed, straight into Will's heart. He fell at her feet, his pride flooding out of him with his life's blood. She remembered dropping to her knees to touch his face and look into his startled eyes as his soul fled his body. She remembered touching the blood over his heart, and screaming.

Pen closed her eyes against the memory, and lifted her face to the warmth of sunbeams. She'd expected bloody madness from this young man, this Tristan. Never had she expected these confusing feelings, this physical disturbance that made sea storms seem calm.

But he had no memory. Most like, he was as full of violence as any young man but didn't remember it. And now she couldn't rid herself of him as she would like, for no good Christian would cast out a man in such difficulty. She considered sending him across the island to Ponder Cutwell, but reluctantly discarded the idea. No one could trust to the generosity and mercy of Ponder Cutwell. Was there no escape?

Tristan disturbed her. She couldn't forget him. She couldn't make these feelings go away.

Mayhap it was his doing apurpose, for he seemed to know how to compel her fascination against her will and regardless of her fear, how to draw her to him without speaking a word. He'd done it even when he lay senseless on the rocks at the cliff.

She had thought to avoid him and thus relieve herself of the disturbance, but the moment he'd gotten to his feet, he'd nearly toppled the keep walls with his shouts for her. And then . . . and then this disaster upon the landing.

Mother of God, he had saved her from a perilous fall only to come so near her that she'd smelled his scent. He'd smelled of the sea, of smoke, of himself. Then she in her cowardice over a near fall had allowed him to touch her in ways unimaginable. And what had been her recompense? Near seduction, and afterward, orders. Nay, commands.

She must keep a distance from him and pray for the early arrival of the supply boat. She would send him away on it regardless of the state of his memory. Aye, that was the wise course, for if his memory returned, most like he'd turn out to be as bloody-natured as all young men, and that she couldn't endure again and remain in possession of her wits.

"Aye," she said aloud. "You can just molt in that room with Nany and Dibbler for company, Sir No-Name."

But if she didn't give him clothing, he'd come after her. This much she had learned. His majesty King Tristan stood for no transgression against his royal self.

Aye, but she wasn't about to allow him to order her around in her own keep, by the saints. And she couldn't keep living in fear of him and what he might do. She had certain affairs that needed tending to. Work had to be done. The castle and its folk cared for. They had no one to look after them but her. By the saints, she'd show Tristan who was mistress of Highcliffe.

With this avowal, Pen picked up a bundle of clothing from a stack recently mended and placed it in a portable chest along with the small collection of Tristan's belongings. Her conscience troubled her over the omission of the serpent dagger. It was safely concealed with all the swords and daggers in the castle. It would remain there.

Snapping the lid of the chest closed, she answered a knock. Erbut walked in looking as vacantly willing to please as ever. At her orders, he picked up the chest and followed her to the tower and upstairs to her chamber. She knocked, praying that Tristan had the manners to be in bed and covered.

"Enter, Gratiana, if you dare."

She felt her face burn. Glancing back at Erbut, she met his appalled stare.

"Cursed arrogance," she muttered to herself, and slammed the door open.

He was in bed, thank God. In bed and smirking at her as if he knew she'd feared he would be standing naked in the middle of the room. Cheeks flaming, Pen marched into the room and pointed to a spot on the floor. Erbut set down the chest and stood shifting his weight from one foot to the other, and gawked at the guest.

Pen opened the chest without looking at Tristan, snatched up his possessions, and carried them to the bed. She dropped them on his lap.

"There, sirrah, are your clothes and other oddments. As you can see, they were in no condition for your use. I, in my foolish desire to see you provided with better, have altered others left here by my father before he died."

At least he had the grace to stop smirking. He even thanked her. She watched his merriment turn to solemnity, and then to concern as he examined the collection.

As he picked up a bundle of shredded and torn clothing, she dismissed Erbut. He wouldn't want the boy to witness his confusion. She watched him finger the remnants of hose of the finest wool, a leather jerkin, wisps of cambric that had once been a shirt, a belt of expensive leather, and a pouch. He opened the pouch, but it was empty.

In silence, Pen produced a shapeless mess that had once been papers. Neither of them could pry apart the fused mass. If they'd succeeded, the effort would have been to no avail, for the ink had run, leaving blots of gray and black instead of words. Even the broken seal on the end of the papers had been crushed into unrecognizable bits.

He shook his head. His expression grew dark, and his mouth tightened.

"Nothing. I remember none of it."

"Mayhap later."

"Mayhap never."

What could she say? Her own anger faded at the sight of his dismay. She thought she heard a sigh, but he'd turned his head so that she couldn't see his expression.

"I pray you, Mistress Fairfax. Leave me."

"It's near dusk and time for our meal."

"My thanks, mistress, but I desire nothing at the moment but solitude, if you would be so gracious."

His very gallantry spoke of suffering. Feeling guilty for her recent uncharitable thoughts, Pen nodded.

"As you wish. I'll send up something along with Twistle's camomile tea. It will help you rest."

She left him lying there, alone, with his face averted from her.

Tristan woke from a dreamless rest some hours later to find the chamber dark. And he still had no memory. Restless, fearing to fall prey to hopelessness, he dressed and went to the window. He climbed onto the embrasure and looked outside. A rolling fog crept across the inner bailey and surrounded the dovecote and beehives. The old glass in the window made the fog ripple. His breath misted on the panes. On the wall walk he could make out a sputtering torch. Dibbler should have been beside it, but wasn't.

There was no surprise in this fact. He was beginning to realize that Pen conducted the running of Highcliffe in hugger-mugger fashion. She had no real men-at-arms, and Dibbler was a poor alternate. If ever a young woman needed a man's guidance and abilities, it was this one. She hadn't the sense to govern her own humors, much less a castle and manor.

Where was the old fool? He'd met Dibbler yesterday, and a more ignorant and know-everything villain had yet to be born. No, that wasn't true. Sniggs, the teller of unbelievably bad lies, rivaled Dibbler. While he was trying to decide which of the two buffoons was worse, a soft thud caught his attention.

He shot to his feet—too quickly—for he wavered and had to steady himself against the wall. He was paying for his day's unwise activity. Once his dizziness passed, he sped across the chamber to the door and cracked it open. Whispers floated up the spiral stairs, growing more and more faint. He followed them.

The stair was so black, he couldn't see his own body. He felt his way down, hugging the wall. Voices sounded on the landing below, and he stopped.

"I get to hold the rope. I'm captain of the guard."

"There be no guard except for me and Turnip and Erbut."

"That's a guard."

"A pox on you, Dibbler. That be a shepherd and a farmer."

"And there's Wheedle," Dibbler hissed.

A snort made its way up the stairs. "Wheedle be a pig girl."

He was about to return to his chamber, when he heard Pen's light voice.

"God's patience! Cease this perfidious bickering. Dibbler will hold the rope. Sniggs, you will bear the torch, and Wheedle and I will follow. We're supposed to meet Turnip and Erbut, and you've made us late with this witless quarrel."

A shuffling noise signaled the progress of the group below him. He crept after them, down past the chapel to the well room. He waited in the blackness of the threshold while Pen and her servitors bustled out of the room, into the entry hall and outside. Fog was lapping at the steep stairway by the time he reached the top of it.

He flattened himself against the iron-studded oak door of the keep and watched Pen's cloak vanish into the rising whiteness. Forgetting his condition, he thrust away from the door and raced down the stairs after her. What lunacy! She was cavorting with those lackwits in the middle of the night. God save him from witless women. Halfway down, his strength disappeared, an anvil broke inside his head, and his knees buckled.

Cursing, he threw out his arms and dropped to the stone steps, bruising a shin. He crouched there, breathing heavily and shivering. By the time he regained his strength and was able to stand, Pen and her band were gone.

Thwarted and out of temper with his own weakness as much as with Pen's recklessness, he regained the stairs. He returned to his chamber, found a cloak and blankets, and slowly climbed the stairs to the top of the keep. Once outside on the top of one of the keep's four towers, he settled himself in an embrasure and waited.

Soon he found it hard to keep his eyes open. Then, after what seemed like hours, he heard a faint whispering. Glancing around, he could find no other person abroad in the night. The whispering faded into a hiss, a pulsing murmur. Tristan covered his ears, but the sound remained. He lowered his hands and turned his head, staring into the darkness. Abruptly, the murmuring faded. He waited for it to return, and in waiting, he fell asleep.

When he woke, he found himself in a world in which the ground had vanished beneath a veil of white clouds. Silence beat at him, and his body was stiff from crouching in one position. He shivered and climbed out of the embrasure. It had been foolish to remain outside in this cloying mist.

He descended the stairs wrapped in his cloak and blankets, but halfway down the flight that led to the floor above his chamber he heard an unholy screech that made him jump. Shrugging off his blankets, he flattened himself against the wall, and reached for a sword he didn't have.

"Rrreeeeeeeee!"

The noise crawled up his spine and made the hair stand up on his neck.

"Rreeeeeeeee! Ree, reee, reee, ugh, ugh, ugh. Reeeeeeee!"

"Wheedle, make her stop that. She'll wake Tristan."

"Yes, mistress, but it be a malignant thing, prodding her up all these stairs."

Wild surmise drew him forward. He pushed his cloak back over his shoulder and walked down the last flight of stairs. On the landing above the floor housing his own chamber, he met a spectacle. A girl in a smock, hose, and boots was crouched with her back to him, tugging on a rope. Attached to the rope was a brass ring; attached to the ring was the largest and most irritated sow ever to grace a castle keep. And shouldering the distraught pig from behind was his golden-eyed savior, Mistress Penelope Fairfax. Tristan forgot his own misery at the sight of Pen grunting and shoving a pig.

"Pull hard, Wheedle," she said between gasps.

Wheedle hauled on the rope and backed into him. She whirled around, dropped the rope, and gawked at him. Behind Pen, Dibbler and Sniggs had been holding torches and urging the pig on with whispers of encouragement. They too subsided. Pen rammed her shoulder into the outraged pig's bottom. Freed from the restraining rope, the sow squealed and twirled around in circles. Pen toppled to the side, knees high and skirts askew. The pig vanished through an open door.

"Saints, Wheedle, what—"

Pen stopped as he left the shadows and stepped into the torchlight. He glanced at her legs; she tugged her skirts down to cover them. Appalled and yet fascinated, he walked down to her with stately grace despite the foolishness of the circumstance. He offered his hand and frowned at her.

"Am I to believe, Mistress Fairfax, that you, a gentlewoman, have opened an inn for pigs?"

Pen scowled up at him, scrambled to her feet, and dusted her hands. Brushing wisps of hair from her face, she shrugged her shoulders.

"Marry, Tristan, I warrant it appears so. Bad Margery!" She dashed past him as the sow appeared in the doorway, pulled the door shut, and returned to him. She brushed straw and dust from her cloak. "In truth, my lord, I've abducted her."

Pen surveyed her retainers with approval, as though she took great pride in their accomplishment.

He rubbed his temples, for his head had begun to ache again. "You stole a pig? A pig?"

Her amusement disappeared, and she turned on him.

"Stole? What mean you? I don't steal, sirrah. I have abducted Margery from my meanest enemy for good reasons."

Tristan hardly heard her as he realized she had been wandering about the island at night, that she had an enemy from whom she could expect danger, and that she'd also risked the welfare of her servants.

"Jesu," he said. "You've hazarded yourself and endangered these people as well? God's breath, woman. You're not fit to command a cattle pen, much less a castle."

He heard her mutter something under her breath but couldn't catch it, for she turned her back and dismissed her servants, who were listening in avid silence. When they were gone, she whirled around to confront him. Gone was the practical manner of an enterprising adventurer. Her golden eyes had taken on the glint of metal, and her breathing had gone shallow and quick. Tristan began to forget his disapproval of her as her fury provoked his senses. He was so distracted that he failed to attend to her words.

"And if you suppose that I'll endure another of your chastisements before my servants, you're deluded, sirrah. You're an ungrateful, sirrah. And you think being a man gives you the privilege of judging me and requiring me to answer to you." Pen looked him up and down as if he were a dog that had soiled a precious Turkey carpet. "I, sirrah, am not a thief."

For a moment he could think of nothing to say. Blood rushed to his face. He was blushing! She'd made him blush like a child. Thoroughly furious, he began to walk toward her, but she sidestepped to keep distance between them.

"Thievery, mistress. Taking something to which you have no right, something that isn't yours."

He took a quick step toward her, and she shuffled backward. She was facing him and feeling behind her with one hand. That hand met the empty space of the stairwell. He grinned as she glanced behind her. Both of them remembered her last experience with stairs.

"Don't," he said as he stalked to her, "call me sir-rah."

He reached for her with both arms. Too late he saw that she'd braced her hand against a wall. Her foot came up and jabbed him lightly in the chest. Air burst from his lungs. He grunted and stumbled back while she whisked around and vanished into the darkness of the winding stair. He straightened, rubbing his chest, and gazed after her half in puzzled irritation at her recklessness and half in admiration for the way she burst into sunlike radiance when aroused.

"God preserve me," he said to himself as he remembered Mistress Fairfax's passion. "I've been rescued from a sulfurous, roaring storm by a most savory and inflaming pig thief."

On the other side of Penance Isle, the foxes, weasels, and hedgehogs of the fields and forests were just recovering from the spectacle of the abduction of the pig called Margery. Many of them still gazed in astonishment upon the stately courtyard house of Much Cutwell, for it was from the rear of this magnificent brick and stone abode that the parade of thieves had come, squabbling and bickering all the way.

Much Cutwell spread itself over four acres, had fifty-two staircases, three hundred sixty-five rooms, and no sow, of course. Within the house, Sir Ponder Cutwell, owner of this sprawling modern edifice, trailed through the gallery and down the main staircase, his sleeping cap askew, his spindly legs working hard beneath the expanse of his belly. His knee joints cracked as he moved, and with him floated the odor of the cloves he chewed to combat his foul breath. He was muttering to himself.

"My Margery, my Margery. Beshrew that girl. I'll have her hanged for a thief, the hagborn piece."

Trailing his yellow bedgown and robe across the floor, Ponder shuffled into a dining chamber like an animated custard. He started and stumbled into a chair upon perceiving that the chamber wasn't empty. His guest sat with his legs propped on the dining table. Beside a candle sat a bottle of wine. Ponder glanced at muddy boots, clothing of black silk trimmed with gold, and a dark visage surrounded by ebony hair and eyes. Disheveled as he was, the guest managed to make Ponder look even older and more ungainly than he was while himself resembling a beautiful blue-black raven.

Ponder glanced at the sword at the young man's side. His gaze slid away and landed on the wine bottle. He found a goblet and filled it. Draining it, he mumbled to himself.

"The devil take her, stealing my prize sow. I should have burned her out of that castle years ago when she spurned my offer of marriage. She spurned me, and after I took so much trouble in wooing her. Cost me, did that wooing. It isn't right. Not right. The vile creature, depriving me of my land, my castle, mine. Old King Harry gave it me, he did. His son had no right to take it away. None."

"Give o'er, Cutwell," the young man said.

"Foul thievery, that's what it was. I've tried salting her fields, poisoning wells, naught avails me."

Ponder's dark-haired guest sprang to his feet. The chair flew back and slammed against a sideboard as the young man roared at his host.

"Stop your tongue, lackwit! By the trinity, I'll hear no more. Why didn't you tell me the girl found a man washed up on the beach?"

"By my faith, what man?"

The guest planted his hands on the table, leaned toward Ponder, and stared like a snake gazing at a field mouse. "Before he sailed for France, my ship's master told me that your steward mentioned a young castaway lodged at Highcliffe Castle. I don't pay you to worship pigs, Cutwell. I thought this man drowned with the rest of those bastards in the storm, and now I find him lolling and taking his ease under my very nose."

"Upon mine honor, I didn't know."

"That, my fat host, is the trouble."

The guest released Ponder from the prison of his gaze and studied the candle flame. He cradled his goblet in both hands, revealing well-groomed, strong fingers capable of snapping Ponder's neck. After a few minutes of silence broken only by Ponder's agitated breathing, the guest spoke again.

"God has brought him near to me, and I will study to make of him an instrument, ere I take his life. For indeed, Mistress Fairfax's guest must not leave Penance Isle alive."

CHAPTER IV

Muttering to herself, Pen preceded Nany Boggs up the stairs the morning after abducting Margery, set two pails down, and paused at a window slit to gaze across the castle walls to the sea beyond. Offshore she could see the fog bank that had crept in early that morning. She glared at the fog and muttered to herself again.

"Thievery, by the saints. And who made him God's apprentice to sit in judgment?"

Behind her, Nany Boggs glared over a pile of clothing.

"No good will come of this, mark you." Nany grunted as she joined Pen on the landing. "You should send him to Much Cutwell."

"I'm no thief. What? Send him to Ponder Cutwell's?" Pen wavered on the brink of temptation, then drew back. "Nay. Ponder wouldn't shelter Christ himself without profit, and there's no profit in Tristan. Mark you, he might hold him for ransom if he could discover who Tristan is."

"So be it, but I like it not." Nany snorted at the view through the arrow slit. "That be another sign. Whoever heard of fog in bright sunlight?"

"Tush, Nany. If I can endure, you can." Pen picked up her pails and climbed to the next floor, where she set them down again and turned to the nurse. "Give those to me and go away."

Nany relinquished the clothing but remained at the door, arms folded over her bosom. Pen entered her chamber. Still muttering under her breath, she tiptoed past the curtained bed that contained Tristan. Placing the clothes on a chest, she crept to the bed and drew back the hangings to reveal a rumpled pile of covers surrounding a long body.

"Good. It would be a blessing if you slept for the next three weeks."

She scowled at the tangle of soft locks just above the covers. In the torchlight last night they had gleamed like polished ebony. Saints, what was she thinking? The owner of those locks had accused her of dishonesty and carelessness with the lives of her folk. She, who had devoted herself to the welfare of Highcliffe, who scraped and saved and racked her wits for means to their survival.

She was trying to teach Ponder Cutwell a lesson so that he'd stop trying to force her off the island. Who was Tristan to pronounce her stratagem worthless and foolish? He knew nothing of how few were the choices of people like Twistle and Dibbler.

"Cursed interfering arrogance," she hissed.

She yanked the hangings together. "Sir No-Name."

Why had she been cursed with this disapproving invader? That storm, it had been some evil enchantment, a phantasm that brought him to Penance to wreak havoc with her peace. He was interfering with the life she'd worked so hard to build, a life far happier than the one she'd left.

Now she could hardly remember her old home in England. It had been too long since she'd left. Of course, her leaving had been a necessity. Too many careless mistakes on her part had revealed her gift. Saints, but people caught the fever of the mad just because she'd been given a gift from God. They accused her of mischief and sorceries when all she did was know things. Even Mother and Father had been frightened. For no reason at all. Well, not no reason, for they would have suffered along with her if she'd been condemned for using sorcery.

Pen remembered her errand and set a pair of newly polished boots beside the bed. She loved Highcliffe and the wild beauty of Penance Isle. She even loved battling Ponder Cutwell. But she had to admit that, after five years, she'd grown lonely despite the company of her servants and the villagers who lived beyond the castle walls. There was no one to share the burdens of Highcliffe, no one with whom she could talk as a friend. Efforts to discuss the doings of court and country came to naught when the only candidates were the likes of Nany, Twistle, Dibbler.

Cousin Osbert, who had inherited her father's title, wrote of the queen, her ministers, and Parliament to her. But neither Wheedle nor Turnip realized the dangers to England from the Catholic kings of France and Spain, nor the death threat that was Mary Queen of Scots. Pen sighed as she stared at the dark blue velvet bed hangings. Now she had some idea of how beleaguered Queen Elizabeth must feel.

If only Tristan had been an old man. She could have endured an old man. But she couldn't spend more than a few minutes in his company without suffering both fear and some kind of titillating possession. Her gift hadn't failed her in its warning. In the past it had saved her life, though she'd been forced to leave home as well.

In the end, she'd acquiesced to her exile when she

was fifteen, because of the young men—like Will. By then she'd realized how impossible it would be for her to bear the company of noblemen who strutted about with their pride hanging from their sleeves, their swords always ready for drawing. And these same strutting coxcombs, how quickly their swaggering turned to slinking when they found out about her. How could she respect a man who feared her?

But now she wished Tristan feared her. Pen picked up her skirts, and with a last glance at the bed left the chamber, still grumbling. She picked up her pails while Nany stood by in red-nosed disapproval. She handed one to her nurse.

"Come, Nany, time to feed Margery."

Determined to lighten her spirits, Pen began to hum. On the floor above, she opened the door to the pig chamber. A mistake, for Margery was leaning against it, and the portal banged against her billowing flank.

"Reeeeeeeeeeeeeee!" Margery's tiny legs shuffled, and she rounded on Pen. "Uff-uff-uff, reeeeeeeee!"

"Hush, Margery."

"Reeeeeeee."

"There's a nice piggy-wiggy. Look. Pen's brought her some nice slops and mash."

Pen stuck the pail under Margery's nose, then emptied it into her trough. Nany did the same, but refused to remain to watch the enriching sight of the island's largest pig partake of her feast. Pen spread hay from a basket left outside the room. She was standing in the doorway, admiring Margery's enthusiasm for her food, when she heard someone speak.

"Upon mine honor, am I never to rest an entire night?"

Whirling around, Pen beheld her guest looming over her, a frown marring his face, his hair disheveled and his clothing only partially fastened. She glanced at the edge of his unlaced shirt and saw black hair. Discomfort assaulted her, causing her foul mood to return. He yawned, and she marveled that he still managed to frown while doing it. Stuffing his shirt into his belt, he glared at Margery.

"I wasn't dreaming. There is a pig below my chamber."

"Aye, and a fine one," Pen snapped as she closed the door. "But concern yourself not with Margery. I won't keep her here long. Just until I find another place to hide her."

Tristan rubbed his temple. "Marry, why keep her at all? You've stolen her from someone. Give her back and allow me some peace."

"Interfering arrogance," Pen began.

Holding up one hand, Tristan stopped her. "Peace, mistress. My condition this morn admits for no quarrels. Just tell me why you can't return the creature."

"I owe you no explanations, sirrah."

He stopped arranging his clothing, leaned against a wall, and grinned at her.

"Verily, you do not. But then, I could always let Margery out of her chamber in the middle of the night."

"Don't you attempt it!"

"I but asked for an explanation. Why not return her?"

Pen threw up her hands. "Oh, the devil take you. I can't do that. Ponder has to learn not to sow salt in my fields, and the best way to teach him is to keep Margery for a while. He loves Margery."

"Who is Ponder?"

"Sir Ponder Cutwell. He owns half of Penance Isle and hates me for owning the rest. He tried to buy

Highcliffe long ago, but Father wouldn't sell it, and when I came, he tried again. He even tried to get it by wooing me. Now he plays the scorned suitor, but I know his pride and his purse were wounded far more than his heart. The Dark Forest lies between our two domains, and my lands stretch through it. The boundary runs north above the standing stones at the western edge of the island."

Pen found herself unable to take her gaze from Tristan's fingers as they began tying the laces of his shirt. "When my parents died and Cousin Osbert inherited the title, I came here to live." Her voice trailed off as his hands smoothed back hair from his forehead. Then she realized how foolish she must seem, and resumed.

"Highcliffe was my mother's and came to me. It's all I have but for a small inheritance which buys spices and such from the mainland. Ponder has nursed a lust for Highcliffe for more years than I've been alive."

Glancing up at Tristan's furrowed brow, she grew confused. He'd done nothing. He merely stood there, his body vibrant with unleashed power. How could his very nearness agitate her and destroy her composure? To cover her confusion, she gave him a falsely bright smile.

"You see, Ponder served old King Harry under his majesty's minister, Thomas Cromwell."

"Mean you he had a hand in ruining the abbeys and monasteries?"

"Aye," Pen said, lowering her voice to a whisper. "It's said that he was a lowly clerk who rose in Thomas Cromwell's favor by helping him conjure up false charges against the nuns and monks and priests. It's said that he once put the torch to an abbey himself, and was rewarded with half this island for his diligence in serving Cromwell and the king."

Forgetting her ill humor in the telling of the tale, Pen hardly noticed when Tristan bent down to catch her next words.

"And they say that to this day he's haunted by the ghosts of the monks who died in the fire. And Ponder also smuggles. He has a carrack, and the funds from his smuggling most likely paid for Much Cutwell."

Tristan bent down to meet her gaze. Pen gulped at finding his lips so close to hers. After a moment in which she forgot what she was saying, she stuttered, then gave him a jittery smile to hide her growing disquiet.

"They say he fears hellfire and the rack of Satan. I say Ponder is a mean old blister who hates folk and loves pigs, no doubt because he and they share so many qualities in common."

She heard her voice trail off into nothing, but couldn't seem to prevent it. Part of her understood that he was doing it again, remaining silent and compelling her with the sheer force of his gaze and the power of his body. That part of her didn't seem to care. She stared into his eyes, fascinated by the darkness she found there. They weren't the deep, dark brown people usually called black, but almost obsidian black—true, sparkling black.

As she held his gaze, his expression changed. Black fire flared in that look. Neither of them moved, and yet both began to breathe quickly. Inside her head, Pen shouted at herself to retreat, to turn and run. But she remained where she was, impaled by the force of Tristan's mere presence simply because he willed it. Eternity seemed crammed into the small space during which they remained motionless. Finally Tristan murmured to her in a voice low with pent-up and brimming excitement.

"Gratiana, reckless mistress of storms. Do you know what a tumult you stir in me?"

As he spoke, he lowered his head. She watched his lips near hers, but he paused with them barely touching.

"I read your eyes," he said. "They speak of need, Gratiana. Need."

Need, Pen thought. Was that what these feelings were? She tried to think calmly, but he was kissing her, and all thoughts dissolved. She would have been lost if a crash outside hadn't made her jump.

"Oh, I forgot Wheedle."

Pen brushed past Tristan and sprang for the stairs. He gave a frustrated curse and caught her arm.

"What is a wheedle?"

"Wheedle, the pig girl."

Grateful for the disruption, Pen raced down the stairs with Tristan close behind. They hurried to the outer bailey, which seemed filled with milling, bloated pigs.

Pen stopped on the edge of the herd near the girl called Wheedle, and Tristan joined her. He surveyed the roiling mass of pork.

"Pigs again."

Wheedle shrieked at two muddy figures swimming in the midst of the herd—Dibbler and Sniggs. "Get out of there, you poxy fools!"

As she shouted, Sniggs bent down to retrieve a rusted pikestaff and a wooden bucket. A pig bumped him, and he fell over Dibbler. They plunged into the mud.

"What happened?" Pen asked.

"Sniggs stepped on that sow," Wheedle said, "and she charged him."

"But what is that he's put on his head?"

"A bucket, mistress. He's cut out one side to leave room for his face, and he's using it as a helmet."

Tristan pointed at Dibbler, who had managed to right himself and put his makeshift helmet back on his head. "God's toes, he's carrying a halberd. You aren't going to allow that knave to carry a halberd, are you?"

"Shh!" Pen hissed. "You'll hurt his feelings."

"Hurt his feelings?" Tristan gaped at her. "What care I for his feelings? The fool hasn't been trained. Know you how long it takes to master the halberd and the pike?"

He was censuring her again.

"How long?" Pen asked with as much mockery as she could summon.

Tristan threw up his arms as Sniggs accidentally poked Dibbler's ass with his pike. "In this instance, longer than those two have left to live."

"Then they must be careful." Pen called to the two men. "You will take care with those weapons. And don't leave Wheedle and the pigs alone. Ponder may try to steal one of our sows. And you know what to do when the time comes."

Tristan's mouth fell open. He closed it. "Are you saying that this Cutwell knows who took his sow?"

"Of course," Pen said with impudent cheerfulness. "Saints, Tristan, who else is there?"

She'd pitched him into speechlessness. Satisfied, she turned her back to him then and watched the parade of the pig guard. Dibbler and Sniggs shouldered their long weapons, fell into step, and marched under the portcullis. Soon they could hear the patter of dozens of pig feet over the drawbridge.

Tristan gave his head a slight shake as the last pig vanished. Wincing, he muttered to himself.

"Jesu deliver me."

"No time for prayers," Pen said, tugging on his arm. "We must hurry if I'm to show your possessions again as you asked. I have more to do than tend your needs."

An unfortunate choice of words. He leered at her. She flushed and set her jaw while waiting for him to bait her.

He unsettled her by smiling as though he would like to meet her needs right there and then, saying, "God protect me. I'm in the lair of a lady thief."

"I," Pen said as she marched along with Tristan in her wake, "am not a thief. I rarely steal things. Hardly at all. And only if necessary."

Perhaps it was a blessing that she was already red-faced, for she couldn't blush any further when he drew everyone's attention with his laughter.

As they strode across the bailey past a line of villagers armed with flails and winnowing baskets, Pen felt as if she would either melt from the heat of embarrassment or scream from provocation. Head held high, she led Tristan back to the keep in search of his possessions, which she'd cleaned and stored away after he'd seen them the first time.

In the well room she paused. He'd disturbed and flustered her so that she couldn't quite remember where she'd put his things. She stopped in the middle of the well room and turned around slowly, gazing at the arras over an archway, at the tattered hangings on the walls, at the well and the bucket hanging from its pulley.

"Hmmm."

Tristan walked over to join her in contemplating the well.

"I know I put them away most carefully."

Groaning, Tristan leaned against the well and rubbed

the bridge of his nose. "Tell me not that you've lost my only possessions."

"Oh, not lost."

Pen tapped her fingernail against her front teeth.

Tristan winced. "God's breath, don't do that."

"Pardon, but it helps me think." When he sighed, she resumed her tapping. After a few minutes, she broke off. "Not here. Perhaps in the hall."

"God protect me," she heard him say. "Addlepated as well as reckless."

She glared at him, then veered away in an attempt to avoid another quarrel in which she played the fool and lost. In the middle of the room she paused once more and looked around at the rounded arches that marched down the long sides of the room, at the trestles and benches stacked against the walls, at the fireplace in the center of the room. On the dais at one end, servants were laying a cloth over a table. Behind the table was the newer fireplace set in the wall, and above it, high on the lofty wall, hung the dusty banner of her mother's family.

"Now I remember."

Not looking to see if Tristan followed, she went to the dais and the fireplace. Beside it rested an old cabinet that had been in her mother's family since the time of Edward I. She opened the battered oak door, and out fell a dulcimer. Tristan stooped and caught it before it could crash to the floor.

Setting it aside, he knelt while Pen rummaged through the cabinet. She handed him a pair of sheep shears, a pile of scarves, and several sleeves of taffeta and grosgrain. Tristan's arms began to fill as she placed a pair of tongs on top of the sleeves and then added a heap of her unfinished embroidery, a spoon, her sewing basket, and a half loaf of old bread.

"You put my things in here with all this, this, this refuse?"

"Do you wish to examine your possessions or not, sirrah?"

"Oh, I wish it, if you can find them."

Pen bit back a retort and reached deeper into the cabinet, finally sticking her head inside and pulling out an old gable headdress. This she tossed onto the heap in Tristan's arms along with a broken clock.

"There it is."

Pen backed out of the cabinet, whirled, and tossed a bundle at Tristan. The bundle sailed at him, but he couldn't see it for the clock, and it hit the timepiece, which fell against his nose, dislodging the gable headdress, which poked him above the eye. Tristan yelped and dropped his burdens.

Tongs, sheers, spoon, and clock crashed to the floor. Tristan followed them. He landed on his ass with the gable headdress planted sideways on his head. As he came to rest, Pen gaped at him, snickered, then covered her lips with her fingers while she tried not to burst into a noisy guffaw.

"For-forgive me, my lord."

Swiping at the headdress, Tristan blew a wispy silk scarf off his nose and scowled at her. "By the rood, Mistress Fairfax. You're worse than any thunderclap or ravening storm."

Pen knelt in front of him, laughing. "Oh, Tristan, you looked so wondrous foolish."

"God's breath, you did that apurpose. I'll teach you to—"

He lunged at her. Pen scrambled away, tossing the headdress at him, then the spoon. He batted them aside and kept coming. This time she scooped up the bundle wrapped in goatskin and slammed it into his stomach as he came at her. His hands locked around it, and he stopped.

To Pen's relief, he seemed to forget their quarrel. He shook his head and looked down at the bundle. She knew his memories of seeing the contents were slightly blurred. It was clear he was trying not to hope too fervently that another look would spur his memory. Pulling at the twine that bound it, he unwrapped the parcel. A belt of fine leather appeared first. This he touched lightly. He ran his palm over the surface but said nothing.

The belt was laid aside along with the pouch that hung from it. Beneath the belt lay a pulpy mass bound in a kerchief. Tristan examined the shapeless stuff, then glanced up at her.

Pen shook her head. "I tried to dry it and pry apart the leaves, but it was hopeless. I hoped the sight of it or the color of the sealing wax might be familiar to you." She felt a jab of pain in her heart at the bleak look he gave her.

"No, I remember it not." He closed his eyes, his lips turning pale at some effort at self-governance. Then he looked at her again. "But I thank you all the same."

There it was again, that courtesy that concealed an agony of mind. Pen felt her own sympathy grow and smother her offended pride.

"Think you not that it's odd that you would wear no ring, no chain or sword by which we could divine your name?" she asked.

Tristan sighed as he held up the remnants of his shirt and stared at her through the holes in it. "Mayhap I left off wearing ornaments aboard ship. Mayhap I had none."

Pen pointed to a worn place on his belt. "You wear a sword."

"Mayhap not in a storm," he replied.

Pen offered him a length of shredded hose and laces and watched him tangle his fingers in a length of expensive wool. "None of these things yet seem familiar?"

His hands clenched into fists. He sucked in his breath and pressed his fists against his forehead. Alarmed, Pen scooted close to him and touched his arm. She could feel the tautness in his body.

"Fear not," she whispered. "The blankness will pass."

Tristan lifted a ravaged countenance to her and hissed, "You know not of a certainty. No one can be sure. What if I'm trapped forever in this soulless void? I have nothing to grasp, nothing upon which to stand, no name, no past, no family—nothing."

Pen hesitated, then squeezed his arm briefly. "If such a thing comes to pass, why, then, you will be Tristan, brought to this isle through the enchantment of a storm. You will begin from there."

He gave her a twisted smile.

"Dare I hope, Mistress Fairfax, to receive your sweet comfort? It seems you're not alone in having needs. Is that not a thunderstroke of a discovery?"

Pen felt heat rush to her cheeks, but before she could recover her wits, the blast of a horn caused both of them to spring to their feet.

"Jesu, what is that foul noise?" Tristan asked, grimacing.

Pen listened to the horn, then burst into a run. "It's Dibbler and the pigs! Come, we must hurry before Ponder gets them."

She burst out of the keep and down the stairs. As he joined her in running across the bailey to the gatehouse, she heard him mutter.

"Pigs again. God deliver me from perfidious storms and pigs."

TO ROAST A PIG

To roast a pig curiously, you shall not scald it, but draw it with the hair on, then, having washed it, spit it and lay it to the fire so as it may not scorch, then being a quarter roasted, and the skin blistered from the flesh, with your hand pull away the hair and skin, and leave all the fat and flesh perfectly bare; then with your knife scotch all the flesh down to the bones, then baste it exceedingly with sweet butter and cream, being no more but warm; then dredge it with fine bread crumbs, currants, sugar, and salt mixed together, and thus apply dredging upon basting, and basting upon dredging, till you have covered all the flesh a full inch deep; then the meat being fully roasted, draw it and serve it up whole.

CHAPTER V

Tristan followed the whirlwind that was his benefactress as she scurried up the stairs within the gatehouse to the battlements. She'd changed on him again, launching into her guise as a kind of madcap female outlaw. No woman should behave so. And while she was doing it, she was wearing blue and white, a gown of fine wool that made her look like a bit of sky and clouds topped by the sunshine that was her hair. He chased strands of gold up the stairway.

Once on top, he found her dancing with excitement and gazing across the countryside in the direction of the wood. Beside her stood the pink and earnest Erbut, grasping a rope that dropped over the castle wall. Both Erbut and his mistress were pointing and shouting.

"Hurry, make haste!" cried Pen.

She jumped up and down and waved her arms. Not a few moments before, she'd been comforting him sweetly. Where was Penelope Fairfax, the gentlewoman?

Tristan watched Pen in irritated disapproval. Then he shaded his eyes and looked over the battlements to see Dibbler, Wheedle, and Sniggs herding their porcine charges down the path that led from the woods to the castle. Beside him Pen hopped and shrieked encouragement as the pig guard tried to hurry animals never meant to go faster than an energetic saunter.

Behind them came five men on foot, all of them armed, all of them limping and stumbling. The spectacle of liveried men-at-arms chasing pigs caused Tristan to squeeze his eyes shut in disbelief. Upon opening them, he watched the pig guard exhort its waddling charges up to the castle and over the drawbridge while Pen and Erbut cheered.

As the pursuers raced toward the drawbridge, Pen tugged on his arm.

"Help us!"

She stepped behind Erbut and grabbed a length of the rope, bracing her feet. He hesitated, knowing her lunatic habits.

"Come, Tristan, before it's too late," she pleaded.

He shook his head, but at her imploring look, he relented and took up the rope.

"Pull now!" she cried.

They all yanked on the rope. Nothing happened. Tristan rolled his eyes and sighed. Then he put his full strength into the chore, pulling so hard, they all stumbled backward as it gave. Then something caught, and the rope stopped. Pen careened into him, and Erbut into her. Tristan crashed to the floor with both on top of him.

Luckily they scrambled off before he suffocated. He leapt up and joined Pen in hanging over the wall. Below, on the path before the drawbridge, the five men-at-arms churned and scrabbled in the dirt. Tristan followed the rope that hung over the wall to where it angled around a post and fastened to a net that had been covered with dirt and straw.

He surveyed the victims with a frown while Dibbler and Wheedle rushed back across the drawbridge. Pen shouted instructions at them as they drew the ends of the net over the men before they could stand. Then the two hurried back inside the gatehouse, and the drawbridge rose. Erbut went to join his comrades farther along the wall walk. Unable to quite accept what he'd seen, Tristan said nothing when Pen clapped her hands and bent over the trapdoor at the top of the stairs.

"Well done, Wheedle," she called.

"Think you so?" he asked, but she hadn't heard him.

He joined her at the door and peered down at the pig girl. Wheedle was one of those girls one could mistake for a boy. She wore heavy, cracked leather boots, hose, and a long smock wherever she went. Her lanky hair was shorn in ragged lengths, and her face seemed permanently begrimed so that her blue eyes stood out against their smudged surroundings.

Wheedle beamed up at them. "Guess who we got in the big net in the woods, mistress."

"Not Ponder."

"Aye, mistress. He's hanging there like a plump Christmas goose."

Pen clapped her hands again and hopped in place. "Right marvelous, Wheedle."

Tristan uttered a curse of exasperation and walked back to gaze at the men struggling in the net. One had managed to free himself and was unwrapping the others. Erbut, Dibbler, and several other castle denizens jeered at them from the battlements and threw sticks and clods of mud. Once freed, the men shouted a few curses at their tormentors before limping back down the path to the woods.

"Come, Tristan," Pen said as she joined him. "I can show you Highcliffe before mealtime." She gazed down upon her handiwork and nodded to herself with a smile.

She expected him to approve! Barely containing his

aggravation, he pointed at the men-at-arms. "Again you engage in this foolhardiness. You set some sort of trap for those men, for Cutwell."

Pen was watching the retreating men-at-arms and didn't appear to notice his ire.

"Marry, I haven't laughed so since Twistle put a purgative in Ponder's favorite wine." Her laughter bubbled over, showering him with its beauty.

Regardless of his disapproval, as she laughed Tristan felt his body grow light. The laughter took on a hollow quality and began to echo until he heard someone else's laughter. Without warning, he felt a jolt of familiarity—a woman's laughter. She was tall, much taller than he, with ebony hair and eyes. Tolerant laughter. *Run away, child. I've much to attend. Run away, child.*

He blinked, then gasped, but the vision was gone and Pen was calling him. He glanced down to find her at his side, her warm hand on his arm, gazing up at him with unfeigned concern. He caught her hand, knowing without thinking the words that the feel of it nestling in his would anchor him. Her gaze darted to their hands. For a moment he thought she would pull away from him, but she didn't.

"Is aught wrong?" There was a tremor in her voice that spoke at once of fear and attraction. "Are you ill?"

"I think not," he said, distracted by the quaver in her voice. Then he shook his head. "There was something, some memory. A long-ago memory, I think. Mayhap from my childhood, but I can't make sense of it."

Pen smiled at him. "Saints, did I not say you would get well?"

"But there was nothing. No names, nothing attached to the vision. It may only be a dream." He dropped her hand, turned away from her, and pounded the stones of the battlement. "God's breath, I can't endure this blankness."

She came to him and touched his arm. "You need distraction. Let me show you Highcliffe."

In the distance he heard Dibbler and his crew chortling. Tristan groaned and turned to her.

"Oh, no. I'll not be diverted again." He fixed her with his gaze. "You haven't any understanding of the proper way to govern a castle and its lands. What demon's whim caused you to send those folk out on such a dangerous errand? This quarrel between you and Cutwell will end in someone's death if you're not careful."

"Saints!"

Pen's cry was so sudden that he started.

"Saints and saints and saints." She paced back and forth in front of him, her arms waving. "Is there no end to your infernal arrogance? You don't know Ponder Cutwell and his lust for Highcliffe. Has it occurred to you that I'm doing what I can with the little I have to defend myself?"

She stopped in front of him and looked him over from head to foot. "And what makes you think, my Lord Remember-Naught, that you know anything at all about governing a castle?"

Taking a step that brought him so close his chest almost touched her breasts, Tristan growled out his answer.

"I know enough not to start a pig war."

Pen tossed her head. "There's naught to be alarmed about. Ponder will be busy trying to get out of that net. He's as wide as a galleon and won't have an easy time of it."

"Then I would advise you to use the time to prepare for attack," he said, bending so that his lips were level with hers. "If you'd trussed me in a net, I'd breach your walls and toss you in your own jakes."

Pen's neck craned back at an awkward angle as she tried to avoid him. This time he was ready for the sudden appearance of apprehension in her eyes. He spoke softly to her before she decided to run.

"What is it you fear, Gratiana?"

She didn't answer, only looked up at him as if trying to find the courage to flee. His own senses were filled with the luminous gold of her eyes, the desire to touch those slight curves. Not daring to break their gaze, he held it until the last possible moment as he sought her mouth. His tongue touched her lower lip. It quivered, sending jabs of craving from his head down to his groin. Something about that trembling excited him past endurance, and he opened his mouth over hers. He felt her cry, though his mouth smothered it. He grabbed for her too late.

She vanished in a whirl of golden hair and flurry of skirts. He darted after her. He emerged from the stairway only to run into her, as she had stopped in confusion in the shadows. They collided gently, and he caught hold of her arms. To his right loomed the upright mass of the drawbridge and portcullis, to his left, rays of sunlight pierced the open doorway that led to the outer bailey. Although there were half a dozen people nearby, they were alone.

"You should have remembered what happens when we come so close, Gratiana." His voice sounded hollow and disembodied in the dark, empty gatehouse. "Look. There's a silver beam of light in your hair. It's turned to wild mist."

She tried to disengaged herself, but he held her firmly.

"I don't want—"

"Jesu, woman, you know not what you want."

He began to move, edging her back into the shadows

and against a wall. He pulled her arms up around his neck and held them there. In the darkness he traced the line of her face with his lips—forehead, nose, lips. How many women had he kissed? Surely never one who made him feel this agony of pleasure. He opened his mouth and delved inside her with his tongue. Yes, he must have done this before, but he couldn't have felt nearly so bemused.

Entwining his fingers in her hair, he felt the ever-present weight of dread at his lost memory lift. Once it was gone, he realized how greatly he'd suffered from it.

Pen's body slid against his, and he realized she was trying to slip away from him.

"Please," he said, and she stopped, listening in the darkness. "Please, don't leave me. I would never harm you, my Gratiana."

Then he nuzzled her nose with his. All at once he felt the stiffness in her body slacken.

She whispered to him. "I never wanted to kiss a man—a particular man, that is. You don't know. You can't understand."

He went still. What was he that her confession of innocence drove him mad with the desire to initiate?

"Marry, Gratiana," he said as he lowered his mouth to hers, "you may know little of what you're doing, but you're doing it right marvelously."

"But—"

His lips cut off her words, and soon he could tell from the way her breasts rose and fell that she'd forgotten what she'd wanted to say. He pulled his lips free, only to find himself unable to resist kissing her neck. God, he loved her flesh in his mouth. When he reached the base of her throat, her fists gripped his doublet and twisted it. "Saints," she muttered. "Saints, Tristan."

He heard the frenzy in her tone and felt a tingle of anticipated victory.

"Mmmm?" He was trying to devour her neck. He pressed his hands against her back and squeezed her against him.

"You smell like sea air after a storm," she said. "And you feel like . . ." She groaned.

At the sound, he suddenly yanked at buttons and laces and slipped his hands inside her bodice. His fingers skimmed over the flesh above her breasts.

"You feel like . . . I've never felt anything so wondrous," he murmured. "Wondrous, wondrous."

Blood rushed to his head, and to his groin, for each time he said the word, she thrust her breast against him.

She gasped. "I shouldn't."

"Oh, aye, you should."

Her voice was low, febrile, and tense, but it must have been his hands working their way up beneath her skirt that finally woke her. She cried out as he began to brush his arousal against her.

Planting her hands on his chest, she thrust him away from her body. "N-no."

"Jesu!" He whirled and pressed his burning body to the wall.

His cheek rested against cold stone. Clawing at the mortar, he forced himself to breathe deeply. Pen came up behind him and touched his shoulder. He flinched.

"Touch me not, woman. Jesu preserve me. Do you want to end up on the floor?"

"No, Tristan."

He whipped around then to stare at her, chest heaving, wishing she hadn't said that word.

Pen put her fingers to trembling lips. "Saints, I

hadn't meant to—there are things of which you know nothing."

"I know what you do to me."

She wasn't listening to him. Poised for flight, she shook her head. Swearing, he lunged at her and captured her wrist.

"I've watched you," he said. "You want me, but you're afraid. Afraid of something that brings only pleasure. God, I think I shall go mad, Gratiana. I feel all swollen and surging—like the surf, only hot. So terribly hot."

She covered her ears and hissed. "Don't. Don't talk to me like that."

He was still so swollen he could hardly walk straight. Blood pounded in his ears. He cursed and grabbed both her wrists.

"No," she said through her teeth. "You don't even know if you've a wife."

"I don't."

"You can't know that."

Her voice rose, and he heard a thin note of pain. "I can't. Dear God, there is peril here as well as pleasure."

"What peril?"

He heard a half sob. Without another protest, he released her.

"As you wish, for now."

Feeling dazed, he followed her into the sunlight of the bailey before balking. When he caught her arm, she turned a questioning gaze on him.

"You must face it, soon or late," he said.

She glanced away from him. "I beseech you, trouble me no more about it."

"Jesu, but you know little of men if you think I can forget what just passed."

"It's not what you think."

"Then make me understand," he said.

She only shook her head and kept her face turned from him, as if she were afraid her will would break if she looked at him. His body ached for release. She was driving him to lunacy. He hadn't been with a woman in—he didn't know how long, but long enough to make him want to howl with it. He began to feel as if he'd been cast into some mad phantasm by that storm, and he had yet to wake. Yet he was awake. God, how he wished he knew whether he was the kind of man to seduce Pen without remorse, or not. And he feared that soon he wouldn't care.

A shout from the battlements jolted him from his musings. Dibbler was on the wall walk next to the gatehouse, pointing to the west. Something in his stance evoked a response in Tristan. That cry, that gesture. A warning he found familiar. Tristan thrust Pen from him and bolted for the gatehouse stairs once more. She ran after him, and Dibbler was gesturing at them with impatience as they joined him.

He pointed again, and Tristan gazed across fields to the woods. For some ill-defined reason, he expected to see a line of men, cavalry, sun on armor and standards snapping in the wind. No, mayhap there should be great stones, huge monoliths. . . . Tristan searched the landscape even as he wondered at this last idea. At first he saw nothing, but in raking the horizon, he glanced at a solitary hill devoid of trees. Upon it sat a man on horseback, his cloak slapping in a breeze that had suddenly churned up the air.

The stranger moved not at all, nor did his mount. Although he was too far away for Tristan to discern his features, his presence somehow roused an unsettled alertness. The cloak sailed out behind the man, flapping and tossing in the wind. The horse's mane and tail danced in the air, yet neither creature stirred. The contrast caused uneasiness within Tristan.

He stared at the motionless rider, and somehow knew the man was staring back at him—not the others on the wall—only him. His skin prickled, and he couldn't look away. If he'd been a hound, his fur would have risen, and he would have growled. Without breaking the link between them, he addressed Pen.

"Who is he?"

"I know not," Pen replied as she leaned over the battlement and peered at the stranger. "He's clad all in black. No livery, no colors. It's not Ponder." She paused, then resumed on a note of surprise. "This is a young man, like unto yourself, and . . . he's a stranger to the isle."

He continued to stare at the figure in black while the breeze increased and lashed at him. Suddenly he leaned out over the wall. He was almost certain the stranger was trying to commune with him. His hand went to his side, groping for a sword, then dropped, empty.

"Why does he not approach, mistress?" Dibbler asked.

"Mayhap he saw what happened to Ponder's men," she said. "And we have shut up the castle. Anyway, I wouldn't let him in if he's an intimate of Ponder's."

"There's something wrong," Tristan said.

"There's much wrong with those who bide with Ponder."

He still hadn't been able to take his gaze from the man. He felt as if the rider were calling to him, demanding something. He shivered and felt a great relief when, at last, the dark stranger turned his mount and vanished over the hill.

"You mustn't stand in this wind," Pen said.

"What?"

"The wind, Tristan. You must come out of the wind."

"You're sure you know him not."

"Upon mine honor," she said. "Now come."

He allowed her to escort him to the outer bailey, where he inspected the brewhouse, the thatched barn and stables, the dovecote, and the smithy. What he noticed was that the castle and its buildings were more than half empty. No one had mucked out the barn yet or lit the fire in the smithy. Pen seemed unconcerned with this laxity. They stepped out of the dovecote and rounded a haystack on their way to the chapel in the inner bailey. Tristan glanced at the quiet smithy.

"Where is the armory?"

Pen hesitated under the rounded arch of the chapel doorway. "The armory?"

"You must have a place to store weapons."

He eyed her as she seemed to hold her breath.

"Oh, yes, the armory. Yes, the armory." Pen waved her arm, indicating the surrounding wall and its towers. "It's in one of the towers somewhere."

"You didn't show it to me."

"We can see it some other time."

Pen opened the chapel door, but he grabbed it to prevent her from entering.

"I desire to see it now," he said.

"Um, I've lost the key."

He glanced at the ring of keys that hung from a chain about her waist. When she walked, they clicked and tinkled as her hips swayed. He'd come to link that sound with her, and usually listened for it when he wasn't with her.

"Mean you that of all those keys, not one fits the armory?"

"Not a one," she said with a tense smile. "No doubt I'll find it eventually."

She tried to open the door again, but he pressed it closed and slipped between her and the portal.

"Pen, I need a sword."

"Fie, Tristan. You're not well yet to need a sword, and most like you won't know how to use it."

He said softly, "I know."

"Well then," she said with another too-bright smile, "we'll find one for you eventually."

"Where?"

"Oh, there are some somewhere."

"No, you obstinate, there are none." He leaned down to hold her gaze with his. "Not even hanging in the hall over the fireplace, not in the gatehouse, where they should be, not in my chamber, or any other chamber of the keep. The arms rooms in the guard towers are empty of blades except for halberds and pikes. The only blades I have seen are kitchen knives and the like. What kind of castle is this that there are no swords or daggers in it, Mistress Fairfax?"

Pen tried to dig the toe of her shoe into the flagstones. "Saints, Tristan, are there none? What a marvel." Her head darted to the side, and she eyed him. "But then, none of my folk can use a sword. That's why I gave Dibbler and the others pikes and halberds."

"Nevertheless, I want a sword." There it was again, that changeable quality that so intrigued and irked him. He refused to answer her smiles and quips, and continued to stare at her. "Take me to the armory."

Breaking the lock of their gazes, Pen gestured at the stained glass rose window above the door. "Like you our chapel? It's much newer than the one in the keep, of course."

He frowned at her as she chattered. Surely she wasn't trying to keep him a prisoner. The idea was absurd. He caught her arm and prevented her from opening the chapel door.

"I want a sword, mistress." He didn't mention that seeing the stranger just now had made him all the more eager to find one. "I may not know who I am, but I know I use a sword and need practice before I lose my skill. And don't bother telling me there are none. No castles lack swords. And after you've found one, you may tell me why there are almost no weapons of any kind in this moldering pile."

Holding on to Pen when she was disturbed was like holding the wings of a butterfly. She fluttered and dipped and swayed and danced on her toes until she realized he wasn't going to release her. Then she settled and began chewing her lower lip while she looked at the flagstones, the ground in the bailey, the foundation of the chapel.

"Well?" he said. She muttered something, but he couldn't hear her. "What?"

"I said no."

A moment passed while he accustomed himself to the idea that she refused him. "God's breath!"

"Prithee calm yourself."

"God's eyeballs! Jesu give me patience."

He released her, then began to back her into the chapel door, where she bumped her head. Shaking a finger at her, he raised his voice.

"By the cross, no woman sets herself up as my master. You have until this evening to produce the key to the armory. Tomorrow I'll find it and break down the door."

Turning away from Pen, he stalked across the courtyard without giving another glance to the woman he so desired and who had saved his life.

CHAPTER VI

Pen remained at the chapel entrance when Tristan had gone. Near to bursting with conflicting urges, she wanted to strike him, but she also wanted to beg him to try to seduce her again. Surely it was a sin to feel so . . . so heated about a man.

She paced beneath the rounded arch and wished she could scream until her voice echoed off the Highcliffe towers. She'd been right from the first. Young men brought peril. Tristan was already driving her mad with his assault on her senses; now he wanted a sword. She didn't know anymore which was the most dangerous—his passion or his desire for a weapon. She was still shaking in reaction to how he'd stalked her in the gatehouse. What was she to do? Tangling and untangling her fingers in the folds of her skirts, she strained to think of some way to prevent him from obtaining a sword.

Her heart beat faster with each step, and she tried not to think about the first time she'd touched a sword and been consumed. It had been soon after she had experienced her first monthly time, when she'd begun to realize that something odd was happening to her, something more than simply becoming a woman. Her father had been cleaning his sword, and she'd touched it by chance when handing him a clean rag with which to polish it.

A jolt of burning cold leapt from the blade to her fingers and arced from her hand to her chest and then to her mind. In an instant she exploded into a different place—a dark, confined place that smelled like metal, leather, and sweat—and she was so frightened that she nearly relieved herself. Her head was encased in metal, and she couldn't move it well. Narrow rectangular slits limited her vision, and what she could see was men fighting and dying.

She glimpsed the standards of Clarence, Gloucester, Norfolk, and Buckingham. A riderless horse galloped by, nearly toppling her. She raised her arm, and heard the click of metal. She looked at her hand. It was encased in a gauntlet of carefully articulated metal plates that fitted the shape of her hand exactly. And in her hand rested the sword. She heard a scream and turned.

A knight on an armored destrier charged at her. His sallet helmet flashed in sunlight as he raised his sword and brought it down at her. Somehow she knew she had to kneel at the last moment and aim the point of her sword up.

Terrified, she waited until the knight was upon her. She knelt. Gleaming metal plates slid smoothly—and shoved the blade up, underneath the man's arm between the breastplate and pauldron, where only gussets of chain mail protected vulnerable flesh. The point pierced the chain mail. She sprang up, driving the blade home.

The momentum of the destrier jerked the sword and her along with it. She flew after the horse and its dying rider, then yanked the blade free. The sudden release of the sword sent her off balance, and she toppled onto her back. Terror seized her as her padded head banged around inside the helmet. Although made to fit her, the weight of the armor slowed her somewhat.

She rolled and maneuvered to one knee, lifted her head—and saw a blank expanse of polished metal. A breastplate and plackart, raised gauntlets. The tip of a sword hurtled at her and rammed into the eye slit. Excruciating pain. Blood that gushed from her eye socket. It spilled over her face and filled her helmet. She was drowning in her own blood. . . .

Pen remembered this vision today as clearly as the first time. After it was over, she awoke to find her parents hovering over her, frightened and confused. When she described her experience, her father told her that the sword had been taken in one of the battles during the Wars of the Roses. From that day, he'd never looked upon her in the same way. From that day, she knew her father's feelings for her changed. They became tainted with apprehension, a little distrust and wariness, and, mayhap, fear.

It was this breach that taught her to conceal her gift, that and the terror of the experience. From then on she took care not to touch swords or daggers, for they seemed to be the greatest threat. And now Tristan wanted a sword. Sooner or later he would remember the dagger—the dagger with the hilt of ruby enamel that seemed ready to melt and drip like blood, and its writhing snakes of gold. Then what would happen? Would the dagger bring with it the terror she feared? Would it transform Tristan into one of those violent young men she found so intolerable?

Pen trod back and forth before the chapel threshold, muttering to herself and wringing her hands. "Saints, saints, saints, saints. I must find a way to avoid him tonight. I'll not dine in the hall. No, he'd come to my chamber. Why must he be so forceful? Mayhap I can distract him." She stopped in mid-stride.

"A feast! I'll stuff him so full of meat and drink he'll be too surfeited to want a sword. His belly will be so full he won't be able to get out of his chair. And if he does, I'll tell Dibbler to rouse everyone for a game of foot ball in the bailey. I can rely upon Dibbler's foot ball to cause a noisy fray."

Delighted with her solution, Pen set off for the inner bailey and the kitchens. As she hurried through the gate of the inner wall, the weakness of her plan dawned upon her.

"But what about tomorrow and the next day, and the next? I can't keep him distracted from his purpose forever."

Or mayhap she could. Pen's steps faltered in the castle yard. Would he forget about swords if she stopped refusing him her body? Holy Mother, what a sinful thought, made more sinful by that part of her that responded with anticipation at the thought of what he might do. God, she hadn't realized how much she wanted him. She had to think clearly, and with logic, not with desire.

Would he forget? Aye, he'd forget. But not for long. For if she'd learned anything about Tristan, it was that once he decided he wanted something, he didn't stop until he obtained it. And now she was beginning to understand that, in his pursuit of her, she didn't want him to stop.

Pen began tapping her teeth with her fingernail. Best not put herself in the path of temptation. Inhaling a ragged breath, she resumed her progress across the castle yard. No, she must thwart him some other, safer way.

The kitchen was in a separate building beside the

keep. She stopped at the open door and muttered to herself. "What to do, what to do . . . ah!" She smiled and rubbed her hands together. Why hadn't she seen it? Tristan couldn't find a sword if there were no swords to find. Tonight, when everyone else was abed, she would have Dibbler, Erbut, and Sniggs throw all the swords and daggers in the moat. No, not the moat, in the sea. Aye, the sea was much better. Less chance that Tristan could fish them out again.

Pen chuckled and stepped into the kitchen. "Twistle, Nany, hark you. We're to have a feast tonight."

The Western Coast of England

From his hiding place in the shadow of a cliff, Christian de Rivers watched the ship master sitting on a horse at the edge of the shore. The man shifted uncomfortably in the saddle. It was dark, and no doubt he hated being alone on this stretch of wild shore. Smugglers and rogues prowled the cliffs and crags along the beach at this hour. The sound of the surf thundered in Christian's ears. As he gazed at his quarry, the ship master's horse sidestepped the wet fingers of foam that clawed at the sand.

What was he going to tell Derry? Greetings, my friend, I've lost your younger brother and I think he's drowned? He never should have allowed Morgan to pursue that pestilence of a priest alone. But he'd been afraid that Jean-Paul had discovered the English queen's involvement in sending that drunken fool Darnley to marry the Scottish Mary Stuart. And now Morgan had vanished.

Without warning, a cloud that had shrouded the full moon drifted away. Christian motioned to the men at his back. He nudged his mount, slithered out of hiding, and approached the waiting ship master. The silver moonglow illuminated him as he came to a halt. The ship master turned and started as he beheld a rider who hadn't been on the beach when he'd last looked. He touched his sword, but Christian nudged his mount again and the animal walked forward. The master squinted at him as he drew alongside and threw back the hood of his cloak.

Scrabbling on the rocks that lay between the beach and the cliffs signaled the arrival of hunched figures bearing torches. Soon they were bathed in golden light. The ship master peered at the rider next to him and furrowed his brow. Christian nearly sneered, for he could imagine what the man was thinking—too young. This man was too young. A pretty gentle used to pomanders and galliards.

Christian leaned closer to allow a glimpse of fine lines about his eyes, the faint gossamer strands of silver in his hair. Then he spoke to dispel all thoughts of prancing gallants.

"You're the sod who lost my Morgan to the sea?"

"God save you, my lord Montfort. It was a black squall."

"Belabor me not with excuses!"

The ship master winced. Christian's stallion danced and chewed his bit at the violence in his rider's voice.

"I beg you, my lord, don't blame me for the storm. It came from nothing and returned there. I wanted to turn back, but Lord Morgan wouldn't have it. He said good Englishmen would die if we didn't catch the priest."

His voice rose. "A pox take you and your ship. Lord Morgan was like a younger brother to me, and you've killed him."

The ship master heard the sliding of metal on metal and found himself looking at the tip of a dagger.

"How do I know," asked Christian, "that you aren't in the pay of the priest and have murdered my friend?"

"Oh, no, no—no—no. No, my lord. Why would I do that and risk my own ship? It will be months before I can afford to repair her."

The dagger vanished, but Christian grabbed the ship master by the neck of his cloak and nearly lifted him out of his saddle. He dearly wanted to commit murder.

"Tell me, ship master. Could Lord Morgan have survived the squall?"

Sweating, his mouth dry, the master shook his head. "I doubt it, my lord. If he clung to a spar or a barrel, mayhap. But the sea was so rough, I fear he couldn't have stayed afloat. And we were blown so far off course, I vow there was nowhere for him to take refuge."

"And the priest's ship?"

"I know not, my lord."

"You know damned little."

Christian thrust the ship master away. "If I find out you've been lying, I'll make you eat your own entrails."

"Before God, my lord, I tell the truth."

"Did Lord Morgan say more about the priest and his designs?"

"No, my lord. Only that if the priest escaped, he'd cause the death of good Englishmen."

"How?"

"I know not, my lord. He didn't tell me more."

Christian wasn't looking at the master. He gazed out at the dark sea and pearly foam. "I'll wait until I myself have searched before I tell his family." He glanced back at the ship master. "Get you gone from my sight, and pray that I never have cause to doubt your veracity."

The ship master turned his horse awkwardly and rode down the beach. Christian forgot the man. Soon he must give up his search and meet with master secretary Cecil, the queen's closest adviser.

The torchbearers had crowded around their leader. In the dancing light of the flames, every one of them was looking out to sea. Then Christian faded into the cliff shadows once again. His men followed, leaving nothing but sand, rocks, and sea foam.

Tristan looked down at his wooden trencher and knew that it should be pewter, or even silver plate. How did he know this? He shook his head and speared a piece of roasted and spiced rabbit. He glanced aside at Pen, who was biting into a slice of roast suckling. Pigs again.

She was trying to distract him with this feast. The more she avoided the subject of swords, the more amused he became. She had an aversion to hand weapons. A squeamishness he could understand. Most women shrank from violence, and Pen was so good-hearted, so gentle—most of the time.

Indeed, sometimes she was wise. He wouldn't put swords in the hands of Erbut and Dibbler and the other madmen she allowed to serve her. She stole a look at him from behind the glistening screen of her hair. He gave her a smile of such contentment and sweetness that she wrinkled her brow.

He couldn't resist confusing her. She'd snarled him in the woolly yarn of her antics for days now, beset and confounded him by provoking this nagging, unquenchable urge to conquer her. It was time for her to be tormented instead of him. When this mock feast ended, he'd insist upon visiting the armory.

"Cod?" she asked, holding out a plate of the fish.

"My thanks." He took a piece.

"Poached capon?"

He nodded again. She was trying to stuff him so that he'd be surfeited and fit for nothing but sleep. She didn't know how much he could eat. He popped a chunk of capon in his mouth. It had been stuffed with bacon and spiced with savory, parsley, hyssop, and sage. He had to admit that the evil-minded wench Twistle could cook.

While he ate, he surveyed the noisy diners below the salt. As usual, Dibbler was arguing with Sniggs. From what he could see, the fools were quarreling over how a carver should rear a goose and whether it was harder than breaking a deer or chining a salmon. Dibbler claimed he'd seen a carver do all three types of carving in "London town" and therefore he was an authority. God's breath, this castle needed a man's ordering.

The meal progressed, as did the merrymaking, until the last pasty had been nibbled, the last sip of ale drunk from a leather blackjack. Tristan drained his own pewter cup. As he set it down and prepared to address Pen on the subject of the armory, a pair of arms came down from behind him, bearing a tray. Upon the tray sat a giant pastry. He started upon hearing Twistle's voice.

"Apple tart," she said with a grunt. The cook glared at him. "Don't know why she had me make it for you. Mincemeat's good enough for the rest of the folk. Ought to be good enough for you."

He narrowed his eyes. "Did you poison it?"

"Not tonight."

"Thank you," he said.

"Might tomorrow."

Twistle stalked off to a sideboard without another comment. Pen smiled sweetly at him when Twistle was gone. She cut a piece of tart for him large enough for three men.

"I watched Twistle myself. All day long."

He offered her a piece of his tart, but she shook her head. "I prefer Warden pie. I love pears."

"Mayhap because they're lush and juicy, like you."

Pen gawked at him. "Me? I'm bony and flat of form. My chin is square and I could pass for a lad if I cut my hair. Nany says I'm a cricket."

"But you're pleasing to me. Ha! You're blushing."

"Eat your tart, Tristan."

He put down the pie, leaned closer to her, and gazed into her eyes. "I would love to."

Her eyes nearly popped from her head when he touched her thigh. She jumped in her chair and gave a little yelp. Slapping his hand away, she picked up the tart and shoved it at him. He was laughing, so he had no chance to close his mouth. The tart jammed between his lips. He chuckled and chewed at the same time while she ducked her head and nibbled on pear pie.

She kept shoving apple tart at him, and he took her challenge. He finished every last dollop of filling and crumb of crust, then demanded another.

"There isn't another," she said in awe.

He filched a portion of her Warden pie and washed it down with half a blackjack of ale. Then he grinned at her.

"If you're imagining that I'll grow drowsy with the weight of all this food, you're going to be disappointed, Mistress Fairfax. I'm going to finish your Warden pie, and after that, you and I are going to the armory."

"Oh, we can't."

"Nonsense."

"We—we can't until Dibbler performs."

Dismay flooded him. "Dibbler."

"Aye, he's composed a song."

"Jesu deliver me."

"Now, Tristan, he's worked hard on it."

He sank down in his chair and rested his chin on his chest as Pen signaled to Dibbler. The aspiring captain of the guard strode between the tables of roisterous castle folk and villagers to bow before the dais. He had oiled his fringe of hair so that it appeared to be painted in a half circle on his skull. The aged, shiny velvet of his best doublet did its best to cover his paunch. His yellow hose sagged at the knees and ankles. Dibbler passed a hand over his hair, then glanced down at it and surreptitiously wiped it on the back of his hose. Looking pinker than ever and breathing through his mouth, Erbut joined his superior and began to strum a lute. Dibbler placed a hand over his heart, extended the other and pointed a toe.

> *Hey ho and fiddle dee dee,*
> *My love comes to tarry with me.*
> *Hey ho and hi nonny nonny,*
> *Skip to the haystack and folly,*
> *folly!*

Tristan winced and buried his chin in the neck of his doublet. "God's breath."

"Hist, Tristan." Pen dug her elbow into his arm. "You'll offend Dibbler."

"How can I offend a churl who simpers and twirls about the place hooting about follies and haystacks in a voice that would offend a deaf adder?"

Mercifully, Dibbler's fourth verse was interrupted when Sniggs came trotting into the hall, out of breath and perspiring into his patched clothing.

"Mistress, Margery is gone!"

Erbut broke a lute string. Dibbler choked on a nonny—and Pen sprang to her feet.

"When?" she asked.

"I know not, mistress. Sometime between her last feeding and just now, when I went to check on her and muck out her chamber."

Pen threw down her napkin and bolted for the stairs in the gallery behind the dais. Tristan, who was beginning to feel the effects of the feast, nevertheless shoved his chair aside and chased after her. At his heels scampered Sniggs, Erbut, Dibbler, Twistle, and most of the party in the hall. He caught up with Pen before she reached the stairs and pulled her behind him.

"You'll not go first. Have you no sense? Cutwell has most likely come for his precious pig and might still be lurking. Did I not warn you of this?"

He ran upstairs to Margery's chamber with Pen close behind him. The door lay open, and the pig quarters were empty. He glanced up the stairs but saw nothing. Behind them, Pen's retainers crowded up the stairs and tripped over each other. He heard Sniggs yelp.

"Ouch!" Sniggs snatched off his cap and slapped Dibbler with it. "You watch your ox's feet, you poxy turd."

Dibbler thrashed at Sniggs with both hands. "Spavined catamite, get out of my way."

Tristan let out a bellow. "Quiet!"

The milling crowd stilled. Tristan gritted his teeth and scowled at them.

"How quiet do you think Margery's going to be with Cutwell trying to hustle her out of the keep?"

Pen frowned at him and put a finger to her lips. Heads cocked to the side. Breaths were held. Dibbler took the opportunity to pinch Sniggs on the arm. Sniggs kicked Dibbler's shin, and the captain of the guard gave a silent howl. Tristan raised his arm as if to back-hand them, and they subsided. Everyone listened.

After a few moments, Tristan heard a far off squeal of protest. "Listen."

He pointed up toward the top of the tower. There it was again. A high, shrill screech of offended majesty. Tristan bolted for the top of the tower. He hadn't gone three steps before Pen snagged his sleeve and held tightly. He grabbed her hand and plunged through a doorway that led to the walk along the outer curtain wall. They were just in time to see, through the open doors of the next tower, a Cutwell man-at-arms hauling on a rope. He spotted them and began playing out the rope frantically.

Tristan ran to the wall and peered over it. Below and to the right he saw men-at-arms holding tapers, a rotund person who had to be Cutwell standing in their midst. Their attention was fixed on something halfway down the wall.

Tristan pointed to it as Pen joined him. "Look."

Her bulk cradled and overflowing a makeshift sling, the pig Margery floated down at the end of the rope. As they watched, her tiny feet paddled the air as the man at the rope lowered her faster and faster.

"No, you don't," Pen said. She ran toward the man with the rope.

Tristan grabbed for her and missed, then leapt after her. She was almost upon the man when he reached out, slipped an arm around her waist, and swung her off her feet.

"No, Tristan!"

The man-at-arms saw them, played out the rest of his rope, then grabbed another attached to the battlements. As Tristan dodged Pen's fists, he vanished over the wall after Margery. By the time Tristan had set Pen down, Dibbler and the rest had arrived and were hurling insults at Cutwell and his men. Pen rounded on him.

"Why did you stop me?"

Tristan swore, but was interrupted, abruptly, when he yawned. "You're not going to attack a man-at-arms while I'm your protector."

"You shouldn't have—" Pen broke off, and smiled at him. "You're my protector?"

He yawned again. "Of course. Jesu, woman, who else could be in this madman's haven? Marry, this running about can't have wearied me."

"You ate enough for three men. No doubt you've jostled your stomach."

Blinking slowly at her, he yawned. Then he put his hand on the battlements for support, for his head seemed to want to travel in circles.

" 'Smatter with me?"

Pen sidled up next to him and smiled a too-bright smile. "Too much food. I warned you."

"Pen?"

"Aye, Tristan."

"My stomach seems to be trying to climb up my throat."

"To bed." She began to guide him back along the wall walk.

"Jesu, don't walk so quickly. I've treacle for ankle bones."

He swayed and dipped his way back to his chamber, where he collapsed on his bed and stared up at the painted cherubs. Their red cheeks blurred, and he closed his eyes. The last thing he remembered was Pen's light voice.

"I'm sorry, Tristan."

CHAPTER VII

That same night, in the spacious apartment next to the stables at Much Cutwell, Sir Ponder watched his pig man empty slops into Margery's trough while he patted her back. As the pig man left, Ponder's ears filled with the glorious sound of a prize pig engaged in her favorite activity. He sighed, left the pen, and closed the gate. Leaning over it, he beamed at Margery. She'd recovered from the distress caused by being trussed in a harness and lowered over the walls of Highcliffe.

The door of the pig shed banged open. His guest stalked over to Ponder, a tall black shadow illuminated by the lanterns hanging from support posts. Ponder tried to ignore the boiling gaze, but failed. Hunching his shoulders, he wished the man would speak and relieve the agony of waiting.

"Your antics have caused the woman to shut up the castle," the young man said. "By our lady, I can't get in, even to talk."

Ponder rubbed his plump hands on his fur-trimmed gown and cleared his throat. "I had to get Margery back before they made her sick. Do you know how hard it is to physick a pig?"

"By the Trinity, I do not!"

Ponder jumped at the rage hurled at him. His guest snarled at him, then whipped a dagger from concealment and stuck it beneath the lowest of Ponder's three chins.

"I told you to make peace with the woman. There isn't much time before my villainous friend arrives, and this matter must be dealt with before that happens." The tip of the dagger touched the end of Ponder's nose. "If not, I assure you my friend will make you wish it had been."

Stuttering and sweating, Ponder tried to nod, but the point of the dagger stopped him. "M-mm-m—Marry, I will."

"You'll begin at once, this morn," the guest said. "Send some placating message. Beg pardon."

"Beg!" Ponder shuffled backward and out of reach of the dagger. "Why should I ask pardon of a woman who's spurned my hand and then stolen from me?"

The young man regarded Ponder as though he were a bloated snail before fading into the depths of a shadow near his host. His voice floated in the air, disembodied, sedate.

"You're well recompensed for the use of this conveniently secluded hole of pestilence, Cutwell, well paid even according to your rapacious needs. But I grow weary of your loutish pursuits and protestations. Mayhap I should spare myself your company."

The guest paused, and the air filled with the sound of Ponder's labored breathing. "After all, it's near pig-slaughtering time. You'd look a wondrous sight hanging from a tree limb with your throat cut."

"I can ask pardon. I can." Ponder wiped sweat from his chin. "Upon the morrow. At sunrise. Before."

"I have great faith in it, my dear Cutwell. Great faith."

•   •   •

After seeing Tristan to his bed, Pen made sure that several of the village boys manned the wall walk in case Ponder returned. Next, she gave certain orders to Dibbler and saw to it that they were carried out. Then she crept back to Tristan's chamber. Pressing open the door, she poked her head into the darkened room. The hangings around the bed had been drawn, but she heard him sigh and turn in his sleep.

She waited until deep, even breathing replaced the sighs, then retreated. Once outside the chamber, she fled quickly downstairs and out of the keep. She drew her heavy cloak around her as she sped out of the castle, heading for the line of torches marching toward the cliffs. She caught up with them just as Dibbler set down a rope-bound packet at the edge of Dead Man's Point.

Greeting Wheedle and Erbut carrying their own bundles, she came upon a cart drawn by Turnip and pushed by Sniggs. She joined Sniggs in shouldering the cart down the path toward Dibbler. The cart was laden with bundles like those carried by the others. Pen gave a last shove at the cart. Straightening, she brushed her hands and pushed back the hood of her cloak.

Dibbler came up to her bearing a torch. "That's the lot, mistress. But it be a terrible waste, for all you're so skittish about them things."

"Let's turn the cart," Pen said. "We need it to face the other way for unloading. And don't complain. I let you save some. Did you put them in the haystacks?"

"Aye, mistress."

Sniggs gave a harrumph. "I put them in the haystacks. You just sat on your arse and watched."

Pen laughed at Sniggs, for she knew Dibbler took every opportunity to repay the fairy incident. She grasped a bundle from the wagon. The rest grabbed bundles of their own.

"You'll have to throw hard," Pen said. "No, wait. Dibbler, you and Turnip throw one bundle between you. Sniggs and Erbut will do the same. I'll count to three. Ready? One. Two—"

"Three," said Tristan.

Dibbler yelped and dropped his end of the bundle. Pen whirled around to face black-eyed fury. She was so goggled, she tried spreading her cloak to conceal the parcels of swords at her back. Behind her back, she waggled her hand at the others, who scurried forward to block Tristan's view of the cart.

She gave Tristan a desperately blazing smile. "Good e'en to you, Tristan. I thought you'd gone to sleep."

Tristan stalked to her, and as she saw him more clearly, she cringed. He seemed to froth and boil, seethe and bubble with anger. He lifted a stiff arm and pointed at her.

"You poisoned my food."

"Oh, no." She tried to smile again, but couldn't in the face of blistering contempt. She cleared her throat. "It was only All Heal, valerian, to help you rest."

"Luckily, I'd eaten far more than you expected. I don't think you used enough, and you're a bleeding liar."

She winced and bit her lip. He wasn't just angry with her, he was in as great a rage as she'd ever beheld. Never had she thought his anger could be so frightening. She jumped out of the way as he pushed her aside and loosened a bundle.

Swords clattered and slithered against each other. He picked up one, discarded it, then chose another. Testing the weight and heft in his right hand, he gave it a preliminary swipe or two. The blade danced in his hand. As he plied it, Pen grew weak with the knowledge that she witnessed unparalleled skill. This man was no clerk. Next he retrieved a scabbard from the pile at his feet, put it on, and sheathed the sword.

Then he turned on her. "Even a bawdy-house drab has more honor than you do." Looming over her, he swept his arm about, indicating her retainers and the swords. "Have you looked at what you've wrought? Do you know you were about to dump hundreds of swords into the sea? The sea! God's breath, I do think you're mad. Nay, possessed. You belong in Bedlam, where you can bang your head against walls and bite your own fingers and toes."

Pen felt the sting of tears. He was treating her like folk had in England, and without even knowing her secret. She grew cold as she realized she'd never thought it could be herself rather than her gift that people disliked.

Tristan was still railing at her, but she remained stunned as another, even more frightening realization came to her. Never had she thought his good opinion would matter to her so. And, dear God, it was important to her because she loved this furious, sensual man.

The skin around her eyes ached from holding back tears. Her throat grew sore from trying not to cry. She heard him order Dibbler to drag the weapons back to the castle.

Dibbler kicked at a bundle. "We're the mistress's men, not yours."

"Dibbler," Tristan said. "I'm going to pull out your tongue and make you eat it."

Pen swallowed, trying to hold on to her composure

in the face of her discovery, and managed to speak. "Content you, Dibbler. There is no purpose now that he's discovered us. Do as he says."

As she finished, she lost the battle to hold back her tears. Oh, God, he was coming for her! She threw out her hands to ward him off, but he gripped her upper arms and drew her to him.

"I hate traitors."

He shoved her from him and was about to continue, but she stopped him with a half sob.

"No, I pray you. No more." She paused to swallow another sob and desperately tried to keep hold of her reason. "I beg your pardon for my—oh, God, I never thought I'd fall in love with you!"

Tristan's expression went blank. Aghast at herself, Pen whirled around, gathered her skirts, and ran. She heard him call to her, but raced for the castle without turning. Soon his voice faded in the distance. She ran all the way to the castle, gained the keep, and stumbled into her chamber. Throwing herself on her bed, she fended off the alarmed inquiries of Twistle and Nany. Upon her orders, they left her alone.

She lost track of how long she cried. It hurt to weep so violently, but she couldn't stop the sobs. She hadn't realized she'd been so lonely, until Tristan came. He'd forced her to understand her real nature, swept her into a maelstrom of love and desire. And now she'd lost him. She burrowed her head under a cushion and stuffed a fist in her mouth while she gulped and sobbed at the same time. Dear God, he hated her without truly knowing her.

And she'd shamed herself before everyone at the cliffs just now, assailing him with mawkish looks and blurting out her feelings. The thought of everyone from Turnip to Nany pitying her was like a malignant growth in her heart and made her cry harder. She was trying to curl into a ball, when the pillow she'd stuffed over her head suddenly jumped out of her hands.

Gasping, she reared up on the bed to find Tristan standing over her with it in his hands. Her misery caused her to snatch the thing and hurl it at his head.

"Go away!"

Tristan dodged the pillow and sat on the bed. He dropped several kerchiefs before her. Taking them, she scrambled away from him to crouch near the bedpost. There she busied herself in sniffing, wiping tears, and blowing her nose on the kerchiefs. She jumped when he began to speak with unlooked-for gentleness.

"I have just spent most of an hour being chastised, rebuked, castigated, and generally put to the horn. Why could you not have told me about your aversion to swords and daggers?"

Pen blew her nose loudly. "Who told you?"

"Every addlepated rogue of an inhabitant of this castle."

"Even—even Nany."

"Especially Nany, who had taken her usual bath in ale this e'en and was eloquent upon the subject."

Uncertain of how much damage Nany had done, and aching with shame, Pen stared at her kerchief. "Oh."

"She was eloquent until I began asking about the nature of your dislike and how it came about. Then she closed her mouth, the foolish old lament."

When he stopped, Pen sneaked a glance at him. He was regarding her calmly, as if waiting for her to offer more explanations. Knowing she couldn't make him leave her alone, Pen tried to think of a way to get rid of him. He wouldn't relent until answered, but she'd never told anyone about her gift. The one time she'd confided in a girlhood friend, she'd lost her to fear and suspicion. She'd lost her father and mother to the gift. She couldn't risk more pain. Pen twisted the kerchief in her fists. She would give him part of the truth.

"I—um—I saw a man butchered by sword when I was a child."

"There's more," he said. "I can feel it. Nany mumbled about a curse."

"Oh, Nany is always seeing changelings and hags and elves and is convinced that behind every misfortune is a curse due to some . . ."

Her voice trailed off under the burden of Tristan's unsmiling gaze.

"I had hoped for the truth from you, but you're frightened. I can see that now. I should have realized it at once, for you never shrink from battling me in other matters. Very well. Then if your aversion is merely that, you won't mind explaining why you kept this from me."

He had been sitting with one leg braced on the floor. He stooped and pulled something from his boot. Straightening, he held the gold and ruby dagger in the palm of his hand.

"Nany asked me how I found my dagger," he said as he held it out to her. "I found it looking for you. How haps it that you never showed me my dagger?"

As he proffered the weapon, Pen widened her eyes. Her breathing stopped, and her vision filled with the hilt. Crimson enamel transformed into a field of leaves so red, they were almost black. In shape they resembled deadly nightshade, and on the leaves writhed golden serpents. Pen shrieked, threw out her hand to ward them off, and hurled herself off the bed. She raced for the farthest corner of her chamber, rammed into stone, and clawed at it.

Tristan's voice called her back from the gold and ruby nightmare. "Pen! Pen, it's gone. The dagger is gone."

She blinked. Her vision cleared, and her sense returned. She could feel Tristan's arms around her. He'd picked her up without her knowing it and was walking to a window seat. He sat with her in his lap, pressed her body to his, and murmured reassurance. Shivering, Pen grasped the edges of his doublet and buried her face in his neck.

"It's gone," he whispered.

"The s-serpents, they tried to get me."

"I've put it away in my chamber."

"Th-that's why I locked it in that casket."

She felt him nod, suddenly remembered where she was, and burrowed her face deeper into his flesh. Calmer, she realized how powerful his presence was. Unlike the other times when visions assaulted her, she hadn't been lost until the images left of their own accord. He'd been able to reach inside the nightmare and pull her from it with his voice, the feel of his hands and body. Why did she have to lose him?

Gathering her courage, she lifted her head and faced him. "Do you, do you really hate me?"

He closed his eyes for a moment before facing her. "Jesu give me strength. No. I was furious, but I shouldn't have said that. I didn't understand, and you'd been so passionate with me that I felt betrayed."

He met her gaze, and Pen began to drown in a darkness of a different kind, one that began to simmer her blood and turn it to steam.

"But," he continued, "you must tell me the truth."

As he said this, he smiled at her, and her misery

turned to rapture. That one smile caused her soul to dance on moonbeams and whirl in starlight, and so she told him the truth, from the beginning, every bit of it. He listened without interrupting until she finished and grew afraid that his silence meant condemnation. She started when he rose abruptly and placed her in the window seat, feeling abandoned. Then he knelt before her and captured her hands.

"You're such a brave little woodcock."

"I'm not mad!"

"I know that, Gratiana."

He bent and kissed her hands. Pen's mouth formed an O, and she wiggled in her seat at the intensity of the tingling that shot from her hands to her heart.

He looked up at her, scowling. "I find it hard to believe that your parents exiled you here."

"Oh, you don't understand. It was the only way. I was a danger, with my visions and portents. If I'd been accused of sorcery, they would have suffered along with me."

"God's breath, a father and mother are supposed to protect their child; instead, you protected them."

Anxiety caused her chest to burn and tears threatened once again. "No, no. You don't understand. They loved me."

He didn't answer. She met his gaze, pleading, and at last he smiled a pained smile.

"Of course they did. How foolish I am. How could they not love . . ."

She angled her head to the side as he paused, and stared at something beyond her shoulder. She glanced back, but there was nothing. Now he stared at her.

"Did you mean what you said?"

Pen avoided meeting his gaze. "I don't remember saying anything of import."

"You little coward. Back at the cliffs, when you ran away, you said you'd fallen in love with me."

He moved to sit beside her, but she scooted back into a corner of the window seat. When he moved closer, trapping her, she hunched her shoulders and crumpled the skirt of her gown in both fists. She felt his breath skim across the flesh of her ear. Tiny bolts of lightning arced through her body.

"Did you mean what you said, my Gratiana?"

He knew anyway, so Pen managed to nod. The breath on her ear grew hot, and was followed by lips, and a soft kiss. Fingers lifted her chin, and she looked at him. He looked back, solemn and gentle.

"Verily, my dear little woodcock, I think I like this shrinking peony almost as much as my lusty sorceress, or my nonsensical mischief."

She licked her lips. "You don't think I'm possessed by Satan?"

"A fairy with a touch of mad blood, perhaps, but never Satan."

She held still when he brought his mouth close to hers, then thought of something.

"You don't think—"

"Jesu, my love, your questions are cursed untimely."

He kissed her then, drawing her lips, pressing them, opening them. Excitement filled her as Pen understood that she was to have what she'd wanted and feared she'd lost. She came out of that corner then, pressing her body to his and accepting his heavy kiss. She dug her fingers beneath his clothing to find his chest. She rubbed her way down and felt each rib until his fingers at the neck of her gown distracted her. They tugged, then ripped, but she was too busy with her own explorations to care.

"Are you sure, Gratiana?"

With shaking hands Pen wrenched his belt free. "Untimely questions."

He chuckled as he lifted her and put her on the bed. Impatient with the delay, she was placated when she perceived that he was going to take off his clothing. She paid attention to each movement, every piece of cloth, every inch of smooth flesh, every vein that stretched over a muscle.

Although she reddened with embarrassment, she looked anyway, for her newly discovered love impelled her. Once he bent to retrieve his trunk hose from the floor, exposing one of the few curved portions of his body. Pen promised herself that she would touch him there, soon. Then he straightened. He turned toward her, and she saw a white scar nestling in the hair on his thigh near his groin.

A jab of fear struck her as she realized it had been made by the tip of a blade, but then her gaze fastened on his hips, and she forgot the scar. The last bit of his clothing vanished. She hesitated, then reached out with both arms. He came to her, surrounding her with hot, unyielding male flesh.

Her gown loosened as he searched her with his hands. His palm cupped a breast. If she hadn't been so feverish, she would have worried that he would find her lacking. But the moment passed quickly when he murmured something erotic and kissed her nipple. She nearly leapt in the bed with the intensity of the arousal his lips provoked.

When he began to suck, she raked her fingers through his hair and lunged against him. Her nipple was forced deeper into his mouth. She rubbed her hands up and down his body, spanning his back, kneading his buttocks. He moved to her other breast, and her desire climbed a higher peak.

She needed something more. Frantic, she searched his body, skimmed his thighs with her nails, then drew them upward. Her hands found his hips, and then his sex. She shied away, but he whispered to her of his love and his need. So much heat, so much urgency.

At last Pen responded to his whispers and began to stroke him. Each movement brought more heat, more urgency, and filled her with greater tension. She was so distracted by her discovery and its power that she felt no apprehension when he pressed his hand between her legs.

As he touched her, a wondrous aching grew and grew. On and on they pushed each other until Pen was sure she was going to burst into sparkling bits. Then he shifted, reassuring her as he moved between her legs. Kissing her breasts, he kept up his caresses.

She reached for him again, but he forbade her. Pressing her open, he touched her with himself. She started, but he reassured her with a pleading kiss. Pen responded to the entreaty and lifted her hips. He murmured to her again, and she obeyed him by remaining still. She felt so swollen and ached so.

This was true madness, and she needed relief. As he slowly inserted himself, Pen at last understood how she could gain release from her agony, and spread her legs wider. She felt a sharp sting as Tristan plunged forward. She gasped and clenched her jaw as he settled upon her.

Assistance arrived when he began to touch her nipples and suck them. By the time he began to move, she was more than ready. His hand slithered down to her core and rubbed her, causing even greater madness to erupt. Her hands stroked his arms and his back. She kissed her way across his neck and shoulder and dug her nails into his buttocks.

At the feel of her teeth and nails he moaned and pumped harder. Pen sank her fingers into flesh, she drove her hips higher and spread her legs as wide as they would go, and still she couldn't get enough. She wanted to scream with the frustration.

Suddenly he stroked her in that maddening spot and then thrust himself into her. She screamed and burst into flames. Through her inferno she heard him groan and felt him pumping so hard she nearly broke through the bed ropes. He plunged into her one last time as she panted and quivered beneath him. Then they both collapsed, chests heaving, weak, and sated.

She opened her eyes to find him staring at her. He rose to his elbows and cupped a breast. He kissed her.

"My love, even if I regain all my memories, none will ever compare with this."

Her eyes filled with tears. She couldn't help it. She let them fall.

"Oh, Tristan. You make me furious and draw me into lurid sin, and I love you."

"And I, my incomparable Gratiana, seem to have lost myself to you without discovering who I am." He nuzzled her cheek. "Don't weep, little woodcock, or I won't tell you I love you as well."

CHAPTER VIII

Tristan watched Pen drift into sleep. He was afraid to doze and miss that expression of contentment on her face. She'd confessed that Nany had given her a surfeit of bawdy explanations about men and women, but that she'd never wanted to find out the truth of it for herself until he'd touched her. That confession had thrilled him and frightened him when he thought of how easily he could have blundered with her.

Jesu, how he wished he could remember making love before. He couldn't, but when he'd touched Pen, his body had known what to do. Therefore, he must have made love to a woman in the past.

From the ease with which various movements and practices came to him, he suspected he'd done it many times—many times, and with many different women. The idea worried him. Was he a lascivious churl?

He stirred, disturbed by the thought. Pen snuggled into the crook of his arm, and he kissed her forehead. Her hair tickled his nose, and he remembered being chained to his own arousal and feeling her hair with his hands.

The memory evoked a twitching between his legs. He resolved to behave himself. Turning onto his back, he closed his eyes.

He hadn't intended to make love to Pen. He'd

awakened at a sound in his bedchamber earlier and realized that he'd been dosed with some herb. Enraged yet bleary, he'd kept still out of caution and peered past the hangings to see Pen's little face studying the bed.

By the time he'd roused himself sufficiently to follow her, she'd gone. He rushed to the armory to find it empty except for a few scabbards and a box, which he broke open. It had contained the ruby and gold serpent dagger.

He hadn't expected to be treated so by Pen, and his anger had been too hot for him to consider why she was behaving so strangely. Then, after he'd confronted her, she'd burst out with her own anguish. She'd said: *I never thought I'd fall in love with you*, and stunned him as if he'd been thrown against those jagged rocks on the beach again. Then Pen vanished and every ragtag villein, from the pig girl to that know-all Dibbler, had chastised him. He heard about how she'd taken each of them in or protected them, or saved them. And from their ravings, he'd gathered that Pen was as perfect a lady as Christ's mother, and that he was lower than pig dung.

Still irate but willing to forgive, he'd followed Pen after threatening Dibbler and the others with thrashing if they didn't return the weapons to the armory. He searched for Pen, but encountered Twistle and Nany on the stairs to her chamber. The two women crowded him against a wall and ranted. Then Nany had said too much.

"You got no right to come here and make her endure them fantastical visions again!"

He'd pounced on this, but Nany closed her mouth and didn't open it except to mumble that if Pen wanted to tell him about the curse, she would. And so he'd determined to find out the truth. Dear Pen. She'd been so afraid he'd think her cursed, as did Nany. Yet as far as he could divine, this ability, this gift, caused no harm to anyone. How could it, when Pen possessed a golden benevolence, a lightness of spirit beyond measure, a nature suffused with compassion.

Since he'd awakened at Highcliffe, he'd been driven near to madness by Pen's antics and apparent heedlessness, and yet fascinated by them at the same time. Desperate to hold himself aloof until he regained his memory, he had fought not to care for her. When had he lost this battle?

Was it when he discovered her wrestling with a pig outside a bedchamber? Mayhap it had been when she refused to let him succumb to black desperation. Or had he lost the struggle when she'd buried him under a pile of oddments—everything from sleeves to dulcimers? Or mayhap it was when he'd opened his eyes and found her floating above him surrounded by cherubs and peacocks.

Musing over his sparse yet colorful collection of memories, he finally lapsed into sleep. As he dozed, he heard that disembodied murmur. It came to him in waves, as though washed to him by some unseen power. He wondered sleepily if he should rouse himself and ask Pen if she heard anything, but the chanting lulled him deeper into rest until he thought about it no more.

He could have sworn he'd been asleep only a moment, when banging at the chamber door woke him. He groaned as Pen sat up, digging her elbow into his chest. He heard the banging again, and his unknown training asserted itself.

He sprang out of bed, grabbed his new sword from its sheath, and faced the door. He braced himself, but Pen flew past him. Glancing over her shoulder, she eyed the weapon.

"Peace, Tristan. Can you not hear? It's only Nany."

He sheath the sword. "Cursed noisesome old crone."

"Now, Tristan."

He turned and bent over a clothing chest and found his hose and shirt behind it. He glanced up to find Pen staring at his hips.

"Saints," she murmured as Nany began to bang on the door again.

He grinned at her and dropped the clothing. She turned away, blushing and opened the door a crack.

"Mistress, there be a messenger without, from Much Cutwell."

"Tell him to go away."

"We did," said Nany, blowing a strand of gray hair off her forehead and waving an ale mug. "He won't go. Keeps howling before the drawbridge. He's upsetting the bees and the doves, mistress."

"Then send Dibbler out to receive the message. We'll be down soon."

Tristan sat on the bed to pull on his boots and heard Nany hiss at Pen.

"Be you well, mistress?"

He glanced up to find Nany scowling at him like a harpy faced with a minotaur. He frowned back at her, stood, and took a step toward the door. Nany scooted back, sniffed, and disappeared.

He and Pen washed hurriedly. Although he was tempted to delay while Pen bathed herself in cold water from a basin, he knew better. Wiser to go slowly after so active a night.

He wrapped his belt and scabbard around his waist as Pen dressed. Soon they stood facing each other. He noted her apprehensive glance at his weapon. Smiling, he extended his hand. She swallowed, then gave him her hand. He knew she was holding her breath. When she released it, he chuckled.

"You see. I'm no different with it on than with it off."

She drifted into his arms and lay her head on his shoulder. "I was afraid the sword might contaminate you with its nature, but you're too strong for it. Thank God you're so strong."

He didn't understand her, but if she was content, he wouldn't question her reasoning. Together they emerged from Pen's chamber, and met a gathering of servants and villagers in the hall. As they entered, he murmured in Pen's ear.

"Last night was no secret, Gratiana."

She gave him one of her blazing smiles. "I care not."

They met a sea of stares. At their appearance, Dibbler broke from the mass and hurried to them. Glancing warily at Tristan, he handed Pen a sealed letter. She opened it, and they read it together.

"What a marvel," Pen said as she finished.

Tristan lifted a brow. "Is this Cutwell so generous a soul as to forgive and offer peace?"

Pen chuckled and raised her voice to the onlookers. "What say you? Is Sir Ponder Cutwell a generous soul?"

The answer was a din of hoots, guffaws, and jeers.

"A most excellent trick, then," Tristan said, taking her hand and forgetting about Ponder Cutwell.

"Aye," Pen said, "a most excellent one indeed. And one we shall ignore. Are you hungry?"

He bent close to her ear. "After last night's labors, my stomach is as shriveled as my—"

"Tristan!"

He grinned as she clamped her hand over his mouth. He kissed her palm, and she removed her hand in order to press it against an inflamed cheek. Glancing about and finding dozens of gazes fixed upon her, she stamped a foot and sent them scattering to their tables.

She turned to him. "I'll not sit in this hall and be gaped at."

"Shall I have Twistle bring food to the well room?"

"Please."

He sent her ahead, and gave orders to Twistle for bread, cheese, and ale, then followed her. In the well room Pen was drawing two chairs to a brazier. He went to the well and began lowering the pail. He hadn't been jesting about his hunger, but his thirst was worse. He began cranking up the pail, and when it reached the top, leaned over the well to grasp it.

As he bent, a heavy weight rammed into him and he collapsed over the ledge of the well. Without thinking, he jammed his elbow backward and reared up off the ledge. He heard shrieking, as if a herd of sheep were arguing with a magpie.

Someone pounded his shoulders, and he fell over the ledge again. He felt his legs being lifted. His head sank into damp blackness. He heard an echoing shout— Pen. The blackness engulfed him, but he gripped the ledge and kicked with both feet.

One foot met a solid bulk that went flying as he jabbed it. Suddenly the weight on his back lifted. He propelled himself up and back over the edge of the well, whirled, and drew his sword.

"Tristan, no!"

Enraged, he didn't respond at first when Pen grabbed his arm and shouted at him. He located his enemies, two of them. He pointed his weapon. Then he recognized his opponents.

"God's beard," he said, breathing heavily. "It's the crone and the cook."

Nany leaned on a broom and puffed while Twistle fermented, fumed, and pawed the ground. He sheathed his sword, at a loss as to how to answer an attack by two women. Pen was in no doubt. Sweeping past him, she planted herself in front of them.

"What mean you by this parlous attack? Come, don't quail and yammer."

Twistle stomped forward, curtsied to her mistress, and pointed at Tristan. "We did fit the action to his, mistress. We took an oath between us that if he stayed with you the night and did not come forth betrothed, we'd drop him down the well and not let him out until he said his vows."

Tristan wanted to rub his ears to see if his hearing had been disturbed by being turned upside down. He glanced at Pen, whose eyes glittered with mirth as she looked from him to her serving women.

"Fie, Twistle. Would you have me marry a man floundering in a well?"

"Aye, mistress," said the cook, pushing up the sleeves of her gown to reveal thick arm muscles. "Shall I push him in and fetch the old priest?"

"Now, Twistle . . ."

Tristan's amusement subsided as he listened, for it seemed as if the well room faded around him. He was aware of a vague feeling of remorse at not knowing whether he could promise himself to Pen, but that feeling dwindled as an image flitted into his mind and began to take on substance.

A crowd of men in the practice yard. He shouted with the rest of them and hooted at the two boys fencing in a circle of cheering men. The two boys, one dark, the other light, fought with the frenzy of long-held grudges and old hatred.

He cheered the dark one, the one whose hair was as

black as his own, who moved as he did, whose voice was a deeper version of his own. He hated the golden one. Then the golden one lost his sword. It stuck in the earth, and the boy bent to retrieve it.

Tristan screamed for the dark one to take his chance. While his hero charged, passing him as he went, Tristan yelled and gave him an encouraging shove. Catapulted by this additional force, the dark one lunged forward just as the light one pulled his sword from the earth. The sword came up. Tristan shouted. The dark one glanced back, distracted—and plunged onto the sword.

Tristan threw up his hand and called out. Someone shook him, and the sound of men screaming dimmed, then vanished. His attention, indeed his whole being, seemed to alter, called back from the twilight of memory by the sound of Pen's voice.

"Tristan, what ails you? Tristan?"

"It was my fault. All this time, it was my fault."

Pen took his face in her hands and made him look at her. "Tristan, take heed of me. What ails you?"

"I've remembered something."

Twistle snorted. "He's remembered two or three wives, no doubt."

"No, just a fragment, some scrap from long ago." Tristan rested his hip on the edge of the well while Pen held his hand. "But no names. Only faces. There was a man. I think he was my father, and two boys, one dark and one light." He stared at his boot. "The dark one died."

Nany Boggs finished a long slurp of ale and wiped her mouth with her sleeve. "But not a hint about your own name. How can he marry without a name? We never thought of that."

He was still trying to stretch and thicken the memory, but it wouldn't grow, except for this new feeling of boundless guilt and remorse. This was no dream. This was a real memory—one he wished he hadn't recovered. If he could cause someone's death in childhood, what was he now as a man?

Where once he longed for his memory's return, he now dreaded it. He was convinced that the dark-haired youth had been someone important to him, and he had killed him as surely as if he'd held that sword. Jesu, of what else was he capable? What other foul acts had he committed?

Pen squeezed his hand, and he glanced up at her. She was studying him anxiously, so he smiled at her. She must never know how terrible was his sin, for she trusted him without reservation. And he didn't think he could bear to see her enraptured gaze turn to a disdainful one if he told her the truth. He would confide only part of the memory to her, but not everything. He didn't even want God to know the whole of it.

Sir Ponder Cutwell labored up the stairs to the first floor and puffed his way to the high great chamber. Pausing on the threshold to regain his breath, he passed sweaty hands over the fox fur that edged the sleeves of his gown. A voice snapped at him.

"Well?"

Ponder stuck his thumbs in the belt that encircled his jelly-pot stomach. "It's been done, but there's been no reply. That cur Dibbler shoved my man out with no answer to the message. He wouldn't let him wait. If I could get my hands on that pig thief, I'd wrap his guts around a cart wheel."

His guest flew at him in a streak of black fury, and Ponder found his neck balancing on the tip of a dagger.

"How long, Cutwell?"

"I know not." He felt a prick, and blood seeped down his throat. "Ouch! But—but—but I've plied the villagers for news."

The dagger retreated. Pulling a kerchief from the sleeve of his gown, Ponder dabbed the nick on his throat and hastened with his explanation.

"The young man at the castle suffers from a blow to the head which has robbed him of all memory. He knows nothing of himself or how he came to Penance Isle."

Snakelike, his guest wove closer to Sir Ponder and hissed. "It's some ruse."

"Mayhap, but every villager and most of the castle folk believe this malady to be real. Even the lady, Mistress Fairfax, believes him, and she's not a woman who can be fooled easily. If she were, I'd have had her and Highcliffe long ago."

Ponder fluttered his hands. "And there is much talk of how Mistress Fairfax is mortal enamored of the stranger. I fear that she won't release him, for she's more than twenty and a maid. To get her to give him up would be like taking a honey pot from a bear."

The guest turned away from Ponder and slithered over to a line of windows that let in great, wide sunbeams. Blinking in the light, he mused for a while, then addressed his host.

"I've no time to besiege that castle."

"Nor have I the engines with which to besiege it."

The guest turned suddenly to scour Ponder with his gaze. "You say that Mistress Fairfax is a loyal English subject."

"Oh, aye. She devours her cousin's letters about good Queen Bess and the doings of the great in England. She's always saying how her majesty has steered clear of war and made policies for the good of her common subjects. Fostered trade and saved money and such."

Ponder watched, entranced by long, clean fingers that drummed on the sill of a window. He studied the short cloak, the black doublet embroidered with gold, the gold and black onyx ring on the left hand. He jumped when that serpentine voice resumed speech.

"Then I must study to make her want to give him to me. I must drive them apart."

"But how?"

The guest smiled a reptilian smile. "By turning him into what she hates."

"But Mistress Fairfax is difficult to beguile."

Turning back to the window, the guest shrugged. "You have a few days to establish yourself as a peace-maker in the eyes of Mistress Fairfax. A week at the most. After that, I shall go to Highcliffe and claim the stranger."

"But how? That Fairfax harpy is more stubborn than a hundred goats."

"And I must have the services of your blacksmith."

"But—"

"Blood of Christ! No more protestations. See to it that you mend your quarrel with Mistress Fairfax before the week is out, for I intend to show her castaway the inside of your deepest, blackest cellar."

POTTAGE WITH WHOLE HERBS

If you will make pottage of the best and daintiest kind, you shall take mutton, veal or kid, and having broke the bones, but not cut the flesh in pieces, and washed it, put it into a pot with fair water; after it is ready to boil, and is thoroughly scummed, you shall put in a good handful or two of small oatmeal, and then take whole lettuce, of the best and most inward leaves, whole spinach, whole endive, whole succory, and whole leaves of cauliflower, or the inward parts of white cabbage, with two or three sliced onions; and put all into the pot and boil them well together till the meat be enough, and the herbs so soft as may be, and stir them oft well together; and then season it with salt and as much verjuice as will only turn the taste of the pottage; and so serve them up, covering the meat with the whole herbs, and adorning the dish with sippets.

CHAPTER IX

Pen left the kitchen building in a hurry, wiping her hands on her apron, and heard the ringing crash of swords. Her steps faltered. She turned toward the sound, which issued from the outer bailey. For over a week Tristan had exercised and fenced in the unused practice yard, and she'd grown accustomed to the sound. She hadn't grown accustomed to what the sight of him sweating in a thin shirt would do to her.

For most of the last nine days she'd walked about in a blithe muddle. She'd fallen in love with Tristan, and the reward felt as wondrous as a storm in sunlight. At the same time, she felt as if she had been wandering, purposeless and without stability, only to suddenly acquire deep, anchoring roots. A part of her, the uncertain, fearful part, quieted, as if to say "We're home." And all the while, she reveled in the discovery of Tristan's physical love.

Which was why she couldn't defy her urge to wander over to the inner gate and peer past it at Tristan as he plied his sword. He stood in the middle of the yard, shirt plastered to his body with sweat, and lunged at Dibbler, who parried clumsily with a sword held in both hands. Tristan danced around his opponent, delivering quick jabs and slices as he circled. Poor Dibbler, in spite of the padding and armor he wore, jumped and yelped at each light touch of the blade. This past week had been a nightmare for Dibbler.

Pen didn't hear Dibbler's complaints, for she was too busy consuming the sight of Tristan's glistening skin. He'd removed the wet shirt and was fending off a new attack by Dibbler. He turned his back to her, revealing that long valley in the middle formed by ridges of muscle over his ribs. She smiled as she remembered the two indentations on either side of his hips just above his buttocks.

Just then, he thrust at Dibbler. One leg stepped out and bent, taking most of his weight, while his sword arm swept forward. In the sunlight, with sweat highlighting it, the arm appeared wrapped in long, thick cords of muscle from shoulder to wrist. She marveled at the strength of those arms, for he could be sitting down and lift her in the air with them. And yet never once during their lovemaking had that power frightened her. His touch was as gentle as his voice.

Pen watched Tristan avoid a swipe from Dibbler's wobbling blade, darting aside and coming under the man's guard. He wielded the sword easily, in the manner of a man who had had the years of practice it took to be able to lift it with no effort and ply it as if it were as light as a riding whip. He must have had that training, the training of a gentleman. Of course, she'd known he wasn't a common man the moment she saw him.

Dibbler squawked and fell on his ass, drawing her attention away from Tristan. She giggled when Dibbler began struggling with the great helm he'd donned to protect his face. Then she noticed a thin man in a robe that resembled that of a Franciscan friar striding across the outer bailey toward her. Father Humphrey!

Pen turned and scurried back past storage sheds, haystacks, and the kitchen, up the outer stair and into the keep. In the hall she sought refuge by the central fireplace, where she skipped back and forth in front of the flames in agitation. Father Humphrey served the island's inhabitants both at Much Cutwell and Highcliffe. He'd been at Much Cutwell attending to several marriages, two births, and a deathbed.

Father Humphrey was an enthusiastic shepherd to his flock. Pen suspected he secretly longed for the holiness of sainthood, and that his ambitions caused him to ferret out and study with fervid intensity any sin no matter how unworthy of the name it was. When he'd discovered a particularly succulent transgression, his walk acquired a spring to it, and he marched about like a lord mayor on coronation day.

The hall doors banged, and Father Humphrey bobbed into the room. His eyes harbored an almost pleased gleam. Everything about him was brown—his hair, his eyes, his skin, and his robe. He threw back his cloak and stuffed his arms in the sleeves of his robe as he greeted her, but the bones of his elbows still showed through the cloth. With barely a nod, he launched into his attack.

"Mistress Fairfax, for shame!"

"Wherefore?"

Humphrey shook a finger at her. He looked so much like an indignant donkey in need of a meal that Pen covered her mouth to hide a smile.

"You have sunk into the pit of carnal sin."

Pen blushed, but felt her chest burn with irritation. She knew she had sinned, but she intended to remedy the transgression as soon as Tristan remembered his name. It wasn't her fault that the wooing had to take place back to front. And she'd prayed for forgiveness each night. After all, she knew now that God had sent Tristan to her, so he couldn't have meant her not to accept him.

"There must be a marriage," Humphrey said as he caressed the cross that hung about his neck. He raised his gaze to the ceiling and lifted one hand. " 'And if a man entice a maid that is not betrothed, and lie with her, he shall surely endow her to be his wife.' "

They both jumped when another voice barked at them.

"What is this prattle of marriage?"

Tristan strode toward them. He'd thrown a cloak over his bare shoulders and was wiping his face with his wet shirt. He joined them, and from the moment he appeared, Pen almost forgot the priest. Standing next to Humphrey, who was all bone and sanctity, Tristan's bare flesh and hard breathing called to mind the raw sensuality of the pagan. Pen saw Humphrey scuttle away from this man who dominated him merely by his height.

Humphrey wet his lips and met Tristan's scowl. "If a man entices a maid and lies with her—"

"Jesu!"

Tristan's bellow made Humphrey gasp and start. Tristan stalked toward him, and Pen caught his arm in an effort to dissuade him.

"Who is this sanctimonious churl of a priest?"

"Now, Tristan," Pen said as she succeeded in halting his advance on Humphrey.

"This is Father Humphrey, and he's only concerned for me."

He glanced down at her, and immediately all anger faded from his expression. She nearly shivered at the crackling tinder in his gaze. When she grinned at him, he sighed and kissed her hand.

"You're fortunate," he said to Humphrey. "My lady distracts all ill temper. As for the other, I'm sure you've heard that I have no memory. How can we say vows until I know who I am?"

"Oh, oh, I hadn't thought of that." Humphrey sidled nearer and appeared to think over this dilemma. "I shall have to study the scriptures. What a perplexity."

Pen felt a joyous bubble of laughter growing inside her, for until then, Tristan hadn't made himself clear regarding their remaining together.

A din in the bailey interrupted Humphrey's babbling. Dibbler rushed in with Sniggs at his heels.

"Mistress! Sir Ponder and his men are without. He's come to make peace as he said he would in his messages."

"Saints, not now."

Tristan squeezed her hand. "Why not? You can't continue to make war on the man forever, Gratiana."

"But you don't know how delightful it is to see him befooled." She bit her lip and examined the toes of her slippers as he stared at her.

"By the rood, you enjoy all these skirmishes and pig wars."

She smiled at him. "The winters are long here, and after the meat-salting is done and the threshing and grinding are finished . . . And Ponder is such a gumboil, and he festers so when annoyed. He provides hours of merriment on long winter evenings."

"I begin to think you provoke him apurpose. No, don't answer. Jesu, allow him in so that I may meet this fool who hasn't enough sense to know how you play him."

She nodded, and he turned to Dibbler.

"Cutwell may enter, but allow him only one companion and no men-at-arms. Conduct him here."

"Aye, my lord."

Humphrey bristled at this address. "My lord? But you said you have no name."

"He doesn't," Pen replied. "But Dibbler says Tristan is a lord because of his manner and the clothing in which we found him. So Dibbler has called him 'my lord' from the first, and everyone followed Dibbler's example."

"Dibbler has a high opinion of his reasoning skills," Tristan said.

They turned to the double doors of the hall as they swung open and a party of men entered. Dibbler led the way while Sniggs, Erbut, Turnip, and several farm lads flanked two strangers. Tristan was standing close to her, and she felt him tense. Glancing up at him, she saw that he was gazing not at Sir Ponder Cutwell, but at his companion. The stranger's coloring was as dark as Tristan's, but his chin was more rounded, his eyes less black and more brown. However, his movements had that same easy quickness, that freedom of motion that comes with constant physical activity. His hair was as black as Tristan's, but he wore an air of entitlement she'd seldom encountered in her own guest.

Sir Ponder navigated toward her slowly, his progress made unwieldy by the thick fur trim at the hem of his gown and the full-length coat of tarnished silver damask that kept getting tangled between his legs. Pen eyed his side locks, which he'd grown long, pomaded, and combed over his bare dome in an ill-advised attempt to disguise his baldness.

"At last, Mistress Fairfax, at last we may end this foolish hurly-burly. God be with you."

Ponder bent over her hand. Pen tried not to grimace as he touched parchment-dry lips to the back of her hand. She refused to give him the kiss of greeting, even if she had to listen to a scolding from Father Humphrey. Instead, she murmured a welcome and looked inquiringly at the stranger.

Ponder gave his companion an apprehensive glance. "Er, Lord Morgan St. John, may I present Mistress Penelope Fairfax."

She curtsied to St. John's bow, but when they rose, she found him gazing not at her, but at Tristan. Ponder was also studying him. She looked at him as well, but he appeared to be waiting patiently for his own introduction and gazed back at Ponder and St. John without so much as an eye twitch of disturbance. St. John seemed to be waiting for something too. He glanced over Tristan's entire figure, noting the sword, the bare chest, the arms held loosely at his sides. At last he broke the silence.

"My name amazes you not?"

Pen felt a growing irritation, for this man hadn't spoken to her at all. An imp of mischievousness caused her to interrupt.

"Fie, my lord, how could so commonplace a name as Morgan cause agitation to one blessed with a beautiful one like Tristan? If it please you, your name seems a quite serviceable one. Not one to be ashamed of at all."

St. John gave her a glance that told her he was speculating on just how mad she might be. Then he'd forgotten her again and was staring rudely at Tristan.

"Now," she continued, "if your name had been Dogdyke or Poxy John or Weasel, then we would indeed have been amazed."

That made him look at her again. She smiled a treacle-sweet smile at him.

"My lord, may I present my guest, Tristan, who has been cast upon our shores in a storm and has lost his memory."

St. John moved closer as he nodded to Tristan. Pen felt rather than saw Tristan's tautness of mood. He inclined his head, no more, at this man who seemed to think himself the superior of all the company. When St. John came nearer, his hand began to rub the silver embossing on the sheath of his sword.

"What a tragedy," St. John said.

What was it that caused the hair on the back of her neck to rise? Mayhap it was the vibrating timbre of that voice, and the way he purred at Tristan. That low thrumming reminded her of a cat that has just dined and is lying on a sun-baked rock contemplating an unsuspecting lizard for dessert.

"Then you don't know my name," St. John said as he trapped Tristan's gaze with his own.

"Jesu, my lord, since I know not my own," Tristan said, "how could I recall yours?"

St. John made no reply, but instead gave Tristan a smile of relish, of gloat, almost of gluttony.

Ponder had been warming his hands by the fire. "Lord Morgan is thinking of purchasing some of my property on the mainland. In Cornwall."

There was another uncomfortable silence while the two younger men surveyed each other and Pen tried to deduce why they'd conceived such an animosity for each other at first sight. St. John startled everyone with another of his odd remarks.

"Then if you've lost your memory, you don't know whether you're a papist or a follower of her majesty's church of England, or even of the teachings of Martin Luther. In faith, you don't know which faith holds the truth."

"Are you saying you do?" Tristan asked.

"By the rood, sirrah. Every good subject of her majesty knows the difference between our Lord's truth and popish lies."

Pen's own experience warned her of the danger of religious quarrels and accusations. "My lords, there is no need for this discussion."

"God's breath," Tristan said without a glance at her. "I hate sanctimony."

St. John gave him another of his gloating smiles and bowed. "Your pardon, sir. I but remarked upon how difficult must be the plight of a man who knows not whether his soul is safe."

"I can manage my own soul."

Pen was caught off guard when St. John looked at her and said, "Or allow Mistress Fairfax to look after it."

She put her palms to her cheeks to cool the flames that rose there. "Oh," she said as she heard Tristan whisper a curse. "Oh, saints, my lord, you really shouldn't have said that."

As Morgan stepped away from her and put his hand on the pommel of his sword, she tried to grasp his arm and missed. This was what she hated about young men. Put them in proximity and they behaved like rams in rutting season. So much violence, so much barely leashed power, so little sense. She followed Tristan as he moved apart from her, closed the gap between them, and lay her hand on his shoulder. At her touch, his body went still, taut muscles went slack.

"Forgive me," she said loudly, causing the men to look at her. "I haven't offered the hospitality of Highcliffe. Dibbler, attend to it. Good gentlemen, please come to the fireplace. Sniggs, bring more cushions."

Without waiting for their agreement, she went to the dais and sat in her chair with the Fairfax coat of arms carved in it. Ponder scurried after her. Thus abandoned, the younger men had no choice but to give up the confrontation and join her. After this, she kept control of the conversation by flitting and hopping from one topic to another and chattered inanities until hot spiced cider appeared along with meat pies, bread, and cheese. Several times St. John tried to engage Tristan in some contentious discussion, but she managed to distract them with her rattled nonsense. Unfortunately, St. John proved the better strategist, for he waited until she took a sip of her drink to speak again.

"Enough of this senseless prattling. Sir, or Tristan, since you've no other name, I would have privy converse with you."

Pen burned her throat swallowing too quickly. "What needs this privacy? What can you have to say to Tristan since he's a stranger to you?" She stopped abruptly as the significance of what she was saying occurred to her.

Tristan was frowning at St. John. He rose without a word and swept an arm in the direction of the stairs that led to his chamber. Not waiting for permission from her or Sir Ponder, he left. St. John bowed to her and followed. As the two men vanished, Pen's apprehension grew. She didn't like St. John. She didn't like him speaking to Tristan alone. Her agitation increased when Ponder suddenly rubbed greasy lips on a napkin, set aside a meat pie, and made excuses.

"So many duties to attend to at Much Cutwell. I will take leave of you now. Mayhap now that we've settled our little differences, we can be friends, though, as you know, I want much more than friendship."

Pen stared at him as he babbled.

CHAPTER X

The trouble with holding a privy conversation in a keep is that there are few privy places. Tristan left the hall with St. John behind him, only to encounter Twistle on her way to the well room and two boys carrying a turnspit. He mounted the stairs in the tower that contained his chamber, only to meet three maids dragging bundles of soiled linen coming down while two more overtook him with clean sheets on his way up. He reached his door, shooed the maids on, and held it open for his guest.

He glared at a boy with a broom who appeared on the landing, and the lad scampered back downstairs. Shutting the door and glaring at it, he turned to St. John and found himself the object of a down-to-the-bone scrutiny. He felt a prickling along his spine, a warning, as if he were back on the castle battlements, caught in that duel of stares.

"What have you to say to me that demands privacy?" he asked.

"Such haste." St. John turned away, went to a window embrasure, and leaned his hip against it. "I agree. Without a doubt we'll have little time before your mad mistress conceives of some excuse to interrupt."

Tristan couldn't rid himself of that prickling feeling.

This man's very presence made him want to snarl and bare his fangs. He waited, but St. John was still contemplating him with the unwavering regard of a snake. Then, suddenly, he burst out with a chuckle.

"*Sacré Dieu, mon ami.* You may abandon the pretense. I fail to see that it gains you anything now that I've found you. Indeed, I fail to see the need to conceal yourself at all."

Tristan frowned. "You're French. Why have you come here pretending to be English?"

St. John sighed and shrugged his shoulders.

"Why think you that I'm the one who is French? Am I not speaking a language you know intimately?" He paused, then laughed. "Come, you've betrayed yourself, so you may as well abandon playing this foolish part."

"I'm not playing a part, and I don't like being lied to, especially by Frenchmen." Tristan turned his back and walked to the door.

"*Arrêtez.*"

Tristan found himself obeying. He turned to face St. John.

"*Si je parle français, tu parles français. Oui?*"

His mind filled with French, and with it came a flash of memory, a brief image of this man standing in the shadow of a ruined abbey, standing over another man prostrate at his feet, a man with golden hair. *Infortuné, mon fils. This quick wit of yours has brought you a death sentence.*

Tristan put his hands to his head, wincing, and heard himself say, "*Arrêtez. Je ne le comprends pas. Je vous implore.* No more."

He started at the sound of St. John's voice, for the man had left the embrasure quietly and now stood too close.

"*Non, mon ami.* It is you who must stop, and you do understand what is happening. Shall I prove it?"

St. John leaned closer, so close that Tristan shoved his cloak aside and dropped his hand to the hilt of his sword. At the movement, St. John arrested his advance and spoke softly.

"If your loss of memory isn't a ruse, then you won't care if I tell you Derry is dead."

Tristan furrowed his brow but could find no response to this new name within himself. He met the challenge of St. John's gaze with an unruffled stare. The silence between them lengthened until his opponent broke off, leaned against the wall beside Tristan, and chuckled again.

"*Dieu.* Mayhap I will believe you after all. Or is it that you're as great a liar as I am?"

Tristan stared at him. "You know me."

"Too well. You are my curse."

He didn't think; he only moved. Grasping the man by the neck of his doublet, he wrenched him upright. "Tell me who I am."

It was like trying to keep hold of lightning. St. John twisted, whiplike, and wrenched free. In a blur of motion, both men drew their swords. Tristan sighted down the length of his blade.

"Damnation to you. You know who I am."

His opponent took several steps backward, bowed, and grinned at him. "Verily, my friend. And therefore you won't risk killing me, or you may never find out who you are."

Tristan slowly lowered his weapon, then sheathed it as St. John sheathed his.

"You can't be a friend," he said. "Or you'd tell me at once. Therefore, you're an enemy. What was it you said, that I'm your curse?"

"I grow weary of this game."

"Then tell me who I am."

"You're indeed wondrous obstinate," said St. John. "But I'll never believe your tale of a memory wiped clean, so you may as well abandon this foolish guise."

Tristan hesitated. "You think I'm a threat to you. Why is that? Why are you so concerned about me? What have you and I to do with each other? And why is an English nobleman lurking on this sequestered isle so far from home and court? I begin to think you're the one playing a part."

In a burst of action, St. John drew his sword and lunged at Tristan. Tristan easily darted back and drew his own weapon before his opponent could complete the attack. They circled each other. Blades twitched, and St. John tried another thrust to no avail. Tristan parried, locked his sword with St. John's, and hurled the other man away from him. St. John stumbled against a table, cursed, and flung himself at Tristan, only to meet the freshly sharpened tip of a sword blade. Tristan smiled calmly as the man darted backward at the last moment, his gaze fixed on that sword tip.

Flushing, St. John said, "Enough of this game. Have you told anyone about this island or me?"

Tristan grinned at St. John as he flicked his blade in invitation. "Why should I tell you aught? The devil take you. You began this little skirmish. Let me end it for you."

St. John widened the distance between them and lowered his sword. "In these past months I've learned much about you. You're stubborn, tenacious. Barnaclelike, you've clung to me from Scotland to England and into the sea, and now here we are. I thought you'd drowned, but instead you reappear, like a lost love. Mayhap I've misjudged you. Did you know more than I thought?"

Tristan kept his gaze fixed on St. John, but lowered his sword in response to his opponent's gesture. "I see we have much to discuss—if I can call what we're doing discussion—but I prefer to do it in the open, where no one else can get hurt. Shall we take this privy conversation elsewhere?"

St. John hesitated a moment, then inclined his head and put away his weapon. Since the man had learned to keep his distance, Tristan led the way out of the chamber. He was listening for that telltale hiss that signaled the drawing of a sword when he saw Pen, Dibbler, and Wheedle coming up the stairs to the landing. He heard the hiss, sprang at Pen, trying to reach her to shove her aside, but he was too late. She saw St. John and the sword.

"Dibbler!"

Dibbler rushed past them with his pike, swung it at St. John, missed, and hit the sword blade. As it fell, Tristan sprang forward, grabbed the sword, and pointed it at his enemy.

Pen seemed to have brought the entire castle with her. Sniggs and Dibbler jabbed their pikes in the air and congratulated each other on their prowess. Erbut gawked blankly at Tristan and St. John while Pen, the girl Wheedle, and Turnip babbled questions at him.

"I knew something was wrong when Ponder scuttled out of here as if he expected the hall to burst into flames," Pen said.

Everyone was talking at once. Tristan growled an order for silence before turning on Pen.

"Jesu, woman, have you no wits? I needed no interference, and you might have been hurt." He shook his head when she would have answered. "Oh, don't protest your good intent. Did you listen at the door as well?"

"No, I was gathering everyone together to defend you and only now reached the stair."

Tristan regarded St. John warily, for the man was too quiet and calm.

"Your guest has been playing games with me. So much so that I begin to suspect that he's not been telling us the truth. I don't think he's who he purports to be."

"At last!" St. John cried. "At last he speaks a few truthful words. Indeed I'm not who I claimed to be, but more. Behold."

Withdrawing folded papers from his belt, St. John handed them to Pen. While he waited for her to read them, he bathed Tristan with a satisfied smile. Pen looked up from the papers. Foreboding settled over him as Tristan met her wild glance. Tremors shook her slight body, and he watched the color of her lips fade from rose to the palest pink. The blush of her cheeks vanished as well, as if she'd been suddenly buried in unseen snow and chilled to freezing.

"Pen?"

She shook her head, and the papers she was holding slipped through stiff fingers. The document almost fell from her hands, but he caught it and read. He read a commission authorizing Lord Morgan St. John to pursue and capture a French priest named Jean-Paul, a priest whose description matched his own down to the small scar on the inside of his thigh near the groin.

Tristan suddenly felt as if he were swimming in hot mist. He clenched his jaw and tried to think. A priest? He was a priest? He didn't feel like a priest, but most of the time, he felt like nothing at all. And how could he believe St. John, who so obviously hated him and wished him ill?

So great was his own turmoil, Tristan hardly noticed

the quiet that settled over the group on the landing. Then Pen's trembling voice brought him out of his thoughts.

"No," she was saying to St. John. "You're wrong. I know Tristan, and he couldn't be what this paper says. He couldn't be a murderer or a spy. Such things are against his nature."

Tristan smiled at her through his own bewilderment, but she wasn't looking at him. She was looking at his enemy, who began to speak again with gentle sorrow.

"Forgive me, but you're not the only woman to fall prey to this man. If I may be plain, you yourself are a witness. Remember the scar."

"Enough!" Tristan put himself between the two and looked down at Pen. "Pen, you're right. There's something wrong here. I—I couldn't have done the things in those papers."

"Oh, God." Pen's voice was a moan. She pressed her palms to her temples and grimaced in pain as she stared at the papers in his hand. "No, no, no."

He tried to go to her, but she veered away from him as she moaned again and looked at him with growing uncertainty and confusion.

"It can't be," she whispered. "Oh, God, please. It can't be. But the scar. The scar."

Wrestling with his own uncertainty and suspicion, Tristan reached for an alternative. "A moment. What if this is all a ruse? What if these papers are false?" He turned on his enemy. "Mayhap he bears a scar as well."

Pen lowered her hands from her temples and looked from Tristan to the newcomer. After a few moments' deliberation, she swallowed and spoke.

"Dibbler, take this man into the chamber and look for a scar."

Tristan gestured with his sword, but his opponent was already headed in that direction. Dibbler followed him, and the two soon returned.

"Well?" Pen said in a faint voice.

Dibbler shook his head and glared at Tristan. Pen caught her lower lip between her teeth, appearing not to notice that she'd drawn blood.

"It matters not," Tristan said to her, waving the papers in his hand. "He seeks to visit confusion upon us all with these foul documents. Pen, you don't know what he said to me when we were alone. You have to believe in me. Surely you don't think I'm such a monster. God, you must believe in me."

She hadn't even heard him. When he finished, Pen seemed to wake from a daze. Her face contorted with pain, and she let out an agonized cry. Lunging at him, she snatched the papers and screamed at him.

"May God damn your soul!"

"Pen, there's some trick here."

She was shaking. He tried to go to her, but she shrank back. At her alarm, Dibbler, Sniggs, Turnip, and the rest shifted, placing themselves between him and their mistress. He found himself surrounded by rusty pikes and furious stares. He considered booting them all down the winding stair, but in the ensuing brawl, Pen might be hurt.

Fighting his own confusion, desperate to make Pen believe him, he decided to bide his time. He could deal with Dibbler and the rest later. Pen was too upset to make sense at the moment. She was still glaring at him, trembling and shaking her head in a stunned manner.

Tristan was contemplating how best to assuage her pain, when St. John went to her and retrieved the commission. He brandished its seal at his listeners.

"Behold the seal of the queen's secretary. William Cecil himself has given me this task. I was pursuing this man at sea, when we were overtaken by a storm, but I've found him at last. This man is a priest, a spy for the Queen of Scots and her uncle the cardinal of Lorraine. He's hatched countless plots against our good Queen Elizabeth and must be stopped."

"No," Tristan said. The word came out faint, for St. John seemed so certain, and all he had to deny the accusations was his own horror at the idea of having deserved them.

He tried to go to Pen, but the point of a pike stopped him. "Don't trust him, Pen. I don't trust him."

Tears streaking her face, Pen shook her head. "Have you been lying all this time? Were you afraid I would discover who you were and turn you over to her majesty's ministers?" She clutched her head as if a sudden pain had lanced through her. "Oh, God, you've been playing a part all along to save yourself. Have you been waiting for the supply ship so that you could escape?"

"Jesu! Listen to what you're saying. Do you believe I would concoct such a passel of lies? How could I do that to you?"

Pen pointed to the commission in St. John's hands. "That is you in that description, even to the most intimate particular. No one could resemble such a finely wrought portrait by chance."

"I don't know how it came about, but can't you see I'm not that kind of man?" He felt himself losing his temper. "I can't be a spy, and by God, I don't feel like a priest. You should know that after enticing me into your bed for the last—" He stopped at Pen's gasp that turned into a sob. "God's breath, Pen, I didn't mean that."

Pen turned her back to him and faced a wall. "Get him away from me."

"I'll take charge of him," St. John said.

Tristan snarled at him. "Not if you wish to live."

Dibbler drew himself up and pounded the staff of his pike on the floor.

"Here now. This lying bastard is our prisoner."

"The commission says he's mine," said St. John.

Pen turned around swiftly. "No. I want him."

Tristan felt relief that soon vanished.

"I want him," Pen continued. "When the supply ship comes, I'm going to take him to England myself and give him to her majesty's minister."

"You can't do that," Tristan said while trying to keep his temper.

She fixed a sightless stare upon him. "I want to see him in chains."

"Give him to me," St. John said, "and you'll see him in chains at once."

"Sniggs, Turnip, Wheedle—escort Lord Morgan from Highcliffe and raise the drawbridge after him."

Sniggs and his companions surrounded their charge. St. John swore and tried to knock Sniggs's pike aside, but Sniggs avoided his blow and stuck the tip of the weapon into his prisoner's doublet. St. John grabbed the pikestaff.

"Hold," Tristan said to him. "If you succeed in breaking through them, you'll still have to face me."

St. John cursed, then released the pikestaff and turned his back on Tristan and Pen. Tristan watched him leave, then returned his gaze to Pen. She wasn't looking at him.

"Dibbler, now," she said.

Dibbler hopped in front of Tristan, raised the staff of his pike, and bashed Tristan on the wrist. His hand went numb, and he dropped St. John's sword. Pain shot up his arm as Erbut darted around him and snagged his sheathed sword. Gripping his wrist, Tristan could only set his jaw and fight the agony while more of Pen's minions surrounded him. One of them prodded him with a rusty halberd. Bellowing, he swung around and tried to cuff the culprit, but all of them scuffled out of reach.

"Penelope Grace Fairfax, you call off these armored mice!"

Pen turned her face to the wall and sobbed. "Dibbler, please, go now. Go."

Dibbler poked Tristan in the back with the tip of his pike. "Look what you done. You bust her heart, you did. Get away from her. A lewd, popish priest in disguise. Makes me want to puke."

Outnumbered, Tristan knew he couldn't escape without a fight in which one of Pen's ungainly defenders would likely fumble and skewer her instead of him. Rather than risk this possibility, he relinquished resistance for the moment and allowed Dibbler to prod him down the stairs, across the hall, and down another flight of steps that led from the well room deep under the keep. Descending into darkness, he was forced down into a room lit by a single lamp.

Someone hauled open a door heavy with iron supports and studs. Dibbler jabbed him, and he stepped into blackness. The door slammed. A bar dropped into place, and he was sealed in a cell without light.

The blackness matched that of his memory. Suddenly he was fighting horror all over again. He quelled the anxiety with his anger.

Pen should have had faith in him instead of believing the lies of a stranger. They were lies. They had to be. And because of them, Pen had abandoned him.

Somehow that feeling of being forsaken drew forth nightmarish feelings—feelings so unthinkably frightening that he hated her for evoking them. Tristan gasped at the assault, then pounded a stone wall with his bare fist to stop himself from thinking such thoughts. He would think about St. John.

Jesu, what a riddle. Out of everything that had just taken place, the only thing of which he was certain was that St. John wasn't telling the whole of the truth. If he had been simply a royal agent, then why that wondrous strange conversation when they were alone? No, St. John hated him for far more grievous and personal reasons than political ones. Why? Doubt assaulted him again as Tristan searched his blank memory for an answer. Was he a priest?

"Dear God, no," he muttered to himself.

Suddenly a small window in the door to his cell opened. Pen's tear-stained, pale face appeared.

"Why did you have to pretend to love me?"

Still reeling from his own dilemma, he had no patience left for *her* doubts. "God's blood, there was no pretense."

He could see more tears glistening at the corners of her eyes. "Don't, Gratiana. Don't. I wouldn't hurt you, ever. Don't believe him. Believe in me. I can't be the kind of man who would betray you so. A priest, by the rood. To befoul my vows. Surely you don't think I could do such things."

"I wish I could believe you," Pen said. "But you're proved false, Tristan, and I think you've killed my heart."

He heard the resignation in her voice.

"St. John is false, not I. You know me. How could

you not after I've put myself inside you? I've poured myself into your body, given myself utterly. There should be no question in your heart about my honor and what I feel."

"I wanted to believe you. I wanted to so terribly. I would have, too, if it hadn't been for the scar. And don't tell me Lord St. John is the priest." She leaned close to him, her eyes burning and her voice expanded in the hollow chamber. "He has no scar, and you do. Don't you think I want to believe you? I tried to prove the man false and failed. And the documents are valid. I know a royal seal when I see it."

Tristan shook his head. "I don't know the truth, but I know what I am, and I know St. John knows more than he's revealed. Don't you see? There must be some confusion."

"Yes," Pen said. "Mine."

He pounded his fist on the door. "I gave myself to you utterly, but you chose to believe him when you should believe me."

Pen wiped a tear from her cheek with shaking hands.

"I don't think you understand," she said.

"Verily, I don't."

"Mayhap I'm a bit unconforming in my ways at times."

"At times? Most times."

"I'm of braver and more solid mettle than you think. And I know what passes in the world. I know that popish France is the enemy of England and the queen. And no French spy is going to use me or my island as an instrument in his designs against her majesty."

Tristan clawed at the door that separated them. "Why can't you believe in me?"

"I learned long ago to face hard truths. I will face your betrayal and your lies, Tristan. I will do my duty as a loyal Englishwoman. No doubt her majesty will have her ministers question you. I know what that means, and I can hardly bear thinking of it."

"Then let me out of this cell."

"You thought me a fool, a mad, prattling fool. You used my compassion against me, but no more. You'll see me merry no more. I'll put away clemency, mirth, and love. And before I'm through, you'll rue the day you decided to make me your fool."

CHAPTER XI

Pen opened her eyes with a gasp and looked around her in confusion. She was crouched on the floor of her old room, Tristan's room, amid the rushes. Sinking back on her heels, she blinked slowly and tried to recall how she'd come to be there. Several minutes' reflection brought no memory.

Her hands hurt. She looked down at them and found them clenching Tristan's shredded shirt. They were bleeding and bruised.

Releasing her stranglehold on the garment, her glance fell on traces of red on the floor. She must have pounded her fists there. Her eyes were swollen and burned. Her hair had knotted in front of her face. She dropped the shirt and made halfhearted brushing movements at the tangles.

She must have been weeping, for her face, throat, and the neck of her gown were damp. Vaguely she wondered how long she'd been crying. Glancing out a window, she found that daylight still reigned.

Her legs cramped, so she got to her feet slowly, like an old crone. All the muscles in her arms and legs ached, as if she'd contracted an ague, and her mind ached as well. Thoughts blurred and trudged sluggishly through her mind—meaningless, obscure thoughts.

Her gaze darted around the chamber without purpose, and finally she wandered out to the landing and up the narrow stair that led to the tower battlements. With weakened arms she shoved open the door and went into the sunlight. She'd forgotten her cloak, and a late breeze nipped at her, causing her to shiver and come partly awake. To the west, the sun sailed low in a blaze of reddening apricot. The sea crashed against the rocks below the walls as if nothing had happened.

Pen looked deep into the churning white froth, watched it crash against stone and batter it. Within her she found a faint echo of the sea's violence, but it was dying, as her soul was dying. Tristan had killed it, and she had helped him.

She'd fallen in love with a priest. She'd lain with a priest. Growing queasy at the thought, she stumbled to an embrasure between two merlons. Leaning into the gap, she buried her head in her arms and tried to reason with herself. But reason played no part in the tangle of her emotions.

No matter that she wasn't a papist, she still recoiled in horror at the desecration she'd committed. Priests of the bishop of Rome were supposed to be chaste. Tristan had touched her with an artistry and skill that belied that chastity. He'd taken her love and used it for his own designs, his own gratification. What kind of man took holy vows and then deliberately broke them in the most foul and dissolute way?

And he was a spy, a French spy. Those documents proved him an enemy of England and the queen. Tristan served the cardinal of Lorraine, the uncle of the Queen of Scots. And Mary Queen of Scots lusted after the English throne. Mary and her uncle were members of the rapacious de Guise family, who sought to rule not only France but Scotland and England as well.

Tristan, a French priest. A priest who had been in

England and Scotland at the behest of the cardinal of Lorraine. Pen knew little of the secret machinations of the powerful, but from what her cousin had written, she understood that the Queen of Scots had been plotting to get herself named Queen Elizabeth's heir.

Elizabeth demurred, giving equivocal answers. Elizabeth knew better than to commit herself to such a course and, as she was fond of saying, set a winding sheet before her face. Declaring her cousin Mary her heir would be issuing her own writ of execution.

Pen could imagine the English queen balancing precariously between Catholic France and Catholic Spain, with the Catholic Mary Stuart lurking, always lurking, ready to pounce and disembowel should Elizabeth falter. Should Mary rule England, the kingdom would fall under the sway of the inquisition. And it was hapless fools like Nany Boggs and Dibbler, who had almost no formal learning, who fell victim to heretic-hunting priests, heretic-burning priests—like Tristan.

Her jaw quivered. Was it from the cold, or from grief? She'd fallen victim to her own confusion and thoughtlessness and made a laughingstock of herself. He never had loved her. She said this thought to herself with little more than a distant ache in response. She must have wept for hours, for she hadn't the strength to weep anymore.

She thought she remembered having put Tristan in a cell beneath the keep. Yes, she had. And in a day or two, when the supply ship came, she would have to take him to England, to the queen's minister, Cecil.

But what would Cecil do to him? The rack, the whip, the brand? Pen lifted her head and stared out to sea. She couldn't turn him over to Cecil knowing what would be done to him. But she had to. Such a spy could cost the lives of good Englishmen, or even the queen. Yet she couldn't bear to think of him being hurt, no matter how terribly he'd hurt her.

"God," she muttered to herself, "this choice will tip me into madness."

Her body quivered as an icy breeze whipped around her. Hugging herself, she left the embrasure and went to her own chamber. After standing beside a chest in indecision, she finally opened it and donned a cloak she found within it.

She left the keep, refusing to glance at the stair that led to Tristan's cell, and went to the kitchen. There she found Twistle and Nany presiding over preparations for the evening meal. Nany was rolling out dough for the crust of a pasty while Twistle made cabbage pottage.

She dropped onions, leeks, and cabbage into a stew cauldron. Then she spiced the mixture with saffron and salt. The vessel held enough stew to feed the whole castle and the village as well. It was suspended on an iron bar inside a fireplace that was almost a cave.

Pen took a stool beside its yawning mouth and noticed a much smaller pot simmering over white embers. From it came a peculiar smell that caused Pen to shift so as to avoid the fumes.

Nany Boggs punched a rounded lump of dough while staring at her charge. "How fare you, mistress?"

"Not well, Nany."

Twistle hadn't said anything. She went to a shelf, turned her back to Pen, and reached for a pepper pot. Nany sniffed and slapped flour on her dough.

"Foul bastard French priest," she said. "Hiding here

in our midst while he spins his plots. You should have
let the queen's man have him, mistress. Sweep him
out the door with the rest of the offal, that's what
I say."

Hugging herself, Pen stared into the flames of the
fire and shook her head. "I can't."

"Prithee, why not?" Nany said.

Pen sighed as Twistle removed a white ceramic pot
from the back of the topmost shelf and brought it to
the table. The pot was so large that it required two
hands to hold it. She emptied dried lumps of root and
leaves from it into a stone bowl and began mashing
them with a pestle.

"He's tricked you," Nany was saying, "and there's no
remedy in marriage with a papist priest. He's soiled and
besmirched and degraded—"

"Please!" Pen covered her ears for a moment, then
straightened her spine.

Nany had the sense to look contrite. "What's the
worst is he's taken the happiness and mirth from you,
mistress."

"I should have remembered what young men are
like, then I wouldn't have gotten myself debauched,"
Pen muttered.

Twistle rammed her pestle into the bowl, causing
the table to shake. "I don't see why we should give
him to the queen's man."

At first Pen couldn't believe she'd heard correctly. Twistle clamped her lips together and said nothing else. She sealed the pot she'd used and placed it
back on the topmost shelf. Pen watched her empty the
ground contents of the stone bowl into the smaller of
the two pots in the fireplace.

The mixture in the pot bubbled sluggishly as Twistle
stirred it. Pen frowned while she watched the mess

roil and simmer. It was a grayish-brown and contained long, wormlike ingredients that surfaced occasionally and wiggled as if alive.

"Twistle, what is that foul concoction?"

The cook rubbed her hands on her apron without glancing at Pen. "Stew."

"You're making more stew? What about that in the larger pot?"

"You said to feed him," Twistle said without smiling. "This is prisoner's stew."

Nany plopped her dough into a pasty pan. "Our pottage is too good for a spy."

Pen glanced from Nany, whose grin made her resemble a vulture with a fresh carcass, to Twistle, who had yet to met her mistress's gaze.

"What kind of stew?" she asked.

Twistle dropped pieces of cabbage into the prisoner's stew without speaking.

Nany wiped her flour-covered hands, grasped a mug, and took a gulp of ale. She wiped her mouth on the back of her sleeve and grinned at Pen.

"Rat stew," she said.

Pen jumped up to peer into the pot. Rat tails, bits of hairy hide, and a paw floated on the top of the concoction. Pen swallowed against nausea and backed away as she caught a whiff of steam. Something in the smell made her whirl and stare at Twistle, who was calmly chopping more cabbage.

"Twistle," Pen said.

The knife clicked rapidly on the table.

Pen knew the young woman too well to expect an answer without a fight. She went to the herb shelf and retrieved the white ceramic pot. Opening it, she sniffed the contents. She coughed, then shoved the pot back on the shelf with a clatter and slowly turned to face Twistle. Undisturbed, the cook strewed cabbage into the large stew pot.

Pen marched up to Twistle, pointed at the rat stew, and said in a low voice, "You put wolfsbane in his stew."

Twistle nodded as she stirred the cabbage into the castle stew.

"You'll feel much better after he's gone," she said calmly.

"I told you not to put things in his food."

"That was before," Twistle said as she tasted a piece of stew meat.

Pen's heart had begun to pound. "Twistle, didn't you tell me that wolfsbane is deadly?"

"Oh, aye, mistress." Twistle's apple-round face took on a dreamy expression of enjoyment. "First he'll feel this burning and tingling and his tongue and throat and his face will go numb. Then he'll puke and he won't be able to see anything but blurs, and he'll have trouble breathing. Then his sight will dim and he'll get chest pains."

Twistle paused as she contemplated the prospect, and smiled. "Then he'll get worse. He'll get fits, and after than he'll grow so cold he'll feel like his flesh has become ice. And then the real pain starts, mistress. And the best part is that he'll be awake to the end."

"No!"

Pen heard herself shouting, but she didn't care. Gone was her concern for the pain Twistle had suffered. Grabbing a poker from the fireplace, she tipped the pot and emptied the rat stew into the flames. The kitchen filled with the smell of burnt food and the hissing and sputtering of quenched flames. Pen shoved Twistle aside and marched to the herb shelf.

Blinking back tears, she snatched the white pot,

opened it, and emptied its contents into the fire. Dried leaves and roots crackled and burst into flames. Pen dropped the pot onto the worktable and faced Twistle.

"You're not to touch him." She glared at Nany. "No one is to harm him."

Twistle swore. "But what he did to you—"

"I don't care!" Pen felt as if her head would burst with pain. She pressed her palms to her temples.

"I don't care, do you hear? I can't bear to think of him suffering. And you're not helping me. Do you understand that? There is more at peril here than my virtue and my happiness. This matter touches the queen, and no matter how much I wish it were otherwise, Tristan must go to England to confess whatever evil machinations he's devised against her majesty."

Nany settled down on a stool with her ale mug and regarded her mistress with a tear rolling down one plump cheek. "But we were happy before he came and wrought destruction upon you, mistress. He should pay for ruining our happiness."

"If we don't kill him, he'll do more harm," Twistle said quietly.

Pen rounded on her. "I'll have your promise not to harm him, or I'll send you out of the castle at once."

Meeting Twistle's defiance, Pen filled her own gaze with all dominance she could command—and won. Twistle muttered her acquiescence and curtsied.

"And to help you obey," Pen said, "I'll take Tristan's meals to him myself."

A few minutes later Pen carried a tray out of the kitchen, where Dibbler and Erbut waited with their pikes. They marched ahead of her to the keep with Nany following behind carrying blankets and Tristan's clothing. Down into darkness they went, until they reached the glow of a torch.

There Sniggs waited for them. Pen nodded to him. Dibbler and Erbut readied themselves and their pikes. Sniggs lifted the bar over the door, opened it, and jumped back, pike at the ready.

Tristan appeared at the threshold and scowled at them with bleary eyes as three pikes touched his chest. He spread his arms to indicate compliance. Pen stepped between two of the weapons. She hadn't wanted ever to face him again. The sight of him called up her shame.

"Stand back," she said.

He stepped deeper into the cell when Dibbler poked him. Pen darted forward, set the tray down, and retreated. Nany threw her bundle inside, and Sniggs shut the door with a bang as Tristan stalked toward them. Pen retreated as he began to pound on the door. She was almost at the stairs when she heard him.

"Penelope Fairfax, if you don't come back here, I'm going to shout a description of what I did to you last night to my donkey's arse of a jailer."

Gasping, she whirled and marched back to the cell. Motioning for Sniggs and the rest to leave, she slammed back the cover of the grille in the door.

"You have more lies to tell me? Speak, sirrah, for I'm not accustomed to trotting about at the hests of spies."

His face suddenly appeared at the window, and she started at the black glint in his eye.

"I've been thinking, trying to remember, but I can't. All I know is that I can't be a priest. Surely I would conduct myself differently, more—more like a priest."

"That commission and your own body have condemned you," Pen said. She began to close the window.

"No, wait!"

She paused as he ducked his head to meet her gaze. She couldn't understand how his eyes could catch the torchlight when he was surrounded by so much darkness. Her glance strayed to his mouth. It had been thin with tension, but now his lips softened.

She remembered how he had placed them in the most unlikely places. Once, he had kissed the flesh at the back of her neck and nearly caused her to leap from the bed. Flushing, she drew herself upright.

"How can you deny such proofs?" she asked.

He came closer to the grille and glared at her. "What if that commission is false, a forgery? Even an antick like you must see that St. John might have twisted the tale around to suit his purpose. Calm your mad blood, Pen, and think. If he's twisted the tale around to suit his desires, if he's lied—"

Pen, furious at being called an antick, folded her arms over her chest and sneered.

"You can't go on because you've realized that even an antick wouldn't believe such driveling."

She met his gaze, but it was as if he weren't seeing her, and his voice was faint.

"If he's twisted the tale . . ."

"Saints," Pen said. "Being found out seems to have robbed you of your skill at lying."

"If he's twisted the truth, and tampered with those commissions, then . . . then it might be as I suggested, that it is he who is Jean-Paul."

"In faith, it's you who are the antick, not I."

Tristan appeared to return from whatever reverie had overtaken him and looked at her again. "If he's Jean-Paul, then—then mayhap I'm Morgan St. John. But the name means naught to me. And he mentioned someone named Derry, which means nothing to me as well. Yet if I'm St. John, then this Derry is important to me in some way, and—and he might be dead." He held her gaze, and his own softened.

"Incomparable Gratiana, my beautiful storm, I think I've found part of the truth. Listen to me."

His tone lowered and grew intimate so that he was murmuring to her as he did when he'd found her alone in some corner of the castle. He'd done little more than look at her, and yet she'd grown hot. She eyed him warily, for she was beginning to realize how dangerous it had been to remain in his presence for so long. Blinking, she started as she found that she'd begun to lean close so that she could hear what he was saying, and that he had touched her face with the tips of his fingers. She jerked her head out of his reach.

"What vile sorceries are you trying to work upon me now?" she said on a cry.

His gentle, seductive expression vanished and he snapped at her. "Afore God, woman, try to use reason. Let us hence, find this man, and force him to tell the truth."

Eyes stinging from unshed tears, Pen clenched her fists and glared at him.

"No, I'm going to tell you the truth. Those documents show no sign of forgery. St. John bears no scar, so he can't be the priest. You are. I know nothing of this Derry of whom you speak, and I'm not going to release you. You made a mistake."

Sighing with impatience, Tristan grumbled, "What mistake?"

"You made a mistake in taking me to bed."

"Did you not take me as well?"

She paid no heed. "You forget that I've seen your body in every part. Did you think me so antick that

I'd forget I've seen the scar. There is no path around this trap the queen's man has laid for you."

"Jesu Maria!" Tristan pounded the door with his fist. "Can you not listen with an unfettered mind? That man and I have the same coloring, and we're almost the same height. He could have added the part about the scar to a legitimate commission he'd stolen."

Pen shook her head. "I won't be gulled a second time."

"Be damned to you!"

"And I'll have no more of your shrewd curses, priest." Pen darted her head forward to scowl at him through the window once more. "Or would you have me believe that this man knows the secrets of your flesh? If this man is your enemy, how haps it that he knows about a scar that's so near the most private portion of your body?"

She heard a succession of vivid curses and more pounding on the door.

"The devil take you, Penelope Grace Fairfax. I'm no man's catamite. God's breath, I wish I could get at you. You need thrashing."

Squaring her shoulders, Pen lifted her head. "Saints, how he cavils when faced with the truth. Mayhap next time I feed you you'll refrain from evil seductions now that you've learned I'll no longer play the fool for you."

She turned on her heel and marched to the stairs.

"Come back here, you unnatural little wretch."

"Cease your ranting and be grateful I didn't let Twistle feed you the rat stew she'd prepared. Good e'en to you, monsieur priest."

CHAPTER XII

They had forgotten to close the cover over the grille in the door to his cell. Tristan listened to the serenade of snores performed by Sniggs and tried to judge how many hours had passed since Pen had left. During this time, he'd forced himself to analyze his predicament with calm and logic.

A stranger, St. John, had come after him, uttering cryptic threats and hinting at knowledge of Tristan's identity while refusing to reveal it. Then, when forced by Pen, St. John revealed that he was a royal emissary sent to capture Tristan, who was a spy-priest named Jean-Paul.

At this point in his recollection, Tristan faltered. That description had been damning. In the past hours he'd writhed with doubt, almost cringed with the fear that he was what St. John accused him of being—a murderous priest. He'd nearly climbed the walls of this black cell in an effort to escape the pain of wondering whether, in truth, he was the brutish soul described in the warrant.

The character of St. John and his actions were what saved him from hopelessness. If St. John were merely a royal agent, why would he play such games with a man he'd been ordered to capture? Why had St. John wanted to know if Tristan had told anyone about him or Penance Isle? This queen's man feared that Tristan had revealed his presence on the island, which seemed a wondrous strange attitude for a royal servant.

Then he'd remembered something even more peculiar, something he hadn't noticed at the time of their privy conversation. St. John had said that Tristan had clung to him from Scotland to England and into the sea. And yet St. John was the one who was supposed to be doing the chasing. If he was Jean-Paul, why would he seek out St. John?

Tristan cursed his lack of quickness in discovering these contradictions. But then, he'd been so amazed at the things St. John had been saying, so desperate to discover his own name and past.

There was another reason far more compelling than these suspicions. This man, who after all was supposed to be a dispassionate official of the queen's government, hated him. In that chamber with St. John, he had seen white-hot embers of cruelty in those dark eyes—cruelty savored, prolonged, relished.

Tristan wasn't sure of many things, but he knew in his soul that this man would have burned kittens alive had not human victims satisfied his appetite far more. And so, whatever the truth about his own past, he had to find out what St. John's real designs were. What cursed luck that the man from whom he must seek the truth was more dangerous to him than a rabid wolf.

Aye, St. John was dangerous. In his gut, Tristan believed that the man was lying about his identity, that the documents he possessed were false. St. John's character was far more in keeping with the actions of the priest—the priest who was a spy.

God's blood, he had to find the truth, and there was no one to help him. In the darkness Tristan tried to control the pained fury that assaulted him at the thought of how Pen had chosen to believe St. John instead of him. She had lost faith in him, betrayed him.

He had to escape. Pen wouldn't listen to him, so he would have to risk hurting someone. But he couldn't wait much longer. Pen was going to try to take him to England, leaving behind the only man Tristan knew to possess knowledge of his past.

That he couldn't allow. Not only for his own sake, but because if St. John were an impostor, some foul plot was afoot that threatened three kingdoms—England, Scotland, and France. Tristan was going to find out what it was if he had to flay the skin from St. John's back to do it.

But he couldn't pursue the truth with Pen harassing him. He needed his freedom. After he'd questioned St. John, he would leave Penance. Where he went depended on what he discovered. Since he'd heard Erbut tell Sniggs the supply ship had arrived at sunset, he had to go now. The ship was anchored in a cove near the castle. He planned to borrow some of Pen's coin and bribe the ship's master to take him when he sailed.

He felt better now that he'd settled on a stratagem. Yet he was again assailed with disquiet, for he couldn't help feeling that St. John had wanted to hurt him by telling him of the death of the one called Derry. When his memory returned, grief might await him. Nevertheless, he couldn't let such concerns interfere with his plans.

Tristan slithered over to the opening in the cell door and peered out. Sniggs had slumped down on the floor beside the cell with his back to the wall. His pike was cradled in his arms. Tristan contemplated the possibility that his ruse wouldn't fool the man, but discarded the idea. Sniggs worried about fairies and imps; he would believe Tristan's performance. If he woke.

Tristan picked up an empty wooden trencher from the tray Pen had brought, turned it on end, and slid it through the bars of the window. He shoved it, and the plate sailed into Sniggs's bare head. The trencher hit with a thud, causing Sniggs to bolt upright and yelp. Tristan quickly upended the tray, spilling its contents about the cell. He moaned loudly and dropped to the floor. Curling into a ball, he moaned louder as Sniggs's dirty face appeared at the door.

"What betides?"

"P-poison. Ohhhhh."

"By the rood!" Sniggs's greasy head bobbed up and down as he tried to see Tristan in the dark cell.

"Help me, ohhhhh—"

Tristan ended his moan with a gurgling choke and collapsed. Beneath his lashes he watched Sniggs.

"Here, knave, what ails you? Priest? Curse you. If you're dead, the mistress will blame me."

He heard Sniggs remove the bar from the door and enter. His arm was grabbed, and he was turned on his back. He waited until he felt Sniggs's hand on his chest. Then he grabbed an arm, pulled hard, and raised his feet. They landed on Sniggs's chest, and he tossed the man over his head. Sniggs crashed into the opposite wall head first and bounced off it. He landed on the floor on his face and didn't get up. Tristan examined him, but he appeared to be unharmed except for the knot on his head.

He closed and barred the cell door again. Finding his sword in a corner, in but a few moments he'd crept upstairs and into the well room. For the first time he found himself grateful for the haphazard nature of the castle guard and resolved to think better of Dibbler in the future.

Shadowlike, he slid across the well room and into the hall. Snores greeted him from servants sleeping on pallets. He tiptoed around these, through the alcove behind the dais. Soon he was climbing a stair in a little-used tower. Pen had mentioned that she called the top chamber her treasury.

The door to the so-called treasury wasn't locked, but the casket containing Pen's coins was. He had little trouble in snapping it from the wood with the serpent dagger, which had remained in his boot, forgotten by his inexperienced jailers. Taking one of the small bags of coins that lay within, he stuffed it inside his doublet and left the keep.

Dibbler's laxity prevailed outside as well as inside. Of the few sentries posted, only Erbut remained awake to walk his post. Tristan stuffed the bag of coins under a rock at the base of the castle wall, where it would be safe until he needed it.

As he slinked into the shadows near the stables, the boy marched past overhead, his attention fastened where it never should have been—upon the stars overhead. Tristan watched Erbut's retreating back, then slipped into the stable.

After saddling Pen's mare, he walked the animal out of the stable, across the outer bailey, and to the gatehouse. He left the mare tethered behind a hay wagon. Inside the gatehouse he encountered the erstwhile captain of the guard. Dibbler was slumped across a table, an empty flagon of ale at his feet. Tristan recognized the man's stupor, brushed past him, and cranked up the drawbridge.

He winced at the noise, but Dibbler was oblivious. Still, Tristan worked quickly to raise the portcullis. As he left the gatehouse, he could see Erbut's dim figure far away on the wall walk. The boy had his back to the drawbridge and was gazing at the moon.

Shaking his head, Tristan mounted and rode through the gatehouse, over the drawbridge, and out of High-cliffe unhindered. Once free, he pulled up and glanced back at the castle. A feeling of loss came over him without warning. It wasn't right, this stealing away in secret, and he hated it.

He wanted his new life back. He wanted Pen. He wanted her to smile at him defiantly while she described some new torment she was planning for Cutwell. He wanted to sit in the hall and listen to Dibbler's tunes even though they made his head ache. He wanted Pen, the Pen who believed in him.

Turning his back on Highcliffe, Tristan kicked the mare into motion. Until that moment, he hadn't under-stood how important Pen and her mischief makers were to him. But now that he knew, he supposed the only sensible thing to do was come back. And when he did, he'd make Mistress Fairfax beg his forgiveness for not believing in him. He would take pleasure in seeing to it that she atoned for her failing, great pleasure indeed.

A little over an hour later, Tristan lowered himself by a rope into the first courtyard of Much Cutwell. He'd encountered only three men-at-arms. Apparently all of them followed the Dibbler school of guardianship. They were asleep.

Much Cutwell's hundreds of leaded glass windows were dark. He'd scouted the entire grounds and found only one lighted chamber, the topmost one in the cen-tral tower of the first courtyard. He dropped to the ground and gazed across an expanse of lawn that must have comprised several acres. In front and behind him marched the red tile and brick of chimney after chimney, and he faced the creamy facade of the west front with its symmetrical towers and three stories of windows.

He glanced up at the lighted chamber in the tower over the arched entryway. A beacon in the darkness, it called out to him. He would find out who was awake, and then search for St. John. He wanted to steal upon the man in his sleep, force him out of the house and into the forest, where he could be questioned without risk.

Hugging the north wall, he slinked closer and closer to the light. When he reached the west front, he heard snores. A sentry slept standing up against the threshold of the entryway.

Tristan walked quietly past him, found a stair, and ascended three floors without meeting another guard. When he reached the landing of the third floor, he opened a window and climbed outside. It was a short climb to the roof.

Stealing silently across the flat expanse, he plastered himself next to the lighted window. It was ajar. He dropped to his knees and inched his head up until he could see inside. There was no one present at the moment.

The chamber appeared to be the workroom of an alchemist. It was lined with shelves cluttered with scrolls, books, ink pots, and quills. Three worktables creaked under the weight of mortars, pestles, weight scales, caskets, and bottles. On the central table a brazier held a fire, and over it was suspended a glass bottle with a round bottom. Inside the vessel bubbled a golden liquid.

Tristan smelled a sweet scent and realized that

the candelabra strewn about the room held beeswax candles. He was studying a table overburdened with cracked pots filled with herbs, when a shadow fell across it. He ducked.

St. John entered the room humming. He wore a long robe of scarlet damask, and a heavy gold chain draped over his shoulders. From it hung a cross of strange design. Tristan's eyes widened as he recognized a pattern of gold serpents on a ruby-red enamel background. His hand strayed to his boot, where the matching dagger still rested. He hadn't used it at Highcliffe for fear of injuring some addled incompetent.

In the chamber St. John had gone to the bubbling glass bottle. He grasped the cross at his chest, reversed it, and slid back a panel. He held the cross over the bottle. A fine white powder spilled into the golden liquid. The mixture frothed and then began spewing clouds of white vapor. St. John studied the churning liquid while Tristan studied him. Suddenly St. John's gaze lifted, and he looked through the white mist straight at Tristan.

"Enter. I've been waiting for you."

"I think not," Tristan said. "Especially if you've been waiting for me."

"I must insist."

St. John's gaze shifted to something behind him, and Tristan whirled, cursing himself. As his hand went to his boot, a man lunged forward and stuck the point of a sword beneath his chin. Tristan stopped, raised his hands, and slowly straightened. A second man-at-arms held a blade over his heart while a third searched him and retrieved the serpent dagger. Then they shoved him through the window.

Once inside, he was pushed to his knees in front of St. John, who remained standing beside the bottle full of golden liquid. A guard handed St. John the serpent dagger.

Tristan glanced at it, then raised a brow at him.

St. John smiled at him. "Yes, I must insist that you join me. Obviously the men I've had watching for you at Highcliffe bungled the task of apprehending you when you left the castle. If Henri here hadn't needed to relieve himself by the north wall and seen you, why, who knows what would have happened."

"You'd be kissing my sword blade and wishing you'd never set foot on Penance Isle."

St. John surveyed Tristan without replying, his hand stroking the dagger. With a smile he thrust the weapon into his belt and turned to the bottle.

With a pair of tongs he grasped the neck and removed the vessel from the flames. Pouring the golden liquid into a silver goblet, he set the container aside and turned back to his prisoner. Tristan knelt motionless with the point of a sword touching his throat.

"I'm going to enjoy wrecking that pride of yours."

"Are you going to tell me who I am?"

"Ah, you still insist upon this game." St. John walked back and forth in front of Tristan, his brow furrowed. He rubbed his chin and mused. "I have given this puzzle much thought. Much thought. There is little time, you see, and so much of great import depends upon finding out what you've been doing. Have you been ill, as you claim, or have you been playing a part?"

St. John stopped in front of Tristan. He clasped the serpent cross and stroked it. Light flashed off the writhing, intertwined bodies of the snakes and caused Tristan to wince.

"I don't suppose you would care to confide in me, *Anglais*? Before you die, that is. A last confession, shall we say? Have you been truly ill, or are you going to bring down a fleet of English privateers upon my head?"

A wisp of a smile flitted across Tristan's lips, and he whispered, "Jesu Maria, you are the priest."

Jean-Paul drummed his fingers on the table beside them and said impatiently, *"Dominus vobiscum."*

"Then I must be Morgan St. John."

The priest's glance slanted sideways and raked him. In that glance Tristan read a lifetime's experience in corruption and iniquity. So jaded was that look that he doubted if the priest could even imagine what innocence and verity were like.

In that moment Tristan knew at last who he was, even without his memory. He was Morgan St. John. From this moment, he had a name. Morgan. And from this moment, he understood what this man had planned for him all along. The only doubt he had was how long Jean-Paul would draw out his suffering before killing him.

Morgan shook his head. "You're so young to have managed so much evil, priest."

"I have five years more than you, so let us not speak of youth." Jean-Paul glanced over Morgan's shoulder and nodded at the guards.

Instantly Morgan felt himself grabbed and propelled backward until he hit something solid. His head flew back and hit wood, and he landed in an armchair so heavy that the force of his entire weight hadn't shifted it. He lunged up, but someone punched him in the stomach. His guts crawled up his throat, and he nearly strangled.

By the time he could breathe again, his arms and legs had been strapped to the chair. His hands gripped the arms of the chair as a guard passed a rope around his chest. The priest had turned his back and busied himself at the worktable. Now he faced Morgan, and in his hand was the goblet containing the golden liquid.

"Mayhap you remember not my studies in alchemy and herbs." He held up the goblet so that Tristan could see its contents. The liquid sparkled as he swirled the vessel. "One of my charges under the cardinal was to study in Italy. Poisons . . . And draughts to tease the mind into delusions."

"Bastard."

Jean-Paul gave him a brief smile. His glance flitted upward, and hands descended to grasp Morgan's head. Too late he tried to dodge aside. Someone pinched his nose closed. Morgan writhed and jerked, but his bonds clamped him to the immovable chair.

His lungs burned, and he opened his mouth, keeping his teeth clenched. He heard Jean-Paul chuckle. The priest bent over him and placed his hands on Morgan's throat. His fingers slid up, pressed a point on either side of his jaw. To his horror, Morgan felt his mouth relax.

Jean-Paul touched the rim of the goblet to his lips and poured the liquid down his throat. The priest's fingers massaged his throat. Then his hand covered Morgan's mouth hard. His fingers dug into flesh as Morgan choked and tried to spit through closed lips. The golden brew burned its way down his throat. Soon he could feel it blistering a path down his chest and into his gut.

He was released, but he had little time to be thankful, for he couldn't seem to catch his breath. His mouth tingled, and he heard the buzzing of wasps. He squeezed his eyes shut because the edges of objects had begun to melt.

Suddenly Jean-Paul knelt and touched his cheek.

Morgan opened his eyes and met a dark gaze filled with pleasure and tranquility. There it was again, that glint that signaled the desire to see a victim's protracted anguish. He blinked rapidly. Then an overwhelming urge to smile assaulted him. He fought against it, but lost. The priest smiled back at him, and Morgan laughed.

"Release him."

Morgan felt his bonds drop away. Freedom seemed the most wondrous event in his life. He bubbled over with laughter, turned sideways in the chair, and dropped his legs over one arm. The toe of one boot distracted him, and he fell to studying its uniqueness. He didn't hear Jean-Paul until the priest touched his arm.

"Tristan."

He turned to find the priest's face close to his. He grinned at the man.

"Am I Tristan? I thought we'd discovered that I'm Morgan. Which is it?"

"*Merde.* I had hoped you were playing a part, *mon amour.* Of what use are you otherwise?"

"I like your cross," Morgan said as he swung his leg over the chair arm. He touched the cross with a fingertip. "I have a dagger like it."

Jean-Paul hesitated, then pushed Tristan's hand away. "*Non,* my addled one, the dagger is mine. *Dieu,* but I've wanted to kill you for months, and I will enjoy it."

"The dagger was in my boot. Pen told me."

"You took it when I attacked you at that inn on the Scottish border. Curse you, don't tell me you've forgotten that. I nearly slit your throat while you slept. How do you think I knew about that scar of yours? I saw it in the moonlight just before I jumped out of the window."

"What scar?"

A guard approached. "Shall I give him more of the potion, *monseigneur?*"

"*Non*, Henri. There is no need. He has lost his memory. There is a curse upon my dealings with Secretary Cecil's young spies. The cardinal wishes to turn one of them into his own creature, but I fear it isn't so easy to control them. And this one has already nearly cost me my life. Have you not, *Anglais? Non*, this one must die, but I can't help wanting to play with him and savor the taste of revenge."

"I'm hungry."

Jean-Paul's voice suddenly rose as he swore. "*Le bon Dieu,* what pleasure is there in killing you if you know nothing of our past? For months I've looked forward to beholding your anguish. I had to use the potion on you to get the truth, but now you're as merry as a babe with sweets, and without your memory—"

"Hmmm? My memory? Then give me some of the truth."

"God's arse, can't you at least remember some of it? You chased me from England to Scotland and back again. And you found me at Holyrood Palace, talking to that pestilence of a Scottish minister."

Tristan was fastening the ties on his shirt. "Who?"

His jaw clenching with frustration, Jean-Paul appeared not to be listening.

"I never would have known you were there if it hadn't been for his mistress catching you," he muttered. "But you heard, didn't you? You heard about the assassin coming from France to kill Cecil, and that's why you tried to throw me out of the window and splatter my guts on those hard Scottish flagstones."

"God's breath," Tristan said on a chuckle. "I mislike these memories you're giving me. And you prattle and peep while I starve. I want a roast goose and a capon, and five or six cherry tarts."

Jean-Paul swept back and forth in front of him, his agitation apparent in his jerking movements, and in the way he ran his fingers through his hair.

"What an incongruity. Here we are, we two mortal enemies, waiting for the assassin to meet us on this cursed pebble of an island, and you care naught for it. If you had your wits you would try to kill the poor creature." The priest paused to glance at Morgan. "I liked you better as your old self."

"Forgive me for causing you such pain," Morgan said.

He grinned at Jean-Paul, and then yawned. The priest threw up his hands.

"It's my own fault for feeding you that potion, but I was so certain you were lying." Jean-Paul came closer to stare into Morgan's eyes. "*Dieu*, how I wanted to see your face when I told you that I'm here to give my fellow countryman a small piece for information—the whereabouts of Master Secretary Cecil, Queen Elizabeth's favorite and most valuable minister."

"And I would like some wine. Jesu, I've had my fill of Pen's ale. She hasn't said, but I think she can't afford much wine. God, my stomach is as empty as Dibbler's head. I crave something to eat."

Jean-Paul straightened and backhanded Morgan across the cheek. Morgan's head jerked back, but he righted himself dizzily. He touched blood at the corner of his mouth with the back of his hand.

"*Mon amour*, you're quite boring in this condition. I prefer you with all your wits, spitting at me and grudging me every living breath."

"I have a wondrous idea," Tristan said as dabbed at

the blood on his face. He began to chuckle. "Let's eat Margery."

Jean-Paul rolled his eyes, bent, and yanked Morgan to his feet. Morgan wobbled and swayed backward, but the priest caught his arm and held him steady.

Contemplating his prisoner, Jean-Paul murmured, "Listen to me, curse you. I really am going kill you."

"But I'm hungry!"

"*Sacré Dieu.*"

Morgan looked down his nose at Jean-Paul. "There's no need to swear, priest." His ankles bent sideways, and he clutched at Jean-Paul.

Henri the guard grabbed Tristan's other arm. "Shall I run him through, *mon seigneur?*"

Jean-Paul shook his head and drew the serpent dagger. Tristan's head wobbled around, and he pointed at the weapon.

"There it is." He wrapped his hand around the blade as Jean-Paul pressed it against his heart. He looked at the priest. "I told you I had a dagger like your cross."

"Let go of it," Jean-Paul said. "It will be easier."

Morgan burst out laughing and released the blade. He glanced from it to the priest's unsmiling face. A musing smile curled about his lips.

"Are you going to kill me, Jean-Paul?" he whispered.

Silence fell as Morgan continued to smile at the priest with his head cocked to one side as if listening for faint music. The serpent dagger pressed into his doublet, distracting him. He glanced from it to Jean-Paul and smiled again. Then the blade retreated.

"I think not, *Anglais.*"

"Then feed me."

"The devil take you," Jean-Paul said as he walked Tristan toward the chamber door. "If we were on English soil, I couldn't risk allowing you to live, but since we're on this isolated wasteland in the middle of the sea, I can wait to see you die in a less merry humor."

"Food, and then a wench."

"You're going to bed." Jean-Paul ushered Morgan out of the chamber. "And then, after the assassin has sailed to England, I will bethink myself of a most evil death for you."

"I don't want to go to bed. I'm going back to Pen. She hasn't treated me well, and I'm going to tell her that you're the priest so she'll have to beg me to forgive her. I have a list of things she can do to apologize, pleasurable things."

"You're going to bed, and later you're going to die, *mon amour*. Just remember. *Dulce et decorum est pro patria mori.*"

Morgan laughed again. "What?"

"It is sweet and seemly, Morgan St. John, to die for one's country."

OF BAKING MANCHETS

Now of the baking of bread of your simple meals, your best and principal bread is manchet, which you shall bake in this manner; first your meal, being ground upon the black stones if it be possible, which makes the whitest flour, and bolted through the finest bolting cloth, you shall put it into a clean kimnel, and, opening the flour hollow in the midst, put into it of the best ale barm the quantity of three pints to a bushel of meal, with some salt to season it with: then put in your liquor reasonable warm and knead it very well together both with your hands and through the brake, or for want thereof, fold it in a cloth, and with your feet tread it a good space together, then, letting it lie an hour or thereabouts to swell, take it forth and mould it into manchets, round, and flat; scotch about the waist to give it leave to rise, and prick it with your knife in the top, and so put it into the oven, and bake it with a gentle heat.

CHAPTER XIII

The night after Tristan escaped, Pen crouched behind a haystack in the kitchen courtyard of Ponder Cutwell's house. Sneaking into the place had been easy because neither Cutwell nor his guest had prepared for an invasion. They had no fear of her.

Until she'd met the queen's man, Pen had forgotten how contemptuous of women some men could be. Even after she'd discovered his treachery, Tristan had never made her feel as if he thought her stupid. Mad, mayhap, but not stupid. But the man called Morgan St. John oozed contempt from his very gaze. Clearly he'd given no thought to her reaction to his holding on to her prisoner.

His disdain was one of the reasons she was paying this little visit to Much Cutwell. The other was that she couldn't bear to think of what might happen to Tristan in that man's power. If he was to be anyone's prisoner, he must be hers.

Beside her, Wheedle fingered the point of a rusty sword and kept watch. Leaping from shadow to shadow, haystack to cart, came Dibbler followed by Turnip and Sniggs. From another direction slithered Erbut. One by one they sprang for the refuge of the haystack.

"We're ready, mistress," said Dibbler.

"You're certain you found the guest's chamber?" she asked Sniggs.

"Oh, aye," Sniggs said with a titter as he produced something from the recesses of his garb. He held up the familiar serpent dagger.

Pen eased back from the weapon and said faintly. "Excellent. Now put it away."

"Thieving," Dibbler muttered. "That's what he's done."

Sniggs's eyes protruded as he mustered indignation. "I did not! And if we're speaking of thieving, what about that pistol?"

Turning to Dibbler, Pen said, "What pistol?"

With reluctant movements Dibbler rummaged inside his doublet and produced a pistol, then rushed into an explanation. "It be a wheel-lock, mistress. Look you at the workmanship. That be an ebony stock, and this here grip is ivory. And this!" Dibbler jabbed a sausagelike finger at a small vise set on top of the pistol. "This here is the striking stone in the cock. You squeeze this little tongue thing—"

"Dibbler, no!"

Pen shoved the barrel of the gun down so that it no longer pointed at her chest.

"Oh, beg pardon, mistress." Dibbler flushed and stuffed the pistol back into his doublet.

Sniggs spat and jerked his head at Dibbler. "No better than a sotted zany. Daft old counterfeit."

"Peace, both of you," Pen said as she tried to quell her startled self. "No more thieving. Dibbler, that pistol is a murderous luxury his lordship will no doubt miss immediately. It's too late to return it, so it will remain concealed. You and Sniggs must light the fires outside the stables and Margery's pen. Where are the torches?"

Dibbler rummaged through the haystack and produced them. "Fear not, mistress. I'll light them meself so they give off mostly smoke. The animals won't come to no harm."

"I get to light them too," Sniggs said.

"Most like you'll bump into a fairy and fall asleep in Margery's pen," Dibbler said.

Sniggs grabbed for one of the torches and missed. "Sod you, Dibbler."

"I'm the captain of the guard."

"Captain of farts, you mean."

"Cease this caviling at once!" Pen snatched a torch from Dibbler and thrust it at Sniggs. "Away with you. And no more fighting. If you fail me, I'll ship you back to the mainland."

Pen and her remaining band settled down to wait. She glanced at Erbut, who even at this critical moment managed to look slack-jawed. She heard a snore. Turnip had fallen asleep against the haystack, and Wheedle woke him with a jab from her sword. Soon after, she heard a cries of warning and the ringing of an alarm bell. Scrunching low, she watched servants and men-at-arms run in all directions. A sudden light illuminated the night as flames and smoke appeared beyond the courtyard wall.

"Now!" Pen jumped up and ran for a door in the wall.

Wheedle was close behind her, followed by Erbut and Turnip. They sped across another courtyard, into the house, and into a man-at-arms on his way to the stables. Startled, Pen hurtled into the man, then ducked and bounded backward. Wheedle whacked him on the head with the flat of her blade. His knees buckled and he fell.

Pen jumped over him only to skid to a halt as they

neared a doorway. She eased it open but shrank back as Ponder Cutwell scurried down the stairs in the gallery of his great hall, screeching as if he were a sow.

"Fire, fire!"

His dark-haired guest appeared from a doorway in the hall screen. "God's blood, Cutwell, stop howling."

Cutwell's mouth popped shut for only a moment, then he put thick fists on his hips and snarled at the man. "A pox on you! You won't bestir yourself for my house or my animals. Mayhap you'll take notice now that your own chamber is afire."

Without a word his guest burst into a run and sped upstairs. Ponder began to screech again and rushed out of the hall. Pen glanced over her shoulder at Wheedle.

"Which archway?"

"To the left, mistress."

They ran across the hall to the pointed arch beside the lord's dais. Pausing to gather her courage, Pen stepped beneath the arch while the others waited. She found herself in a paneled alcove guarded by a man-at-arms. When she appeared, he gaped at her, then drew his sword.

"What are you doing here?"

Pen whirled and raced back through the archway. The man gave chase, but as he crossed the threshold, Turnip clubbed him on the head with the broken end of a plow handle. The man swayed dizzily, then crumpled when Erbut whacked him across the neck with the staff of his pike. At Pen's direction, they dragged the man into the alcove with them.

There was only one other exit from the alcove, a door set in the paneling. It had a lock, but the key was in it. Another sign of her enemy's contempt for her abilities. Pen felt a jab of irritation that a person couldn't possess a merry nature without people thinking her negligible of wit. She turned the key and opened the door while her companions flattened themselves against the wall on either side of it.

Opening the door quickly, she sprang back. No one emerged. She approached the threshold and poked her head into the darkness beyond the alcove. She edged inside, searching with her feet for the first step down. Once she'd taken several steps, she perceived a faint light. She beckoned to Wheedle, and they all crept down until they reached the last stair. Ahead she could see a cellar filled with ale barrels, wine casks, wheels of cheese, and other foodstuffs.

To her astonishment, one of the largest wheels of cheese appeared to be singing a bawdy song.

Come my pretty shepherd maid,
I'll be thine only ram . . .

Pen followed the voice, which sounded hollow in the vastness of the cellar, rounded the bulk of the cheese, and found Tristan. He was sitting on the floor with his back propped against the cheese wheel. His clothing and hair were in disarray. He held a silver goblet in one hand and waved it in time as he caroled. When Pen appeared, he finished his verse and beamed at her.

"Pen, me own true love, I've missed you."

Erbut joined her along with the others, and they all stared at Tristan. He staggered to his feet, only to sit on the cheese abruptly and blow a lock of his hair from in front of his eyes.

"Tristan, you're besotted."

She felt her jaw unhinge in imitation of Erbut when she heard Tristan giggle. She turned to exchange horrified glances with Wheedle.

"He's giggling," Pen said.

Wheedle swallowed and gaped at Tristan. "Right marvelous."

Pen twisted her hands. "What does this signify?"

Tristan began to sing again. Pen lost patience, darted at him, and snatched the goblet. Sniffing its contents, she wrinkled her nose.

"Some foul potion. Tristan, quiet you and come with me."

Tristan shook a finger at her. "My name is Morgan."

Snagging his wrist, Pen tugged on his arm. He was too heavy for her and dug in his heels.

"My name is Morgan. The priest admitted it." He paused to chortle. "I was too clever for him. He confessed his evil. And you, Mistress Fairfax, must beg my forgiveness for being so foolish as to doubt my honor and my affection. I will hear your apology anon."

He yanked his wrist free and folded his arms over his chest as if settling down to listen to a soliloquy from her.

Pen uttered a strangled gasp of frustration. "Not now, Trist—"

"Morgan! Morgan, Morgan, Morgan, Morgan, Morgan."

Wheedle had been watching at the stairs.

"Mistress, I hear noises. We should fly."

Looking like a belligerent colt, Morgan scooted around on his cheese and turned his back to her.

"Very well. Morgan. Do you hear me? Morgan. Now will you come?"

"Shall I hit him on the head?" Turnip asked.

"We don't want to carry him," Pen said. "He's too heavy."

"I am waiting," Tristan said after turning around, "for you to beg me to forgive you."

Pen closed her eyes and prayed for forbearance. "Tris—Morgan. Morgan, my dear sweet lord, may I beg after we go home?"

"Home!" Tristan jumped off the cheese, swayed, and clamped a hand on her shoulder. "Will you feed me?"

"A dozen roast geese and two dozen apple tarts."

"Then I'll come."

True to his word, Tristan gave them no more trouble. Pen grasped his hand and led him up to the hall, down the gallery, and outside. They shrank into the shadows as servants bearing water buckets rushed by. Racing from tree to shadow to alcove, they made their way to the rear of the grounds. Dibbler signaled to them from the shelter of a hay cart sitting near to the back wall. Pen heard shouts in the next courtyard. Discovery!

Hauling on Tristan's arm, she raced across the courtyard with her companions close on their heels. At the cart she shoved Tristan from behind. He climbed onto the cart and up the pile of hay in it with her prodding him.

A rope had been secured from the cart and draped over the wall. Sniggs waited on the other side with their horses. Tristan stood on top of the wall and swayed. Pen grabbed him before he fell and he giggled at her again.

At her urging, he climbed down the rope, and soon they were all mounted. Pen snapped at Tristan to hold on to the saddle. She took the reins of his mount, kicked her own horse, and they rode away. She glanced back at Much Cutwell, but the wall and courtyard seemed deserted.

Grinning to herself, she wished she could see her enemies' response when they discovered the true cause of tonight's havoc. She looked at Tristan, who seemed to be enjoying himself. His legs hugged the saddle, and he clutched at his horse's mane. Leaning over the animal, he moved easily with the pace of the gallop.

Mayhap the effect of the potion they'd fed him was fading. Still, he was in no state to make the journey to England. No doubt the trip would have to be delayed a bit.

She considered the bemused expression on his face. Part baseless merriment, part evil relish, he seemed to embody the tales of black sorcerers Nany used to tell her. She hoped he wouldn't recover his wits too quickly—not until she'd gotten him clapped in a tower. Despite his traitorous nature and his evil toward her, she really didn't want to bash him on the head just to get him locked up.

Pen put Tristan in the tallest tower at Highcliffe, the Watch Tower. Situated at the rear of the keep, it was the farthest tower from the drawbridge. It contained another of those beautiful rooms created by her mother's ancestors and left neglected when the family moved to the mainland.

Called the Painting Chamber, the room lay at the top of the tower. Its walls were covered with oak panels. Painters from Italy had been employed over fifty years before to illustrate the four elements—earth, air, fire, and water, as well as the seasons, the laws of nature, and the mysteries of alchemy. Even the ceiling bore paintings of fantastical animals—griffins, dragons, and leopards. Tristan belonged in such a room, for he was as magical and brilliant as the chamber itself. Besides, he couldn't get out of it.

The next afternoon, when Wheedle informed her that he'd awakened and recovered from the potion, Pen went to visit Tristan. She took Dibbler with her.

Dibbler took his pike. She unlocked the door and gave Dibbler her ring of keys, then slipped inside. Tristan was sitting in the deep-set window embrasure, gazing out at the sea.

"My preparations for our journey are progressing well now that I don't have to chase you all over this island. So many instructions to give before I leave, so many problems to anticipate. Good morrow to you, Tristan."

His head darted around and he glared at her. "Morgan. You may as well accustom yourself to my real name."

She lost her breath for a moment. "You remembered?"

"No, but the priest admitted who I was. I told you that."

"You said many things last night. Nonsensical things."

"So," he said. "You still disbelieve me."

"I weary of this game."

"And I weary of being locked in chambers and cellars and dungeons. I warn you, Penelope Fairfax. You won't find me so tolerant or temperate if you don't begin to see reason. I've been careful of your safety and sparing of your pride, but no longer. There is great danger here, and not just to me. This man plots against England, and I must find out how."

"You said you remembered naught."

"I remember something of last evening—not all. But I've just spent a night and a day conversing with a French priest who's hatching evil against the queen's chief minister. I hope I dreamt it, but I think he said he'd sent for a French assassin to kill Cecil."

Pen bent her head and studied the patterns of wood grain on the floor, then she lifted her gaze to him.

"Marry, sirrah, you must think me simple indeed.

You spin tales and expect me to believe them because I fell under your spell and loved you once. Contrary to what you and most men think, love doesn't rob a woman of all sense. I can still reason, and my reason tells me you'd contrive any outlandish fable that would convince me to release you."

Tristan uttered a curse and thrust himself out of the window embrasure. He stalked toward her, but halted when she held up her hand.

"My guards are without. If you touch me, they have orders to skewer you."

"You think I would hurt you?"

"I know not."

He sighed and held out his hands. "I but wish to propose a test."

"What manner of test?"

"Now, Pen, I know how afeared you are of my serpent dagger, but if you held it, you might find the truth."

"No."

He came to her, but she stepped to the door, and he stopped.

"Pen, there's little time."

"No," she said, biting her lip. "I can't."

"But it's mine. You might sense the truth about me from it."

Pen pressed her back against the door and shook her head. "It's a perilous thing you ask of me."

"I know," he said softly, "and I wouldn't ask, except that I'm desperate to prove my innocence and foil the priest's designs against Cecil."

Pen chewed on her lip. "The supply ship has docked. The ship's master brought a letter from my cousin. He says the Queen of Scots' half brother, Moray, has rebelled now that she's married Darnley, whose

mother was Elizabeth's cousin. Mary is furious and
has chased her brother across the border to England
with her army. She accuses our queen of aiding her
brother and his allies and threatens to pursue him into
England. Tristan, there might be war."

"Jesu Maria," Tristan said.

He pinched the bridge of his nose and lapsed into
silence. Then he spoke as if to himself. "Her majesty of
England, she balances between two evil choices. If she
supports Moray, she will be aiding a subject who has
rebelled against his lawful sovereign, a dangerous pre-
cedent considering the number of English Catholics.
If she does nothing, she may lose her most valuable
ally in Scotland."

"How do you know this?" Pen asked.

"I know not. I seem to have much perplexing and
important knowledge, but I don't know why I have it.
I suspect it's because I, not Jean-Paul, am the queen's
man."

Pen shook her head. "I don't know."

"Gratiana, Mary of Scotland has the blessing of Philip
of Spain to seek the English throne and set up the
Catholic church again. Should Elizabeth appear weak
in any way, it will be a signal to Spain or France to
throw their strength behind Mary and destroy our
Queen Bess. Which do you want, an English queen
or a foreign one?"

"Saints, I can't think."

Tristan reached out to her, but she feared his touch
and darted aside. He withdrew his hand and waited.
Pen rubbed her forehead while agitation made her
mouth go dry.

"Very well," she said at last.

She rapped on the door and ordered Dibbler to bring
the serpent dagger. They waited for it in silence. When

Dibbler returned, he brought Sniggs, Erbut, and Turnip with him as well as Wheedle. Sniggs bore the dagger in its sheath. The men filed into the chamber while Wheedle remained outside and locked them in. Tristan kept his distance at the point of their pikes.

With them between her and Tristan, Pen approached Sniggs, who held out the dagger. She tried to keep at bay her aversion to blades, the old memories of drowning in blood. But every step that brought her closer to the dagger sapped strength from her legs until she thought they would fold under her. Fighting queasiness, she took a last step that brought her within touching distance of the dagger.

Pen held out a trembling hand and touched the sheath with her fingertips. She stared at the hilt. She saw the tail of a serpent twitch. A minute ruby eye flashed. Freezing, breath stopped, she fought the vision until the writhing stilled. Then she spoke to herself sternly of courage and grasped the sheath.

All at once she was sailing in the air above a jewel-blue river. A chateau floated in the midst of the waters, and, like a bird, she flew to it and through an open window, and up a winding alabaster stair. At the top she soared through an open door of polished mahogany and into a room decked with Flemish tapestries. Beneath lay the myriad hues of a Persian carpet. She came to rest upon the carpet. Across the room, before the arched window, sat a carved table upon which lay a silver quill holder and ink pot, a golden drinking cup inlaid with amethysts and pearls.

There was a flash of yellow light, and heat. She squeezed her eyes closed against the pain of the sudden brightness. When she opened them, she realized she was staring into the flame of a candle in a gilt wall sconce, and shifted her gaze to look past it.

Out of the darkness of a shadow came a man dressed
in scarlet. A lean man, golden of hair, a priest. The man
stopped in the splash of torchlight. He was smiling,
and that smile, so like that met in dark alleys after
midnight, made her flesh grow cold. To her surprise,
he withdrew his hands, which had been tucked into
the flowing sleeves of his robe, and touched her face.

"*Acheté, cher, Jean-Paul, mais très beau.*" The man in
scarlet withdrew the ruby and gold dagger from his
sleeve. "*Un cadeau.*"

The torch flared, and Pen blinked. When her sight
cleared, she was in the midst of ruins illuminated by
moonlight. Fighting men surrounded her, and she faced
a man with golden hair and hell's fury in his gaze. They
confronted each other across the length of their swords
while she fingered the hilt of the serpent dagger.

"Jesu, *Anglais*, you have cost me much this night."

"And the Cardinal of Lorraine, I hope," said the
other.

"*Infortuné, mon fils.* This quick wit of yours has
brought you a death sentence."

She grew dizzy, and the night blackened. When she
could see again, she was perched outside the window
of a bedchamber. She glanced around, and found herself clinging to a wall of white stone above a moat.
Above her rose the towers of a chateau with its conical
slate roofs, gables, and turrets. She stepped onto the
sill, shoved the window back, and dropped silently into
the chamber.

A bed hung with blue and gold silk sat on a dais. A
dying fire crackled in a fireplace. She floated over to
the bed, palmed the dagger, and with the tip of the
blade parted the hangings. The owner of the chamber
lay within undisturbed. She parted the hangings and
calmly pulled the covers from the sleeper.

They revealed an old man with the tonsure of a
priest. He snorted, then turned over on his back. The
dagger seemed to leap in her hand. It descended. She
felt it hit and pierce flesh. It slid between ribs and
embedded itself to the hilt. The old man grunted. His
eyes flew open even as he died. His last sight was
of her.

She smiled, pulled the dagger free, and wiped the
blade on the man's chest and the covers. She wiped
spots of blood from her own black garb. Then she withdrew. Taking her time, she straightened the hangings
and took a last look at the body. The blood looked black
and gleamed wetly at her. Pen shook her head. Nausea
curdled her stomach, and she grew dizzy again. Her
gorge rose, and she doubled over.

"Pen!"

She heard Tristan, but she was too concerned with
the dizziness and sickness to answer. She heard her
own teeth chattering and her sobs. At the sound,
she opened her eyes. She was on the floor cradled
in Tristan's arms with her men gathered around
them. Sniggs had grabbed the dagger and shoved it
into his jerkin. Summoning every last bit of her will,
she lunged upright and out of Tristan's arms. Once on
her feet, she swung around to confront him, quaking
and shivering.

"Pen, what happened?"

"Murderer."

At this, Dibbler and the others surrounded Tristan
and pointed their weapons at him. He gave them but
a glance and returned his gaze to her.

"Pen, I'm no murderer. Why say you such things?"

Pen pointed a shaking finger at him. "You took a
desperate gamble and it failed. You should have known
better, but no doubt you thought my gift would show

me only what I wanted to see. You've destroyed your-self, priest, for now I know the true depth of your evil."

Tristan tried to approach her, but was stopped by the point of a pike.

"I have to stop this assassin here, before he sails to England. He could be on Penance at this moment."

Pen barely heard him. Calling to Wheedle, Pen paused on the threshold when the girl opened the door. "It will kill me to do my duty, but I will do it. You sail with me to England, where I've no doubt the queen's ministers will clap you in the Tower and rack the truth out of you."

"God's blood, woman!" Tristan knocked a pike aside, but another took its place. "Penelope Grace Fairfax, you're allowing a French spy to roam free and helping him to murder Cecil."

"Belabor me with no more colorable tales, sirrah." Pen felt weaker than a plague victim, but she kept her back straight and her head held high. "You'll spin no more enchantments upon me. Your magic is as dead as my love."

CHAPTER XIV

Christian de Rivers looked out a window in the high great chamber at Falaise, his gaze fixed on the edge of the forest beyond the grounds of the manor. Morgan had been missing for almost three weeks, and he awaited word from Inigo on the success of the search at sea. He heard the click of heels on polished wood. Turning, he saw his wife Nora entering the chamber, a fencing sword in her hand.

Smiling, she came to him and plied the blade in a figure eight. The sword buzzed in the air, then she saluted him.

"Lessons over?" he asked.

"For me," Nora said. "But the twins have begged to be allowed a chance."

Christian frowned. "They're too young."

Nora put a finger to her lips, then laughed.

"The fencing master has given them wooden blades, and I left orders that he's to watch them every moment. Elizabeth and Jehan have both promised to obey. No word?"

He turned back to the window. "None—wait."

He leaned out and squinted against the afternoon sun. A rider had emerged from the tree line and galloped toward the manor. As he approached, Christian

made out the scrawny figure of Inigo Culpepper. The
thief galloped close to the moat, wheeled, and waved
a black kerchief.

Christian's heart plummeted to his knees. He closed
his eyes for a moment, then returned Inigo's wave. The
thief nudged his horse and galloped back the way he'd
come. Christian remained in the window, staring at
nothing. Morgan was lost. Morgan, who had been in
his care since the boy's father, Viscount Moorefield,
had asked him to foster his youngest son.

He felt Nora beside him. "It was my fault."

"No."

"Aye," he said. "I sent Morgan to help his brother,
hoping they would reconcile. They did, but then he
met that bastard priest and went after him."

Nora slipped her hand into his. "Morgan wanted to
serve the queen as you do. You know how the viscount
tried to destroy both him and Derry. And you most
of all know how desperately Morgan was running from
his past."

"I should have made him stay at court."

"The queen was furious with him for allowing her
favorite serving woman to seduce him."

Christian waved a hand. "She would have forgiven
him. He but needed to attempt to seduce her with
his courtly graces and she would have been placated.
I should never have let him go."

"You couldn't have made him stay with you forever,
my love."

"What am I going to tell Derry? He's at Moorefield
Garde, taking possession of his father's title." Christian
turned to Nora, caught her hand, and brought it to his
face, stroking his cheek with it. "What am I going to
tell Derry?"

Nora kissed him. "Nothing until after you have come

back from your meeting with Cecil. If Inigo hasn't returned by then, we'll know Morgan's lost."

Morgan shouted at Pen through the locked door of the Painted Chamber. "Penelope Grace Fairfax, you come back here!"

"I'm going to get your supper."

Morgan kicked the door and glared at it.

"I knew you couldn't stay away." He raised his voice so that she could hear him as she left. "Because you love me, damn you."

"I do not," came the faint reply.

Morgan cursed, drew back his fist, and punched the door. A bolt of pain shot up the bones of his arm. Yelping, he grasped his fist with his other hand. He ranted at himself and panted with the pain.

"Witless sod. You're a fool, Morgan, or whoever you are. A witless crackbrain—"

Morgan stopped in mid-rant. He stood beside the door without breathing as all of existence picked itself up, shifted at right angles, and sat down again. Without fanfare, without a sign or portent, his memory popped back into his mind. He didn't even hear his own breathing stop, speed up, and then grow faint.

"Bloody everlasting perdition," he whispered.

Absently he shook his aching hand and began to stroll around the chamber as memories deluged him. Disjointed thoughts stumbled through his head. He'd been chasing Jean-Paul. Jean-Paul, the bastard, had said his brother Derry was dead. By God's mercy, he'd said Derry was—no, he wouldn't believe that. He couldn't and keep his reason intact.

All he could do was hope the priest had been lying. It would be like Jean-Paul to conjure up such a falsehood to torment him. Somehow he had to submerge this ravening worry about Derry. God, he'd been so close to killing the priest twice. Each time, Jean-Paul had escaped, and now he was glad, for he'd discovered the plot to kill Cecil.

So much killing. Morgan's steps faltered as he remembered his own part in the death of his oldest brother, John. For so many years he'd blamed Derry for it, and hated him for it, tried to make him suffer for it, when all along *he* had been the one who caused John's death.

Morgan dropped his face into his hands, almost unable to bear the floods of remorse and guilt. After John's death their father had blamed Derry for John's death and used Morgan against him. He encouraged Morgan to blame Derry as he did, to hate him, even tried to coax him into killing his brother.

At first Morgan had been comforted by his father's attention. He'd been the youngest, the one always left behind, the one forgotten and pushed aside in favor of his older brothers. The viscount's sudden attention was like water to a shriveled and drought-ridden young plant.

But the years passed, and Morgan gradually realized that his father wasn't interested in him except as a tool to be used against Derry. Once he understood the meanness of his father's affection, he gave up trying to attain it. An act of wisdom.

Sensing Morgan's withdrawal, the viscount sent him from Moorefield Garde to be fostered by Christian de Rivers. It was Christian who had told him just how unfair Father had been to Derry. Christian had revealed how Derry, more interested in books than in fighting, had forced himself to forsake the pursuits he loved for the bloodthirsty occupations his father respected. All in search of the love of a man whose heart was as small as his wit.

At first Morgan hadn't believed him, but now he knew the truth. He owed Christian de Rivers an unpayable debt. With Christian's rough tutelage and viperish affection, he grew to manhood. He learned courtly dances, how to kill a man with a stiletto, how to kiss a lady's hand—and more—and how to cross London by rooftop. This last skill might prove useful, for he was leaving Highcliffe at once.

His disastrous encounters at Much Cutwell had yielded valuable knowledge. Jean-Paul awaited an assassin with the location of a meeting between Christian de Rivers and William Cecil. The assassin had been expected at any moment. He had to return to Much Cutwell and find the man.

He wanted to kill the murderer here rather than risk chasing him by ship and by land in England. And he still had to rid himself of Jean-Paul. The priest was far too dangerous to be allowed to live. He'd almost succeeded in his plots against the queen several times. Sooner or later he might accomplish one of them.

Enough useless musing. He needed to convince Pen to let him go—Pen.

"Oh, no."

Morgan winced as he remembered the last three weeks with her. Tristan had fallen in love with Pen, a woman who ultimately had no faith in him. Morgan clawed the paneling beside the window embrasure as thoughts of Pen brought back memories of what he'd become on this island. Lost, vulnerable, exposed.

He felt as if he'd been stripped naked and whipped before a jeering crowd. By the bloody cross, he never wanted to feel that way again, never wanted to be that helpless. His loss of memory had peeled all his protective layers away to leave him raw and bleeding. Morgan cringed as he understood how near to madness and dissolution he'd come. Only Pen had stood between him and death.

But that had been Tristan, not Morgan. Tristan had been in love with Pen, but he wasn't Tristan. Tristan had been lost and alone. He was neither.

Morgan paced around the Painted Chamber, past masterpiece after masterpiece, assuring himself of his strength and how unlike Tristan he really was. He needed no faithless woman to protect him. God, he'd survived duels with five men and been in more skirmishes in his service under Christian de Rivers . . . No, he wasn't vulnerable at all. He didn't need Penelope Fairfax.

And since he'd discovered the truth about himself, he'd sworn to atone for his great sins by serving his queen and country. By risking his life to protect others, he might achieve some kind of salvation. But he couldn't do that on Penance Isle.

Nor could he remain in this backwater, even without the need to atone. For he craved the activity and splendor of court life, not for the power or the riches, but for the unfailing attentions of the women. At court he basked in a sunlight of female admiration that soothed old hurts.

These hurts lodged in his soul in the form of memories of a lady of great beauty, with a waterfall of ebony hair and quick, agitated movements who had died too soon, before he could capture her attention. And when he was quite young, he had needed that attention so desperately.

But she'd been too busy to do more than pat his head and mutter, "Run away, son."

No woman ever told him to go away now. Female attentions fed a part of him that had starved as a child. If he had to forgo them, he felt a gradual emptying of his being, and he had to return and fill himself up with the affections of women. Mayhap the emptiness left by both his father and mother was limitless, for no one of his women had ever been able to fill him up.

If he tied himself to Pen, he risked feeling like a starved cat in a cage with a mountain of fish just out of reach. What would a man like that do to Pen? And anyway, if she ever found out about what he'd done to his own brother, she would hate him.

No, he didn't need Pen. Not at all. He didn't need a woman who had no faith in him, who believed he could be that monster Jean-Paul. She'd abandoned him, and he owed her nothing.

The vulnerable and desperate Tristan needed her, not Morgan. Sighing, trying to ignore the feeling that his heart had become a spiked mace bashing against the walls of his chest, Morgan plopped himself down on the cot that served as his bed and waited for his jailer to return.

Jean-Paul sat across a small table from his long-awaited guest. A single candelabrum sat between them as they dined. The candle flames flickered in a draft that wended its way from behind an arras. He lifted his goblet and saluted the one called *Danseur*, the dancer. Few knew what Danseur looked like. To his knowledge, only two or three of these lived.

"*Bien*," Jean-Paul said. "So you understand. You have the map to this country manor where Cecil will lodge.

You are the cook's cousin from London come to help out with preparations for this important guest who is to arrive within a week."

"*Oui.*"

"And you understand that Christian de Rivers must die first. His death is as important as Cecil's."

He got no reply this time other than an annoyed glance.

Jean-Paul shifted uneasily in his chair. "*Maintenant,* I have a small task for you to accomplish before you leave."

Golden brows lifted. Pink nails traced a design on a silver plate as silence grew around them.

"This is unexpected. I detest the unexpected."

"The *Anglais,* Morgan St. John, is lodged at Highcliffe Castle. He must be killed, for he knows about you."

"How does he know?"

Jean-Paul lounged back in his chair to cover his agitation. For all Danseur's golden appearance, there was a certain reptilian quality to that gaze that disturbed, that caused one's senses to sharpen with alarm.

"Morgan is a spy," Jean-Paul said. "His business is to ferret out secrets. For your own protection, you must kill him."

"Why haven't you?"

"Ill fortune has plagued my dealings with Lord Morgan. *Naturellement,* I will pay the usual fee."

He met a contemplative gaze that scoured its way into his brain and retrieved the truth.

"A mistake, *monseigneur.* I dislike mistakes more than I do the unexpected. You would do well to remember this."

"Don't threaten me," Jean-Paul snapped. "I'll pull your spine out through your throat and then make a meat pie out of you."

"Then mayhap we're more alike than I thought, *monseigneur.*"

Pen stepped into the Painted Chamber bearing a tray of food and drink. Erbut shut the door behind her, but she hardly heard it lock. Tristan, or Morgan, had lit all the candles in the wall sconces so that the room glowed. The paintings that had sky in them reflected various shades of blue from azure to sapphire.

Opposite her, in the window embrasure, her prisoner lay on his back with his arms bent to pillow his head. He'd changed clothes and wore black again. One leg stretched out so that his booted foot was propped against the embrasure wall.

He hadn't moved when she came in, yet Pen grew more uneasy as the moments passed and she continued to study his body. All she could hear was his even breathing. He hadn't spoken, but she sensed a change. The quiet lengthened.

Then he stirred. He didn't open his eyes. Instead, he stretched. Slowly, as if his muscles were made of cool honey, he unbent his arms, arched his back, and thrust his boot up the wall. She watched the knot of muscles above his knee surge. Then the sinews along his thigh began to work, and her gaze followed the river of motion up his leg to his groin. It skipped to his face, and she found him staring at her in amusement.

A chill rippled up her back. He was looking at her strangely, as if he knew her breasts were stinging. He'd never made her feel the awkward virgin before. Pen jutted out her chin at him. And he laughed at her quietly, as though he'd expected her to behave as she had.

Without warning he rose from the embrasure, mov-

ing like sea foam over a beach, and Pen's agitation
turned to alarm. Somehow he was different. He even
moved differently.

She'd never known Tristan to be quite so blatant.
This man deliberately set out to entice. Or was it her
own fantasy? He hadn't said a word, and yet as he
approached he exuded sexual menace. Walking toward
her, he seemed to fan the flames of excitement each
time his legs parted for another step.

To her relief, he took the tray from her and set it on
the cot. But then he came back to her, took her hand,
and bent over it. She felt no kiss, only his warm breath.
He straightened, cocked his head to the side, and gave
another soft laugh that displayed the roughness in his
voice.

" 'Alas, how oft in dreams I see/ Those eyes that
were my food. . . . ' Sooth, don't be afraid, Mistress
Fairfax."

Pen opened her mouth, but words seemed beyond
her. Even his voice had changed. Where before it
reminded her of the summer sea breeze, it now took
on the quality of a distant yet relentless storm. And
he was quoting poetry at her as if they were in some
palace garden. In addition, he walked about the Painted
Chamber as if he were accustomed to being surrounded
by the beauty of great art, by polished oak fit for the
withdrawing chamber of a king.

"We never met in ceremony, did we?" he said. "No
matter. I am Morgan St. John, brother of Viscount
Moorefield."

She said nothing, but he appeared undisturbed. He
was glancing over her face with interest. Then he burst
out with a chuckle, causing her to start.

"Beshrew me," he said, "but Tristan has marvelous
improved upon my light tastes. He found himself a

maid of more virtue than beauty, and yet you're a pleasing chuck, Mistress Fairfax. You're no fair Helen to launch ships like some I've danced with, but that's just as well for your sake."

He touched her chin with the tips of his fingers. Pen gasped and slapped his hand away.

"What foul masque are you playing at now?"

She glared at him, but he only smiled at her and plucked a small loaf of manchet bread from the tray. Tearing it, he took a bite.

"Are you offended?" he asked between bites. "Marry, if you knew me, you would be pleased not to be included among so many kissing and heaving cherries. I remember one, she was a Douglas, I think. She had such ripe lips and thighs like soft . . . but she wanted to use a whip on me. I tried to oblige, but I found the amusement lacking."

By now Pen was shaking with outrage. "Dissemble no more! This pretense disgusts me."

"Ah, dear Pen, so guileless and unaware, like unto Persephone."

He smiled at her, dropped the bread on the tray, and scooped up a goblet of ale. Where before his movements had been graceful, now they also contained that sureness and swiftness of a man accustomed to command. Turning from her, he went to lean with his back against the wall beside the window. He studied her, and she grew uncomfortable under his stare.

"I had hoped that you told the truth when you said you loved me not."

"I did."

He shook his head and gazed at her with compassion as he sipped his ale. "I'm afeared for you, mistress. Don't think that I'm ungrateful to you. You saved my life and gave comfort while I went a little mad.

Sooth, I thank God and you for my recovery, and wish I could remain longer to make you understand how much I regret leading you to believe there was more than thankfulness in my heart. But you do understand that I was injured."

Tears stung her eyes. "This is another trick, and may damnation take you for using it."

She watched his gaze stray to the tray and back to her. He sighed, then dropped into the embrasure and hooked an arm around a bent leg.

"This is a wicked tangle, chuck, and one of which I'm heartily sorry to have been the cause."

"Stop it."

"Matters of grave import call for my attention. I cannot spare you for fear of risking lives." He regarded her solemnly. "I beg you to remember this in times to come—I hold you in great affection. For your love of me, remember this."

"You make no sense. Whether I love you or not, and I do not, can have naught to do with your foul designs upon the peace of England."

Making no answer, he cast down his gaze as though in grave deliberation, then he lifted his head and smiled at her. It was a smile of tousled bed sheets and spice wine, of laughter behind a haystack, of assignations in deserted alcoves. And it was so unlike Tristan that Pen took an unthinking step back, away from the sensual knowledge it signified. Her confusion was so great that she didn't respond when he suddenly appeared at her side.

"Come, chuck. There's no need for this pretense."

Wrinkling her brow, she tried to summon her composure, but he was too near, and he was talking so softly in that lion's purr of a voice.

"There is no shame in honest desire."

He laid his hand on her arm, a gesture that should not have aroused heat in her most private parts. He leaned down, lifted a long corkscrew curl, and kissed it. Disbelief arrested any movement she might have made as he began to whisper to her.

"You are the one who is dissembling. I, sweet mistress, tell you the truth. 'How fair and how pleasant art thou, O love, for delights! / This thy stature is like to a palm tree, and thy breasts to clusters of grapes.' "

Pen whirled away from him as, at last, she comprehended his words. He followed her, and she retreated.

"A pox on your lush and lusty speech, sirrah. I'll have none of it or you."

"Fie, chuck," he said as he pursued her, "not long since, you made me feel the hunted stag."

"No doubt through your own contriving. Our encounters happened only because of some foul enchantment of yours."

He stopped in mid-stride and glared at her. Pen glanced around the chamber to locate the door. She scurried toward it, knocked, and turned to confront offended male pride.

He planted his hands on his hips. "Admit the truth. You wanted me."

The door opened, and Erbut stuck his head inside, then retreated and stood with his pike pointed at the prisoner.

"It was your doing," Pen said as she squeezed out the door. "You're a foul player of parts, and this one is your most evil invention yet. In faith, I marvel that you haven't grown horns and a tail with all the evil you've done. Do you sit at the right hand of the prince of hell at night?"

Before she could close the door, he was there, scowling and rigid with fury, yet his tone was light.

"God's breath, chuck. What monstrous tales you spin. If you wanted me not, you wouldn't have burst into feverish panting when you came upon me just now. I did nothing but lie in a half doze, and yet the sight of my body inflamed you. Verily, I wonder that you didn't leap upon me as you were wont to do not a few days past."

"A pox on you!" She slammed the door in his face.

She heard him shout through the oak that separated them.

"Come back. I'm willing to submit myself to your intemperate cravings."

Pen fled before she could hear more. Running downstairs, she tried to think of epithets foul enough for him.

"Cloven-hoofed devil's spawn. Hagseed. Even the rack is too gentle a fate for such as you."

CHAPTER XV

Late that night Morgan listened at the door to his prison. In his hand was the knife that was the prize he'd obtained by baiting Mistress Fairfax. As he had planned, she'd grown too agitated by his lustful manner and taunts to endure his presence and had fled, forgetting the tray and the knife. Neither she nor her servants had ever made good men-at-arms.

By filing the knife against a stone on the ledge outside his window, he'd shaped it to be inserted in the lock. At the moment he was listening to Erbut's shuffling feet as the lad marched up and down the landing.

He'd suffered a little regret at offending Mistress Fairfax, but not enough to keep him from his plans. After all, she didn't believe in his innocence, and she was interfering in the fate of England. His other choice had been to hold her hostage for his release. Lackwitted as they were, he didn't wish to face all the castle folk and try to drag Pen past them and risk causing her or them a dire hurt.

The chamber was dark, for he wanted Erbut to assume he was asleep. Working the slim blade inside the lock, Morgan listened for Erbut's footsteps—and heard them where they shouldn't be, behind him. Someone was in the room with him, someone who had apparently slipped in through the window. Never had he been so grateful of his training at Christian de Rivers's hands.

He remained as he was. Straining his senses, he heard a footfall, closer this time. He was kneeling. He swiveled around without standing, shot out a leg, and rammed it into something directly behind him.

A knife hit the door and embedded itself there, quivering. At the same time, a light body buckled under the impact of his foot. Instead of falling, it cartwheeled over him, turned, and delivered a blow to the side of Morgan's head with the hilt of another dagger. Stunned, Morgan fell into a pool of moonlight.

He expected an attack, and knocked aside the dagger that aimed for his heart. A backhanded blow caught him on the side of the head, but he gripped on the dagger arm of his attacker. The man was sitting on him. Morgan had little time to give thanks that his opponent was so light. Through pain and dizziness, he felt his opponent's blade pierce his doublet and shirt.

The man pushed the dagger, using his whole weight, and Morgan moved back. He stopped the blade, and he heard his enemy grunt with effort. Bleeding from the wound to his temple, and furious, Morgan turned his head and blinked to clear his vision. All he could see was a figure wrapped in a dark cloak and hood. There was no face within the hood. It was shrouded in a long black kerchief except for gaps at the eyes and mouth.

The man heaved with his entire body. The dagger jabbed Morgan hard enough to prick his skin, but not hard enough to kill. He heard a laugh, then the hiss of breath being drawn in as his attacker moved so that he no longer blocked the moonlight, and it illuminated Morgan.

He heard the man suck in his breath. Then, abruptly, he reversed the direction of his force, pulling instead of pushing the dagger. The blade withdrew from Morgan's breast and touched his throat. Again Morgan's strength halted the blade easily, and he realized with some surprise that his enemy was already tiring.

Without warning, his attacker bent down and placed his lips upon Morgan's. Morgan froze, feeling the edge of the blade at his throat and a hot mouth and tongue ravaging him. At the same time, the blade began to slice into the skin at his neck. All at once his sense returned and he realized that a man was kissing him.

He swore, bucked, and thrust with his arms. The man flew up and back, hit a wall. His hood fell back, and Morgan caught a glimpse of long golden curls. Wiping blood from the corner of his eye, he rose unsteadily. "A woman? You're the assassin!"

Her arm moved, but Morgan easily dropped to his knees again as a knife flew at him. It jabbed into a painting. The assassin flew to the window. He saw the straight line of the rope she'd used to enter the room. She must have stolen onto the tower roof, tied the rope around one of the merlons, and then climbed down. Poised on the ledge holding a climbing rope, she chuckled while he struggled to his feet.

"It's my ill luck. You should have been asleep like everyone else, and you should have been neither so skilled nor so tempting. You may call me Danseur, *mon corbeau*. A weakness of mine, to allow the prettier of my victims to die upon a kiss. It's my misfortune that for once I was distracted more by the kiss than the killing. We will meet again for the experience, *non? Adieu.*"

Morgan lunged at her. She vanished as he moved, and the door slammed open. Erbut charged in, waving his pike at Morgan, who was forced to dodge its sharp tip before it sliced his ear off.

Cursing, he grabbed the pike and banged Erbut on the head with the staff. The lad dropped to the floor. Morgan rushed to the window, but he was too late. All he saw was a rope dangling down the length of the tower to end a few feet from the rocks that abutted the foundation of the castle.

Morgan returned to Erbut, relieved him of his sword, and donned his own cloak. Without another glance at Erbut's prone body, he lowered himself over the window ledge after the assassin called Danseur.

Pen marched upstairs to the Painted Chamber with another tray in her hands, the final one. After the previous evening's confrontation, she was looking forward to avenging herself by having Tristan hauled aboard the supply ship. He would doubtless try another of his manipulations upon her. However, he would find her no more easy to deceive than she had been the previous night.

The little sleep she'd managed to get had come at the expense of hours of remembering Tristan's removed and yet derisive demeanor, his sad pity for her. His remoteness had frightened her. Not a few hours before, he'd shouted at her about their love.

Now he'd evidently given up the pretense, and she found that she preferred the former lie. To have him confront her with his indifference, that had been like wading through the fiery lakes of hell. And his pity had washed over her like burning oil.

It was the thought of his condescension that provoked her rage, and she welcomed it. Pen marched up the last steps to the landing and paused as she beheld the half-open door to the Painted Chamber. With a clatter she set the tray down on the floor and rushed inside. Erbut lay on the floor, his head cradled on his arms, snoring.

"Erbut!"

The lad snorted and snuffled himself awake. He sat up, wincing, and cradled his head in his hands.

Pen stood over him with her hands on her hips. "Erbut, what have you done?"

"He hit me, mistress."

"But why did you enter the room? I told you not to come near him."

"I heard noise, mistress. Like fighting. I seen someone at the window with his lordship—er—the priest. But he hit me. I woke up, but I was so woozy. Right befuddled, and me head ached, and then I fell asleep."

"Oh, Erbut, how could—what is this?" Pen rushed to the window and gazed over the ledge at the length of rope. "The supply ship! Hurry, Erbut."

Pen lifted her skirts and flew upstairs and out onto the top of the tower. She ran to the space between two merlons and gazed out to the southeast. Almost to the horizon, a speck in the midst of the pearl of dawn, she discerned the outline of the supply ship.

An inarticulate cry of fury burst from her. Erbut gaped at the retreating ship, his jaw nearly at rest on top of a merlon to which was fastened a rope. Pen swept back and forth across the roof and cast enraged glances at the rope and the ship while she berated herself for not setting more men to guard Tristan.

"I never should have waited for him to regain his wits. How did he get a rope?"

"From the devil," Erbut said. "I saw one of his imps crouched in the window."

"Oh, Erbut, no fantasies now. You sound like Sniggs." Pen smacked her fist into her palm as she walked back and forth. "I must think of a way to catch him."

Across the castle, on top of the gatehouse, Dibbler shouted and signaled to her. Pen ignored him and increased the speed of her pacing.

"I know. Ponder's carrack. It's much faster than the supply ship. Aye, the carrack. Ponder will just have to forgo his smuggling for a while."

She turned at the sound of many footsteps. Coming toward her across the wall walk were Dibbler and his motley castle guard. Dibbler waved a pistol, his acquisition from their raid of Cutwell's house. Between the erstwhile captain and Sniggs strode the queen's man. Trailing behind came Turnip, Wheedle, and several farmers.

He came to a halt in front of her, stuck out a bandaged arm, and snapped, "I have come for an explanation, Mistress Fairfax. I should arrest you along with the priest. I've got myself nearly scorched to death and succumbed to the perilous humors of smoke. You have interfered with her majesty's sworn emissary. Deliver the priest Jean-Paul unto me at once."

He glanced aside at Dibbler. "And that knave has my best pistol. Return it to me before he kills someone."

"Beshrew the pistol. You're too late, Lord St. John."

St. John smirked at her. "What has happened? Is he dead? Have you killed him?"

"No. The priest has fled." Pen pointed to the supply ship as it vanished over the horizon.

St. John gazed at it, then burst into curses. Pen stared at him as his face turned the color of a ruby.

"I should have attended to this matter myself!" he shouted.

"What?"

He glared at her, then looked away. "Never mind. Now I must pursue him all over again. By the cross, you had better pray I kill him before he reaches England."

St. John turned and tried to leave. Pen signaled to Dibbler, and the queen's man found himself in the midst of a circle of pikes and pitchforks. He rounded on Pen.

"What mean you by this?"

"You said you were going to kill him."

As though speaking to an inhabitant of Bedlam, he said, "You have left me no choice, mistress."

"I cannot allow you to kill him," Pen said.

"Allow? Allow? God's testicles!"

"Cease these foul ravings, my lord, or I'll have you clapped in a cell."

Turnip poked the man's backside with his pitchfork. St. John clamped his mouth shut and glared at her.

"As I said, I cannot allow you to kill him, but I will help you capture him again."

"I need no assistance from a foolhardy such as yourself. You may chase him all you like, but only I know where he's bound."

Pen contemplated her triumphant opponent for a moment, then sighed with mock regret. "If you won't help me catch him, then I'll go without you. Alas, then I shall be forced to put you in a cell until I return."

St. John eyed the pikes and pitchforks again. "What do you propose, mistress?"

"You and I shall take Ponder's swift carrack and hunt down the priest," Pen said.

"I shall gather my men."

"Nay, my lord. You'd be too tempted to o'rthrow me. My men will suffice. Prithee, make haste, for I wish to sail at once."

St. John made a sweeping bow. "I am at your command, mistress, although when we catch the priest, I vow you'll regret ever setting foot off this God-cursed island."

Her preparations for a voyage were already complete. Pen visited her treasury, which consisted of an ancient worm-eaten casket stuck in a dusty room below the Painted Chamber. It was during this search for travel funds that Pen realized she'd been robbed and by whom. The pitted and rusted lock on the casket had been breached, and nearly a third of her store of coins was missing. Gathering up the rest while she cursed, Pen set off with her retainers and St. John.

They rode to the Cutwell dock on the other side of the island with St. John scoffing at the idea of her stealing a ship. Pen paid him no heed. Dismounting from her horse, she marched down the dock to the ship's master with her men right behind her. She handed the master a bag of coin, spent a few minutes in intense discussion, then boarded the ship with a chastened St. John at her heels. She'd used most of her meager store of winter coin. But her need was dire.

The voyage to England took little over a day, most of which she spent at the prow of the ship straining to catch sight of the supply vessel. She never did. They anchored in a secluded inlet on the coast of Cornwall the following night and were rowed ashore. At the master's instructions, she found lodging in a village nearby and was up before dawn the next morning.

They hired horses and set forth on a road that led north according to St. John's guidance.

As they rode, Pen came out of her grim silence and cast a glance at the queen's man. "Why did you dose Tristan with that evil potion?"

He shouted over the thunder of their horses' hooves. "Think you that I wanted to waste time in prizing from him his foul secrets?"

"So this tale of an attempt upon Cecil is true."

Turning his head to look at her quickly, he didn't answer at once. He kicked his horse into a faster gallop.

"Aye. Why do you think I'm chasing after him at the risk of my own life? He purposes to murder the queen's minister. This is why I must get to the meeting place before he does."

It took all Pen's strength to keep up the bone-pounding pace, while her thoughts seemed to slow as though dipped in chilled syrup. Tristan, a murderer. She remembered how he'd been in the Painted Chamber—all calculating sensuality, manipulation, and connivance. She had lied to herself about him. She couldn't trust her own judgment, not about him. God help her, Tristan was going to—she didn't even want to think the words.

They slowed a bit to rest the horses, and she came out of her misery. "You may as well tell me where we're going, then."

"North, mistress, north and east for more than a day's ride. To a remote domain far from the queen's reach, deep in the countryside. Secretary Cecil and his escort Christian de Rivers, Lord Montfort, are to arrive at a place called Beaumaris at any moment. Pray God we reach them in time to stop the priest."

"Beaumaris," Pen said. "I know it not."

"The seat of Baron Rochefort—a secret and reclusive man. But that isn't important. What is important is that Cecil will be there, and, if we are unlucky, so will the priest. Then, mistress, despite your scruples, I am going to kill him."

Pen stole a look at St. John. His eyes frightened her. They held no compassion, no regret. Looking into them was like looking into the eyes of a stalking wolf, where no meaning dwelt, only the relentlessness of a predator. By the heavenly Father, she couldn't let this man get to Tristan. They rode through the night—Pen, St. John, Dibbler, and her retainers. They left two of the farmers behind. Unused to riding, they both took falls and were left at a hamlet to nurse sore backsides.

Changing horses when they could, they rode late into the next afternoon. It was all Pen could do to keep her eyes open and her bottom planted in the saddle. Only her determination to stop Tristan and at the same time prevent him from being killed kept her upright.

She woke from her daze of weariness when St. John slowed his horse to a walk. They had left the main road that stretched all the way to the border hours before and took a narrow path that wound through field after field of stubble. At midday they plunged into a forest that seemed as deserted as a crypt at midnight.

The track they followed dipped into a ravine, the floor of which was covered with limbs and leaves dropped from the trees above. Now they could no longer rush their horses without risking a fall. At a point where the ravine came to its narrowest point, they pulled up at a site of slaughter. Beside the path lay the bodies of two men, blood from sword wounds drying on their chests. Not daring to take the time to stop, Pen signaled her people and they rode by, taking care to watch the sides of the ravine for attackers.

St. John, who was riding ahead of her, turned in his saddle. "You see? He's killed already. No doubt those men were sent by the queen's minister to guard this path, and he found them."

Pen said nothing. Her gorge rose, and she felt unable to take in more horror. St. John couldn't know that Tristan killed those men. They wore no livery, so they might have been thieves, not a minister's guards. Was she lying to herself, trying to absolve Tristan of any crime because of what she felt for him? She fell deeper into a state of tortured uncertainty.

Eventually they halted, and St. John appeared to lapse into fervid thought. Pen heard the trickle of a stream. She dismounted and led her horse off the path and through trees bare of leaves. As they'd ridden north, frost covered the ground more and more frequently. This afternoon the sun's pallid rays had failed to burn it from the ground.

She was watching her horse drink, when she heard shouting. On the path she saw the queen's man punch Dibbler in the jaw. As Dibbler reeled, St. John snatched his pistol from the holster on Dibbler's saddle. He rammed his boot into Dibbler's chest.

Dibbler hurtled from his horse's back. St. John quickly slapped the rumps of the horses that surrounded him, causing most of them to bolt, with their inexperienced riders either falling or wrestling in the saddle as the animals fled.

Pen shouted at her men, but they were too concerned with saving their own necks to pay heed. St. John vanished down the path as she scrambled back to her horse. Turnip came bustling up to her through a screen of bushes fastening his clothing.

Only Wheedle had managed to keep hold of the reins of her horse. Pen gazed about her, wanting to cuff the ears of everyone, including herself. Instead, she mounted her horse. Calling to Wheedle to gather the rest and follow, Pen galloped after St. John.

The man hated Tristan. He'd already said he wasn't merely going to prevent a murder. He was going to kill Tristan, and he didn't want her interfering with his blood lust. But she couldn't let St. John hurt Tristan, no matter what he might have done. She had to stop St. John and at the same time keep Tristan from harming anyone.

Leaning over her horse's neck, Pen strained to see a sign of the queen's man, but the path twisted back and forth, and the forest loomed close on either side, blocking her view. Wheeling into right-angle turns, dodging low-hanging branches, she plunged down the track and hoped she stayed in the saddle.

With no warning the trail broke free of the trees. She faced an expanse of field. Across it she spotted St. John. He was heading for the gates of a great house that someone had built in the midst of this wilderness.

Pen raced after him as the sun began to drop toward the tree line behind the house. It was sinking quickly, and she could make out nothing of Beaumaris except soaring square towers turned black against the red-gold light of the dying sun. St. John suddenly veered to the side and skirted the redbrick wall that surrounded the house.

In spite of her haste, Pen noted how deserted the house appeared. She saw no servants or sentries through the gateway. When she careened around the house to the back, she saw her quarry dismount before a door in the wall. Evidently it was barred, for after trying it, he stepped back and leapt for the wall. His hands gained purchase at its top, and he began to draw himself up.

Pen hardly waited for her mount to slow before she sprang to the ground, running. St. John had gained a foothold between the bricks at his feet and was hauling himself up the wall. Pen stopped a few yards from him and called his name. He kept climbing. She rushed to him and grabbed his leg. He cried out, looked down at her, and rammed her in the chest with his knee. Pen flew backward, hit the ground, and lay there for a moment, stunned.

She sat up to find St. John had dropped back to the ground. He drew back his fist and rushed toward her. Pen gasped, and her hand, which was planted on the ground, fastened around a palm-size stone.

As St. John hurtled toward her, she prayed for skill gained in aiming at Ponder Cutwell's men-at-arms. She hurled the stone at his head and heard a smack. St. John plummeted to the ground at her feet.

Stooping over him, she removed Dibbler's pistol from his belt and stuck it in her girdle. If anyone was going to prevent Tristan from murdering a royal minister now, it would be she. It was the only way she might save his life.

In the distance she heard a horse whinny. Someone was arriving. Pen gazed up at the wall. If St. John could scale it, she might. But she also might flatten herself against it.

Running back to her horse, she led the animal to stand next to the wall and mounted. Then she took a risk. She slipped her legs under her, stood on the saddle, and grasped the ledge on the top of the wall before the horse had time to become startled. As she gripped the ledge, the animal snorted and danced out from under her.

She hung from the top for a few moments. Finding a toehold between the bricks, she lifted herself to the ledge and crouched there. Before her lay a deserted kitchen yard. Through an open shutter she could see a cook with his back to her, kneading dough at a worktable.

On a door stoop sat a scullery boy. Pen went still, knowing he would look up soon and see her. The cook shouted, and to Pen's relief the boy jumped up and bolted inside the house.

What now? She had given little thought to her actions after this point, for she'd been too concerned with keeping her eye on St. John. The clatter of hooves on flagstones out front spurred her. Someone, possibly Cecil, was riding into the front court. As she listened, Pen scoured the lines of the house for a way inside. Her gaze traveled over a symmetrical arrangement of eight square towers and row after row of gridiron windows.

As she looked at one of the highest sets of windows, she perceived movement. Directing her gaze upward, she spied a black figure on top of the central tower at the front of the house. Tristan! Pen swung her legs over the wall and dropped. She landed hard on packed earth, jarring her entire body.

The pain failed to stop her from racing to a door beyond that of the kitchen. Trying it, she found it locked. Alarmed and frightened, she nearly lost her composure and banged on it.

Then she composed herself. The room she sought to enter was deserted. Looking around, she spied a woodpile nearby. She selected a slim piece. Swallowing her anxiety, she went to a window, covered the end of the log with her skirt, and punched a hole in it.

Pen dropped the log. Slipping her hand inside the hole, she unfastened the latch and climbed into the chamber. It was but a moment's work to creep across the chamber and peer through a series of doors and successive rooms until she found the great hall.

As she watched the room, a man crossed it, a tall man with silken locks that were at once dark and yet streaked with luxurious silver. He walked with the gait of a man used to exercise, while his skin had been tinted by the sun. He was heading for the front court.

There was no time to waste. As he left, Pen raced across the hall to a marble stair, went up a flight, and found another door. Praying that she'd guessed correctly, she flung it open to find another stair leading up to the central tower. She clutched her skirt and churned up the stairs.

Halfway up she stumbled and clutched at the sill of one of the tower windows. As she regained her balance, she glanced outside to see the silver-haired man walking toward a party of men dismounting in the court below. One of the guests was slight and balding, the other much taller and younger. This younger man glanced in her direction. Pistol in hand, she saw his startled expression as he beheld her and the weapon. Then he suddenly bolted for the house.

Lungs aching, Pen raced on. Through the clatter of her own footsteps she heard others ahead of her. Who else was on the stair? She charged up two more flights and through a narrow doorway that stood open.

She burst out onto the roof of the tower to find herself unexpectedly on the heels of her quarry. What was he doing on the stair? Tristan raced across the roof toward a cloaked figure. This was the person she'd seen from below. Tristan stopped suddenly. Her gaze fixed only on him, Pen shoved aside all concerns except stopping him.

Knowing what she was being forced to do, Pen began to tremble. Tears threatened to obscure her vision. Her fear turned to horror when she saw his arm cock back and glimpsed a dagger. St. John had been right. He was there to kill.

Hands quivering so that she could hardly hold the weapon, she lifted her pistol and aimed. "Tristan, no!"

His head jerked around, and he met her tortured gaze. His own face was devoid of expression. Turning from her, he threw the dagger as Pen screamed and fired. Over her own scream, she heard another, and it wasn't Tristan.

"God's mercy, no, no, no," she cried as she rushed toward Tristan's fallen body. "I beg you, Lord, no."

Pen had vaguely realized that the third person on the roof had been wounded, but at the moment she cared only about Tristan. Dropping to her knees beside him, she touched his bleeding shoulder as he struggled to rise. She clutched his good arm, but he shoved her away while trying to draw his sword, his gaze fixed upon the dark figure at the edge of the roof.

Satisfied that she hadn't killed Tristan, Pen finally looked at the stranger. Shrouded in a dark cloak, masked, it had dropped a crossbow and was pulling the dagger from its arm. The mask slipped, and Pen beheld the golden eyes and curls of a young woman.

Swaying slightly, the woman faced Tristan while she wiped blood from the dagger and gripped the blade in order to throw it. "*Mon Dieu,* what a curse you are, *Anglais.* Greet the devil for me, will you?"

CHAPTER XVI

The woman with the golden hair wiped the blood from the dagger. Then she gripped the clean blade. Pen shrieked and tried to shove Tristan aside, but he lunged at her, throwing his body over hers. Pen fell beneath him. As she landed, he arched up, his gaze shooting past her in the direction of the tower door.

"Christian, duck!" Tristan shouted as he covered Pen, and a shadow knifed across them both.

Pen felt his weight crush her for a moment. Then he was up and lurching to his feet. He reached down and jerked her upright. Pen landed beside him to see the man called Christian bending over the prone body of the woman. She lay with a knife protruding from her shoulder. She cursed at Christian like a bawd from the London stews, before going limp.

Beside Pen, Tristan weaved on his feet. She clutched his arm, and Christian rushed to them. Putting his shoulder under Tristan's good arm, he supported the wounded man and glanced at Pen.

"My vanished raven. How fortunate for you that I saw this maid through the tower window. I thought you drowned, you black-haired little pestilence."

"Near drowned, near stabbed, a multitude of near deaths," Tristan said.

Pen hovered in front of them, confused and grieved,

tears now flowing freely. Both men seemed to have forgotten her, and she hesitated in a frenzy of bewilderment.

Christian glanced at the wound in Morgan's shoulder before nodding in the direction of the assassin. "What a direful spectacle you've made of yourself. And who is that murderous wench? Shall I let her bleed to death?"

"I know not who she is," Tristan said, "but she's French and would make a most useful prisoner."

He sucked in his breath and pressed his hand over his wound. Sweat beaded on his forehead as color drained from his face.

Pen found her tongue at last. "Tristan, how do you fare?" She looked to Christian. "Will he be well?"

"If we care for him at once." He tried to open Tristan's clothing with one hand.

Tristan seized his wrist with a bloody hand. "Derry, how fares Derry?"

"Marvelous well, my raven. Why?"

Letting out a sigh, Tristan swayed, winced, and shook his head.

Pen plucked at the folds of doublet over the wound. "Tristan, I don't understand. Why were you trying to kill that woman? The queen's man said—"

She cringed at the scalding glance he turned on her. The tendons and muscles of his jaw worked, and he grimaced with pain. He was growing more and more pale as the moments passed.

"God's blood, you tried to kill me. Go back to your island, witch."

"But, Tristan—"

"Get out of my sight!"

Pen gasped at the furor behind that shout. The strain of it showed as Tristan's features contorted with pain. He sagged against Christian, who slipped his arm around Tristan's waist and supported him almost completely.

"You seem befuddled, lady," Christian said. "Morgan was trying to stop that woman from murdering Secretary Cecil, but this is no time for quarreling. Morgan needs tending at once."

Dazed, Pen helped Christian support his friend. "Morgan? He is Morgan?"

"Aye, of course," Christian said as they carried the wounded man toward the stair. "Ah, there you are, Rochefort. Help me. And have your men tend to our lady murderer over there."

The silver-haired man sheathed his sword, gestured for the men behind him to attend the assassin, and took Pen's place. Pen followed them down the tower stair, up another, and into a bedchamber. She watched them lower Morgan to the bed and wrung her hands. More men-at-arms posted themselves at the door, but Pen paid them no attention. She went to the bed and shouldered her way between Rochefort and Christian.

The three men stopped talking when she joined them. Through his grimaces, Morgan managed to glare at her.

"How did you find me?" He broke off to wince as Christian cut his doublet and shirt from him. "Bleeding hell, Christian! Leave off. I think she's brought the priest down on us."

He half rose in the bed and gripped Pen's sleeve with bloody fingers, drawing her down so that his face almost touched hers. "You came with Jean-Paul, did you not?"

"I—I made him take me here, but I didn't know. Upon mine honor, I thought you were the priest."

"Jean-Paul is here?" Christian asked quickly.

Morgan bit his lip and nodded. Christian exchanged glances with Rochefort, who left at a run.

Pen called after him. "I left him senseless by the back wall."

Christian gently pushed Morgan back onto the bed even as he laughed. "By the rood, Morgan, a goodly jest. You, a priest. Ha!"

"There's an even goodlier jest." Morgan lunged upright despite Christian's restraining arms.

"She claimed to love me. By God's entrails, she set me afire with her—" He sucked in his breath as a spasm of pain raced through him.

"But when the priest descended upon us with his foul lies, she proved herself faithless. By the cross, her love is easily shaken. It's a thing of mist and vapor, dissipating with the smallest of breezes. She believed every tale he spouted, even thought me capable of murder. And because she's so faithless, she tried to kill me!"

Pen's tears were flowing again. She could hardly bear to look at Morgan's wound, and he was growing more and more impassioned.

"Please," she said. "How could I have known?"

"You made love to me," Morgan said between grinding teeth, "and then you tried to murder me. God, I want to strangle you."

Morgan tried to sit up again, but Christian held him down.

"Mistress Fairfax," Christian said. "Pray leave us, for I must dress this wound. I won't be able to do it if he keeps hopping about like this."

"Let me whip her first," Morgan said.

Pen nodded to Christian while biting her quivering lower lip. Turning away, she heard him growl at his friend about seeing how she liked his riding crop.

Christian was trying to soothe him. "Peace, my raven. You shall have your revenge when you're well."

Pen left, passing a footman on his way upstairs with water and linens. In the hall she encountered Baron Rochefort, who was at the center of a group of liveried men-at-arms.

"Ah, the lady," Rochefort said. "Mistress Fairfax, I've imprisoned the lady murderer and sent men to search for the priest, but I believe this brood of guinea fowl must be yours." He waved a hand at a bedraggled and bruised group in one corner of the hall.

"Mistress!" Cap in hand, Dibbler rushed to her. "They say the queen's man was a priest all along. He punched me in the nose, did that poxy bastard. And then he kicked me. A devilish cruel blow it was. He had the strength of forty men. I told Sniggs to watch him."

Sniggs scurried over to them. "You did not! And I was watching him, but he was right quick, like the devil's imp he is. I near got me neck broke when he scared me horse."

"I did so tell you to watch him," Dibbler said, swelling.

Pen was too distraught to bear this squabbling. She shook her head and waved a hand at them, but it was a loud male bellow that quieted them.

"Silence," roared Baron Rochefort. "Get you gone to attend your horses."

They all shuffled out while Rochefort finished giving orders to the men-at-arms. Soon they were left alone.

"I will show you to a chamber, mistress, and then I must leave you."

Feeling as if she was in an evil dream, Pen nodded. "The minister, is he well?"

"Aye. The moment we realized there was danger, we dispatched him to one of Christian's strongholds."

He conducted her to the threshold of a blue and white chamber. Glancing inside, Pen noticed that Lord Rochefort's expression had turned even more grim than it had been.

He kept his gaze away from the chamber and addressed her as he left. "I'll send someone to you."

Once alone, Pen closed the door to the chamber and sank to her knees, then back on her heels. Doubling over, she burst into tears as she remembered firing the pistol. She saw again the way Tristan's—no—Morgan's body jerked with the impact of the shot, how he spun around to give her a look of such incredulity and pain. She cringed at the vision of him collapsing and then, with an unmatched force of will, summoning the strength to face that horrible woman with the golden hair.

Vaguely Pen realized that he'd been telling the truth all along, and that the woman had been the French assassin. She had only wanted to prevent a disaster for her queen and country. She'd been so stalwart in forcing herself to choose duty over love, and instead she'd nearly destroyed both. Over and over the image of Morgan's agony flashed before her. Pen covered her face with her hands and moaned.

Morgan. Morgan St. John, emissary of her majesty. No, not emissary, but something more, something much more dangerous.

Between bouts of dread over Morgan's condition, Pen recalled something else—the change she'd seen in him, it was real. He'd been telling her the truth about himself all along. He had said he wasn't Tristan, and it was Tristan who loved her. He'd said Morgan felt only gratitude.

And now, thanks to her lack of conviction in him and her interference, she'd made him hate her. Had she destroyed all trace affection in him for her? Oh, why couldn't she have been made like other women who trusted the men they loved blindly? Mayhap she'd been made too wary by what had befallen her before she took refuge on Penance.

Tears snaked down her cheeks, and Pen wiped them with the backs of her hands as she sat on the floor. Through the machinations of that evil priest, she'd betrayed and hurt Tristan. Holy Mother, would he forgive her? Pen felt the heat of her body drain from her as she remembered Tristan's rage. Terrifying to behold, it had nearly sent her fleeing from the room with its force.

She had been wrong, but not by design. Surely he would understand that once he'd calmed. And she would have to begin to know him anew. If he would allow it. He wanted nothing of her at the moment, yet she had no choice but to remain. For he held her heart, and even if she so desired, she couldn't leave it and him.

Yes, she would remain and hope that Morgan's rage would ebb enough for her to convince him to allow her to make atonement. She sniffed and began to search her costume for a kerchief. A knock startled her, and she let in the scullery boy from the kitchen. He bore a pitcher of water and bathing cloths. Setting them on a sideboard, he pointed to a wardrobe.

"Prithee, lady. His lordship said there be garments for you in there." Smiling shyly, he bowed and ran out of the room.

Worried about Morgan, Pen snatched the first bodice and kirtle that met her hand. She washed quickly and donned the garments, which were of white silk shot with silver. The tight undersleeves and the fitted bodice gave her trouble.

She found shoes, but they were too large, and she resorted to her riding boots. She nearly tripped over the kirtle until she found a farthingale of buckram that made it stand out enough. For warmth she had just pulled on a fitted overgown of black trimmed with pearl and jet, when another knock heralded the entrance of the man called Christian de Rivers.

"Is he well?"

"Aye, mistress, and resting." He led her to sit on a stool by the cold fireplace. "I had to force a sleeping draught down his throat, the stubborn little canker. So now, with my men and Rochefort's hieing themselves across the countryside, it is time for you and me to talk. Explain yourself, Mistress Fairfax. Why have you nearly murdered my sweet raven?"

Pen looked up at him. "I pray you, sir. Why should I tell you?"

"Marry, lady, because I near killed myself fostering that lad, and in a few weeks' time you seem to have undone much of my work." He paused to study her before saying softly, "And because you must."

Pen narrowed her eyes and contemplated the man standing before her. What convinced her wasn't the sword master's body, or those hotly violet eyes fringed with heavy lashes, or his habit of ruthlessness in language that reminded her of Morgan at his worst. What convinced her was the certainty with which he said those last words—because you must. There had been no trace of supplication. And he waited for her to answer as though there had never been any doubt that she would comply. Whoever this man was, she knew he had the right to command.

Having surmised his authority, Pen began to confide her story. When she finished, Christian made no comment. He appeared to lapse into deep contemplation, leaving her to wonder if he believed her. Then, suddenly, he chuckled.

"God's eyebrows. Only Morgan could rise from the sea in spite of hell's own thunderclaps and foil a murder plot designed by that catamite of Satan, Jean-Paul." He grinned at her. "And find a cunning lady possessed of phantasms and charms as well."

Pen grew alarmed. "I'm not a witch, Lord Montfort."

"As you say."

"I'm not!"

"My sweet raven says you are. He was perilous adamant about it just before he succumbed to the sleeping draught."

Pen pursed her lips, clasped her hands in her lap, and refused to answer.

He chuckled again. "Don't fret, sucket. I blame you not for Jean-Paul's machinations. He's a dragon breathing flame upon the kingdom, a master of deception, as you well know from that forgery of his. I've lost several good men to him."

"Trist—Morgan says I should have believed in him rather than trusting the priest," Pen said.

Christian leaned against the mantel. "Ah, yes, Morgan. Morgan, my dear sucket, has had a surfeit of betrayal in his life. Though your mistake wasn't of your own making, he feels only the hurt, and the pain blinds him to reason."

For the first time since her ordeal began back on Penance Isle, Pen smiled. To her delight, Christian returned her smile.

"He's a stubborn arrogant," she said. "And seeks to ply me as he does his sword, but I love him. I begin to think that storm brought him to Penance for me apurpose."

Christian whistled softly. "Christ, lady. If this is how

you deal with him, I shall tell him to surrender the moment he wakes."

"None of these disasters you speak of have been my doing."

"Not the pig?"

"He told you about Margery?"

"Nor being tossed down a well?"

"Only half tossed!" Pen glowered at him. "Saints. I vow he must have chattered like a squirrel while you dressed his wound."

"*Ranted* seems a better word."

Pen covered her mouth with the tips of her fingers but couldn't hide her smile. "You should have seen his face when he first saw Margery."

They grinned at each other.

"When may I see him?" she asked.

"He should wake upon the morrow. His wound is clean and quite shallow, and no bones have been damaged. His body will heal quickly, but I fear his heart and his temper won't."

"I shall woo both."

"I shall witness your progress with interest," Christian said.

Although Christian assured her there was no need, Pen kept watch over the sleeping Tristan throughout the night. Finally she fell asleep in her chair with her head resting near his shoulder on the bed. She woke late the next morning when he stirred beside her. As she rose, he tossed his head and tried to shove away the sheets and blankets that covered him.

Flushed, he opened his eyes when she drew the covers back over him. Pen touched his cheek and found it hot. His lips pressed together, and she could tell he was fighting pain.

"What do you want?" he snapped.

"Naught but to care for you, Trist—Morgan."

At the name, he cursed and lifted himself on his elbows. The covers fell away, revealing smooth brown flesh and bandages. Pen glanced at his bare shoulders, the long line of his chest as it tapered toward his hips, then met his angry gaze. As they looked at each other, his eyes began to glitter, and a slow, torrid smile crept over his lips.

"Even when you thought me a spy, you wanted me. Did you not, Gratiana?"

Flushing, she ignored his barb. "How could I have known? I beg you to understand that I was deceived."

The smile vanished, and he lay back, breaking their gaze. His jaw clenched, and he closed his eyes.

Pen settled in her chair again, not daring to speak. He didn't want her there, not only because he was furious with her, but because he didn't want her to see him fighting the pain. Dear God, he'd looked at her with almost the same ruthless disgust he reserved for the priest.

"Go away, Pen."

She started, for he'd opened his eyes again and was raking her with that intimidating black gaze only made more frightening by the blaze of fever. When she didn't move, his hand shot out from the covers and snatched her wrist. He yanked her from the chair and hauled her close so that she felt the heat from his body. Dear God, how could she be aroused when she was scared? His lips were so close to hers when he spoke, his jaw set.

"I said, go away."

Pen felt her heart skitter and thud, but she hung on to her valor. Placing her hand flat against his bare chest, well away from his wound, she pressed hard. He swore, released her hand, and dropped back onto the bed. Gasping, he continued to hurl epithets at her.

Pen straightened the covers once again, then prudently moved her chair beyond his reach and sat down. "You'll never get well enough to avenge yourself on me if you don't rest."

Her answer was a torrent of curses that faded quickly. Tristan glared at her, but his eyelids drooped. His mouth clamped into a thin line, and he finally turned on his side away from her. The sheets fell away as he moved, and he kicked at them, leaving one long leg bare. Pen swallowed and contemplated drawing the covers over him, if only to spare herself the sight of flesh she couldn't touch. She didn't want him to grow cold. But she didn't move.

If she touched him again, he might fight her. And if they fought, he would put his body against hers. She already longed for him, and he knew it. He had taunted her with it, and from what she'd seen of Morgan St. John, he was capable of using her longing to torment her, of using his body and his allure as a weapon to gain the vengeance he so clearly wanted.

No, she must wait, wait and hope that as his body healed, his wrath would fade. If instead his anger grew, she didn't want to think about what he would do to her once he recovered.

TO MAKE HIPPOCRAS

To make hippocras, take a pottle of wine, two ounces of good cinnamon, half an ounce of ginger, nine cloves, and six pepper corns, and a nutmeg, and bruise them and put them into the wine with some rosemary flowers, and so let them steep all night, and then put in sugar a pound at least; and when it is well settled, let it run through a woollen bag made for that purpose; thus if your wine be claret, the hippocras will be red; if white, then of that color also.

CHAPTER XVII

Morgan woke with a clear head for the first time since he'd been wounded. He lay on his stomach with his arm flung out across a lump beside him in the bed. Raising his head, he recognized Pen's frail jawline and swore to himself.

No blessed loss of memory saved him from recalling his folly of the past few days. He'd given in to weakness and tolerated her presence. It was the fault of the fever.

Pain and the heat within his body had robbed him of anger so that he craved the touch of her cool hands above all else. He'd become vulnerable again, exposed. But now the fever was gone, and he was left in bed with a woman who had tried to kill him and nearly precipitated a tragedy for England. Even if he could have forgiven his own betrayal, he couldn't forgive what she'd almost cost the queen.

After he'd escaped, he'd chased after the Danseur to the cliffs near the castle. He saw her wade out into the surf to greet men rowing a boat to shore. As he expected, the boat then met a ship, which sailed immediately. He wasted no time in retrieving his bag of coins. He'd found the supply ship and roused its master. The man had been furious at having his slumber disturbed, until he realized that Morgan came bearing gold. After he'd caught sight of the coins, he'd almost drooled while giving orders to set sail.

Sailing in the wake of the Danseur, he reached England hours behind her. He drove himself near to exhaustion once he reached land, and had been close to catching up with her when those men ambushed him in that ravine in the forest. If he hadn't been so furious, he would have admired the woman for setting her mercenaries on him. He'd escaped, to her misfortune, but now he knew that the delay had allowed Pen and Jean-Paul to catch up with him.

He'd reached Beaumaris only to find it all but deserted. Evidently Rochefort had opened the house only to provide a meeting place for his friends. As Morgan had approached the house, he saw Cecil and Christian passing through the distant entry gate and riding down a long avenue toward Beaumaris. At the same time, Danseur was slipping around the back. The visitors were still too far away to warn. Tristan had been forced into a race to stop Danseur before she found a hiding place and her victims arrived unsuspecting.

He followed her into the house only to see her disappear while he had to duck inside a pantry upon the appearance of the cook. By the time he came out, Danseur was nowhere in sight. He was forced to waste precious minutes searching for her. His luck changed when he noticed that the door to the tower stair stood slightly ajar. Then he realized that instead of taking aim from some front-facing chamber where she might be interrupted, Danseur had gone to the roof.

He raced up the stairs in desperate haste. He'd had no idea Pen had followed him, until she appeared on top of the tower with him. He remembered her shouting at him, and how astonished he'd been to see her. But he couldn't afford to listen to her. When she threatened him, he'd made a choice. He'd gambled that her love would stop her from hurting him. He'd lost.

She'd betrayed him. Trusting someone dear to him had always resulted in betrayal. Morgan winced at the small spiked thought that lanced through his heart—people he loved betrayed him because he deserved nothing better. Quickly he stepped on that thought, swept it off the edge of his awareness and down a bottomless crevice. But the pain stayed with him, deep and unbearable, and so, to save himself from destruction, he acted.

Inching his hand from beneath the covers, he took a corner of one sheet and touched it to Pen's nose. She wriggled it, but slept on. He tickled her again, and this time she rubbed her nose, sighed, and opened her eyes. As she did so, he withdrew and pretended to sleep.

He felt her bend over him. He remained still and breathed with the even pace of sleep. Then he felt her slide from the bed. Hearing her walk to the door, he slightly raised one eyelid to peer at her from beneath his lashes.

The door opened to reveal Christian de Rivers. Pen put her finger to her lips and whispered.

"He sleeps still. I thank God his fever finally broke."

"I told you it would. Wound fever is a common happenstance. Run along to your chamber, sucket. I'll watch him while you dress and eat. I've left off asking you to rest. Mayhap you will now that he's better."

Pen left, and Christian came into the chamber, all bright and vigorous in his movements. He walked over to the bed, drew a chair close to it, and sat. He swung booted feet up and onto the mattress, jarring Morgan's legs.

"You may open your eyes, raven. She's gone."

Morgan turned over and kicked at Christian's legs. "Jesu. What manner of care is this for a wounded man?"

"The kind you deserve. I can see by your color that you fare well, and you've the look of a cock trapped by a wolf."

"Am I to have no compassion from you for all my trials?"

"Spare me your sacrificial postures," Christian said as he lay back in the chair and gazed at Morgan. "Mistress Fairfax hopes that you've forgiven her. She doesn't know you as I do."

Morgan glared at Christian, who continued.

"You're going to take aim with that poison-tipped arrow of a tongue of yours and wound her more fatally than she ever wounded you."

"You know naught of it. And if I've a poisonous tongue, it was you who gave it to me."

"And I did my work too well. I know your character, you loathsome colt. Why can you not listen to me? I've told you that in running away from her you condemn yourself."

"What know you of running and women? You've been married to Nora for years and years."

"And when I first met her, I made the mistake of not believing in her." Christian's gaze dropped away and fastened on another corner of the room. "I made a mistake that near cost me her love."

"Love?" Morgan suddenly became restless and began slapping at his covers and straightening them. "What has love to do with Penelope Fairfax? I told you what happened. How I was before, that was a phantasm brought on by my lack of memory. If I wish the company of women, there is Lady Ann in London and Maria at my country house."

Christian swept his feet off the bed and yanked the covers out of Morgan's grasp. "Now, you listen to me, my raven, for you're about to make a perilous bungle. I've watched you with Mistress Fairfax."

"And remember that I've seen you with your Lady Ann and your Maria as well. Neither of them ever made you furious. Marry, no woman has ever made you more than slightly vexed. I watched you when she left, raven. I saw your eyes when you dared to open them."

Morgan sat up in the bed, glaring at him. "I don't love—"

Christian cursed, planted a knee beside Morgan, and shoved him back into the pillows. He gripped Morgan's good shoulder and hissed.

"Shall I tell you what I saw, how you feel about her in truth? Like this: 'Godlike the man who/ sits at her side, who/ watches and catches that laughter/ which (softly) tears me/ to tatters: nothing is/ left of me, each time I see her, . . . tongue numbed; arms, legs/ melting, on fire. . . .' "

Morgan knocked Christian's hand aside and met his mentor's taunting gaze with a glare. Christian disturbed him by answering his glare with a chuckle. He dropped back into his chair.

"God's beard, raven, you remind me of how I screeched and clawed and railed against my fate when I met Nora."

"The comparison is false. Pen never listens to me. She refuses to use good sense."

"The priest slipped through our grasp again," Christian said.

Blinking at this sudden change of subject, Morgan said, "I don't marvel at it, for where Pen interferes, you may be sure of disaster."

"Her majesty is busy trying to avoid war with Scotland."

"If you hadn't given succor to her half brother when he rebelled, the Queen of Scots would have no pretext."

"I'd rather give succor to her bastard Protestant brother than to the legitimate witch who plots her majesty's death. The key, my dear fury, is not to overbalance in favor of either."

"And Cecil's death would have overbalanced . . ."

They regarded each other silently.

"Then you see how Mistress Fairfax nearly caused a war as well as my death with her infernal hindrance," said Morgan.

"That was not my point," Christian replied. "Mistress Fairfax is unschooled in the machinations of papists, especially those like Jean-Paul."

"Then she should have kept out of it," Morgan snapped.

He heard the door creak and glanced up to find Pen looking at him over a tray full of food. She gave him a sorrowful look and stood on the threshold as though uncertain whether to enter. Morgan fixed a scowl upon her, leaning forward, and felt something tug at his shoulder. The covers had dropped down to his waist, and for the first time since waking he looked at his wound.

A bandage wrapped around his chest and shoulder, holding a poultice of some sort in place. He touched it. As he inhaled, he caught a whiff of such tartness that his eyes watered.

"Jesu, what is this?"

Pen hesitated, then came forward with a determined smile and set the tray on a chest at the foot of the bed. "It's a poultice of mandrake root and other healing herbs. Your wound began to corrupt, so I spoke with Wheedle."

"Wheedle?" Christian rose and gave them both a startled look.

"Wheedle?" Morgan cried.

"Aye," Pen said, brightening as she went on. "You see, she knows all manner of remedies for pigs. They ofttimes wound themselves because they're so clumsy of form."

"You stuck a pig poultice on my shoulder. A pig poultice!"

He stopped because Christian burst out with a raucous laugh that built into a guffaw so strong that he had to lean against his chair for support. Morgan's temper snapped. He felt as if his hair were standing on end and crackling with the force of his anger.

He began tugging and pulling at the bandage. Pen cried out and rushed over to slap at his hands and try to prevent him from removing the wrappings. He shoved her hands aside and tore the bindings. He lifted the padding, squeezed his eyes shut against the fumes, and thrust it at her.

Pen took the wrappings from him. "Look what you've done. Wheedle says you must keep the poultice on the wound for another day."

"Wheedle can go—"

"Morgan," Christian warned.

Morgan pounded the bed. "Jesu, next you'll be roasting me in wine and spices like a loin of pork. Fetch clean cloths and hot water at once, woman."

His irritation expanded when she gave him a contrite look.

"Fear not. That's what I intended."

As she spoke, a serving man entered with the required items. He bore a request from Lord Rochefort that

Christian join him at the stables, for his men had returned from searching for Jean-Paul. With a glance of admonition at Morgan, Christian left with the serving man.

He was so distracted with glowering at Christian that he started when Pen began to bathe his wound. For an instant he was back in the chamber that she'd made his, surrounded by a dome of painted azure sky, peacocks, and winged putti with round pink cheeks, soothed by the chimes in her voice. Then he fell back into the present with a jolt that bruised his heart. The pain evoked fear and an overwhelming urge to strike out at the one he blamed for it and his confusion.

Pen began to wrap a bandage around his shoulder. Each time she touched his bare flesh, prickles of awareness crawled across his body and darted to his groin. His gaze seemed anchored to her full lower lip. He tried to look away, and failed. The failure reminded him of his vulnerability, and the urge to lash out at the cause of it overpowered him.

"Saints, Tristan, what a tangle," Pen was saying. "I shall never be able to forgive myself for hurting you."

He heard that old name, the one that didn't belong to him, that he didn't want. Pulling free of her grasp, he turned on her.

"Damnation. When will you learn to call me Morgan?"

Pen covered her lips with her fingers. "Forgive me, but I have a passing fondness for Tristan."

"Then go find him," Morgan said in an even tone. "For he's not here."

"When we return to Penance Isle, you'll find him."

"How haps it that you think I'll ever return to that gravestone in the middle of the sea?"

Occupied with smoothing sheets, Pen sighed, causing his glance to drop to her breasts. His unruly body began to stir.

"You're fretful, Tris—Morgan. It's the wound and the weakness from the fever that make you so querulous."

"I'll not be quibbled at like a teething babe."

He heard himself growling at her. He was losing governance of himself. Quickly dampening his anger, he hid it behind another urge. He took a pillow from her hands and shoved it aside when keeping hold of her hand. His gaze held hers as he evoked his own particular kind of sensual enchantment with the intensity of his regard.

"I need solace after enduring so much pain, Gratiana."

"But your wound."

"It troubles me not, and I assure you I won't feel it with you to distract me."

As he whispered to her then, murmuring with his lips close to her ear,

> I have decked my bed with coverings
> of tapestry, with carved works,
>   with fine linen of Egypt.
> I have perfumed my bed with myrrh,
>   aloes, and cinnamon.
> Come, let us solace ourselves with loves.

He drew her close and covered her mouth with his. She responded by lacing her arms around his chest and stroking his back. He'd misjudged himself and her power over him. Her hands felt so small against him, but everywhere she stroked him, he burst into dry-tinder flames.

He nuzzled behind her ear, into the hollow of her throat. She was murmuring to him now in that enraptured, chimelike voice that spurred him deeper into arousal. His hands worked at her bodice until it hung loose. He pressed his chest against hers and sighed as if he'd been starved and had suddenly found a banquet.

Burrowing down her neck and shoulder, he captured a nipple in his mouth. His skin smoldered with heat. His fingers danced at her ankle, then skimmed up her calf and thigh to find heat and blessed moisture. The feel of her excited him beyond endurance.

He shoved the covers from his body. Rising over her, he yanked skirts aside and pressed the length of his body to hers. Their flesh touched, melded, and he settled between her legs. Aroused to the point of pain, balancing on his good arm, he arched his back. He moved, stroking himself and her. She clawed at his back and sank her teeth into his breast.

She was murmuring to him again, but all he caught was one word.

" . . . Tristan . . ."

The name battered its way past his defenses like a siege ram, grinding his desire to powder. He'd closed his eyes against the torture of holding back in order to please her. Now his eyes flew open and he stared ahead in alarm.

Disgusted with himself for falling prey to weakness, he drew back from Pen. His hands fell away from her body. She opened her eyes and gazed up at him from the pillows upon which he'd pressed her.

He regarded her with distaste. "Tristan is a fantasy of your own making. If you wish to make love, do it with me, Morgan."

Rising, Pen brushed a lock of hair from her eyes. "I love you both." Her hand strayed to his chest and kneaded the flesh over his ribs. "Saints, but you're right marvelous made."

He shoved her hands away before she engulfed him in a black squall of desire again. Seeking refuge beneath the covers, he held her off with one hand.

"Are you ill?" she asked. "Have I hurt your wound? Dear, beautiful Tristan. Forgive me." When he didn't answer and only stared at her, she shook her head and smiled.

"Upon mine honor, you've worked upon me so I have no maiden's timidity left at all. Did you know that the very sight of you suffices to make me long to touch your most pleasureful parts."

"Jesu, keep silent!"

He had to get away from her. His flesh sizzled, and the pain in his gut and groin raked his temper. He was so distracted by his own anguish, he failed to notice that Pen had slipped beneath the covers with him. Thus, when she put her hand on his bare inner thigh, he jumped and shoved it away.

She turned her head to the side and regarded him with a confused look. "Don't you want me, Tristan?"

"No, God curse you!" He winced as his movements jarred his wounded shoulder. "Can you not leave me be?"

"But—"

"Hasn't it sufficed that you've almost killed me? Must you also ravage me on my sickbed?"

Pen sprang out from the covers, knelt on the bed, and put her hands on her hips.

"You were the one who began—"

"Pleasureful parts." Morgan was sneering now.

Pen lapsed into silence and gazed at him with dismay. Taking care not to jar his wound, he yanked a sheet from the bed, wound it around his hips, and sat down before he lost strength. The more she pleaded, the more she inflamed his anger.

" 'I long to touch you, Tristan,' " he mimicked in a high voice. Then he swore. " 'Shall I lay myself down on the bed and part my legs for you? Come. I've lost strength and can't fight you. Have me.' "

He leaned closer so that he could sneer into her face. "Then perhaps you'll have your fill of my body and leave me in peace."

Through the black mist of his rage, Tristan barely perceived how the last vestiges of color drained from Pen's face. She hadn't spoken. Like a butterfly dashed by the wind against a stone, she remained motionless.

At last, eyes glittering with moisture, she left the bed. Her movements disjointed and uneven, she fastened her clothing. With the deliberate actions of a priest conducting mass, she gathered up old bandages, cloths, and a basin of water.

Turning from him, she walked to the door and opened it without making a sound. Not once did she look at him. As the door shut, he noticed that she'd been careful to close it gently so that the latch slipped into place with a muffled click.

It had been like watching a ghost. Remorse enveloped him but faded when he reminded himself of how he'd believed in her only to face betrayal. And now she could expose his vulnerability merely by whispering a name. He felt as though she'd flayed the skin from his body and rubbed salt in the raw flesh. He knew without question that to avoid feeling this way, he would never be able to touch Penelope Fairfax again.

CHAPTER XVIII

Once she'd seen a leaf from a beech tree, still green, frozen in ice at the edge of a brook. She felt like that leaf—chilled into lifelessness. Yet her thoughts wouldn't keep still inside her frozen shell. They wandered afar, as if to seek warmth and shelter from the familiar.

She should never have left Highcliffe. She'd missed All Hallow's Eve. At Highcliffe, the end of harvest brought feasting and merriment. Great platters of mutton and roast suckling were passed around the great hall along with custards and spiced ale. And of course there was an enormous frumenty-pot of hulled wheat boiled in milk.

Then arrived the night when spirits roamed abroad, the night when they were the easiest for mortals to see. All work came to a halt while the Highcliffe's denizens indulged in pageantry and mummery. Lads and lasses ducked for apples. Pipe and tabor played lustily so that all could dance.

Mayhap it was better to be in this foreign house after all. She had no merriment left. And nothing could induce her to listen to music, not even a dirge.

Pen glanced about her. After Morgan had attacked, she had fled without looking where she was going. Without interest she noticed that she'd taken refuge in a bay in the long gallery. She had been blindly staring out across a courtyard through one of the diamond-shaped panes in a bank of windows that ran almost from the floor to the ceiling. The window was sweating, and she watched a drop of water trickle to the next pane.

He had turned on her like a maddened destrier.

She remembered being hurt, shamed, and she remembered nearly screaming with the pain of his assault. But then numbness had seeped into her. With it came relief. Vaguely she perceived that this winter of the soul preserved her from torment, and so she clung to the deadness, took care not to shatter the icy coffin that contained her emotions.

"Mistress Fairfax."

She turned her head to find Christian de Rivers standing behind her. He held out his hand but dropped it when she shook her head.

"I am going home."

"Marry, lady, I haven't come to stop you."

He held out his hand again and gave her a look of such command that she placed her own upon it without protest. Conducting her down the gallery, he led her into a withdrawing chamber. She took the chair he offered before a snapping fire and stared at the marble mantel.

"Warm your hands, sucket. They're like ice."

"I'm going home," she said without taking her gaze from the marble. "You don't need me to hunt down your priest-spy."

Abruptly Christian knelt beside her and covered her hands with one of his. She started at the sudden warmth.

"I feared Morgan would try to murder your love. I tried to stop him."

Pen heard herself speaking in a dead voice. "I don't care about him anymore."

"Yes, you do. It takes much more to kill a love such as yours, my sweet comfit. I assure you that cruelty is foreign to Morgan's nature. I'm surprised he hasn't been driven to it more by his family. No, he hasn't killed your affection yet."

Christian squeezed her hands. "No more than he's succeeded in vanquishing his love for you. That is what drives him to lash you with such ruthlessness."

A crack appeared in her icy shroud. It grew, branched, and spread until she was left wearing slivers like a cloak of diamonds. But now she could feel the pain again. Pen turned her face away from Christian.

"He made me feel disgust for myself. I'll never forgive him, and I don't want ever to see him in this life again. I should have known no one can force another to abandon long-held fears. I learned that just now."

"Aye," Christian said. "But we can provide Morgan with the opportunity to learn to abandon them of his own will. And believe me. I'm a formidable teacher."

Pen turned to give him a vexed look. The more this man spoke, the more his barbs fragmented her icy cloak.

"I told you, my lord. I have no wish to amend Lord Morgan's character. Indeed, I heartily hope that someday a lady of great beauty and wit takes his heart and grinds it beneath her heel. By the cross, I've never hated anyone in my life, but I do hate Morgan St. John."

"But you'll forgive him."

"Not if God himself begged it of me."

"I shall have to, as God is occupied elsewhere."

"No, my lord."

Christian sighed. "Very well." He glanced at her from

beneath thick lashes. "But I'm grieved, for I had hoped to distract my raven from his predations among English gentlewomen. God's blood, sometimes I fear for his health, he so overtaxes himself."

"What gentlewomen pray—no." Pen hugged herself. "I care not."

She refused to meet his half-amused stare. After a few moments, he sighed and spoke again.

"Then mayhap you can help me in another matter." He held out something in his hand. A cross dangled from a chain, a cross about which slithered ruby-eyed, golden serpents.

"The companion piece to the serpent dagger," Christian said.

Pen stared at the cross in horrified fascination. He held it out to her, but when she touched it, evil crawled up her hand, spiderlike, and she jerked her fingers back as if burned.

"I can't," she said. "It's Jean-Paul's, is it not? To touch it is to bathe in corruption and evil."

"Ah, yes," Christian said as he stored the cross in a pouch on his belt. "Morgan mentioned your power. But I can't help wishing you could manage it. Just to see if we could track the bastard with it."

"I would end in madness and you would be no better off." Pen sighed. "I can be of no help to you."

"Yes, Morgan told me of the dagger, but you can help me. My dear raven is of no use to me as he is, all snorting rage and passion, but he won't admit that he craves you. Now, don't interrupt. I've a stratagem to work upon him."

Christian patted the pouch that held the cross. "You sail to Penance Isle. I'll tell him when you've set sail that I let you go knowing that Jean-Paul fled to the island for refuge."

"Blessed saints, no."

"He will chase after you like a hound after a bitch. He'll perform the labors of Hercules to get to you."

"He will come for the priest, not for me. But he'll find out he's been deceived. I want no part of this foolish design."

"Come, Mistress Fairfax, don't let a moment's anger ruin your heart's future."

Pen stood and faced Christian. "Upon mine honor, I have no love left in my heart for Morgan St. John. Do me the courtesy of believing what I tell you, my lord."

"Are you certain?"

"Unsurpassed certain."

Shaking his head, Christian bowed over her hand.

Pen almost smiled at him. "You've a kind heart, my lord, and for your good wishes I am obliged to you. You've tried to quicken my dead heart with hope. And though the effort came to naught, I will always remember you for it."

"In time you may reconsider."

"No, my lord. I'll not risk letting him hurt me again, for if he did, I don't think I would survive the pain."

Several days after he'd nearly bedded Pen, Morgan was dressing in his chamber. He hadn't seen Pen at all. When he wasn't sleeping, he caught himself listening for the sound of her footstep outside his door. Each time someone entered, he glanced up expecting Pen.

Each time, he'd been wrong. Rochefort had assigned the scullery boy to serve him, for Pen no longer took an interest in his welfare. Instead of soft, cool hands and a perilous bright smile, he got a runny nose and pigeon-toed feet that stumbled over each other.

He spent much of his time furious at her and yet listening for her. Now he'd decided that he couldn't bear this chamber. A walk was what he needed. And he'd take care not to go near Pen's chamber. Of course, he didn't know where it was, so he might come upon her by chance.

Pulling his belt tight, he grimaced as he strained his shoulder. It was healing well, but not because of that loathsome pig poultice. Morgan glanced up as Christian came into the room bearing two cups of hot cider.

"Good morrow, raven." He handed Morgan one of the cups. "Well rested from your labors at tearing innocent maids' hearts in two, I see."

"She sent you to plead with me no doubt."

Christian leaned on the fireplace mantel, sipped his drink, and gave Morgan a wicked smile. "Have I ever pleaded with you?"

Morgan shrugged and set his cup aside while he drew on his boots.

"Go to Hades, Christian. You've been trying to reconcile me with her from the first."

"True, but much as I might desire to play Eros, even I can't do it if the lady vanishes."

Tugging at a boot top, Morgan paused. "What mean you?"

"She's bolted. Gathered up her flock of crackbrains and sailed off to that island of hers. A pity, too, for she amuses. Yes, she amuses and yet defies sanity. 'A bird full sweet/ For me full meet . . . ' "

Morgan swooped down and grabbed his sheathed sword from the bed. "You guard your tongue, Christian de Rivers."

Christian spread his arms wide, grinning.

"Peace, raven, peace. She'll trouble you no more." He eyed Morgan as he drank. "No more pig stealing, no more concealing nets to trap Ponder Cutwell, no more getting tossed down wells or slapped with pig poultices. No more merriment at all. You may bask in an utter lack of mirth for the rest of your days."

"Go fu—"

Christian clicked the tongue against the roof of his mouth and wagged a finger at Morgan.

"For shame. How can you be so discourteous after all my years of fostering? Have I not sheltered you and drawn you into manhood?"

"You're worse than Pen," Morgan said through gritted teeth. "I remember once you left me at the mercy of a passel of drunken louts at the Bald Pelican after telling them I was a tax collector. I near got my head broken."

Christian waved his hand. "Merely a test of your fighting skills."

"Ha!"

Donning his sword, Morgan walked away from Christian on his way out of the room.

"Are you not interested in the progress of our search for Jean-Paul?"

Morgan turned. "What news?"

"Rochefort has had word that the priest has left England."

"When?"

"Oh, certainly before Mistress Fairfax sailed." Christian stared into his cider.

Walking slowly back to stand before Christian, Morgan scoured his mentor with his gaze.

"What has Pen to do with it?"

"Oh, naught."

"Jesu give me patience." Morgan drew closer. "I know you. You have that pleased-viper look, so spit out your venom."

Christian gazed at the ceiling, then smiled at Morgan as he sipped his drink. "That fever has slowed your wits or you would have understood me from the first." He set his cup on the mantel. "Mistress Penelope has fled from you, but a far more deadly creature awaits her on Penance Isle."

"Sodding bastard, you let her leave knowing he was going there!"

Morgan lunged at Christian, drawing his sword, but Christian was ready for him. He leapt forward and knocked the sword out of Morgan's hand while drawing a dagger. Morgan jumped at him, but came up short when the tip of the dagger touched him beneath his chin. He froze, breathing hard.

Christian laughed. "Such fury from a man who vows he cares naught for Mistress Fairfax." His smile vanished and he squinted at Morgan. "I suggest, my sweet raven, that you waste no time avenging yourself upon me and ride hard for the coast."

Morgan jerked his head aside, cursing. Christian chuckled again and sheathed his dagger.

"You did this apurpose," Morgan said, "to make me go after the priest. You knew I wouldn't go near Pen unless you forced me. God's breath, Christian, I think you'd sleep with the devil if it would serve the queen and the kingdom."

Without waiting for a reply, Morgan turned on his heel and headed out of the room.

Christian laughed. "Fare you well, raven. Your horse is saddled and waiting in the courtyard along with a few of my men."

Morgan climbed down the ship's ladder and stepped into the boat carrying five of his men. They had reached Penance Isle just after sunrise. He settled at the prow while two more boats loaded men. Early morning mist

obscured the island, but he could see the battlements
of Highcliffe arching out of a sea of white vapor.

In the distance he could hear the crash of the surf, an
indistinct, watery shattering. For a moment he thought
he heard that strange murmuring. He went still and
searched the mists and the tops of Highcliffe's towers
that floated amid the whiteness.

Nothing. Odd how he hadn't heard it in England,
only here, on the island—Pen's island. No doubt the
trouble with his hearing was due to his ordeal in the
shipwreck. He disregarded it, for he had far more urgent
concerns.

He'd had almost a week to agonize over Pen's safety while he rode west and then sailed for the island.
Never had he experienced a terror so great as when
he imagined careless Pen stumbling upon that spawn
of the unholy, Jean-Paul. His agony became physical.
He prowled the deck, endlessly raging against the crew,
the captain, the winds.

Only in the last few hours had it occurred to him
that Pen might have hoped he would follow her. Mayhap she'd even thought he would so fear for her that
he would forget her faithlessness, forget that she'd
almost betrayed England. She was reckless enough to
do such a thing. But he wasn't fool enough to trust
her a second time.

His rage festered, kept alive fed by suspicion and by
old hurts. Yet, despite his anger, he couldn't make his
body stop craving her, which made him all the more
furious. Only the night before, he'd dreamt a vision so
real that he could have sworn he felt himself inside her,
clasped in moist warmth, his back and buttocks raked
by her nails.

Morgan felt his unruly self stir at the recollection.
Then he remembered how, despite his love, when he'd

been so confused and alone, Pen had chosen to believe Jean-Paul rather than trust him. God, after she turned on him, he'd almost lost faith in his own worth. The boat rocked on a wave, and he nearly bit the inside of his cheek as he set his jaw and pushed away the memory.

The mists cleared, but as they neared the island his anger could have boiled the sea into steam. He stood up, gazing at the clear space between the rocks. While he watched, Pen walked around one of them. Under her cloak she wore a loose kirtle and gown of bronze-colored wool that made her appear to be part of the fabric of the island, at once of the earth and the sea. She paused in the gap between the rocks, waiting.

Her presence condemned her in his eyes. She had expected him to fear for her and thus to forgive. The boat slid ashore, and Morgan leapt into the surf. He could see Pen waiting for him, her hands folded in front of her. She made no effort to call to him. She didn't try to meet him.

Behind him, to the east, inky clouds popped over the horizon and tumbled toward the island. Morgan's cloak skimmed the water as he stalked up to Pen, planted his hands on his hips, and glared at her. The surf hissed about them as if his anger were turning it to steam.

Pen spoke before he could begin his tirade. "Go back. He's not here."

"This is a useless machination, Penelope Grace Fairfax. Even love sickness doesn't excuse you. I am here only to hunt the priest, so there's no use hoping— what say you?"

Pen hadn't moved. "I said, go back. The priest isn't here. I told Lord Montfort not to play this game, but it seems he's done so against my wishes."

"Are you saying Christian told you to return to Penance, into Jean-Paul's path? Come now, my pretty mischief. He's played a few evil tricks, but never any so evil as those you've served to me. And he wouldn't endanger a woman."

The rage that had simmered inside him combined with the knowledge that all the time he'd been worried about her safety, she'd been sitting in her castle, warm and comfortable.

"God's blood," he said. "I didn't want to come here, and the only reason I have is to find the priest. Belabor me not with tales of Christian's designs. You should at least have enough honesty to own your sins. A few more won't matter, nor will a few less make me forgive what you've done."

Lifting one brow, Pen remained motionless as the wind increased and cavorted through her hair. "Perchance I should explain something to you. Despite your notion that God has blessed all women by sending you to them, you're mistaken if you think I number among your idolaters any longer."

He lost all hope of governing his anger, but even as he felt his rage erupt, his body began to betray him. Her breasts rose and fell as her breathing quickened, and his gaze strayed to them. He took a step that brought him within whispering distance of her. He gave her an evil smile that contained anger as well as lust when she stood her ground rather than skitter backward. He would jolt her from aloofness. He lowered his voice, knowing that his breath brushed her cheek.

"Have you dreamt of me as I have of you?" She wouldn't look at him, the little coward, but he'd made her blush. "I remember things well now, especially how you shivered when I kissed your inner thighs, and how your mouth feels on me."

She retreated several quick steps then, and he grinned as he heard her suppressed gasp.

"I remember," he said, "how you begged me to forgive you, to bestow my favor upon you."

"Remember it well," Pen replied with a lift of her head. "For I doubt you'll ever hear such words again, and assuredly not from me. I'm sorry, my lord. There's no one here who cares to worship at your feet. Go back to your ship. If I cared what happened to you, I'd hope you fall overboard and sink to the deepest chasm beneath the sea."

She turned then, and without another glance at him walked between the two rocks toward the cliffs. Morgan stared after her. Had Christian deceived him, or had Pen? Jesu, sometimes there wasn't much difference between the two.

He heard a bark of laughter and glanced up at the cliffside. Ranged along it, sniggering and whispering, were most of Highcliffe's inhabitants. Morgan gave them a disgusted look. She'd brought them along to witness his dismissal, like some craven unworthy to kiss her toes. His gaze darted to Pen's retreating back, and he tracked her withdrawal. While he watched her, he forgot the noise on the cliffs, for he was trying to fight off the maddening concoction of fury and desire. He hadn't considered that Pen wasn't the only one who succumbed to arousal when they came close.

Morgan's gaze never left Pen's slight figure. It would be only what she deserved if he left her to her own devices and Jean-Paul really had come back to Penance. God's toes, he wanted to sail away this very moment, but he also wanted to toss Penelope Fairfax into the surf and watch her sputter and spew seawater.

He turned his back on Pen's retreating figure, then stopped. He had to search the island for Jean-Paul even if Pen had been telling the truth. Also, if he stayed, he could accomplish two things—assure himself that the priest wasn't here, and drink a goblet full of the sacramental wine of vengeance. He thought for a while, and as he did, a smile returned to his lips, a smile Derry had often compared to that of the devil when counting sins.

Above him he could hear Twistle taunting his men. He heard a muffled sound behind him. Turning, he saw his sergeant at arms shaking his fist at the cook. Then he glanced back at Pen, who was climbing the terraced stair. He misliked so many witnesses to what he was going to do to her. His men could wait elsewhere until he needed them.

"Sergeant, take the men back to the ship."

He turned then and ran up the beach after Pen.

CHAPTER XIX

Jean-Paul dismissed his serving man and tugged on the sweeping folds of silk that covered his shoulders. The man had brought the news that Mistress Fairfax had returned. Mistress Fairfax—*Dieu*, how he longed to slit her throat for her interference.

He'd slept late, exhausted by his flight across England. His own rage at Mistress Fairfax and Morgan St. John had wakened him. The night had been filled with nightmares of the ruin of one of his most elegant designs. From the top of the wall at Beaumaris he'd witnessed the defeat of Danseur. What a waste.

Padding across the chamber, he sat at a desk, took out a sheet of paper, and found a quill. His fingertips slid down the length of the feather as he gazed out the window in thought. He couldn't decide which he hated most, St. John or his mad bitch.

Their names had joined several others on a list he'd finally decided to commit to paper. He would send it to Mazarin along with the news of his half sister's capture. Mazarin would be desolate and enraged at the news.

A small, mean smile crossed Jean-Paul's lips at the thought. He might be able to turn this calamity to his advantage, for Mazarin was his sister's lover and would crave vengeance upon those who mishandled her. He was in the Netherlands at the moment, causing havoc for the mighty King of Spain.

However, Jean-Paul was sure that after this latest setback, the cardinal would agree to recalling Mazarin and sending him to England. Certain of his other plans had been more successful. He didn't want Montfort or any of his band to interfere in these as they had in the past few months.

He trailed the feather across his palm, then dipped the quill in the inkwell and began to write to the Sieur de Mazarin. He progressed from the doleful announcement to a description of Danseur's wounding and capture. Jean-Paul sighed, for Danseur, who really should have been called Danseuse were it not for the need for secrecy, had been most useful. No doubt by now she was on her way to London, the Tower, to be tortured for information and executed. His pen progressed to a list of those responsible for her downfall.

Here Jean-Paul paused. It would be as well to include everyone. As long as he was coming, Mazarin might as well attend to the whole lot.

He began with Cecil and Lord Montfort. Then came Blade Fitzstephen and that bastard Lord Derry. No, Derry was Viscount Moorefield now. Jean-Paul carefully traced out the letters of the title in his Italianate script before listing Morgan's name. He added the name of Penelope Fairfax, blew on the damp ink, and finished by writing Baron Rochefort's name at the bottom.

Once finished, he sealed the letter. As he pressed his signet ring into the wax, he glanced out the window again, for it had suddenly grown dark. Across the successive courtyards, over the tops of the forest trees, a rumbling mass of clouds tumbled toward him. A thunderclap shook the window in its frame. Wind rushed into the room, picked up the flowing silk of his robe, and billowed it out behind him.

Jean-Paul rose and shut the window. Below, he saw Ponder Cutwell scurry, grunting, across the flagstones in the direction of Margery's pen. He tapped the letter against his palm thoughtfully.

The fool had provided a useful refuge when he'd first left France on his commission. If Much Cutwell hadn't been compromised, he would have let Ponder be, but now—now the oaf presented a danger. He would have to be dispatched. But not immediately.

Noting the way the thunderclouds blotted out all light, Jean-Paul sighed and returned to bed. He needed to retrieve a parcel from its hiding place before he attended to Mistress Fairfax and left the island. When he'd first arrived, he'd concealed certain valuables from Ponder's curious gaze. It was time they were unearthed. But if he had to wait out the storm, he would do it in bed.

Her eyes watered from the severity of the wind. Pen snatched up hunks of skirt and stomped down the path to Highcliffe. She had begun to lose mastery of herself the moment she distinguished Morgan from the rest of the men in that boat.

It had been as if she were seeing him for the first time, for indeed, for the first time he had dressed in his own clothing. He wore blue-black damask slashed at the chest and sleeves to reveal gold beneath. He sat at the prow of the boat, taller than the rest of the men, hand clamped on a sword that hung from his left hip.

Although clouds obscured the sun, he seemed to shine with the richness of his attire, from the patterned damask to the black fur that lined his cloak. Heedless

of the damage to his black kid boots, he'd jumped out
of the boat and stalked toward her, the wind whipping
his cloak back to reveal the damascene ornamentation
on his sword hilt.

When he'd reached her, she had noticed a gold ring
bearing an emerald-cut onyx bezel. Upon the bezel had
been mounted a heraldic device, a raven addorsed so
that it was shown in profile with its wings spread back
to back. She had taken in the way he wore his cloak
thrown back over one shoulder, the angle of his sword
worn so that it slanted behind him toward his right leg,
the uncommon richness of leather—and realized what
she should have known long before.

Tristan wasn't just a nobleman, he was a polished,
well-bred aristocrat who could duel to the death with
calm while wearing silk and jewels. He wore black damask and gold braid the way gentlemen wore wool.

They had argued, and all the while she'd been thinking to herself. This man belongs in a palace, not in my
keep with the holes in its roof. The gold and black
ring had gleamed at her, and, beneath her anger and
hurt, a little voice said, *He's too far above you, too
wondrous.*

She wanted to crumple and slither away in the face
of this man who looked more like a prince than any royal portrait she'd ever seen. Even while he angered her,
a feeling of unworthiness grew and grew until she'd
clamped down on it out of desperation. She clung to
her wrath and hurt.

Now she wanted only to hide away in her chamber
and regain that blessed tranquility that came with the
absence of feeling. She strained to direct her attention
to his sins. Tenacious in his anger, he still blamed her
for their misunderstandings and yet dared to look at
her with a disconcerting lust. He played the disdain-

ful nobleman well and treated her like some mixture of harpy and convenient bawd. Humiliated anew, she barely heard shouts of derision behind her. Dibbler and the others were taunting Morgan and his men.

Pen hurried away from the cliffs. She'd left without glancing back to see how he'd taken her dismissal. Her life would now be devoted to making true her claim that she no longer wanted him. After all, she had a castle to run and servitors for whom to care—great responsibilities. She wanted no damascened nobleman.

"Penelope Grace Fairfax!"

She stumbled over a rut in the path at the sound of Morgan's voice. She felt a sting in her ankle. Wincing, she stooped and gripped it. She hobbled around to face the cliff. Morgan was striding toward her. Dibbler, Sniggs, and Erbut rushed to meet him.

As she glared at Morgan, Dibbler lunged with his pike. Morgan paused. His arm shot out to knock the weapon aside. His hand slid down the shaft, gripped and yanked it from Dibbler's grasp. He swerved, pike in hand, and brought the weapon up to meet a swipe from Erbut's pike.

Making a sound that was part annoyance, part sneer, Morgan flicked the pike on end and jabbed it into Erbut's stomach. Without breaking his movement, he spun, aimed at the approaching Dibbler, and cracked the staff against the man's head. Dibbler made a croaking sound. His legs folded beneath him, and he dropped to the ground.

Morgan didn't wait to see him fall. He whirled around and swiped at the gathering Highcliffers, making a half circle with the tip of the pike. Sniggs scrambled out of reach only to lose his footing and land on his arse. Morgan was upon him at once. He bent, snatched the serpent dagger from where it had been stuffed into

Sniggs's belt, and cuffed the man when he protested. The dagger vanished into Morgan's boot.

At Morgan's order, Turnip hauled Sniggs out of danger. The rest of their fellows scuttled out of the way as well. Morgan snarled at them, meeting each of their gazes with his own in expression of his mastery. All avoided challenging that stare.

All except Pen. When he turned his glare upon her, Pen sniffed, turned on her good leg, and limped on her way. She hadn't gone far, when she heard the crunch of boots. She felt him grasp her arm. Jerking free, she whipped around and faced him. Morgan had that glittering smile on his face again, that smile that said he was thinking of how he could make her moan with pleasure and was considering doing it right then. She could tell that he'd discard his rich furs and leather in moments.

"Pen Fairfax, you're an obdurate and most tasty little liar."

She tried to laugh, but her voice sounded so shrill and hollow. "Upon mine honor, you're making a direful spectacle for all to see. I marvel that you don't shrink at revealing your conceit to all and sundry."

"I know women, Pen Fairfax, and I know you. I'd wager my London town house I haunt your dreams as you haunt mine."

"You don't."

The words were defiant, but her voice shook. He wasn't touching her, but that smile, the way he stood with his black-clad legs planted apart so that she was reminded of how they felt against her, the very power of him routed her. He began to speak again in a rough voice that made her want to run from him for fear of crumbling at his feet.

"Come, mistress mine, admit what I already know.

After all, since we've been apart, you torture me with visitations in my dreams that leave me increased and surging until I think I shall roar myself into madness for lack of relief."

Dear God, she was growing redder than a rosebud. How could she let him whip her into this furor of craving and fear?

Morgan took her hand and kissed it, molding his lips to the back of her hand. "The least you could do is atone for your sins against me. What's past is unchangeable, but my anger might be assuaged by a little pleasure. Come. You want to beg me for forgiveness with your body. I can see it in your eyes."

Pen yanked her hand free again. This man had taken her trust and love and dropped it down a garderobe. As the wind swirled about her, she flattened her hands against her skirts and lifted her brows at Morgan.

"Verily, sirrah, if you suffer from such curious imaginings, they are of your own making, not mine. All I will say is that I had nothing to do with Lord Montfort's plans to lure you here. Go back."

It would be easier to defy him if she didn't have to look at blue-black damask that brought out the inky depths of his hair. Dear Lord, she'd given him her father's old clothes. When he regained his memory, he must have been offended upon beholding the faded garments in which she'd dressed him.

She turned away from him once again. Her ankle felt much better, and she began to walk without limping. But as she did so, a gust of wind hit her in the back. It was so powerful that it nearly shoved her to the ground.

She threw out her arms and stumbled, driven by the force of the wind and its suddenness. She would have fallen had Morgan not grabbed her and pulled her to his body. Shielding her with his greater height and bulk, he wrapped his arms around her and braced himself against the furor as the wind sliced and ripped at them.

A shout from Erbut drew their attention. Morgan turned, and Pen nearly choked as she faced into the wind.

"Curse it," Morgan said. "You've distracted me, and now we're caught."

He swirled his cloak around her. Never had she been wrapped in anything so warm or so soft. It smelled of the exotic spices in which it had been packed.

With Morgan's help, she trudged against the force of the wind to join the others. Erbut pointed out to sea. Off the coast, Morgan's ship had set sail and was rounding the tip of the island, running ahead of the storm that was almost upon them. A line of blue-gray haze that was rain ran toward Penance, and thunder announced its arrival.

"Everyone take shelter!" Morgan shouted.

He slipped his arm around Pen's waist and guided her back down the path to the castle. Dust picked up by gusts hit her face and stung. Her hair whipped wildly, and she felt the first drops of rain coming sideways.

The wind veered, changed direction, and whipped back and forth. Then the hair on the back of her neck prickled and stood up. She looked up at Morgan in alarm. He grabbed her wrist and bolted.

"Run!" he bellowed.

Legs churning, she flew after him down the path. Behind her she heard a sudden crack and explosion that seemed to pierce her eardrums. Morgan didn't stop, but hurled himself and her across the drawbridge and into the bailey.

So quickly did he run that Pen lost all hope of catching her breath. Her surroundings blurred until he slowed at last. They stopped as the rain hit, soaking them in moments. She had no chance to rest, however, for Morgan picked her up and ran up the stairs to the keep, not stopping until they reached the well room.

Wet to her skin, Pen felt a jar as Morgan set her on her feet. She wobbled, but he caught her, then pulled her against his chest. Unable to catch her breath, she lay her cheek against his doublet and gulped in air.

As her legs weaved, her hands fastened on his forearms. He supported her without effort. For a moment she was too muddled to think of anything but how comforting his strength was. Around them servants and Dibbler's company trudged in, weary and dazed. Twistle stalked past, sputtering and vowed to brew a hot posset for everyone—except Morgan.

The sound of Twistle's hate-filled voice disturbed Pen. She drew back, afraid that her dependence upon him had misled Morgan. She straightened her spine, stepped away from him, and sneezed.

"I could have escaped the storm on my own, my lord."

"You'd be a smoldering heap of ashes if I hadn't saved you from that lightning," he said as he shoved his wet hair back from his forehead.

"Mayhap we wouldn't have had a storm if it hadn't been for your foul presence," Pen snarled.

"By God's entrails," Morgan said. "I must have been born under an inauspicious star to have to endure the rantings of this lady of mischief. Think you I have leisure to skulk about this keep? I've a murderous French spy to catch."

"Then catch him, sirrah."

"The devil take you," Morgan said. Then he chuckled. "No, I'll do the taking."

He took a step toward her. Pen scowled wetly at him, but refused to move. He glanced at her heaving breasts, gave her another of his maddening smiles, and walked past her.

"And where, pray tell, are you going?"

He tossed a glance at her over his shoulder. "To the kitchens. I can't hunt the priest in this storm. I'm hungry. I'm going to eat, and no Twistle is going to taint my food with her malignant potions."

He sauntered out of the well room. Onlookers shrank away as he passed. She stood shivering and listening until she heard a door slam. Then she trudged to her chamber. Nany awaited her. She'd stoked the fire and had hot water and dry clothing at hand.

Pen was so agitated, she didn't notice what Nany was doing until the woman pinned a cap on the back of her head. Pen reached around and felt the cap. Her fingers touched silk and pearls.

"Nany, what has betaken you? I need no fanciful garb."

Pen glanced down at her gown and kirtle and beheld more crimson and pearl-shaded samite. While the storm battered the room's closed shutters, her fingers lifted the glossy silk as she fixed a suspicious gaze upon Nany.

"What are you about?"

Nany's backside presented itself to her as the woman gathered washing cloths and linens from the floor and mumbled her answer.

"What say you?" Pen asked.

Turning around, her face flushed from exertion, Nany spoke over a pile of cloths. "There be no harm in adornment."

"When have I pranced about this castle in such raiment?" Pen paused, then gasped. "It's because Lord St. John is here, isn't it?"

Nany dumped her load of cloths outside the chamber door, then found her ever-present ale cup and took a deep sip. Pen waited without speaking and continued to blast Nany with an accusing stare.

"Weeeeeell," Nany said. She glanced at the bed, a clothing chest, the floor. "Oh, very well. You be in need of a husband, mistress." Nany hurried over to Pen, touched her sleeve, and lowered her voice. "Your honor's in need of restoring, and now that we know he's a rich young lord, we must have him for you."

Pen shook off Nany's hand. "God's patience! What is this turnabout?"

"I've had time to ruminate. A maid who's no longer a maid has to be sensible, mistress."

"Nany, go away."

"But what about—"

"Out of my sight."

Nany scurried out of the room.

"Traitor," Pen called out as the door shut.

Soon Pen was huddled in a chair by the fireplace, toes curled with fury inside her slippers. Her anger, already sizzling from Nany's suggestion, burst into flame again as she contemplated Morgan St. John. She wished she could howl as loud as the wind that raced around the keep.

He had the effrontery to accuse her of wanting him. He was trying to punish her for mistakes she'd made honestly, and now she feared he wanted to do so by making her his leman. Assuredly he was above her in rank and birth, but that gave him no right to demean her.

Why had God cursed her with his presence again?

He was stranded on her island because of this storm, determined to taunt and seduce her at the same time. His manner to her was like unto that of a man visiting a bawd—amusement covering a deep and unchangeable contempt. But she wouldn't let his opinions hurt her. She would soon show him he would get no more mewling, simpering adoration from her and no pleasure either.

She had to convince him of her desire to be rid of him, and soon, before his sensuality burned through her prudence and her hurt, leaving her once again vulnerable. In spite of his meanness to her, she had to acknowledge to herself that she wanted him. The trouble was, he knew she wanted him.

When they were together, she would have to preserve her chilly facade much better. Morgan also thought she'd plotted with Lord Montfort to get him there. And it appeared that the only inducement that would get him to leave her alone was his quest for the priest.

Mayhap—yes—that was a way to show him that she didn't want him there. If she were to help him on his way and on his mission to catch the French priest, that would prove to him that she wanted him gone. She had to do both—convince him that she didn't want him and convince him to leave. How to convince him, how . . .

Pen's breathing stopped, then resumed, shallow and rapid. Did she have the courage to do it? The course was a perilous one, but she was desperate to be rid of him before she grew so distraught that she abandoned her defenses against him.

Someone banged at her door. Twistle burst into the room, interrupting Pen's frightened thoughts.

Folding her arms, Twistle rocked back and forth on her heels. "That man is making me cook supper."

"You always cook supper, Twistle."

"Not at his bidding, I don't." Twistle reddened. "He said I was to cook or he'd roast me over my own fire."

"Oh, Twistle," Pen groaned.

"And he said you were to come down to the hall and eat in two hours' time."

"What!"

"There's to be a meal in the hall for everyone. He's ordered it."

"Ordered? In my keep?" Lips pursed, Pen felt her temper crackle like the fire. "Go you back to the kitchens, Twistle. Say you to my lord St. John that I'll not be ordered about in my own castle. I'll sup in my chamber this night, and that is *my* order."

When the appointed time arrived, Pen was still in her room, tapping her fingers on a sideboard as she tried to read a book of hours. She had ventured halfway down the stair and listened to the preparations in the hall a few moments earlier. Nany should have brought her a tray by then. The emptiness in her stomach was growing painful. She heard the clearing of a throat and glanced up to find Erbut gawking at her, lower jaw adrift.

"I knocked, mistress."

"Where is my tray?"

Erbut stuck his thumbs in his belt and fixed his gaze on the floor. "Lord Morgan says if you don't join us, we don't eat. We been sitting at table forever, mistress."

She felt a pang of sympathy. Poor Erbut hadn't finished growing and needed gallons of food while he was shooting up like a new onion. A flush stole into her cheeks when the boy raised a pleading glance to her.

"Very well, Erbut. I won't make you miss your food."

Erbut broke into a grin. "Thank you, mistress."

Marching ahead of him, Pen searched for some speck

of indifference with which to fight the coming ordeal. By the time she walked through the archway into the hall, her head was high. She hesitated when she saw everyone gathered at their tables and Morgan seated in the largest chair on the dais, his cloak thrown over the back of it to dry. Then she summoned her most brilliant and insolent smile.

"Saints," she said to Nany, who waited by her chair. "Why wasn't I summoned to table? I'm so hungry, my gut is clanging against my backbone."

She stood at her chair without looking at Morgan. "Where is our chaplain? Off doing good deeds? I shall say grace."

"Everyone," Morgan said in a loud voice as he rose. "Bow your heads for grace."

Snapping her mouth closed, Pen shot a killing glance at Morgan, but he'd already bent his head and was saying the prayer. After that, the meal proceeded in silence with everyone from the pot boys to Nany eyeing the silent pair on the dais.

Pen refused to look at Morgan. She bit into her venison. Twistle had spit-roasted it and seasoned it with wine, verjuice, pepper, and ginger. Pen glanced down at her trencher. Twistle rarely had a deer killed, for the island's supply was small.

"Twistle, how haps it that we're dining on venison?"

The cook paused with a tray of chicken pasties in her hands and glared at Morgan. "He made me cook it."

Morgan stuffed a hunk of venison in his mouth and grinned at them, chewing with enthusiasm. Pen managed to conceal her irritation by looking away. Through the screen she saw a boy carrying a mountain of pork tartlets. Behind him came another with poached capon. Then she swiveled her head.

She smelled buknade, a pottage made with hen and

seasoned with more of her dearly bought spices—mace, cloves, saffron, salt, and pepper. And was that ginger she smelled again? Pen took a quick gulp of ale and set her goblet down so hard, the drink sloshed onto the tablecloth. Morgan's chuckle made her grip the edge of the table.

Turning her head away from him, her glance met that of a roasted salmon as Twistle set it down beside her. Salmon too! Twistle's salmon required ginger and cinnamon as well as chopped onions. Pen imagined her stores of dearly bought spices vanishing in the progress of this one meal. She began to tap her foot.

She shoveled venison into her mouth, alternating it with sips of ale, and muttered imprecations against waste. Her plan to rid herself of Morgan was growing more and more palatable the longer she sat at a meal of his devising. The man had no sense of frugality. High and mighty lords didn't have to count every grain of wheat, every leek, and each pinch of ginger. High and mighty lords needed only order dishes prepared and cast aside the honest affection of innocent maids!

Pen muttered to herself. "Loathed spendthrift, wastrel."

"Did you say something, Mistress Fairfax?"

"Naught, my lord."

"I could have sworn I heard you say something."

"You mistake yourself, my—what is that?" Pen gazed at the ceremonial progress of a new dish into the hall, a tall silver flagon set on a napkin-covered tray.

"Oh, that?" Morgan said. "It's only hypocras."

Pen whispered in disbelief. "Hypocras?"

"Aye, hypocras. Twistle made it last night. Fortunate, think you not? Although she mentioned she couldn't put in as much ginger as she's wont to use."

Twistle usually conserved hypocras and measured

it out sparingly. Pen's foot tapped harder as she reviewed the number and type of spices that could go into hypocras. Dear God, sugar, cinnamon, ginger. Then there was nutmeg, marjoram, and cardamom along with ground pepper and grated galingale. The movement of her foot stopped as she remembered that Twistle might have used the long pepper and grains of paradise, and spikenard as well. Saints. Nearly her whole winter's supply of herbs and spices must have vanished when Morgan invaded her kitchen.

Her hands twisted in her napkin. Her glance slid to the side, and she glared at Morgan through the slits her eyes had become. Then she saw Twistle bring in her most valuable piece of plate, a silver serving bowl, and it was filled to the brim with rose pudding.

The last vestiges of her awe at his intimidating and rich appearance and demeanor vanished. Pen thrust herself up from the table. Her chair shot backward, overturned, and clattered to the floor. The whispered conversation in the hall ceased. Pen turned to Morgan, her arms held stiffly at her sides.

"Is something wrong, mistress?" asked Morgan in the manner of a cat surfeited on butter and the fright of mice.

"I would speak with you."

"I thought you might."

"At once."

Morgan grinned at her and bowed. "Thy wish is my charge, Mistress Fairfax." He took her hand and placed it on his arm. "Shall we withdraw to your chamber?"

"The well room will do."

"As long as you don't try to drown me."

Pen removed her hand from his arm and swept past him with a sniff. "After this meal, my lord, drowning is too merciful a fate for you."

CHAPTER XX

As he followed Pen into the well room, Morgan reflected on how much he liked vengeance wine. She wanted to rail at him, and soon he'd have her screeching and spitting at him. Then he'd take unholy pleasure in subduing her.

The well room contained a circular central fireplace. Pen walked to it and stood with her arms folded across her chest. Jesu, but she near glistened with bright wit, defiance, and half-concealed desire. She fumed because of the costly dishes he'd ordered. He gave her a smile often seen on the lips of grand inquisitors. His smile melted when she began to speak.

"My lord, I shall leave aside your meanness in robbing me of coin and now dearly bought stores, for I've no doubt you'll recompense me. Hypocras, by my troth!"

He stared at her. "I hadn't thought—"

"Aye, you seem to have left your reason at Beaumaris," Pen said. "However, I've considered well these past hours. Someone had to. I told you to go back, but you didn't. You no doubt think to avenge yourself upon me by—by seducing me and then casting me aside."

"Why, Pen, how could I seduce you? Did you not assure me that you want me not?"

He chuckled when she refused to answer him.

"I want you gone," she said, "but it seems you'll only quit my island if I convince you of how mightily I desire your absence."

Her voice was calm and even, her expression likewise. For the first time he considered the notion that he'd imagined her desire, that her manner was no pretense, and that no matter how much he might provoke her desire, she really wanted no more of him.

"Pen, mayhap we should both—"

"Please allow me to continue," she said in that removed way that was enraging him. "Knowing Lord Montfort, he sent that serpent cross with you on this journey."

Confused, Morgan felt inside his doublet and brought out the cross. Pen reached for it, and he yanked it away.

"God's breath, Pen. You can't touch it."

Pen opened her mouth, but then looked over his shoulder and exclaimed, "Ponder Cutwell!"

He glanced over his shoulder, and felt the cross plucked from his grasp. "Pen, no."

He clutched at it. He was too late. She held the cross in both hands, eyes closed, limbs rigid. Then a shiver traveled the length of her body. Pen threw her head back and screamed. The sound seared his body and caused him to leap at her and pull the cross from her hands. Flinging it aside, he grabbed Pen and wrapped his arms around her. He felt her body jerk with convulsive sobs.

Each movement made him hold her more tightly, as if his strength could banish the horror she witnessed in her mind. He would rather have faced the rack than endure seeing her in such pain. Her sobs faded slowly as she wept on his shoulder.

Morgan closed his eyes and buried his face in her hair, when he heard a whimper. At last she lifted her head and tried to stand away from him. He kept his arms circled around her and watched her summon her reserve of courage.

Wiping her eyes with the back of her hand, she sighed and said, "I was right."

"What mean you? Curse it, Pen, why did you do that? The horror could have killed you."

Not answering at once, Pen stepped out of the circle of his arms and placed the hearth between them.

Drawing in a shaking breath, she said, "I did it to find the priest."

"But why?"

"Weren't you listening to me? I did it to hasten your departure."

Morgan shook his head. "You're lying, mayhap to yourself as well as to me."

"I told you," Pen said. "I no longer suffer from your enchantments. The most seemly description of my feelings for you is indifference."

She added as if on an afterthought, "Except when you waste my food. Then you're irksome."

He tried to look into her eyes—wide, golden, and as warm as fire flames. She avoided his gaze.

"My stubborn-sweet mistress, I don't believe you."

She gazed down at the fire and warmed her hands before the flames. "I care not whether you believe me or no."

"Pen." He walked around the hearth, but she moved with him. "Pen, come here."

"Don't growl at me like a tomcat, Morgan St. John."

"You're making me hotter than this fire just by standing there."

"Stop!"

She shouted the word so loudly that he obeyed out of surprise, but not for long.

"Gratiana," he said as he resumed his slinking around the hearth, "do you remember that time in the gatehouse?"

"We'll not speak of it."

"Oh, aye, we will," Morgan said softly. "You enjoyed it, you wanton, and surged against me until I was ripe and ready to burst."

Pen batted her hand at him to ward him off as she skittered around the hearth.

"And when you put your hands on my—"

"The priest has hidden something at the stone circle!"

Morgan stopped circling. "What? What stone circle?"

"I saw the standing stones that lie past the forest. You haven't been there, but I think they're important to Jean-Paul. I think he'll return to Penance because he's left something valuable behind. I didn't allow him to leave my charge once he came to the castle, so he couldn't have removed it. He'll have to come back to Penance Isle."

"Jesu," Morgan whispered. "Are you certain?"

Pen gave him an exasperated look. "Of course not. This gift isn't like reading a book of psalms, Morgan. All I know is that we should go to the standing stones. Though we'll have difficulty convincing Dibbler and the others to go with us. They say they're haunted. It's a place of fell magic from forgotten times."

He nodded. "I'll go. You will remain here."

"You don't know how to get there."

"Tell me."

She put her hands on her hips.

"Pen, tell me."

"If you go alone, I'll only follow. After all, this is my island. The standing stones are on my lands."

"Damnable, obstinate wretch."

"The storm has faded," she said. "We should go at once, for who knows how long it will take Jean-Paul to elude Lord Montfort and make his way back to Penance."

"How can someone with such a merciful nature be so stubborn?"

He considered locking her in her room, but then he'd have to lock everyone away to keep her there. "Very well, but you're to do as I say and keep behind me. And if by chance he's there, you're to leave. Promise, or I'll not go at all."

"I give you my vow. You've no need to fear. If I see him, I'll run behind you with pleasure. That man consorts with the devil, Morgan."

In less than an hour they were walking their horses through the forest. Dibbler and his company followed behind them on foot, their steps growing more reluctant the closer they came to the standing stones.

The forest dripped all around them. Morgan felt icy drops land on his head, penetrate to his scalp, and slide down to his neck. The air was wet and sharp with cold. His gloves felt stiff with the chill.

He glanced aside at Pen. A few moments past she'd directed a glance at the square-linked chain of his belt and muttered something that sounded like "black damask and gold" in an offended tone. A mysterious comment.

Pearl-shaded moonlight illuminated her profile, and he almost smiled at the lift of her square little chin. She'd guessed what he was about and sought to deny him his revenge. What rankled was that she was also trying to deny her desire for him.

Still, the more she defied him, the more he wanted her, and the more he had to admit she provoked his admiration. Jesu, the woman had more courage and audacity than a gyrfalcon.

Behind him he could heard Dibbler hissing orders at Sniggs, and Sniggs muttering protests. Turnip slipped on a pile of wet leaves on the forest floor. Erbut sneezed, and was shushed by all three who made more noise than had Erbut. Morgan shook his head, then pulled up his mount as Pen lifted her hand. She dismounted, and he joined her.

"The circle is but five minutes walk ahead in a plain that lies south of Much Cutwell." She eyed her quarreling band of blunderers. "We should leave them here."

"Wise advice," he said, trying not to let the mockery in his tone become too apparent.

She wouldn't take his hand when he offered it. Walking ahead of him, she led the way through leafless black trees that creaked in the wind. It wasn't long before she paused at a point where the forest began to thin.

He joined her to look out onto a great plain that stretched from the edge of the forest to the western cliffs. Flat and featureless, its only landmark was an eerie arrangement of massive boulders. Upright stones stood in a circle, capped by a continuous horizontal lintel. They surrounded an inner horseshoe of giant stones, and around them both stretched a trench. The moonlight caused the stones to shine with a faint silver hue.

Pen moved, but Morgan held her back, waiting. He listened to a forest quiet after the ordeal of the black squall. Here and there on the plain lay limbs broken from trees. An owl circled over the standing stones and screeched, the call resounding in the vastness of the sky.

When he was certain the standing stones were deserted, he began to approach them with Pen at his side. Pen directed him toward a pair of slabs that appeared to mark the entrance to the structure. Before them stood a great conical stone, standing guard over the whole edifice. As they walked between the slabs, he saw Pen pause, then turn to look back at the conical stone.

"This is the heel stone," she whispered. She gazed at it, frowning, then stepped past the slabs.

Morgan walked between the two stones, roughly hewn, upright rectangles. As he moved, the wind rushed through the narrow space. He heard something far off. That sibilant hissing.

Cocking his head, he strained to make sense of the whispers. A cloud moved across the moon, then floated on, and silver light illuminated the circle of stones. Long shadows stretched across the space between Morgan and the stones, forming a pattern of dark and light bars. That far-off whispering seemed to commence from inside his head rather than from any outside source.

"Are you coming?" Pen said.

Morgan started, then regained control of himself as the hissing vanished.

"Aye."

He joined her, and they walked beneath the stone lintel. Pen walked around the half circle of inner stones to pause at the tallest. It consisted of two uprights surmounted by a lintel stone that must have weighed thirty tons. She stood in the resulting arch and gazed up at the stars. Morgan kept looked outward at the plain, watching for anyone's approach. His view in the direction of Much Cutwell was blocked in part by several standing stones. He was about to move so that he could get a better look, when Pen spoke.

"No, this isn't right."

"What isn't right?"

"Not here," she said, and she walked past him, back the way they'd come.

He followed her. "God's breath, Pen. Say you we've come for naught?"

"No," she said without looking at him.

The rebuff stung. He sped up and almost caught her at the slab entrance, but as he passed between the two stones, that hissing came back to him. He slowed, then stopped, gazing about in an effort to find the source of the sound. Without warning the noise burst at him, loud, invasive, and painful.

He covered his ears, but the sound came from inside him. He planted a hand against one of the slabs for support—and glimpsed sunrise. He was floating above the plain, hovering over the standing stones. Grayish light covered everything, and the sky was beginning to glow with the first of the sun's light. Long shadows stretched from the base of the standing stones toward the entrance slabs.

Men and women in coarse clothing stood about the circle. A young man in warrior's garb holding an ax of bronze approached the conical stone. Another man in a long robe joined him. Together they turned toward the rising sun as those near the standing stones chanted.

Their voices buzzed inside Morgan's head as the sun cleared the horizon and cast its light from the standing stones on a direct path through the entry slabs and onto the heel stone. The young man with the ax gave a shout. He turned toward the heel stone, and Morgan saw himself, arms raised, battle-ax held high. He found himself looking into his own eyes.

He gasped, recoiling, and then someone hit him. He blinked, and glanced down to find Pen clutching his arm. He touched his cheek.

"You hit me!"

"You were babbling like one possessed."

He grabbed her by the shoulders. "It was like a waking dream. I saw people, and a holy man, and—and a warrior with a bronze ax who looked like me." Even to himself he sounded crazed.

"Saints." Pen gaze up at him in wonder. "Do you know, I begin to think your own enchantment drew you to Penance."

"I've been hearing these strange murmuring sounds, but I thought them only manifestations of my illness." He felt a minute tremor of apprehension. "What does this portend? Am I possessed?"

"Fie," Pen said. "Once, in times forgotten, your ancestors must have sprung from this island."

Morgan cursed and shook his head. "I'm well repaid for how lightly I considered your suffering because of your gift." No wonder Pen feared her own power. He felt besieged by devils and furious at being at the mercy of phantasms. He shook his head again. "Jesu, what ails me? We've no leisure for visions. Have you brought me here for nothing?"

"Arrogant wretch, I have not."

Pen shrugged off his grip and went to the heel stone. She walked around it, then joined him to stare at it in silence. Morgan was still feeling slightly confounded by the experience of his vision, so he made no objection when she placed her hands on the flaked surface of the stone. Nor did he express vexation when she rubbed it as if it were a cat, then knelt at its base. Suddenly she dug her hands into the wet earth.

Morgan stood over her. "What has possessed you?"

"There's something here."

At this, he dropped to his knees and helped her. His hand dug into the earth and hit a slick shape.

"I've found it," he said as he pulled a package from the mire.

Wrapped in oiled cloth and bound with twine, it was caked in grime. Morgan cut the twine. Pen pulled away the cloth to reveal a leather document case. They wiped their hands on the clean side of the protective cloth, then Pen opened the case and withdrew a sheaf of unfolded papers and a heavy velvet pouch containing gold and silver coins.

Morgan found another containing jewels. Into his hand spilled an enameled gold pendant set with diamonds and rubies, a gold ring set with an onyx cameo of Mary Stuart, and a heavy shoulder chain of silver bearing sapphires and pearls. He and Pen exchanged glances.

"A wealthy priest," Morgan said as he stuffed the contents back in the pouch. "What have you?"

Pen rose, holding the papers. She held them so that they caught the moonlight. "Can you see?"

He looked over her shoulder, but there was little light. He glanced to the bottom of the page.

"This seal," he said. "It belongs to the French ambassador at the Spanish court."

He strained his eyes to catch some of the writing, then drew in his breath. "Jesu, Pen. Mary of Scotland is seeking funds from his majesty of Spain for her troops." He maneuvered the pages to catch the light again.

Pen pointed to a line on the page. "She says she'd raised the army and wants him to help her keep it together so that—Almighty God . . ."

"I told you the priest was dangerous," Morgan said.

"*Oui, Anglais*, I am," said Jean-Paul. "Especially to you and your witch of a lady."

A BREAST OF MUTTON STEWED

Take a very good breast of mutton chopped into sundry large pieces, and when it is clean washed, put it into a pipkin with fair water, and set it on the fire to boil; then scum it very well, then put in of the finest parsnips cut into large pieces as long as one's hand, and clean washed and scraped; then good store of the best onions, and all manner of sweet pleasant pot herbs and lettuce, all grossly chopped, and good store of pepper and salt, and then cover it, and let it stew till the mutton be enough; then take up the mutton, and lay it in a clean dish with sippets, and to the broth put a little wine vinegar, and so pour it on the mutton with the parsnips whole, and adorn the sides of the dish with sugar, and so serve it up: and as you do with the breast, so may you do with any other joint of mutton.

CHAPTER XXI

Pen gave a little cry as she heard the priest's voice. No one had to remind her of her promise; she scurried around to Morgan's back even as he snatched her wrist and pulled her in that direction. On tiptoe she stared over his shoulder at Jean-Paul.

Dressed for riding, shrouded in a dark cloak, he stood between the entrance slabs. Two men-at-arms flanked him and pointed swords at her and Morgan while another stood behind his master. Jean-Paul walked toward them.

"Truly God watches over his servants," the priest said. "I had just set Henri to watch for intruders, when he glimpsed movement in the trees. A few minutes' patience, and I was rewarded. The prey trotted into my lair."

Pen felt Morgan's body tense as the priest drew near.

"Where were you?" Morgan asked.

"Why, in back of the outer stones you couldn't see behind. Each is large enough to hide three men. I knew I was right to come to this place afoot. But I have no desire to converse with you, *Anglais*. You and the witch have cost me much, but I've learned. You'll not befuddle me with diversions again, and I'll offer you no opportunity to escape. This time I've learned not to try to hold on to a devil's tail. Henri, separate them."

Pen was shoved farther behind Morgan as he backed up to draw his sword.

"*Non, Anglais*, look."

They both followed the direction of Jean-Paul's glance to see that one of the guards had drawn a knife and was aiming it at Pen.

Jean-Paul laughed. "Come, I am in haste. If you make no trouble, I'll forgo my vengeance upon the lady."

"Why should we believe you?" Pen snarled.

The priest smiled sweetly at her. "Look at your lover, Mistress Fairfax. Look into his eyes and read the truth. You have little choice, and he knows it. *Alors*, he must take the only chance there is."

Pen moved to face Morgan and gazed into the depths of placid blackness—and saw resignation.

"Don't," Pen said as Morgan's hand fell away from his sword. "They'll kill us anyway."

She grabbed at him as he stepped from her, but he pulled her hands from him and set her aside. She clutched him, but the man with the knife captured her. He wrapped his arms around her shoulders. Pen ground her teeth, fighting the desire to bite his hand until she hit bone.

"Morgan, don't!" she cried.

He didn't listen. Stepping toward Jean-Paul, he allowed the men-at-arms to relieve him of his sword. Pen held her breath as they stepped back, her spirits rising. But Jean-Paul caused them to plummet when he approached his prisoner, felt in his boot, and withdrew the serpent dagger. Jean-Paul shook his head at Morgan, then impaled the weapon in the dirt at Pen's feet.

Morgan shouted and lunged, but two men jumped on him. Pen wrestled uselessly with her own captor as the third pummeled Morgan in the gut. Morgan bent over, suspended between the other two guards. The third cuffed him, and Morgan swayed dizzily. Jean-Paul said something in French, and Morgan was dragged to the heel stone and slammed against it. Each guard grabbed a wrist and stretched Morgan so that his chest was exposed to Jean-Paul, who drew his sword.

Pen shrieked at the priest, but he paid her no heed. He walked toward Morgan, who was panting and shaking his head as if trying to regain his vision. Pen screamed at Jean-Paul as he passed her, then realized that she was doing Morgan no good. Desperation cleared her thoughts of terror. She had no time for fear; she couldn't afford it, for her fits of terror would cost Morgan his life.

The serpent dagger remained embedded in the wet earth at her feet. Pen looked down at it. The golden serpents began to writhe. She nearly whimpered, and her bones threatened to crumble into the consistency of ground ginger. What saved her was one unconquerable desire—to save Morgan. The serpents coiled as if to spring.

"Oh, no," she said in a quivery voice. "I won't have it."

She glared at them, and they stopped moving. Relieved, she sagged within her captor's arms. Overbalanced by the sudden increase in weight, the man grunted and stumbled forward. They toppled over, and he threw out a hand to stop himself from hitting the ground. Pen had been waiting for her chance. When he loosened his hold, she grabbed the dagger, dropped to her knees, and curled into a ball. Rolling on her shoulder, she twisted and kicked the man in his face. She felt a crunch, and blood spurted from his nose.

Not waiting to see if he pursued her, Pen whirled and ran. As she ran, she screamed.

"Morgan!"

She gripped the dagger in her fist and aimed for Jean-Paul. She couldn't throw it, but she could stab with it. Jean-Paul turned as she screamed and lifted his sword. Realizing the danger, Pen swerved without stopping and leapt for one of the men struggling to keep hold of Morgan. At the same time, she heard a clamor from beyond the standing stones.

"Mistress, we're coming!"

Jean-Paul cursed and turned from his pursuit of her to face Dibbler and his Highcliffers.

Pen dashed at one of Morgan's guards, jabbed with the dagger, and sprang back. The man yelled, dropped Morgan's arm, and clutched his own. Morgan's free arm jerked, and his fist punched into the face of the remaining guard. The guard released his hold on Morgan, who kicked him in the head. The man dropped to the ground senseless.

Pen had watched during the few moments it took Morgan to free himself, but she whirled to face Jean-Paul as he ran at them. Behind the priest lay Dibbler, Erbut, and Sniggs, nursing sore heads and wounds. Jean-Paul was almost upon them, and she couldn't throw a dagger. She felt the serpents begin to writhe beneath her hand, but before she could succumb to the horror, Morgan snatched the blade from her.

Jean-Paul was charging at them, sword pointed at her. Pen stared, unmoving. Then she felt a blow to her shoulder as Morgan knocked her out of the way, cocked his arm, and threw the dagger. The blade hit the priest in the chest as he raised his sword over his head and let out a cry of triumph. There was a thud as steel pierced flesh. Pen saw the triumph in his face turn to astonishment, then a grimace of pain and disbelief.

Transfixed by the sight of life fading from this malignant scourge, Pen barely realized that Morgan had snatched her into his arms. He half led, half carried her to stand between the priest and Dibbler. Pen looked from one to the other of her men.

They had managed to overcome the man who had held her before the priest got to them. Dibbler was bleeding from a sword cut on his arm, while Erbut nursed a cut in the head. Sniggs was already whining as he rocked back and forth and clutched a bleeding foot.

She felt a tug on her skirt and glanced down at Jean-Paul. "Morgan!"

She clutched Morgan's arm as they knelt beside the priest. Pen could feel her skin crawling, so she disengaged her skirt from the man's grip. His hand flailed, then gripped Morgan's, and, with unexpected strength, he pulled his enemy down to stare into his face. Blood seeped from the corner of his mouth. He gazed into Morgan's eyes, and Pen nearly drew back at the exultation she saw there.

"I was shriven before I came to this cursed land," he whispered to Morgan. "So you haven't robbed me of my place in heaven. God . . . God will reward me for my work against heresy." Lips quivering, Jean-Paul smiled at them. "His Holiness has given me a dispensation."

"You think God will welcome you?" Pen asked in disbelief. "No man, even the bishop of Rome, can dispense for murder."

Jean-Paul never left off his transfixed stare at Morgan. "I've already seen to it that I'll be avenged upon you and your witch, upon all of you who interfered. When he comes, remember me." His hand clutched at the neck of Morgan's doublet as his throat rattled. "Remember me . . ."

Pen strained to hear more, but all she caught was a faint hiss. All sense left Jean-Paul's frenzied gaze. Those brown-black eyes stared up at her without sight. She looked away as Morgan passed his hand over the lids to shut them. Shuddering, she leaned against Morgan, now suddenly reacting to the battle. Her entire body trembled as she realized how near Morgan had come to losing his life. And yet Morgan seemed almost calm.

"Jesu," he muttered. He squeezed her against his body. "If he'd killed you, I don't—"

Through the murk of horror that had engulfed her, Pen heard the way Morgan stopped himself. She scraped together the dregs of her composure, for she wanted to throw herself against this man and weep into his neck. Swallowing the knot in her throat, she straightened and got to her feet. She drew a deep breath and stood alone with all the determination of her soul.

"A near calamity, my lord, but I thank God we're all alive."

He was looking at her so strangely. His voice dropped and grew rough.

"You saved my life. You risked your own to do it."

Was that wonder she heard, or disbelief?

He reached for her. "Let's have done with this pretense, Pen."

She stepped out of reach and headed for Dibbler.

"What pretense?"

Kneeling beside her captain of the guards, she examined the cut he was trying to bind. She heard Morgan swear, but he busied himself with tying up Jean-Paul's guards. She kept herself from bursting into tears by caring for her men and keeping Sniggs and Dibbler from blaming each other for not stopping Jean-Paul.

Sniggs moaned. "Let us begone, mistress. There be ghosts of unholy heathens about this place."

She and Morgan spoke little as they prepared to leave, except once, when he ordered her to say nothing about his vision at the standing stones. If she hadn't been so distraught, she would have laughed. What need was there to warn her of the dangers of revealing such an experience? To her it was a sign from God that Morgan had been brought to Penance for a purpose. What that purpose might be other than to make her existence a misery, she couldn't see. However, Morgan seemed most reluctant to explore the experience, and she feared to do so as well.

The journey back to Highcliffe was slow due to the wounded and the prisoners. By the time Pen had disposed of the injured men, Morgan had shut the guards in the cells in the Saint's Tower. He had Jean-Paul's body interred in a temporary grave at the village church. If the priest wasn't already in hell, he was writhing at the thought of being stuck in among so many English heretics.

Pen wondered what would be done with Jean-Paul, for she couldn't imagine Morgan writing to the Cardinal of Lorraine saying, Your Eminence, I've just killed your emissary; please send someone for his body. Or, could she? Morgan was far less gentle and peaceloving than Tristan. Mayhap, after all, she could imagine him doing something that brazen.

Whatever his plans, she was certain he would design them without a thought for her opinion. Exhausted, lower in spirit than at any time since she'd lost Tristan, Pen retreated to her chamber, bathed, and crawled into bed as the gray haze of dawn washed over the island with the promise of morning.

She slept until late the next afternoon, and woke to the sinking sun's long shadows that cast a golden pall over the castle. Nany brought the news that Morgan's ship had returned, having weathered the squall with little damage. As Nany helped her dress, she looked out on the castle rooftops, the wall walk, the dovecote. Wheedle strolled across the bailey behind a troop of pigs. She could hear the gentle purring of birds from the dovecote.

Like an anvil dropped from a belfry, her spirits plummeted. So short a time ago she'd loved her life among the ragtags and buffoons of Highcliffe. Why, even Ponder Cutwell had been something of an enjoyment. His latest folly had been to send yet another marriage offer as soon as she'd returned from England. Now, not even the thought of yanking Cutwell's tail could bring relief from this heartbroken misery. She went to another window and glanced down at the castle garden, almost bare of greenery.

A door in the garden wall opened, and Twistle walked between the rows of herb beds with a basket on her arm. It was full of bright green holly. Holly. December and the holy season was almost upon them. Usually she served as her own Lord of Misrule, for no one conducted the riotous merriment and mumming so well as she. This year she would appoint another. This year there was no merriment in her soul.

Her eyes stung. She hastily wiped them, muttering to herself.

"Enough, Penelope, my good woman. Enough of feeling pity for yourself. What an indulgence, and a weakness. What if Morgan sees you? Saints, do you want him to know the truth?"

Her hands were cold and stiff. She rubbed them together, then clasped them in front of her and gave herself a long rebuke. Hadn't she seen how determined Morgan was to torment her? A man accustomed to the idolatry of women, he'd been only amused and challenged by her refusal to bend to his will. Perverse, evil creature. He admitted he didn't love her, but he felt entitled to use her for his own gratification. How many women had he treated in like manner?

She hadn't forgotten Lord Montfort's comment about all those English gentlewomen. And Lady Ann. And Maria.

The lascivious, harlot-chasing debaucher. Pen's anger flared. Its blessed fire warmed the chill in her bones brought on by sorrow. She took comfort in the heat, for it submerged her pain and enabled her to think of facing the world outside her chamber—and Morgan.

What she needed was a device, a plan by which she could hasten Morgan's departure before she broke and crumbled at his feet in abject grief. For she sensed within herself a brittleness, a fragility that couldn't long withstand his presence. Each time he looked at her with that gaze of black fire, each time he engaged in that sinuous dance that made his more than a simple walk—each time, she endured such pain that she thought someone was jabbing her heart with a stiletto.

He moved as he did apurpose. He moved like a hawk gliding over fields searching for innocent, plump mice— with practiced and deliberate skill. If he remained much longer, she would go mad dwelling upon how he'd gained his lover's skills. She would begin to wonder about those gentlewomen and why they waited for him so eagerly. The wondering would lead to imaginings, and those imaginings would drive her into a frenzy. She might even scream at Morgan and demand to know who

Lady Ann was, and Maria as well. *She might succumb to him.*

She must be rid of him or suffer even greater humiliation and pain than she had already. Pen rested her arms on the windowsill, oblivious of the chill wind blowing across the garden. Clouds the color of Damascus steel scudded across the sky. The breeze burned her cheeks and made her shiver, but it also jolted her senses so that she came awake from her unhappy daydreams.

Her new design would have to be much more clever and above all indirect, for ordering about such a domineering wretch was useless. The wind whipped her curls into her face. Pen sucked in her breath at the impact and ducked inside her chamber. Donning a heavy cloak and pulling its hood over her head, she made her way to the wall walk.

She nodded to Erbut, who was pacing around the walk with a heightened sense of importance as the only man-at-arms besides Turnip fit to perform his duties. The shallow cut on his head had afforded him an unlooked-for opportunity to preen and speak about his battle experience to the maids of the village.

Pen made sure Erbut had wrapped himself up well and sent him on his way. Then she wandered back and forth along the wall walk, trying to think of a way to force Morgan to leave the island. It seemed he was intent on forcing a confession of passion from her. On the way home he'd spoken of the need to question their prisoners. He could do that aboard his ship, and he was needed in England, not on Penance Isle.

No, he was staying on the island to force himself on her, to make her his—his doxy. Pen flushed as she thought the word, for in truth she deserved the appellation. In her bemusement with Tristan she'd behaved like a trull, and now he was treating her like one. This thought evoked her rage at him anew. It fed her anger at herself as well.

Pen uttered a cry that was half distress and half fury. Whirling, cloak and skirts whipping in the wind, she raised a fist and pounded the battlement. The bones and flesh of her hand crashed against stone. She yelped, grabbed her fist, and did a small dance of anguish. Tucking the fist under her arm, she bit her lip and gazed out across the bailey.

Wheedle had returned to the piggery. Pen heard her crooning and purring as she coaxed an enormous sow out of a pen. The pig waddled into sight followed by six small, madly trotting offspring. It was Perdita, the pride of Highcliffe.

Unlike Margery, Perdita was black with a streak of white on her belly, and one of her ears drooped while the other stood up straight. Also unlike Margery, one of Perdita's tusks had been chipped in an altercation with another sow in her younger, more high-spirited days. Taken altogether, Perdita, with her misfit ears and flawed dentition, belonged to Highcliffe. Margery, in her porcine perfection, had not.

A door slammed somewhere in the keep. Pen's gaze shot from Perdita to the keep stairs. Morgan ran down them flanked by several of his men. He stalked across the bailey to one of the towers that held Jean-Paul's men, his jaw set, his gloved hand gripping the hilt of his sword. Suddenly he turned back to stare at the keep. His gaze swept along the battlements with precision and fixed upon Pen. He didn't move, nor did he acknowledge her. He just stared.

His men stopped and followed his gaze, then began to nudge each other and whisper. One spoke to Morgan, who nodded, causing the others to chuckle. Morgan didn't laugh, though; he simply continued to stare at

Pen as if willing her to melt into a puddle of sighing, simpering ardor.

In response, Pen lifted her chin a bit higher, folded her arms over her chest, and glared. To her chagrin, Morgan smiled at her and spoke to his men, who guffawed loudly. Pen wanted to toss them all into the piggery headfirst. Her temper wasn't helped by his having donned cloth of silver studded with pearls. Glaring at him, she refused to be intimidated by visions of him attending the queen and dozens of beautiful court ladies. At last Morgan turned away, leaving her to stew in her rage.

Pain and fury stabbed at her, and Pen clutched the folds of her cloak over her heart. Then Perdita squealed in outrage as Morgan kneed her aside without regard to her bulk or her tusks. Pen scowled at Morgan's retreating back.

Her gaze darted to Perdita, and back to Morgan. Pigs. Morgery. Ponder Cutwell. Saints in heaven, she was so desperate, so weary, and she would solve so many worries if she could bring herself to make such a sacrifice. She would no longer have to fear that one mistake, one drought or plague would plunge Highcliffe into starvation. Mayhap she'd been selfish to delay so long.

Pen searched her soul, all the while remembering what Morgan planned for her.

After a while, a suggestion of a smile hovered about her lips. It was the kind of smile most often seen on Trojans who have just finished wooden horses, the kind of smile one imagined seeing across the bubbling contents of a cauldron at midnight. She was weary of drinking the ale of shame. If she was going to make this sacrifice, she might as well enjoy a last bit of retribution by outwitting that sensual despot, Morgan St. John.

CHAPTER XXII

He had searched for Pen from the top of the keep to the piggery and back again. She was deliberately evading him since their battle of stares this afternoon. The stubborn little mischief. He'd tried to tell her what her actions at the standing stones had done to him. She wouldn't listen.

In that one heedless dash to save him, she'd shown him how ignoble had been his anger at her. Mayhap it was his past, the example of his unforgiving father, that had made him so unwilling to pardon the woman he loved. Aye, she'd been ready to sacrifice her life for his regardless of how he'd tried to punish and humiliate her. In the face of her selflessness, his rage vanished.

He'd been left reeling with sudden change, and now he wanted to find Pen and change things between them somehow. Yet he cringed inside at the thought of what she would say if he simply told her he was wrong. A man didn't abandon his pride and grovel before a woman, even one who'd saved his life. There had to be another way of reconciling with her.

Clapping his sword to his side, Morgan ran down the keep steps for the third time and almost collided with Nany at the bottom. He caught a whiff of ale as he threw out his hands to keep from falling into her prominent bosom.

"Nany, where is Pen?"

Nany slapped his hands as if he were an errant scullery boy. "Mistress Fairfax she be to you, my lord."

He'd perceived a tincture of goodwill from the woman until Pen had come back from the standing stones. Once Nany had seen the flatness in her mistress's gaze, she had again looked upon him as the spawn of fiends.

"Quibble not, woman. I've no patience left after dealing with those cursed Frenchmen."

"Mistress is in kitchen," Nany sniffed.

"But I just came from there not a few moments past."

"Afore that she was in solar."

"I looked there as well."

"And then we was in buttery."

"But I—"

"The mistress has more to do than await your pleasure, my lord. There's a manor to run. Tasks don't do themselves."

He refused to argue with a tipsy old woman. Turning on his heel, he headed for the kitchen. He was in a quandary, for he had to sail the next morning with his captured Frenchmen and documents. He had to tell the queen that she'd succeeded in preventing the King of Spain from openly supporting Mary of Scotland.

Faced with the threat of the Queen of Scots and her army, Elizabeth had maneuvered to distract the King of Spain and prevent him from intervening on Mary's behalf. Her strategy had been to dangle the possibility of marriage in front of the king's candidate, the Archduke Charles of Austria. The careful Philip would rather have Elizabeth in his pocket than waste money aiding the Queen of Scots in an uncertain and expensive war.

If Jean-Paul had lived, no doubt he would have given this information to his master and Mary of Scotland. Now it seemed the danger from the Queen of Scots had lessened. A great weight had lifted from Morgan's heart, and yet he felt no lighter in spirit, for he wasn't sure he could make Pen listen to him.

Reaching the kitchen, he thrust open the door. A blast of heated air warmed his cheeks. He heard the clatter of pans, the creak of a spit turning, the chatter of voices. He stooped as he entered and pulled the door closed as his eyes adjusted to the dim light. The din in the kitchen faded. Scullery maids and turnspit boys gawked at him.

Pen was bending over a pot simmering in a fireplace. She tasted something in a wooden spoon without turning to see who had entered.

"The mutton stew needs more rosemary, Twistle," she said in a raised voice. "Or has his lordship squandered that as well?"

"We've scant portions of everything we need for mutton, mistress." Twistle counted the ingredients on her fingers. "There's scarce any ginger or thyme or marjoram leaves and savory and almost no coriander."

"Ah, well," Pen said as she stirred the stew. "No doubt his lordship will recompense me. Let us hope he's sailing upon the morrow, for the sooner our stores are replenished, the better we'll withstand for winter."

Twistle grunted. "He don't care."

"Why, Twistle, whatever makes you think his lordship is so callous, so uncaring of other folks' feelings?"

Morgan stalked over to Pen. "Enough of this mockery."

"Why, my lord," Pen said. "I thought you were in the tower torturing your prisoners." She dipped the spoon in the pot and held it out to him. "Would you like to taste the stew? Marry, it's a bit like pasty dough, since we've so little ginger or rosemary or marjoram or—"

"Damnation to all spices!"

Pen gave him one of her burnished smiles as she stirred the stew, but he'd seen the real ones enough to know that this one was of gilt, not pure gold.

"I would have a word with you," he said, trying not to growl.

"I've a meal to oversee, my lord."

He leaned close to her and whispered. "You may join me or be carried out."

The spoon had been circling the stew pot. It faltered. Then Pen handed it to Twistle.

"I shall return anon," she said to the cook.

Walking past him without a glance, she donned her cloak and marched across the court, into the keep and up to the solar. She went to a cushioned chair, took up a piece of mending, and jabbed her needle into the fabric. He followed her without objection and stood over her, watching the needle stab into wool.

"I've come to tell you I've decided there's been a misunderstanding."

Pen yelped as she jabbed her finger. Sucking on the wound, she gazed up at him in disbelief.

"I have been thinking, and it seems Christian is at his old game again, teaching rough lessons for the good of those in his care and near killing them as he does it. I've often thought I wouldn't live through the evil he did me in the name of teaching me good. It seems he's included you among those who need instruction. I see now that he devised this encounter between us without your knowledge."

"I told you that from the beginning."

Morgan held up a finger to stop her. "However,

Christian wouldn't have interfered had he not been convinced of one thing." He dropped to one knee in front of her and gazed into her astonished face. "Come Pen, admit it. You love me."

Something hard hit him in the chest. Pen shoved with her foot. He sailed backward and landed on his arse as she sprang to her feet and charged past him. He watched her stride back and forth across the solar, sputtering and gesturing in her fury.

"Saints! How do other women keep from slapping that smirk from your face? Did you drive your brother to distraction this way? It's no wonder he—"

Morgan sprang up and lunged at her. "What know you of my brother?"

Pen halted as he planted himself in her path.

"Has Christian told you? God's breath, he has, hasn't he? He told you what happened, what I did."

He'd been stripped naked, his sin unmasked, all without his knowledge. He heard his own voice falter and dwindle. He felt as if his soul were shrinking, withering, drying up in the furnace of exposure.

He wet his lips and managed to speak, although without hope. "How long have you known about John's death?"

"John?" Pen cocked her head to the side and furrowed her brow. "Who is John? I speak of the viscount. Lord Montfort calls him Derry."

"Jesu, you don't know."

"Are you speaking of your older brother? Lord Montfort mentioned him." Pen paused as if gathering her patience. "Make yourself clear, my lord."

"It's of no importance."

"True, since your brother died so long ago, and due to his own stupidity."

Stunned, Morgan didn't answer at once. "Not stupidity. He was a great swordsman, and I . . ."

"Whatever his talents, it was the work of a fool and a callous lout to force Derry to a match and then to try to do him so grave an injury. He was trying to hurt Derry grievously and ended up dead." Pen shook her head in disgust. "I know I may sound unfeeling, but in truth John received the portion he was trying to dispense to someone else. But what has this old business to do with the matters before us, my lord? Let me repeat—no, I do not love you. When are you leaving?"

Still bewildered by Pen's unexpected view of his shameful past, Morgan didn't answer at once. Abruptly, understanding burst upon him. Pen thought that the whole calamity with John had been his father's fault, and John's. Indeed, he had to admit they'd devised the confrontation.

They had forced it. They had even used him in their design against Derry. He'd known this for a long time, but hearing Pen discuss the results so calmly somehow changed the way he looked at his own part.

Suddenly he was weary of old hurts, and surprised at how the pain now seemed muted. Could it be that he no longer bled, but simply ached from old scars? Mayhap he'd healed since encountering Pen, without even knowing it. Or mayhap he'd grown, and in growing, outgrown the need to make good out of something that could never be anything but tragedy.

By the holy cross, he'd been a fool. He needed her.

The depth of his need came crashing down upon him with the violence of the Penance surf, threatening to engulf in a new, frightening, and inescapable dependence. He nearly shivered with the need to, somehow, preserve himself from vulnerability. Yet he had to have her.

"My lord, have you lost your hearing? I asked when you would leave."

"What?" He blinked at her. Then, as she planted her hands on her hips and gave him one of her sparkling looks of defiance, he suddenly smiled and laughed. "Pen, Penelope Grace Fairfax, Gratiana, my fabulous madcap, I want you."

Pen took a step backward as he spoke and gazed at him as if he'd suddenly grown a tail. "You mock me."

He caught her hand and kissed it. When she tried to pull it away, he squeezed it in both of his.

"Only for you will I say this. Forgive me, Pen. I've been monstrous evil to you."

"Aye, you have," Pen said, staring at him.

"I beg to make amends, my love."

"You? You beg? Have you been at Nany's ale?"

"Forgive me, Pen."

He kissed the back of her hand, noting the way she shivered as his lips touched her flesh. He breathed on her skin, then grazed his lips across her knuckles.

"Morgan?"

There it was, that softening of tone, that quiver in her voice. Saying nothing, he drew her into his arms and kissed her, drowning in the pliancy of her lips. Blood churned to his face and down to his groin as she seemed to dissolve into his arms. He breathed in the scent of her hair and sighed. He could be with her if he strove to preserve a small distance and thus protect himself from his own need.

He murmured against her curls. "God, I missed you, Gratiana. I won't be gone long. When I'm in London or in the country, you'll be here."

"I will?"

"I'll send provisions and funds."

"You will?"

He nuzzled her neck. "Jesu, I'm pleased you won't be like the others."

Pen tilted her head back to look at him. "Others? Prithee, what others?"

"Oh, no one of importance."

"By all the saints in heaven, I think you mean Maria and Lady Ann."

"What know you of Maria and—Christian again." Morgan sighed. "Forget them."

Pen stepped back and folded her arms across her chest as she stared at him. "Make yourself clear, my lord."

"I but meant that you should remain on Penance, where it's safe."

"Safe! Safe for you to prowl about other cats while I'm in a cage by myself. I'm not quite the antick you think me."

"Jealous mistress, I didn't purpose to—"

Pen wasn't listening.

"By the cross," Pen said. "I understand now. You think me unworthy of your magnificence. You have the temerity to assume that I will sit on my island all chaste and pining for your glorious presence while you rut and spew every time your cock—"

"Penelope Fairfax, you watch your tongue." He began to lose patience as Pen's voice deepened and boomed at him.

"By God, sirrah, I'll not have it. I'll not be your common doxy."

She stalked toward him, and at the look on her face, Morgan's ire increased. By God's wounds, she didn't trust him—again!

"That's not what I meant," he snapped.

"Puffed-up, rutting, deceitful bawd!"

He halted and planted his hands on his hips. "Puffed up? Now, you hold a moment, Penelope Grace Fairfax. You wanted me almost from the beginning. My memory works now, and I haven't forgotten one kiss or one moan. Was it a dream that you bathed every part of me with your mouth?"

Pen gasped and whirled around to her chair. Scooping up her mending, she threw it at him. It sailed onto his head. He clawed at it and emerged to find Pen sailing past him on her way out of the solar. He charged after her only to come up short when she rounded on him.

"I thought some wondrous enchantment brought you to me, but now I see that I was cursed by some wicked fiend of hell when that storm brought you to my island."

"Belabor me not with such yammerings," Morgan said. He leaned toward her, grinning. "You want me as much as you always have. I may sail upon the morrow, but I'm coming back. And when I do, it will be to your bed."

"When the devil sits at the right hand of God!" Pen shouted.

He would have retorted, but Pen rushed out of the solar and slammed the door in his face. He almost kicked it. Instead, he whirled and began to stomp back and forth. The little pestilence had done it again. She'd lost faith in him. God's breath, but she made him want to bellow and howl with her intransigence. How dare she accuse him of such foul stratagems, when he'd offered himself freely? He loved her, but she was still a woman, and should trust and be guided by him. Why wouldn't she bend to his will as had other women?

He couldn't tell her the truth about why he wanted her to remain on Penance. He almost shuddered at the thought of revealing his craven fear of endangering her. But she knew about Ann and Maria, who hadn't entered his thoughts in weeks, not since he'd seen Pen.

Still, he wished Pen would conduct herself more like they did. Usually he had but to threaten to withdraw and they hastened to accept affection according to his dictates. With Pen, the more he tried to govern their dealings, the more she tried to banish him from her. This was not the way matters were supposed to progress.

Morgan bent and picked up Pen's piece of mending. Tossing it on her chair, he began to smile. God's breath, she was as inconstant as a black squall, and as rousing.

There was no other like, nor would he care if there was. His smile turned to a grin. He'd seduced her before. He but needed to persevere, and she would change again, and finally succumb. Then he could look forward to a tolerable arrangement—he pursuing his work with Christian and Pen waiting for him here, away from danger. His craving for her wouldn't go away, but he would keep it in check. If he didn't, he was much afraid he would drown in his need.

Before dawn the next morning Pen huddled in her warmest gown and heaviest cloak beside the fireplace in her chamber. She read a long document while Father Humphrey warmed his hands. She glanced up from her reading. "You're certain he won't relent about issue?"

"Certain," said Father Humphrey.

Pen glanced over the document once more, then sighed. "Ah, well. I won more points than I'd expected. Come, Father, before the others wake."

They left her chamber and crept from the keep without meeting anyone. At the gatehouse they found Dibbler, Sniggs, Nany, and Twistle waiting with horses. At a signal from her, Erbut lowered the drawbridge. As its rusty chains screamed, Pen cringed and glanced back at the keep.

She expected Morgan to descend upon her at any moment, but he didn't. She led the way out of the castle, walking her horse until they were clear of the bridge. Then she kicked the animal and trotted off in the direction of Much Cutwell with Father Humphrey and her Highcliffers close behind.

Her course was set. It banished any chance of love, but after Morgan had played with her so brutally, she wanted no more of love. And she believed his threat to return and take her to bed. She wouldn't be misused. Bending to Morgan's will would lead her to more hurt, more shame. For a too-short moment she'd hoped for reconciliation and marriage. What amazement. Of a certainty, the world would have thought her a wretched match for the exquisite Morgan St. John in any case. Too plain, too poor.

Yet in the last few weeks she'd learned something about herself—something inside her refused to endure maltreatment anymore. She'd admitted to herself, but to no one else, that her father and mother had sent her away rather than put themselves at risk on account of her gift. She didn't want to be hurt like that again. Therefore she had to insist that Morgan treat her with regard. She didn't want adoration, but neither did she want disrespect, but he didn't seem to understand that.

Marry, all he seemed to understand was rutting. She'd searched deep within herself and come to the perception that although she must admit to longing for Morgan, she could not have him. And so she must protect herself. Which was why she was going to Much Cutwell. After all, she'd neglected the welfare of her people too long.

Her mood worsened the closer she came to Ponder's manor. By the time she dismounted in the outer court, she might as well have been a new-made widow. Ponder was waiting for her on the front steps, garbed in his best raiment.

The sight of Cutwell in yellow and red satin jolted Pen out of her fugue. The sun had risen and glinted off the gold braid that edged his robe. He wore a flat yellow cap with a jaunty red feather in it secured by a diamond pin. Pen gaped at the diamond buckles on his shoes as he conducted her into the house with great ceremony.

"At last you've seen reason," Ponder was saying. "Although I mislike the haste upon which you insist. I'm willing to abide by your wishes for the sake of harmony."

He paused as they entered the great hall. "Behold. I've managed to make some preparations, my dear."

The hall was bursting with Ponder's retainers and decked with Ponder's best tapestries. Tables had been piled with enough beef, mutton, cakes, and ale to feed the entire island for the winter. In the musicians' gallery three fiddlers supplied tunes more appropriate for a May festival. Serving men passed among the guests, supplying everyone with wine. Pen gaped at a lad bearing a large silver cup trimmed with a branch of gilded rosemary.

"Allow me to help you," Ponder said as he pulled on her cloak.

Pen shrugged off the garment while staring at the bunch of rosemary tied with ribbons and stuck in his belt. Ponder noticed her preoccupation.

"The traditional token of manly qualities, I believe."

Pen swallowed hard, then turned to face Father Humphrey. She hadn't thought Ponder quite this foolish. Dibbler was eyeing the man as if he were beholding a dancing pig. All at once the ceremony began, and she heard herself repeating vows she never thought to take.

Refusing to think upon the consequences, she gave her promise. After that, she lapsed into a kind of stupor.

From a distance she heard Ponder repeating his own vows. His small red mouth moved wetly. She couldn't seem to look away from it, even when she heard a jostling sound behind her. She was watching those plump lips wiggle, when a silver blade descended past her to point at the chin below them.

"If you complete those vows, they will be the last words you speak."

Pen fluttered her lashes, struggling to comprehend what had happened. Gasping, she whirled around to face Morgan as Ponder yelped and skittered out of striking range. The group around them hastened to increased the distance between them and Morgan. The priest barked a protest, which Morgan ignored.

"Cutwell," he said evenly as he followed his prey, "you're not going to marry Mistress Fairfax. If you so much as kiss her hand, I'll geld you."

"Peace, my son," said Father Humphrey.

"There will be peace, Father, as soon as Cutwell gives me his word not to come near Mistress Fairfax."

Pen suddenly found her composure and her voice. "You're too late."

Morgan smiled at her with toleration. "I think not."

"She speaks the truth," said Father Humphrey. "The purpose was clear, and most of the ceremony completed before God."

The sword blade faltered, then dipped. Morgan turned away from Ponder to stare at the priest. He searched the man's face for the truth, then looked at Pen. She met his gaze with a defiance that barely concealed her own misgivings. Around her the guests muttered and whispered in small groups.

He swooped at her and grabbed her wrist. "You lackwitted little fool, why have you done this absurd thing?"

"To prevent you from making me your doxy!"

The last word echoed in the hall and banished all whispers. Morgan paled and went silent. His gaze became distant as he appeared to lapse into inner converse for a brief moment. Pen bit her lip to keep from bursting into tears, suddenly aware of how mad her conduct must appear. But what else could she do to protect herself? She heard a curse from Morgan as he suddenly wakened from his silent dialogue. She tried to shrink back as he turned the full blast of his rage upon her.

He yanked her close and shouted at her. "God's blood! This wouldn't have happened if you'd listened to me instead of losing your wits to jealousy. You're not marrying Cutwell. I won't allow it."

Setting her jaw, she stared back at him without flinching.

"You've no choice."

He glared at her while the entire hall seemed to hold its breath. When his eyes seemed to turn to black ice, several men-at-arms took a step back from him. All at once he smiled a smile that made Pen want to duck into the nearest cupboard and wait for mountains to crumble.

"Father, this marriage is unlawful."

"How so, my son?"

"Because the lady has given herself to me. Surely you knew that, Cutwell."

Pen felt herself redden as a collective gasp traveled around the hall. Ponder began to sputter.

"I knew this not. What—how—my honor!"

"Oh, close your teeth," Morgan said. "I but meant that

the lady promised her hand to me. A prior betrothal takes precedence over any later agreement."

"Why, you arrogant plague of a man."

She pulled free of Morgan's grip, picked up her skirts, and turned her back to him. Shouldering her way through the crowd, Pen left the hall and marched to the stables, where her horse stood, waiting to be unsaddled. Dibbler and the others trailed after her. She was shivering and attempting to mount her horse, when someone threw her cloak around her shoulders.

"A wise course, my love."

Pen gasped as Morgan picked her up, thrust her into the saddle, and stood grinning up at her.

"We'll be more comfortable marrying at Highcliffe."

"Marry?" Pen squawked. *"Marry?"*

"Aye, Gratiana. After all, I have to prevent you from marrying that pig-lover Cutwell. Cutwell, ha!"

She stared at him as he burst into a loud guffaw.

"Cutwell, you and Ponder Cutwell. By my troth, what a thought."

Rage blistered through her veins, but she waited until his laughter subsided. Gathering her reins, she frowned down upon him.

"Laugh as you will, my lord, but harken to this." She spoke calmly and carefully. "You may have ruined my chance of becoming a wife, but you haven't won. And do you know why? Because, my lord, despite your belief in my undying love, I'd sooner marry Margery than you. I believe your ship is waiting. Good day to you."

CHAPTER XXIII

Having galloped all the way back to Highcliffe, Pen charged into her own hall, hands twisting, body trembling. Morgan had subjected her to derision and mockery, and she wished she could take a switch to his backside. Arrogant knave. She stomped over to the fireplace and thrust her hands near the flames. The others weren't three minutes behind her. Morgan had followed at a more tranquil pace, and she had to regain her calm before he arrived.

"Spiteful curse, evil-minded lout. If he thinks he can ride me with a whip, I'll teach him otherwise. Hagborn ruffian."

"Ah, you must be speaking of my raven."

Pen swung around to find Christian de Rivers mounting the dais, followed by a man with the most glorious blond hair she'd ever seen.

"What a marvel," the blond man said. "Morgan usually manages to trample women and yet keep them in thrall," the blond man said.

Christian bowed to Pen. "Mistress Fairfax, well met. Viscount Moorefield, may I present Mistress Penelope Fairfax."

Dazed, Pen curtsied as Christian continued.

"I discovered too late that the priest had indeed sailed for Penance, and so I came after you and Morgan. I rejoice that all is well with you." Christian's eyes sparkled as he smiled at her. "Your good woman Nany and the lad Erbut told me what has happened."

Before he could go on, a tidal wave of Highcliffers crashed into the hall. Scuffling and jostling, they rushed at Pen and came to an unsteady halt before her.

"He's coming, mistress," puffed Dibbler.

"And he's bringing the priest," Sniggs said.

"Penelope Grace Fairfax!"

"Ah," Christian said, "the call of the raven."

Morgan charged into the room with Father Humphrey in tow.

"Prepare yourself," he snapped at Pen, never taking his gaze from her. "We're taking vows at once. There'll be no more sneaking about, trying to marry Cutwells."

Pen would have answered, but the viscount stepped beside her.

"Control your tongue, little brother.'

"Derry? How came you here?" Morgan glanced from his brother to Christian and then to Pen. "Did you send for them?"

Outraged, Pen turned her back and refused to speak to him.

"Peace, raven. We came of our own will. And a fortunate thing it seems to be."

"Aye," said the viscount. "God's toes, Morgan. Christian tells me you've managed to make an unyielding enemy of this sweet lady."

"Sweet, my arse," Morgan said. "What would you know of Pen's sweetness? It's all vanished. She only has sweetness for some phantasm named Tristan."

Pen announced to the hall, "Tristan deserved sweetness. You, my lord, deserve bile and pitch."

Morgan threw up his hands. "Mark you, Christian,

Derry. See what I endure? She bites and swears at me after I've saved her from marriage with a lover of pigs. I offer to marry her, and she scorns me. Scorns me when not a fortnight before she doted on my boots."

Pen twisted around to face him and said through grinding teeth, "I never doted upon any stitch of your clothing, much less your useless self."

"Where," Morgan said, looking down at her through his lashes, "is my sweet madcap, my bright and merry mischief? Where is the woman who craved me as she craved food and drink?"

Pen raked his body with her glance. "I know not. In some bawdy house in London, no doubt."

"Enough of this," Derry said.

While Pen and Morgan glared at each other, he conferred with Christian. With a sweep of his arm, Christian sent Pen's servants scattering so that the four of them were alone in moments. Then Christian took Pen aside while Derry cornered his brother. Pen slumped into a chair beside the fireplace and lapsed into misery.

"Mistress Fairfax, do you trust me?"

"What? Oh, yes, my lord."

"You're certain."

"Aye, my lord. You've been so kind to me."

"Then I want you to let me help you."

"Will you make Morgan go away?" she asked as she gazed at Morgan, who was talking to his brother.

Lean and dark, his black eyes glinting with anger, he turned abruptly and walked away from Derry. His body glided, like that of a panther on the hunt. Without warning, he turned and caught her looking at him.

His brows drew together in that alarming way that signaled peril for whoever had gained his disfavor. Then he gave her one of those I-can-make-her-beg-for-me

smiles and started toward her. Derry caught his arm
first and whispered something to him. Morgan glanced
at her, then nodded to Derry and turned away from
her. Not wanting to admit her relief, Pen tried not
to sigh.

Christian went on as Derry and Morgan left the hall.
"I promise to help you resolve this turmoil into which
you've cast yourselves, but only if you'll promise to tell
me the truth when I ask you a few questions."

"What questions?"

"Do you promise?"

"Aye, my lord."

Christian came to stand beside her chair. He glanced
at the screen and the opening that led to the alcove
behind it. Pen watched him, dreading his questions.

"Do you love Morgan?"

Her mouth fell open. Christian fixed her with a stern
glance.

"Do I?" Pen avoided his gaze.

"You gave your word, mistress. The truth."

"The truth is that he's a—a lover of bawds. Morgan
St. John wanted me to sit on this island like a mush-
room while he cavorted with his women."

"Now, Pen," Christian said. "Perhaps I asked the
wrong question. Do you love Tristan?"

"Of course," Pen said without hesitation.

"But Morgan is Tristan."

"He protests that he's not, and labors not to be."

"Nevertheless, the one encompasses the other, just
as your love encompasses both."

"But Morgan is monstrous evil to me."

"For good reason," Christian said. "Those who have
been close to him have caused him great harm. And,
after all, you did betray him, even if it wasn't through

your own fault. Can you bide awhile, hold on to your patience a little bit longer?"

"Why?"

"If I ask it, can you?"

Gazing at Christian in confusion, Pen nodded. "Yes, my lord, as long as you refrain from asking me to abide Morgan's foul idea of marriage where I keep vows and he does not."

"Then come with me."

She followed Christian up the winding stair that led past her chamber and out onto the wall walk. At the top they paused, and Christian put a finger to his lips. He pushed the door to the wall walk open so that a sliver of light appeared in the dark stairwell. He pulled Pen up beside him, and she heard Morgan's voice.

"The truth? I always tell you the truth."

"Then tell it to me now," Derry said. "Did you really think to keep Mistress Fairfax on this island while you cavorted about England, spying and bedding?"

Pen strained to hear, but Morgan seemed to be muttering. Then he spoke more clearly.

"I liked not the force of my need of her." There was a pause before he went on in a chagrined voice. "I gave not a thought to other women, and then she accused me of wanting them. Jesu, she inflames my temper with her doubts."

Derry chuckled. "For all your skill with women, you seem to be blind about this one. Think. She knows the dominion you have over her. She's heard of your reputation with other women. Can you censure her for being afraid you might be tempted? And you haven't told her you no longer care about Maria and Ann."

"What matter Maria and Ann when this morn Pen tried to marry Ponder Cutwell!" Morgan's voice grew louder. "I was trying to tell her I'd forgiven her, that I'd reconsidered."

"How gracious of you," Derry said.

"Hold your tongue," Morgan said. "Oh, very well, I was trying to tell her I was wrong, and somehow we misunderstood each other. She wouldn't listen to me. Later, I could have taken a whip to her when I saw her riding off like that. God, Derry, I wanted to run my blade through Cutwell's fat gut. I wanted to—Christ, Derry—my mind went black. I never came so near to murder, not even with you."

"Why?"

"What?"

"Why, Morgan, and remember you promised me the truth."

Pen gripped the edge of the door and turned her ear to it as the silence lengthened.

"Damn you, because I love her. I love every maddening, addled, mischievous, obdurate inch of her. Jesu, I don't know how I ever contemplated leaving her. Look what she's tried to do when I haven't even set sail."

"Then why haven't you told her?"

Another silence. Pen started to open the door, but Christian barred her way with his arm and shook his head.

"Very well," Derry said. "I can read the answer in your face. You haven't told her because of John. And because you're too proud to admit you've succumbed to a woman."

Pen had to strain to hear Morgan's reply.

"Worse," he said. "I was afraid."

Pen heard him sigh.

"Do you know how frightening it is to be so, so utterly and witlessly enamored? I suppose that's why I contemplated living away from her when I knew I could never do it. God, Derry, I love her. Do you know how hard I tried to stop? Do you know how much power over me that gives her?"

"Of course I know. It was the same for me with Thea."

"But—"

"I've but one more question," Derry said. "Morgan, my dear, suspicious brother, can you honestly imagine that Mistress Fairfax, the Mistress Fairfax who fell in love with you the moment you washed up on her island, do you believe that this woman could ever use your love against you?"

Pen held her breath as she waited. Her fingers turned white from pressing against the door.

"I never thought of it so," said Morgan. Then his tone seemed to lighten. "God's breath, Derry, you're right."

"Now," Christian said, and he pushed Pen through the doorway.

She stumbled into the sunlight, then shrank back against Christian as she saw Morgan turn and gaze at them in surprise. Then his expression blackened.

"Damn you, Christian, you're playing at being a god again."

Ignoring Morgan, Christian went to Derry and clapped him on the back. "I'm hungry, my friend. Shall we find that cook with the absurd name?"

"Interfering bastards," Morgan said quietly.

Pen joined Morgan in staring at the two as they vanished down the stairwell and closed the door after them. When the door shut, Pen tried to look at anything but Morgan—the battlements, the sky, the tips of her riding boots. Her gaze fastened upon a scuff in the leather.

"Pen."

She jumped at the nearness of Morgan's voice. He'd come close while she wallowed in confusion. Flushing, she managed a nod, but couldn't make herself raise her head.

"Pen, mayhap we've been tricked to our own good. I—I heard what you said to Christian."

She looked up, startled, then retreated from the tenderness she found in his eyes.

"Pen, Pen, don't be afraid."

She felt his fingers graze her chin and tried to turn away from him. He stopped her by putting an arm around her shoulders. She heard him draw in a long breath, as if girding himself for some act of courage.

"I was wrong," he said. "Pen?"

Frightened, Pen heard herself stutter. "H-how can I believe you?"

She felt a tug on her arms. Morgan dropped to his knees in front of her while holding her hands.

"I give you my vow, Pen. Mayhap I've been lying to myself. I am Tristan. I think, yes, I think I was afraid to admit it to myself. I'm Tristan as much as I'm Morgan, mayhap more. And, my love, if it will bring me your love, I'll be Tristan until Judgment Day and after."

At this, Pen found the courage to look at him. To her surprise, Morgan was looking at her with apprehension. All at once she understood that he feared losing her as much as she feared losing him. An uncertain smile began to curl about her lips. At its appearance, Morgan rose, taking her with him in a sweeping movement that lifted her off her feet.

"Pen!" he shouted. "Pen, Pen, Pen. Marry me, my madcap star."

She shrieked as he whirled around in a circle. When he set her down, she tottered with dizziness and fell into his arms again. He squeezed her until she gasped, then chuckled and kissed her.

"Oh, Morgan."

"Yes, my joyful madcap."

"Those women."

"What women?"

She put her hands on either side of his face. "I should have listened to you instead of falling into a fit, but when you spoke of leaving me here, I just knew it was because of those other women."

Morgan turned his head and kissed her palm. "You're the only woman who has ever become more necessary to me than my own life."

"I—I know what I look like compared to your fabulous court ladies, a nettle among lilies." Pen stepped away from him and hung her head. "That's the truth of why I was grievous vexed. You see, you're so wondrous, and I am such a plain old shoe."

Morgan grasped her hands and kissed the tips of her fingers. "You have to believe me, and not yourself. You're my bright and wondrous siren, and I'll hear no more talk of nettles and plain shoes." He pulled her closer. The tip of his tongue touched her ear. "What luck for you that you rouse me so with your vexation."

She shivered, and she was turning red again. Someday she would learn how to keep her cheeks from displaying her passions. To distract him and herself, she ducked her head so that he couldn't continue his seduction of her ear.

"Um, Morgan, what of Highcliffe? It's all I have, you know. Hardly a proper dowry for you." Her voice lowered so that he had to lean down to hear her. "After all, I'm only Mistress Fairfax."

"Pen, look at me."

She tried, but her gaze seemed pinned to the floor. He sighed, then drew his sword, knelt, and held it hilt up like a cross. He raised his voice.

"Upon mine honor and before God, I say that Mistress Penelope Fairfax is a match of unparalleled richness."

"Oh, Morgan, get up! You're making me seem foolish."

"Not you, your fears."

Her worries faded as she perceived the indignation upon his face. "But there are still my Highcliffers to consider."

"Ah, yes." He kissed her cheek. "You know, my love, that not one of your servants has anything more than pig slops for wits. And I do have lands of my own."

"But I love Highcliffe."

Morgan shook his head. "I know, and I confess, your band of unworthies has somehow captured my affection, except for Twistle."

"Then what are we to do?"

"No doubt Christian or Derry will know someone who could look after the place during the times we're away."

"Someone capable of dealing with Ponder Cutwell."

"And Twistle."

Morgan said nothing more while he took one of her hands, opened it, and kissed the palm. Then his gaze went distant.

"There have been no more visions." he said.

"Mayhap there never will be."

"Know you for certain?"

Pen shook her head. "I don't even understand my own gift, but mayhap now that you've been to the standing stones, nothing more will happen."

"God's eyes, Pen, I like not this visitation of past

happenings. It's like living with ghosts. And don't smirk at me, you little mischief. You've had years in which to accustom yourself to it."

Pen laughed anyway. Morgan stood back from her and folded his arms over his chest, then gave her a slow assessing look graced with a smile.

"No doubt," he said lazily, "no doubt God sent me these visions apurpose as a sign that I'm needed to govern this island and its willful mistress."

"Or they're a sign that you're in need of governance, my lord Morgan St. John."

He came closer, tangled his fingers in a strand of her hair, and bent to kiss it. "Mmmm. I believe I'm going to enjoy your trying to—govern me. Come. We'll go to your chamber so you can begin."

Before Pen could protest, he took her arm and turned to leave the wall walk. They had gone several steps before Pen stopped and danced away from him.

"Your brother and Lord Montfort await us!"

"They may continue."

Morgan gave her one of his long I'm-going-to-consume-you looks and she felt another of those damnable blushes creep over her face.

"Please, Morgan." She put her hands to her burning cheeks and refused to look at him.

He laughed. "This once, I'll relent."

Pen eyed him warily. He was capable of doing just as he pleased.

Morgan sighed, gathered her in his arms, and gave her a leisurely but thorough kiss that forced her to regret her protest. Then he released her.

"If I must suffer, you'll suffer as well, my stubborn-sweet mistress."

Her voice faint, Pen straightened her gown. "That seems only fair."

She summoned her wits. Saints, but this man could rout them simply by looking at her. Govern him indeed. He took her hand and pulled her to the battlements, and they gazed out at the sea. A breeze played with her curls, and he captured one in his fingers. Pen covered his hand with hers.

"Morgan, Tristan, I love you."

She barely got the words out before he covered her mouth with his lips. When he ended the kiss, she touched his mouth with wondering fingers.

"Morgan?"

"Aye, my love."

"There's going to be a storm."

He looked out at the cloudless sea.

"I see nothing."

Pen smiled at him with her old, bright smile. "Believe me, my sweet, sweet Tristan, there's going to be a storm."

ABOUT THE AUTHOR

SUZANNE ROBINSON has a doctoral degree in anthropology with a specialty in ancient Middle Eastern archaeology. After spending years doing fieldwork in both the U.S. and the Middle East, Suzanne has now turned her attention to the creation of the fascinating fictional characters in her unforgettable historical romances.

Suzanne lives in San Antonio with her husband and her two English springer spaniels. She divides her time between writing and teaching.

THE VERY BEST IN HISTORICAL WOMEN'S FICTION

Iris Johansen

_____	28855-5	THE WIND DANCER ....$5.99/$6.99 in Canada
_____	29032-0	STORM WINDS $4.99/5.99
_____	29244-7	REAP THE WIND $4.99/5.99
_____	29604-3	THE GOLDEN BARBARIAN $4.99/5.99
_____	29944-1	THE MAGNIFICENT ROGUE $5.99/6.99
_____	29968-9	THE TIGER PRINCE $5.50/6.50
_____	29871-2	LAST BRIDGE HOME $4.50/5.50
_____	29945-X	BELOVED SCOUNDREL $5.99/6.99
_____	29946-8	MIDNIGHT WARRIOR $5.99/6.99

Susan Johnson

_____	29125-4	FORBIDDEN $4.99/5.99
_____	29312-5	SINFUL $4.99/5.99
_____	29957-3	BLAZE $5.50/6.50
_____	29959-X	SILVER FLAME $5.50/6.50
_____	29955-7	OUTLAW $5.50/6.50
_____	56327-0	SEIZED BY LOVE $5.50/6.99

Teresa Medeiros

_____	29407-5	HEATHER AND VELVET $4.99/5.99
_____	29409-1	ONCE AN ANGEL $5.50/6.50
_____	29408-3	A WHISPER OF ROSES $5.50/6.50

Patricia Potter

_____	29070-3	LIGHTNING $4.99/5.99
_____	29071-1	LAWLESS $4.99/5.99
_____	29069-X	RAINBOW $5.50/6.50
_____	56199-5	RENEGADE $5.50/6.50
_____	56225-8	NOTORIOUS $5.50/6.50

Ask for these titles at your bookstore or use this page to order.

Please send me the books I have checked above. I am enclosing $ _____ (add $2.50 to cover postage and handling). Send check or money order, no cash or C. O. D.'s please.

Mr./ Ms. _____

Address _____

City/ State/ Zip _____

Send order to: Bantam Books, Dept. FN 17, 2451 S. Wolf Road, Des Plaines, IL 60018

Please allow four to six weeks for delivery.

Prices and availability subject to change without notice.

FN 17 - 7/94